A WELCOME SURRENDER

"May I remind you that you warned me against touching you?" Greyson said with a teasing smile. "You informed me that when you wished me to touch you, you would let me know."

"I remember," Victoria answered, nodding solemnly. " 'Twould be difficult to enjoy the fullest pleasures of the traditional wedding night without . . . touching."

"Yes . . . 'twould be . . . difficult." They gazed at each other for a long moment, then he lifted her and swept her off to his bed. With agonizing slowness, he gently undressed her, caressing her creamy flesh with possessive devotion, feathering hot kisses where his fingertips had been.

Victoria felt hot tides of pleasure coursing through her. Her heart pounded, sending liquid fire through her veins. She was bathed in fluid hunger as she gazed up at him, her eyes lucent with desire.

"Are you very sure," he rasped, needing to hear the words.

"I am," she breathed, drawing his lips down to hers. . . .

SURRENDER TO THE
PASSION OF RENÉ J. GARROD!

WILD CONQUEST   (2132, $3.75)
Lovely Rausey Bauer never expected her first trip to the big
city to include being kidnapped by a handsome stranger
claiming to be her husband. But one look at her abductor
and Rausey's heart began to beat faster. And soon she found
herself desiring nothing more than to feel the touch of his
lips on her own.

ECSTASY'S BRIDE   (2082, $3.75)
Irate Elizabeth Dickerson wasn't about to let Seth Branting
wriggle out of his promise to marry her. Though she de-
spised the handsome Wyoming rancher, Elizabeth would
not go home to St. Louis without teaching Seth a lesson
about toying with a young lady's affections — a lesson in love
he would never forget!

AND DON'T MISS OUT ON THIS OTHER
HEARTFIRE SIZZLERS FROM ZEBRA BOOKS!

LOVING CHALLENGE   (2243, $3.75)
by Carol King
When the notorious Captain Dominic Warbrooke burst into
Laurette's Harker's eighteenth birthday ball, the accom-
plished beauty challenged the arrogant scoundrel to a duel.
But when the captain named her innocence as his stakes,
Laurette was terrified she'd not only lose the fight, but her
heart as well!

Emerald Enchantress

Carol King

ZEBRA BOOKS
KENSINGTON PUBLISHING CORP.

ZEBRA BOOKS

are published by

Kensington Publishing Corp.
475 Park Avenue South
New York, NY 10016

First printing: February, 1989

Printed in the United States of America

Salem, Massachusetts, 1692

A whisper of smoke rose like an obelisk against the moon-silvered night. The thatched roof of the weathered cottage seethed. At once, without warning, a dark flare exploded upward, and an angry red flame pierced the sky. With a roar the cottage erupted into a fiery cauldron that illuminated the seaside village.

Men circling the scene, their cragged and perspiring faces alight with righteousness, held their panicked horses in check. A woman screamed, the shrill ululation echoing over the rock-bound landscape. She broke from her captors and ran toward the one man whom she knew to be the motivating force in this horror. In a frenzy that equaled the force of the voracious inferno that was consuming her home, she snatched out wildly and dragged the astonished horseman from his mount. Without the tether of its master's rein, the animal reared, shrieking in terror. The man shot up, and with the full power of his wrath, he struck the woman, knocking her to the winter-chilled ground. Her mobcap fell, and a tangle of bright, spun-sugar curls tumbled out to frame her pale face. The emerald green of her hate-fevered eyes flashed virulently. She grabbed a rock from the ground and, before anyone could react, hurled it at her assailant. It connected with his forehead with a sickening crack. His gouged flesh spit weals of blood as he

5

tottered wildly and dropped to the earth. The other men gaped. The woman pushed herself up, and in a delirium of desperation, she screamed once more, the sound lifting to meet the roar of the blaze and the pounding of the ocean beyond the cottage.

The men, horses dancing in fear, backed away. The woman looked from one to the other, her teeth bared, flashing brilliant glisters as her scream became shrill, hysterical laughter. Each man gave in to a primal terror, as she looked from one to the other, singling them out, remembering. Their lives would not be defensible if she called forth her vengeful gods. The flaxen-maned demon must be destroyed. They knew it to a man, yet none had the courage to act. Seeing the feeble dissolution on their faces, the terrorized impotence, the woman snarled malevolently. Then, her mass of pearl-frosted hair spinning dizzily out, she pivoted and ran for the abandoned horse. In one swift motion, she mounted the animal, wheeling and spurring it to a pounding gallop toward the sea.

Angry shouts followed her as the men regained their courage. She must be stopped! The evil must be exorcised! The men spurred their horses, leaving their fallen comrade to lie in his own blood on the fire-scorched ground. They followed the luminescent beacon of the woman's hair until, at last, they reached the silvered shoreline of the ocean. They saw in the misting distance the horse prancing on the sand near the moonstruck water. All was silent . . .

The woman had disappeared.

Chapter One

Kolhapur, India, 1773

Brightly colored garments flew like startled birds about the room. Victoria Quayle stood in the center of the chaos, tossing orders, shifting boxes, ripping through piles of tissue paper. Just that morning, a ship laden with cargo for the Darby plantation had disembarked along the West Indian shoreline. Under exacting orders from the young mistress of the plantation, scores of footmen had seen to the cargo's immediate unloading. They had trundled it by oxcart up the hilly terrain from the coast within hours of its arrival. Once deposited on the porches of the main house, the shipment was instantly transfused by yet more general servants into the mansion, up the massive cedar staircase, through long, ornately appointed hallways and into the bedroom suite of the lady of the house. With very little in the way of organization, and with a great deal of youthful glee, her ladyship had torn into the elegant freight and found herself now entangled in a dazzling pandemonium of gowns, shoes, petticoats, scarves, gloves and bonnets.

"Oh, Kat," Victoria squealed in delight, "isn't this extraordinary!" The young woman held aloft an extravagantly plumed bonnet. Its deep emerald color matched the exquisite glitter of her delighted gaze. The cascade of teardrop pearls sewn into the curve of the sweeping brim at the

7

base of the plumes imitated the long, fleecy luminescence of the girl's hair. She placed the hat over her shimmering curls and twirled for her audience of one. "Am I not the loveliest maiden in Kolhapur?"

Katje d'Aumerle smiled tranquilly from the comfort of her rush-caned, easy chair. "You are indeed," she affirmed. She waved a fan languidly near the roundness of her well-exposed bosom.

"And what of this, Kat!" the girl bubbled. Her attention had darted to another bundle. Scattering the wrappings, she plucked out a dressing gown of pumpkin-colored silk and held it up to her lithe form. "Did you ever see anything more exotic?"

Katje laughed lightly. "I hope you do not plan to wear it with the hat," she teased.

Victoria's answering giggle was suddenly cut short as a sobering thought assailed her. "Oh, Kat!" she gasped. "I've not seen the yellow taffeta." She began ripping through the tumult of boxes in a frenzied search. "I ordered it especially for the ball tonight! I prayed so hard that it would arrive in time." Desperation mounted in her tone. "Where could it be?"

"Are you looking for something in particular, Miss Victoria?" A small, brown, matronly woman had entered from the dressing chamber.

"The yellow taffeta, Mrs. Jafar, I cannot find it!" Victoria wailed.

"I hung that one up along with the other frocks, Miss Victoria. I thought you would want—"

"Oh, Mrs. Jafar, thank you!" Victoria dashed past the woman, placing a quick peck on her cheek, and into the other room. The Indian woman eyed Katje dubiously.

"I fear the child will explode before the day is out," she said worriedly.

Katje nodded wearily. She brushed at a dark blond curl that in the humidity of the West Indian afternoon, was clinging to her cheek. "Why don't you bring us some tea, Mrs. Jafar," she said. As the woman started from the room, Katje stopped her with a second thought. "Have

David bring it up," she said gently. "You stay downstairs and have some tea yourself. Get off your feet for a while."

The Indian woman smiled gratefully. "I believe I shall do just that, Mrs. d'Aumerle," she said as she made her way among the cartons and heaps of tissue paper. "And thank you."

"Thank *you*," Katje answered, offering the beleaguered servant an amiable wave as she left the room.

"What do you think, Kat?" Victoria twirled from the dressing chamber, holding before her the frenziedly sought-for gown. Katje pondered the lemony shimmer—it could hardly have been called merely yellow—of the voluminous garment. It glistened jewellike against the pale cream of Victoria's complexion. The underskirts and delicate appliques were a richer, brighter primrose, and light aureates of lace clouded the heart shape of the neckline and drifted airily from the edges of the long, fitted sleeves.

"You have made an excellent choice, as usual," Katje proclaimed softly, understating her own admiration.

"I am certain no one will have thought of yellow," Victoria mused seriously. "Everyone is considering mauves and lavenders this season." Her fair brows winged in puzzlement. "Whatever shall I do about gems, Kat?" she wondered.

"You might think about wearing the opals," Katje offered.

Victoria's responding smile of agreement lit up the already sunny room. " 'Tis a perfect choice, Kat," she agreed. She scurried to her jewelry chest and rifled through the drawers. "Did I put them back in the safe?" she reflected with a small frown when she could not immediately find the pieces for which she searched.

"Try one of the small cases," Katje advised. Victoria drew a morocco etui from a shelf, and with a triumphant smile, she pulled out the opal choker and ear-drops. "You may wear my bracelet as well," the older woman said.

"Oh, thank you, Kat." Victoria ran to her friend and embraced her. She knelt next to the woman's chair. "Tonight will be the most important night of my life, I am

9

sure of it," she said earnestly. "I just know Steven is going to ask me to marry him. Naturally," she added with an impish lift of one slim shoulder, "I shall refuse him." She giggled in pure and innocent enjoyment of what she had in store for Steven Kensington. "I shall make him implore me." She laughed. Her eyes widened then, and her green gaze became solemn. "You do think he *will* implore me, don't you, Kat?"

The older woman touched the girl's smooth cheek. Arching an elegant golden brow she said, "Steven Kensington would be a fool to do otherwise."

"And Steven is no fool," Victoria asserted. "He has been to Oxford University." Her voice lifted in wonder. "Where is Oxford University, Kat?" she asked.

" 'Tis in England, darling," the woman said through a small, gentle laugh. "Uncle David has told you of England."

"And of China, and of Arabia, and mostly, Kat, mostly of America." Victoria stood hugging herself. "That is where I should like to go someday. I should like, more than anything, to see the colonies of North America!"

" 'Tis cold there, I hear," Katje said softly. She waved her fan against the moist unmoving heat and gazed out over the sunny expanse of sky beyond the opened French windows of Victoria's chamber. " 'Tis cold everywhere but here in Kolhapur," she sighed.

Victoria lifted a bright, fringed shawl from a yawning crate and draped it, with dramatic flair, around her slim shoulders. "If I went to America I should need a stout woolen cloak," she said, her tone dreamy. "Can you imagine, Kat, I do not even own a woolen cloak?"

Katje d'Aumerle swept a gaze around the scattered wealth of rich garments. " 'Tis hard to imagine," she answered mildly. She plucked a sweet from a crystal plate and popped it with elegant dispatch into her mouth.

Victoria's green gaze registered sudden anxiety. "You do think they have dressmakers in America, don't you?" she asked.

"Of course they do," Katje answered soothingly. "Other-

10

wise, where would the ladies get their gowns?"

Victoria's expression lightened considerably, and she smiled the golden smile that had made her the ornament of the district for the last seventeen years. She plunked herself onto the feather counterpane that covered her teak-postered bed, and tissue fluttered up like puffs of brightly colored air. Boxes tumbled to the floor at the bouncing action. She smoothed lovingly at her gown which she'd laid at the foot of the bed. "Someday, Kat, I will see America." She glanced up at the older woman. "I do not think that is so eccentric a dream, do you?" Her eyes were now solemn, her tone earnest.

Katje's gaze clouded. In many ways she had known the day would come when Victoria would, in actual fact, leave for America. But that day was far. The older woman rallied. "I have heard of more eccentric dreams," she said evenly.

"I wonder what it is like there, Kat?" Victoria continued.

"My friend, Vivien, writes that 'tis . . . pleasant enough," Katje answered, praying for some diversion. "You know, love," she added hastily, "the more I think on it, the more I wonder if the emeralds would not be more appropriate with the gown. What do you think? You may wear my pale ones, or your deeper colored jewels. Either set would be—"

Lost in some distant, liminal train of thought, Victoria continued in a dreamy tone. "Are there Indians—American Indians—there, Kat?" she asked.

"Not many, love," Katje replied as though defeated. The girl's curiosity about the North American colonies always filled her with a sense of resigned dread. "You will recall Uncle David telling us the story of the smallpox epidemic of 1633. The Indians, having little resistance to the disease, were almost completely wiped out—at least from the northeastern coast."

"If you wish to worry about something," said a small, nattily attired gentleman from the threshold of the room, "worry about the French."

11

Katje laughed and raised herself from her chair. Taking the large brass tray the man carried, she swept it onto a low table. "Come in, David, if you dare," she invited. David Newton stepped neatly around the litter of Victoria's newly arrived plunder and made his way to a chair near the tea table. With a disdainful lift of a thin, dark brow, he eyed the cluttered seat cushion.

"May I sit here?" he inquired, remote disparagement in his tone. Victoria bounded from her bed, scattering empty boxes and small lacy things.

"Of course you may, Uncle David." She giggled. She swept a clump of mismatched shoes from the seat. "There," she indicated cheerily, "an empty space for my esteemed uncle." She saw him into the chair with a brightly suspect deference. "Comfortable, darling?" she asked, mocking courtesy.

"Quite," David Newton replied drily. Shifting himself, he drew a dainty kid boot from beneath the cushion and dropped it with Olympian detachment into a heap of ragged tissue paper on the floor. He accepted, with the same distance, a cup of tea. Victoria laughed lightly, the silvery sound brightening the already sunny atmosphere, and plumped herself onto a pillow near her uncle's feet.

"We cannot all be as tidily disposed as you, Uncle David," she said impishly.

"You are so correct, my girl," rejoined David Newton, sniffing icily. "That is precisely why I keep to my own rooms for the most part."

" 'Twill all be over one day, David dear," said Katje as she handed a porcelain cup and saucer to Victoria. "One day you and I shall have his house all to ourselves. Our little Victoria is talking about America again." She eyed the man, and her gaze held a discreet warning.

Victoria was nodding her bright head. "One day I shall be on board a sailing ship bound for America, Uncle David, and you shall not have to put up with my messes ever again." She laughed. She did not note the sadness that clouded the marble darkness of his eyes. He sat above her in reined silence. Katje glanced at the man as he sat stir-

12

ring his tea. Their memories, separate but shared, wandered to the sun-shimmered day nearly eighteen years past when Victoria had first entered their lives.

Theirs had been a quiet existence in 1755. The British settlement at Kolhapur, newly colonized then, thrived and prospered beneath the life-nurturing West Indian sun. Thriving most prosperously was the plantation of Lord Trevor Darby in the green hills along the shores of the Arabian Sea. His tea fields ripened in crowning profusion on these lush acres. Once settled, Trevor Darby had transported into this felicitous environment his most treasured friends, the elegant citizen of the world Katje d'Aumerle, and Major David Newton, recently decorated officer of the British forces in the colonies of North America, to share the warmth and wealth of fertile fields and British gentility. Together the three friends formed the nucleus of a community of like-thinking expatriates who dined together, communed together on things British and luxuriated together in the pearl in the crown of the Mother Country.

Lazy evenings were spent on breezy verandas where the neighbors would gather to tell lighthearted tales of their lives before Kolhapur. They related nostalgic stories of London, of Greenwich, of Surrey. And they agreed, with bittersweet resolve, that for all its misty beauty, England could not compare with India. Peace, serenity and wealth could be enjoyed here without the pressure and, some might say, falseness of the aristocratic society to which many of them had been forced, by circumstances of birth, to conform. These were men and women of rare and vital individuality. They savored their freedom, lived their lives in gentle celebration of the freedom of others. Though these wealthy and landed people had come to represent a sort of ruling class in this benevolent land, their authority was benign and beneficial. They kept to themselves for the most part in 1755, and those born in India gratefully accepted the bounty engendered by the newcomers. It was a happy time, a time of careless autonomy, for nearly everyone in Kolhapur. The day the child arrived at the

13

Darby plantation was punctuated with rain, but the afternoon had turned hot and steamy. The wriggling bundle was held awkwardly in the sea captain's arms.

"Your pardon, sir," he'd said to Lord Darby who had been hastily summoned, "her parents died at sea, sir. I can't keep her on the ship."

"I cannot imagine what you want of me," Lord Darby had replied. "Surely you do not expect me to take responsibility for the babe."

"No, sir," the captain replied hesitantly. "I just don't know what to do with it."

"Well, take it to an orphanage," the nobleman said in dismissal. David and Katje had arrived, curious, at the doorway and stared at the squirming, wrapped thing.

"What is it?" asked Katje.

" 'Tis a babe," the seaman said helplessly. "Its parents died at sea; they were half starved when they boarded," the man added as if to alleviate any suspicion that he'd neglected his passengers. "I haven't the foggiest what to do with it. As we were unloading cargo here anyway, I thought I might get your advice, sir." His eyes, set in deep sockets in his weathered face, shifted uncomfortably. "Have you any suggestions?"

He held the child toward the threesome, and they backed away imperceptibly.

"Just what we need around here," said David Newton, rolling his eyes toward the heavens. It was Katje, childless in her failed marriage, who leaned forward at last and timidly folded back the tatters of the swaddling blanket. The three of them peered down into the dark folds. They found there a fragile, sallow-faced, squalling cherub. Her skinny arms and legs thrashed the humid air. She was grimy from travel, and she was covered with heat rash. The three non-conforming, freedom-loving Britishers fell immediately, unashamedly, hopelessly, slavishly in love.

They pieced together the little girl's past from the captain's sketchy recollection.

"The parents boarded at Salem or Boston," the man said. "I remember that because I didn't pick up passengers

14

anywhere else. That's about all I can tell you," he apologized. "We don't keep passenger lists, you know. They were just listed as three among the 'Saints and Strangers' that paid their fare. The father died first—one night—then the mama. I don't know anything about them. We buried them at sea. A fellow said a prayer or two over them. I remember someone saying their name was Quayle. That's all I know." Again his eyes shifted. He looked from one to the other of the three well-appointed, carefully decorous people. He adjusted his stance so that they were better able to view the pitiful bit of new life. He sensed their dawning receptivity and held the babe just a bit closer to them. It was Katje who at last received the bundle, cradling it tenderly. She smiled up at first Lord Darby and then at David Newton. Both men were finding it difficult to retain their stern and dispassionate miens. The captain wisely took the moment to thank them all for their kindness in relieving him of the responsibility and disappear down the path from the plantation.

It was decided that the babe would be called Victoria, signifying her victory over the fate of her parents. Her surname would be Quayle, the three decided, though Lord Darby was to very quickly agree to adopt her and raise her as his own.

As the years passed, the pale down that feathered the babe's head became milky ringlets and then a thick, lustrous mane of soft, pearl-frosted fleece. Her wide blue eyes had changed almost immediately to a rich, fiery green, her lips and cheeks had taken on the blush of newly budded azaleas and her skin, beneath the West Indian sun, had ripened to an ivory-gold luster.

Victoria Quayle had thrived on the plantation as the verdant fields thrived, as the fragrant ornamental flowers thrived, as the elaborately adorned birds thrived. And she became as welcomed and as treasured among the families of the community as nature's glorious bounty. Lord Darby was the proudest, most protective father that had ever been known. He adamantly insisted that the child be treated as though she had been born his own. She roamed

15

at will from plantation to plantation, cossetted, adored, protected and loved.

The girl was adorned with every material possession Lord Darby suspected a child might desire. More importantly, he had loved her as profoundly as any man had ever loved a child. Katje and "uncle" David became her adoring champions as well. Throughout her young life, Victoria had known only deference, adoration and affection. She had only to imagine a preference, it seemed, and it became a thing fulfilled.

It was small wonder that she had grown into a young woman who was blessed with the self-esteem of the greatly loved. She was confident, ingenuously high-spirited and . . . irreconcilably spoiled

Katje watched the girl over the gilded rim of her teacup.

"If Trevor Darby were not already dead," David Newton was saying, "he would die to think his barony and considerable wealth had fallen to such a ungrateful little chit."

Victoria's winged brows lifted in puzzlement. "Ungrateful, Uncle David?" she gaped. "How am I ungrateful?"

"Think of it, my girl. You have been endowed with wealth, 'tis true, but more importantly than even that you now carry Lord Darby's family name. You are Lady Noelle Darby and that is no small thing to be." David's tone was appropriately haughty as he explained the obligations of the nobility and why Victoria could never even think of sailing to the American colonies. "Beyond that," he added, "you have a plantation to run. You dare not allow it to languish while you go traipsing off to some godforsaken little tract of land on the other side of the world." He sniffed righteously.

Victoria could not suppress the giggle that bubbled to her softly curved lips. "Oh, Uncle David." She laughed. "This plantation has needed no one to run it for years. Why, the tea practically grows itself."

"It was a nice attempt, David," Katje said languidly, "but that is the last argument you might have put forth, especially this season. Our plants have outdone themselves in prolificity for the past three seasons as a matter of fact.

The British East India Company is buying our crops almost faster than we can grow them. I suggest you think of some other way to sway the girl's thinking on this subject."

"Very well," David answered stiffly. He targeted Victoria with an admonishing glare. Before he could frame his new tack, however, a rustle of taffeta and lace at the threshold of the room roused all three people. They glanced toward the doorway to find Lynnie Franklyn and Marguerite Lunden peering gaily into the chamber. The two young women, from neighboring families, had been Victoria's dearest friends for all her life.

"We could wait no longer to see your new things." Lynnie giggled.

"You won't hate us, will you," Marguerite asked shyly and smiled a pale glance toward David Newton.

"How could I hate my two darlingest friends in the world," Victoria assured them. The two girls bubbled noisily into the room and gleefully inspected the newly arrived booty. Promises were made that this or that item could be borrowed, and at last the young ladies settled onto the floor, gathering around David like a richly blossomed garden. Stirring great heaps of sugar into their tea, they eyed the gentleman expectantly.

"We really ought to be ashamed of ourselves," demurred Marguerite as she noted his stern gaze.

"To tell you the truth, Uncle David," Lynnie chirped, "we did not want to miss your teatime story." The three girls giggled together.

"You *were* about to tell a story, were you not, David?" asked Katje in mild amusement.

"Tweak me if you will, Katje darling," David answered, "but I was about to make an observation . . . before I was so rudely interrupted." He sipped at his tea and offered the girls an arch-browed glare. Marguerite glanced abashedly away. Lynnie smiled boldly. She knew he adored them both.

"Do let us hear your observation, Uncle David," Lynnie said brightly.

"Well, as you put your request so sweetly," he said,

lifting Marguerite's hand into his, "I shall do just that." One of his rare smiles curved his lips as he noted Marguerite's shy answering smile of gratitude. "I was about to observe that the American colonies are, quite simply, not fit for civilized habitation." He glanced around the room, assuring himself that he had the rapt attention of all. Once satisfied, he continued. "You know, of course, they've had no English tea there for nearly ten years." He raised his thin dark brows in Victoria's direction to emphasize his point. "They drink that awful Dutch rot, but the simple-minded brutes refuse to buy *English* tea. Now, we all know what that says about them, do we not? It says," he went on, cutting off any potential response, "that those people are tasteless, unrefined, uncivilized barbarians."

Victoria laughed. "Dear Uncle David, the Americans' refusal to drink English tea does not automatically place them in the category of barbarians."

"They are barbarians, my dear," David Newton rejoined adamantly. He accepted more tea as Lynnie poured all around. "There is not a lady or a gentleman among them."

"I have heard that," Marguerite observed worriedly.

"Daddy says those people are bent on—" Lynnie's brow wrinkled delicately as she attempted to recall her father's exact words. "Oh, yes," she said brightening. " 'The Americans are bent on destroying the very concept of colonialism,' " she recited.

"That is so true, my dear Lynnie," David affirmed. "The creatures do not seem to realize that they are on British soil *for the benefit of the Mother Country.* They seem to imagine they are pulling their own strings." He shook his head in disgust. "They are little more than savages."

"They are British subjects just as we are, Uncle David," Victoria reminded him. "No Englishman can be called a savage."

David Newton sipped languidly at his tea. "Would that were so," he said after a pause. "You forget, however, that I was there. I have observed these people at first hand. Have I ever told you about my experiences during the war

18

with the French?"

Katje rolled her eyes, invoking the deity who had endowed her dear friend with such an ubiquitous memory. Everyone had, of course, heard the oft-told tale of David's soldierhood in the colonies of North America. Nevertheless, the young ladies eagerly welcomed each narration. Each time the story was told it was expanded, embellished, heightened until it was as thrilling as any English fable of knights, round tables and dragons. Victoria listened, as always, fascinated.

For her the knights wore woolen cloaks and tricorns; the round tables were rectangular, wide-planked, trimmed of ornamentation, and gate-legged. The dragons were fearsome, painted creatures, wrapped in bear skins. The brooding medieval forests became the uncharted Ohio Valley. The heraldic pennons became Union Jacks, the lances and halberds, muskets and breech-loaders. For Victoria this was no tale of mythic knights and their romantically embattled campaigns, but of authentic living, breathing people. These were people with whom Victoria shared a history, in whom she felt—dare she even think it—a certain pride. Charging rivers, forbidding mountains and mist-shrouded chasms, lush with ancient vegetation and stalked by crouching shadows were not the stuff of dreams for the gently bred Victoria Quayle; they were the stuff of which her ancestral history was made.

She had been told very early of her beginnings. Her guardians had thought it best to apprise her of the circumstances of her birth. What information they could not supply, Victoria had imagined. She was enthralled that she was part of those vast expanses of wilderness that remained untouched to this day by human experience. With the help of the ever inventive David Newton, she had constructed an entire retrospection for herself. At first this game was fun for all of them, but as Victoria grew, the intensity of her desire to discover the truth of her origin increased. Since Lord Darby had passed on a year ago, Victoria had seemed more determined than ever to act upon her resolution to one day travel to the American colonies. That determination had become the spur of her imagination, the lodestar of her perception of the future. David and Katje had seen, and attempted to discourage, that no longer adolescent fancy for for all that time.

"Of course our little Victoria has always been infatuated with those inhospitable shores," David Newton was saying.

"She has positively doted on them," Lynnie concurred cheerily.

"But I tell you this," David continued, "if George Hanover himself strode into this bedchamber and ordered me to do so, I would not go back there. These days a colony is not simply a colony. While we in the West Indies cherish and perpetuate our good English traditions," he warned, "those wretched Americans challenge them at every opportunity. They are just like the quarrelsome landscape they have chosen to tenant—spiteful, repellent and . . . dangerous." The last word was spoken directly to Victoria. David reached down and touched the petal softness of her cheek. His voice, when he spoke, took on a husky and uncharacteristic gentleness. "Do not think of going there," he declared quietly. " 'Twill break your heart."

Victoria swallowed the sudden ache that rose to her throat. She was not unaware of the campaign that had been launched by David and Katje. She loved them for it, understood that they believed it was in her own best interest, but each time she thought of the rock-bound obstinacy of the people who had tamed the forests, the rivers, the mountains of the American colonies, her heart filled with pride. " 'Twas not so long ago, Uncle David, that you bade me cherish the stories we told each other about my heritage. You spoke of my parents as heroes. You said I was part of a grand English tradition. You told me—"

David rolled his eyes to the neatly beamed ceiling. "For heaven's sake, child, did you docket all I said for perpetuity?" He paused and regarded her pointedly. "First of all, I never dreamed you would actually consider going there. In the second place, we all promoted a requisite loyalty in you to the homeland of your parents because, when you were a child, that homeland was worthy of loyalty. The colonial

Americas have changed, and not for the better. They are not the quiet happy lands of your ancestors' days when George I chopped trees in the northern forests. The lands and their people have grown thorny and willful. They must both be subdued. Until that happens, America is no place for a finely bred English lady." His tone seemed to tell Victoria that that was, indeed, that. Katje added her own confirmation.

"Back in the fifties, when your parents were there, love," she said softly, "there was pride to be taken in your colonial ancestry. But eighteen years have passed. It is 1773 and there is no longer reason for pride. The Americans are a belligerent lot. First there was that nonsense over sugar, then over stamps and now over tea. Where will their contentious attitudes take them?"

Lynnie regarded them all solemnly. "Daddy says war is inevitable."

"I hardly think we need go that far in our consideration of the darker possibilities, Lynnie dear," said David Newton blandly. "However, I do agree with 'Daddy' to the extent that some sort of clash is quite likely to occur. The colonies abound with wretches who seem to wallow in quarrelsome ideals."

"But, Uncle David," Victoria interjected, "you said three years ago that there was hope for the Americans."

"You did say that, Uncle David," Marguerite reminded him shyly.

"You debated with Daddy on that very subject," Lynnie affirmed.

"You said there was a fellow in the colonies who might prove a gentleman after all," Marguerite added with unaccustomed boldness.

David Newton offered the girl a withering glare, and she hastily concentrated her attentions on a tea cake. Nibbling furiously, she lowered her eyes, praying someone would speak and draw his attention away from her. Katje smiled in sympathy and came to the girl's rescue.

"The girls are quite correct, David," she cajoled him. "You told us all that Mr. John Adams was nothing if not a

21

gentleman. Those were your exact words." She eyed him impudently. "Do not attempt to intimidate me with your dark glares," she said waving long, elegant fingers at him. "If you make a statement, you ought to be prepared to stand by it." She laughed.

"Whose side are you on, Kat," he muttered.

The woman merely shrugged and offered Marguerite another cake. " 'Twill not hurt to admit you conceded one gentleman to the American colonies," she said lightly. "Besides, 'tis a fascinating story."

"It seems to me you ladies record verbatim everything I say," he grunted.

"Only the important things, Uncle David," Victoria rejoined with a small giggle.

David Newton set his cup on the tea table with a decided click. "I cannot deny stating—at one time, though I recall the words only vaguely—that Mr. Adams was, in fact, a gentleman."

"You told us about an incident that occurred in the town of Boston," Lynnie reminded him. She was not even attempting to conceal her happy anticipation of another story. "You said the incident was referred to as a massacre," she went on with horrified relish.

David Newton, ever the storyteller, warmed to his tale. " 'Twas called the *Boston* Massacre, Lynnie dear. And, despite what you may have heard, it was no massacre." He shifted himself, crossing his neatly breeched legs and steepling his long fingers before him. " 'Twas a bitterly cold night in March of 1770," he began, "the fifth as I recall. A group of local hooligans, having drunk very late at the Bull and Crown—a notorious and shamefully iniquitous haunt—decided to cause a bit of mischief with the British sentries that had been sent by Lord Hillsborough to occupy the town. At the time, you see, mobs of lawless ruffians were going about harassing the tax officers, holding symbolic public tea burnings and generally engaging in ruffianism of the most devilish sort. Well, as I mentioned these young pranksters had decided to have a bit of fun for themselves. They well knew that our boys had been ordered to forbear any and all aggressive behavior. The American miscreants went charging up King Street, taunting the sentries along their way. They began flinging snowballs at the poor freezing soldiers. Well, that was harmless enough, but then they began to fill the snow with chunks of ice and then with rocks. Finally the bloody rabble abandoned the snow altogether and started hurling just the rocks. Naturally, our lads took a defensive stance. What could they do? The drunken American blighters became more and more aggressive, the assault escalated and by some unforeseen chance a fire was lit in a nearby warehouse. Someone — no one knows who — shouted 'fire,' and the British boys raised their guns and did so." David Newton was leaning forward in his chair. His voice lowered, and the girls listened raptly. "No one knows who started the fire, and to this day, no one knows who yelled fire. The only thing anyone knows for sure is that standing at the center of the crowd of ruffians was a man in a red cape. 'Tis thought by many who witnessed the occurrence that the man in the red cape was the instigator of the whole affair and that unholy villain caused the entire catastrophe. To this day, it is believed by many that that man may be the key to every frown of fortune where the American colonists are concerned." David eased himself back into his chair. "The identity of the man has never been revealed," he said pointedly.

"No one knows who he is?" asked Victoria in awe.

"No one," repeated David Newton. "Everyone has his suspicions, naturally, but those Bostonians are a closed-mouthed lot when it comes to the protection of their own. The point is, my dear young ladies, that this 'massacre' everyone speaks of with such relish was nothing more than a squabble between some scruffy, drunken Americans and a few of our weary lads.

"John Adams, American though he may be, understood the situation quite clearly. The English soldiers fired spontaneously — in defense of their lives — and that was all there was to it. Having been a soldier myself," he added decorously, "I well understood their necessity. Mr. Adams also

23

seemed to understand. He agreed that the altercation was nothing more than an infantile expression of frustration and anger. Injudicious as the use of firearms was, murder was not the intent. Mr. Adams also agreed, therefore, to become the attorney for the British defense." He paused significantly. "You ladies can no doubt understand why I refer to the man as a gentleman. His integrity is beyond reproach. After all, one cannot help knowing where his sympathies must lie. But he believes in absolute impartiality under the law, and that is most admirable. His cousin, Samuel," David added, waving a dismissive hand, "a notorious rabble-rouser, pressured Mr. Adams mercilessly concerning his decision to defend the British boys, and, I am told, he suffered a great deal of condemnation for his decision. But the man's unyielding sense of fair play produced a magnificent defense. No one recalls that, of course. Now, to make a long story short — " Katje arched a brow, but David continued unperturbed — "that incident was not dubbed a massacre until a young engraver by the name of Paul Revere published a nasty little cartoon that depicted the appalling tragedy in a most uncomplimentary fashion. He made our young sentries out to be nothing more than a vicious firing squad. He depicted the American hooligans as defenseless innocents. The blighter even placed a little dog in the picture with the British troops firing on it. Can you imagine such a thing? Anyone who would shoot at a little puppy . . . why, the thought is untenable. But there it was for all to see. This most inflammatory piece of dogerel was circulated throughout the colonies, and the incident was denounced ever after as the Boston Massacre." David Newton took a long breath and closed his eyes briefly. "The great irony of the whole affair was that the thing the Bostonians were so angered over, the Townshend Act duties, was repealed on the very day the incident took place. Naturally, the colonists did not hear of the repeal for several months. But the fact is, the disaster might have been avoided had the rebellious young scalawags employed just a bit of patience. Their impetuosity caused the whole bitter rout."

24

"That was three years ago, Uncle David," Victoria said defensively. "Surely, after the British soldiers were acquitted, the Americans realized their mistake."

David regarded her sadly. "I would not place one ounce of British sterling on such a wager," he said. "For one thing, Mr. Adams is the exception not the rule. I will say, with a bow to optimism," he added, "that there have been few hostilities since then."

"Let us be thankful for that," said Katje, rising and moving to the tea table. She gathered up the remnants of the light meal, and it was tacitly understood by all that teatime was at an end. Lynnie and Marguerite lifted themselves and brushed out their skirts. The older woman eyed the two girls with an indulgent smile. "If you would like," she said to them, "you may come back here to dress for the ball. Have Joel bring your things over."

Lynnie squealed delightedly. "Oh, thank you, Kat," she bubbled. Both girls hugged her and then David and Victoria before they bustled from the room. At the door, Lynnie stopped and blew a kiss to the room in general. "Thank you so much for another wonderful story, Uncle David. Teatime is always such *fun* at the Darby house." She laughed. "We shall be back as soon as we find Joel and retrieve our gowns." Both young women descended the staircase with noisy delight. Katje eyed Victoria who had bounded to her feet, no doubt in anticipation of some intervening "fun" before she dressed for the ball.

"You, young lady, are to rest for at *least* an hour," she admonished. "Come, David." Katje swept from the room, carrying the tray.

David stood tiredly. "You are not the only one who needs a rest," he said ruefully. "I fear I have exhausted myself once again with my long-windedness." He laughed in self-deprecation as he placed Victoria's delicate hand in the crook of his elbow. He kissed her lightly on the cheek. "I hope I haven't bored you, my dear," he said.

"You could never bore me, Uncle David," Victoria said.

"About the American colonies . . ." he began.

"I understand, Uncle David," she said softly. "But you

25

are not to worry, you know. Before I go there, I have several things to do." She tilted a glance toward him as they walked among the scattered tissue, and smiled mischievously. "The first thing I must do is get Steven Kensington to propose."

"That will not be difficult," David rejoined with a dry grin of his own.

"Then, of course, we must be married," Victoria went on playfully. "By the time we start a family, Uncle David, I shall probably have forgotten all about America."

"Let us hope so," he said, kissing her once again. Adopting his usual jauntiness, he turned to the door. Glancing back at her, he offered a little wink. He knew, as did she, that his hope was a vain one. "See you at the ball," he said, and he stepped with sprightly vigor down the long hallway to his own apartment.

Chapter Two

Rest, Victoria thought derisively. She plumped down on her bed among the bright derangement of tissue paper, boxes and finery. Lifting a pair of ecru lace pantalettes, she fingered the delicately woven fabric disinterestedly and at last tossed the garment aside. She swung the small, pointed toe of her shoe, and a cloud of tissue riffled into the air to form a papery rainbow at her feet. Curious, she began to swing both feet. She laughed at the froth of fluttery color the action produced. But even that pretty display soon lost its appeal. She plopped back onto fluffy pillows and watched the golden fringe of late afternoon sunlight fall on the lawn outside her open windows. The green, moist world beckoned to her as it always did. She pushed herself up and stepped out onto her balcony. Passing from the confinement of her room into the dawning twilight offered a sense of release that exhilarated Victoria. Hot breezes ruffled the coronet of her hair, and lightly feathered her skirts.

She glanced back into the confusion of her chamber and made a hasty, and many would have said rash, decision. Lifting one leg over the rail, she reached out to grasp the limb of a nearby cashew tree. As she swung herself out over the lawn two stories below, the brittle wood snapped, and Victoria knew a heart-clenching thrill of excitement. She grappled with the hem of her gown as she secured a

27

toehold and wrapped her fingers around slim sturdy branches. Descending quickly, she lighted onto the damp grasses and sprinted across the lawn to the back of the house. Spotting her favorite Arabian gelding alone in the pasture, she ran to him. He responded with a wicker of recognition and pranced to meet her. Victoria slowed, fully appreciating with her reverent gaze the clarity of form, the elegance of musculature of the regal steed. When she reached him she stopped and took a moment to caress the velvet of his muzzle. With answering affection, he nuzzled the palm of her hand. Victoria led him to a flat rock which she used as a step-up to swing onto his unsaddled back. Her movement was fluid and practiced; the horse sensed her unaffected grace and waited patiently as she whisked her petticoats from beneath her and entwined the coarse strands of the animal's mane in her fingers. She prodded him gently, and he swung into a spirited trot. It was not long before Victoria urged the unbridled Arabian to a muscle-stretching gallop. Horse and rider swept together in joyous harmony over lush rolling lawns, past sun-sparkled pools and ornamental gardens until at last they reached the towering canopy of the teak forest that bordered the Darby plantation. Victoria led them to a favored glen. Twilight came sooner there than anywhere else. In that shaded nest, she had spent many hours thinking out her complex adolescent dreams. The horse was not in the least perturbed when she dismounted. She watched with affectionate pleasure his immediate partaking of the lush and familiar grasses that patched the rich earth. Satisfied that he was content, she wandered off.

Victoria moved slowly into the cool depths of the forest's untouched simplicity. Its moist, fertile smells, its delicate and ever-changing music carried her very far from the manicured life she knew as favored child of a deferential household. And, just now, Victoria needed to be very far from that life. She did not understand her reasons. It was not that she disliked or objected to her status as reverenced daughter; she had known, after all, no other existence. She only wished sometimes that she were not quite so adored, and adorned. Daily she was visited by dressmakers, displaying their little doll models from France, or shoemakers, displaying their finest silks and kids, or glove makers, milliners, hairdressers, diamond merchants and lacemakers. Materially, her every whim was fulfilled. If she expressed a longing for a certain food, the world was turned in search of it. If she took delight in a certain author, volumes of his books were delivered to the plantation. Travelling players and musicians, clowns, jugglers and minstrels were invited, whenever they appeared in the district, to entertain Victoria and her friends. It was only here, it seemed, in the dusky serenity of this quiet wood, that the world of certainty—of determined gratification—evaporated. Here Victoria experienced a drifting sense of possibility. In this dim and vaguely mysterious haunt, time seemed pendent, indifferent to necessity. Here Victoria was allowed the indulgence of her dreams.

She stood before the ancient, gnarled bole of her favorite tree. Touching its golden bark raptly, she wondered how long this old fellow had been around. What stories he could tell, if God had allowed him the gift of speech. She gazed up into the wide-spreading limbs and smiled a greeting. "Hello, noble sir," she whispered as she tenderly patted the ancient bark. Then she knelt at the tree's base where a stone covered a crevice between earth and roots. Lifting the stone, she reached inside the aperture and withdrew a sheaf of papers and a small, nearly consumed stick of charcoal. She must remember to bring more next time she came, she thought. She nestled cross-legged on the mossy earth in a curvature of the tree's old trunk and began to write:

> Many lovers have craved the time I waste
> Waiting for the soul of my desire.
> I sigh the hours lost I've sought in haste
> To find the perfect mate and lived inspired.
> I sleep for dreams of love to help me dream
> To wake and rise and lift my heart that cries
> For a hand as soothing as a June stream,

Flowering fresh with warmth from the springtime
   tide.
Is there a hand so strong that needs my soul
To caress and mold the way one should feel?
Do I belong where hearts at last turn whole?
Or must I die before my heart is real.
   The dream stream flows with my hours in haste,
   To find that love may never lift time's waste.

She said the words aloud as she composed, and their
significance was not lost on an observer nearby. The young
man who watched and listened, tapped his riding crop
thoughtfully against his long, buff-breeched thigh. His
intense gaze took in the soft planes of Victoria's profile,
the luminescence of her upswept curls and the gentle
curves of her trim form as she lingered over her diversion.
In the dewy shimmer of the twilight air, her essence
seemed diffused and translucent. She might have been a
vision, quicksilver, a will-o'-the-wisp, an apparition that
could vanish at any moment. The young man's blood
heated. He stepped from his hidden post, and Victoria
glanced up, startled by the shadowed figure. Their eyes
locked. The forest was silent, the air heavy and fragrant
with promise.

"Steven," she gasped, "is it you?" He stepped farther out
into a shadowed rill of gold that escaped the forest's leafy
cover.

"It is, Victoria," he said softly. "I am sorry if I frightened you."

"You could never frighten me, Steven." She smiled in
welcome. The sun was behind him so that his golden hair
formed a shimmering halo around his face.

"I did not wish to disturb your work."

She lowered her gaze. " 'Tis a diversion I keep to myself," she murmured. "I had not intended that anyone
should know—"

"That you write poetry?" he inquired. " 'Tis nothing to
be ashamed of." He studied her, cocking his gaze. "I have
known you since we were children," he said, "and I was

not aware of your gentle pastime. How long were you planning to keep it from me?"

Victoria's smile deepened. She looked up at him through the veil of her lashes. "I suppose until you found out." She paused and her expression sobered. "The truth is I sometimes feel that people will think me silly or capricious, or even . . . unstable if they know." She lowered her eyes and her smile returned. "Now that you've discovered my guilty secret, I hope we can still be friends," she said softly.

"Oh, yes," he answered and lowered himself onto one knee beside her. "I have always hoped we could be . . . more than merely friends, Victoria," he added. His voice was a warm caress.

"I have hoped that, too," she answered. Since she had been a child, Steven had been the personification of all her girlhood longings. She had loved him innocently, purely. She had expressed her adoration abandonedly, laughing at his jokes, including him in her picnics and parties, choosing him first when they paired up for hares and hounds. When he had left for Oxford, she had wept inconsolable tears, and she had begun that day to compose long letters expressing exquisite sadness on the enforced separation of friends. But since he had returned, their relationship had changed. She was shyer with him, less willing to share her suddenly grown-up expectations. Her friends had cajoled her, assuring her that she and Steven Kensington were headed for marriage. They were the perfect couple, after all. It was roundly and avidly decided that their match had been divinely inspired. Publicly Victoria agreed, but in the most secret recesses of her soul, she knew only that she longed to feel his arms around her, to know the enchantment of a man's embrace. More than that, she longed to be with Steven in places where earthly amenities were altered, where time and place and courtesies were visitors not residents. She longed to feel the sweep of rapture carry her like angel dust on the wind.

Steven's fingers touched the tip of her small chin, and he turned her gently to face him. "Where have your reflections taken you?" he inquired with a half smile. He studied

31

her for a long moment. "You have always been a rhapsodizer, Victoria."

"Have I?" she asked, answering his smile with a smile of her own. "I never thought of myself that way."

He laughed lightly. "Oh, but 'tis true. Do you not recall our childhood games? They were always your inspiration. Lynnie and Marguerite and I were merely players in your grand plots."

Victoria wrinkled her smooth brow in concern. "I had no idea I was so demanding, Steven."

"Not demanding, Victoria," he assured her, "imaginative—more imaginative than the rest of us. Your games took us to far places where dreams thrive best. Your favorite game was pilgrims and Indians; do you remember it?"

Victoria offered him a piquant smile. "I do," she said. "I was always a pilgrim mother—courageous, purposeful—"

"And fruitful." Steven laughed. "You insisted upon gathering your dolls around you, pretending that you had at least ten children to provide for."

"A perfect saint." Victoria giggled. "And you were my husband, a fearless hunter."

"And we lived in a little thatch-roofed hut on the Plimoth Plantation."

"And then we moved to the Shawmut Peninsula where there was fresh water and a generally more healthful environment for the children," Victoria rejoined, in mock seriousness. "And we grazed our cows on the common land—"

"And ate pumpkins," Steven finished, laughing as he settled himself next to her on the ground. He placed his arms around her slim shoulders and drew her to him. They sat for some moments in silent recollection of their childhood game. When their quiet laughter had ceased, Steven spoke. "But now we are grown, Victoria. The time has come for play to end." Her head resting against his wide chest, she nodded. He looked down, breathing in the fragrance of her soft curls. " 'Tis no longer possible for us to live in a world of dreams. Certain realities must be faced."

She lifted her gaze to look directly into his eyes. "I

understand, Steven," she murmured.

"Do you . . . truly?" he asked. Again, she nodded. He continued solemnly. "We have always loved each other, have we not?"

Victoria's heart thumped in her chest. Was he going to propose now? Was he not even going to wait for the ball tonight? A swelling excitement trilled beneath her flesh. *Oh, Steven,* she thought in a delirium of joy, *how can I refuse you? How can I make you implore me?* Her mischievous resolve vanished. Something serious was happening here. Victoria readied herself. Her answer ripened on her lips. "Yes," she breathed at last. "Yes, yes, yes." But he had not proposed, she reprimanded herself. He had only asked if they had loved each other. "Yes," she repeated hastily and less avidly. "We have loved each other, Steven." She glanced down and smoothed at the parchment that lay on her lap with trembling fingers. Her poetry, her phrases of hope and promise and, in a sense, urgency drifted before her. *Ask it, Steven,* she impelled him. *Oh, please, ask the question. Just say it.* Instead, he turned his gaze from her. "We must always be truthful with each other," he said at last. "Wouldn't you agree?"

"Yes," she assured him with less patience that she had meant to display. When he did not immediately respond, the evasion in his last question struck her. She cocked her gaze. "Is something wrong?" she asked.

"Yes," he answered softly. He stood and moved slowly from her, an air of resignation in the slump of his broad shoulders. Victoria felt an apocryphal chill. She shuddered involuntarily. Lifting herself from the forest floor, scattering her poetry, she followed Steven and placed a small hand on his broad back.

"Tell me," she urged him quietly. He glanced back at her and then quickly away. "Tell me very quickly," she said, fear thrilling up from her stomach.

Steven fixed his gaze on a distant point. His words came like flat stones dropped on flat rocks, straight down, unwavering in their terminus, insoluble in their conclusion. "We cannot be married," he said. Victoria's eyes widened.

33

She felt the blood drain from her face. Steven quickly turned to steady her. "There is nothing I can do," he rushed on. "My father has already negotiated a contract with Barbara Meriam's family."

Slowly, Victoria backed away from him, shrugging off his supporting hands. Pain and puzzlement warred in her shimmering gaze.

Steven stepped haltingly toward her. "You must try to understand, Victoria," he said. " 'Tis not my decision. I have always assumed—"

"Whose decision, then?" Victoria asked him.

"My father's, of course." Steven's tone was desperate. "Do you think for one moment, I would choose that cow for a wife?"

Victoria stopped. An emerald fire seemed to flare in her eyes. Her shoulders squared rigidly. "Does Barbara know you consider her a cow?" she asked.

Steven attempted a half-smile. "Of course not," he said, his manner seductive and bantering. "And I certainly hope you won't mention it to her." Victoria's gaze swung away from him. He stepped forward. The initial shock of his words diffused, he felt more bold. He, once again, took Victoria's shoulders in his hands. His regard tilted. "This does not have to mean the end of our friendship," he said softly, "surely you realize that. Oh, I know that right at the moment you are stunned and even, perhaps, a bit angry. But that will pass."

"May I ask why such a decision was made, Steven?" Victoria's tone was like crystal in the deepening darkness.

"Well, I thought you might have guessed," Steven answered, his words coming uncertainly.

"No," said Victoria evenly, staring up at him. "I have not guessed."

"Well . . ." he said tentatively, " 'tis a matter of . . . form, I suppose."

"Form?" asked Victoria.

"Yes, you know . . ." his voice trailed off. He turned suddenly and raked his long, aristocratic fingers through his golden hair. "For God's sake, Victoria, look at this from my father's point of view." He glanced back to find her regarding him steadily. "He is a very wealthy man; he has a great fortune to pass on." He looked away from her. "My father has a profound sense of responsibility," he said sullenly. "Is that so hard to understand?"

"In this context, yes," Victoria answered.

"Well, I think you would do well to try," he rejoined. "He cannot leave his fortune to just anyone."

"Am I . . . just anyone?"

"I didn't mean that," Steven muttered.

"Yes you did." Victoria's voice had dropped almost to a whisper. "I have no 'family' no . . . pedigree, is that it? For all my wealth, for all my adoptive nobility, I am still just a member of the common herd, a peasant."

"You begin to understand," Steven said, facing her. "My father is a Viscount *by descent*. Upon his death I shall inherit that title, and upon my death my son will inherit. Can my father be so careless as to infuse that noble line with God knows what vulgarity?" He stopped suddenly. "I do not mean to imply that *you*—" He stopped again and drew in a long breath, closing his eyes in an attempt to regain his composure. "I do not mean to imply," he went on evenly, "that you, in and of yourself, are vulgar, Victoria. 'Tis only that for all your benefactions you are . . . unblooded."

"And Barbara Meriam has . . . blood." Victoria managed a twinkle of a smile.

"More than enough," Steven said, seeing humor in Victoria's perception of the circumstance and feeling emboldened by it. He smiled as well, even offered a diffident laugh. "You and I both know how foolish all this seems, but picture this, Victoria. How valuable would that animal of yours be," he asked, gesturing in the general direction of Victoria's horse, "if he had no pedigree?" Victoria stiffened but made no response. Steven moved toward her. He took her face into his hands. "These words have been hard to hear, I know," he said gently. "I would have done anything to have spared you this pain." He regarded her carefully as though he were contemplating a rare jewel. "I do love you, you know." Hesitating, he lowered his lips, but she turned aside so that his kiss fell upon the silk of her cheek. "Please try not to be angry," he said.

"I will try," Victoria answered slowly, "but I cannot help thinking that the loss may be yours, Steven." He lifted his brows and questioned her with an expectant gaze. "Barbara is only the daughter of an earl. For all either of us knows, I might be the daughter of a king."

Steven burst into appreciative laughter. "'Twould not surprise me in the least," he said lightly. He placed his arm around her waist and started them in the direction of their tethered horses. "I am glad you are taking this so well, Victoria," he said. "It gives me the courage to make the suggestion I came here to make to you in the first place." Neither of them noted the soft rain that began. "Since my father announced his plans to me concerning Barbara, I have searched my mind for a way to resolve this problem." They were walking slowly beneath a sonorous thunder that sounded in the distance. "My proposal is quite simple," Steven was explaining. The forest misted with sheets of fine droplets. " 'Tis not unusual for a man of my rank to take a mistress." The thunder pounded above them. "And there is no shame in a gentlewoman agreeing to such an arrangement. Think of Mrs. d'Aumerle and Lord Darby." Plump raindrops splashed down from the tips of large leaves overhead. A glister of lightning ripped through the clouds. "I was thinking, this might be the perfect arrangement for us." The sky opened. Rain crashed through the canopy of the trees. Thunder split the sky with a deafening crack. Lightning raged against the darkness, tearing with jagged teeth the moon-grimed clouds. "We had better head for cover," Steven hollered and dragged Victoria through the deluge and toward the horses. Mounting quickly, they headed out of the forest at a pounding gallop.

Much later, as night descended, a hush resonated over the wood. As the storm whispered to an end, as the purling breezes soothed the battered land, a bit of parchment murmured faintly as it was lifted by the wind and carried across the leaf-scattered earth. Noiselessly it was set down

36

a few feet away. A blurred message trickled over its surface, but the words themselves, the promise, the hope had disappeared.

Chapter Three

The high-ceilinged room eddied with swirling color. Radiant Chinese silks and fluttering Indian cottons mingled to form a diaphonous indoor garden which spilled out onto the verandas. Music filled the succulent air of the West Indian night.

Victoria, at last bathed, perfumed and coiffed, and of course, magnificently gowned, greeted her guests. She moved about with fluid grace and with no hint of the monolithic conversion just performed. Katje, Lynnie and Marguerite stood apart, silently congratulating themselves that the transformation had so eloquent a result. That it had taken place at all, Katje decided, was nothing less than a miracle. The child had come in out of the rain, dragging her muddy skirts and looking generally like a drowned cat. She had been properly scolded, plopped into a tub of steaming water and then handed from lady to lady until she was at last deemed fit to be seen.

It had not gone unnoticed, by Katje at least, that the titanic process had been accompanied by an uncharacteristic passivity on the part of Victoria. And there was something else, too. . . . Had soft tears melted the girl's gaze when Lynnie and Marguerite mentioned Steven Kensington? When they had spoken of his anticipated proposal, had Victoria remained inexplicably spiritless? Was her silence during the transformation due to embarrassment over her rash behavior, or was there some other reason for her almost stoic acceptance of the zealous attentions of

38

her friends? Victoria was not prone to embarrassment, thought Katje. The reason for her subdued attitude of earlier must lie elsewhere. The girl seemed fine now, but yet there was a certain want of . . . something about her; some unnameable facet of the gently exuberant Victoria was missing. Or perhaps something had been added. It was impossible to know. She was fast growing up, Katje sighed inwardly, and subject to changing moods lately. Katje hoped that either the mood would pass or that the girl would soon confide in her as she always eventually had. The older woman waved her fan and offered a relieved sidewise smile toward her two assistants as Victoria was introduced to Robert Clive, the foremost builder of the British Empire in India.

Sir Robert bent low over Victoria's hand. "Thank you for including me in the festivities this evening, Lady Darby. It gives me the opportunity to say that you have, indeed, grown into your fabulous promise." At forty-seven, Clive was a tall, distinguished soldier and statesman. He lifted his wide shoulders and arched a gaze at Victoria. "You have had an excellent role model, may I add." His eyes wandered to Katje, and that woman nodded and smiled in delicate modesty. "By the way," Sir Robert said, swinging a sober countenance back to Victoria, "David Newton tells me that you speak often of travelling to America." Victoria glanced quickly to David, whose innocent shrug merely served to confirm his guilt, and immediately back to Robert Clive. She managed her prettiest smile.

"I have an interest in that land, 'tis true," she said mildly. "Both my parents were apparently born there."

"I know that, Lady Darby," answered Clive sternly, "and for that reason your interest is certainly understandable. But I make this appeal to you, nevertheless." Victoria repressed a deep sigh and gazed raptly at her lecturer. "This America to which your thoughts seem to turn is a place where Englishmen turn their backs on their own countrymen. At least here in India, we British stand together—against the French, against the native rulers, against the

Brahmins. For over twenty years I have seen the most valiant unity among our people. Here in India, we know the value of loyalty to the Mother Country."

Victoria nodded solemnly. "I am not unaware of the tradition of loyalty to the Crown that exists here, Sir Robert," she said, gathering her determination in the face of the warnings of this fiercely patriotic gentleman. "You will recall I have grown up with that tradition. I have no intention whatsoever of ever abandoning my love for the Sovereign rule." She managed a piquant smile. "If I ever do go to America, I shall manage, I assure you, to turn a few insurrectionist heads." Her smile sweetened. "I am rather famed for my own rebellious ways, and you know that when one rebel meets another rebel the soil turns red with combat, the air blue with invective, the lip white with fury; those colors, Sir Robert, symbolize all that I hold dear. I shall always be unbending in my support of them."

Thoroughly charmed, Robert Clive smiled warmly. He took Victoria's small hand in both of his. "You might well turn out to be our most effective ambassador." He brushed her cheek with an affectionate kiss. "And now, if you will excuse me?" He turned to Katje and she took his arm. They made a handsome couple as they strolled out onto the dance floor. Victoria wasted no time in impaling David Newton with an accusing glare. He merely shrugged once again.

"You cannot blame me for desiring him as an ally," he said defensively. "The problem is," he added, leaning toward Victoria and speaking in a confidential tone, "Bobby Clive has absolutely no damned subtlety."

Victoria could not stop the laughter that bubbled to her lips. "Neither, it would seem, have you, Uncle David," she cajoled him. She swept him a curtsy, and before he could answer she was off to mingle with her guests. She had made a grand show of gaiety since the ball had begun, she prided herself. She determined to continue that charade. She had lost everything that afternoon—everything that was important to her—but she still had her self-respect. And hope raged within her. Steven could not have meant

40

what he had proposed that afternoon. She had, no doubt, misheard him. Her sudden and most ill-advised anger had blurred her judgement. Steven would see her tonight acting the celebrated hostess, she reasoned, and he would know her for the elevated lady that she was. He would reconsider. In the end, he would marry her. In the meantime — until he came to his senses — she would carry herself pridefully, secure in the knowledge of her exalted position in the community.

"We are all expecting an announcement tonight," said the young and vibrant Lady Louise Arnold as Victoria approached her. She waggled a fan near her plump bosom. " 'Tis long overdue, if you ask me. Why, everyone has known for years that you and Steven Kensington . . ." her voice trailed off.

Victoria's confidence blossomed at Louise's words. There could be no question! There could be no doubt! Everyone *knew* that Steven and she had been made for each other. Victoria offered her a characteristically coquettish smile. "What sort of announcement were you planning on, Louise?" she asked.

"Well . . . you know . . ." she intoned obliquely, her eyes darting to Steven, who was standing nearby with Barbara Meriam on his arm. Noting their attention, Steven offered a small wave in greeting and a playful half-smile. Next to him, Barbara stood tall, cramp-shouldered and, for all her regal height, decidedly unregal. Victoria noted with some misgiving Steven's cavalier attitude toward the woman as he excused himself from her company with barely a nod and strode nonchalantly to Victoria's side.

"Good evening, ladies," he said to the young women in general, but his gaze was for Victoria only.

"Good evening, Steven," said Louise. "I notice you have accompanied Lady Barbara this evening. This is quite an unexpected surprise." Her tone was reproving. "We had all thought you would escort Victoria." She arched a brow, making her displeasure at the circumstance abundantly clear.

"I assure you, Lady Arnold, Victoria understands." His

41

glance glinted knowingly in Victoria's direction. Her heart clenched. She offered him an apprehensive smile. Steven went on grandly. "Victoria and I have a relationship that transcends . . . form." He laughed slyly at what—Victoria could only assume—others were expected to consider a private joke between her and Steven. She stiffened, dread rising, but held on to her composure. Louise Arnold waggled her fan more vigorously and looked astounded.

"I hope you do not realize how that *sounds,* Steven," she asserted.

Another lady, standing nearby intoned, "It *sounds* positively illicit."

"So it does." Steven laughed.

Louise closed her fan with a decided click and tapped him reproachfully on the shoulder. "You always have been a tease," she chided him with a small nervous laugh. Then her expression sobered, and she moved the two of them a few steps away from the possible attention of others. "You know you really ought to avoid that sort of humor, Steven," she said, her tone hushed. "One must be very cautious. This is a small community. One can never be too careful of one's reputation," she finished.

"Your advice is most welcome, Louise," he said, his tone matching hers, "but Victoria and I know exactly what we are doing."

The woman's eyes widened, and she flashed a puzzled look to Victoria. "What in God's name is he talking about?" she blurted.

Victoria's smile narrowed. Her gaze glinted emerald fire. So, she thought resolutely, there had been no mistake. There was a certain satisfaction in tearing up an unfinished poem, in discarding a troublesome swatch of embroidery, in laying to rest an impossible hope. "I haven't the foggiest notion, Louise," she said with finality.

"Well, I should think *not!*" Lady Louise humphed. "And you, Steven, ought to have your mouth washed out with soap."

Steven offered a deferential nod, but his lips remained half curved in an insolent smile. Barbara Meriam sidled toward them, her head, as always, slung low between her bulky shoulders. Victoria noted, with a pang of sympathy, that the dress she wore was woefully inappropriate to her burly dimensions. Barbara invariably chose the laciest, most diaphanous gowns and the rudest colors. Tonight she was disarranged in royal purple. Steven cleared his throat and grasped Victoria's arm, and pretending not to have noticed Barbara's approach, he led her smoothly onto the dance floor. Eyes turned and conversations ended abruptly as the perfectly balanced couple made their way to the center of the ballroom. Whispered comments roundly approved the partnering of the district's most prized couple. Only Barbara Meriam remained impassive.

Tall, broad-shouldered, youthfully virile, Steven bowed proprietarily, and Victoria, dainty, ivory-complected and elegant tipped a curtsy, their shimmering blond heads dipping regally toward each other. The musicians, awed by the attractive pair, seemed to linger over their music with an excess of poetic expression. Together Steven and Victoria danced in eloquent circles on the parqueted floor. The gathered company watched mezmerized and commented on what lovely children the two would create and on how perfectly they complemented each other. When the music ended, the star-kissed couple stepped out onto the veranda with the collective approval of the assembled guests.

The usually docile Barbara Meriam, it was reported, displayed an uncharacteristic bit of temper at just that moment, and everyone was curious as to why the girl swept from the room, her mother bustling worriedly at her heels.

Fragrant breezes encloaked the young couple as they strolled together over the rolling lawns of the plantation. Locust trees formed a silvery canopy above their heads, and low, arching shrubbery brushed their feet gently as they passed. Well-manicured hills and hollows stretched out before them like a moon-shadowed ocean. The scent of bougainvillea and gardenia whispered a welcome to the terraced gardens that surrounded the house.

"These people," said Steven with a derisive chuckle. Victoria tilted him a glance. "Well, you know," he continued as they seated themselves on an ornately scrolled iron bench, "they like to imagine themselves *so* sophisticated. You did note Louise's reaction to our arrangement," he confided expectantly. Victoria shifted her gaze to a near-distant flowering shrub.

"I thought Louise was appropriately surprised," she murmured.

"Did you," Steven inquired in bemusement. Victoria nodded. "I cannot imagine why," he went on. "What did she—or any of them, for that matter—expect?"

"I suppose they expected, as I did, that we would be married." Victoria's gaze swung slowly back to him. Steven paused. Victoria's upturned face was bathed in moonlight. He gazed down into the emerald depths of her eyes which were framed by thick lashes. He found speech difficult. As this was an unaccustomed condition for him, he did not immediately know how to handle it. He stood abruptly and turned from her. Gathering his composure, he managed a small laugh. "I thought we had this all worked out this afternoon," he said.

"*You* had it 'worked out,' Steven," Victoria said evenly. "I agreed to nothing."

Steven took a long breath. *Damn women!* he thought resignedly. Just when you imagine you have them under control they allow their unstable tempers to nettle the es-tablished amity and unsettle everything. Sometimes the creatures were more trouble than they were worth. "I thought I had explained this to you already," he said, rolling his head back in exasperation. "Marriage is a seri-ous business, Victoria, and I can do nothing less than take it seriously. Please do not start being childish about this." The sudden rustle of skirts caught his attention, and he turned. The slap was both unexpected and forceful. Steven grasped his jaw in astonishment. "What in the bloody hell do you think you are about, Victoria!" he burst out. "How dare you!"

"How dare *you*, Steven," she clenched out. "How dare *you*!" She turned and stalked from the garden. Steven grappled with his emotions. He was torn between outrage and apology. Apology for what? he challenged himself. He's done nothing wrong.

"Victoria," he called, his tone surly. He strode to her side, taking up her crisp pace. "I am perfectly willing to acknowledge that there might have been a different outcome to our relationship had circumstances been different. But, dammit, I have a responsibility to my family. I am not about to abandon that responsibility for some trifling dependency of yours on formality. My marriage to Barbara will change nothing between us. We will proceed as planned. I shall even arrange a honeymoon for us, if that will soothe your ruffled dignity."

Victoria's abrupt halt set Steven off balance. She swung to face him. "Dignity?" she blazed. "You speak of dignity? Where is Barbara Meriam's dignity in all this? What will she be doing while you and I are off on our 'honeymoon'? In dignity's name, Steven, marry the woman if you must, but leave me out of your shameful plan." At her quick turn he grasped her shoulders, swinging her back to face him.

"Dammit, girl," he grated, "I have had enough of this. What is so bloody shameful about me wanting to spend my life with you? I love you. And you know you love me. Beyond that, what makes you think you'll get a chance at marriage? I am not the only man who feels this way, you know." His voice went on relentlessly. She struggled against Steven's hold, or perhaps she struggled against his cruel words. He held her more fiercely. "Why do you think no one has approached David Newton? Do you imagine any family of quality in this settlement would welcome you as the assurance of its succession? Be realistic, Victoria. You are common. You rose up like a bloody mushroom, no one knowing where you came from. Deference was showered on you because of your winning ways, because of your extraordinary beauty and because of Lord Darby's prestige. But, by God, do not imagine for a moment that deference will get you a husband. I am your best hope and don't you forget it." Her struggles had ceased. She gazed

45

up at him now, her expression one of disbelief. She could not credit Steven's words, and yet they made a horrible kind of sense. If all he said was true, her whole life had been a lie. Tears of humiliation and denial welled in her incredulous gaze. Steven relaxed his hold. Victoria jerked away from him, unwilling that he should witness her shame. Steven grabbed at her, dragging her toward him, but she resisted him. Her foot shot out from beneath the sweep of her petticoats and connected soundly with his shin. He let go of her to grasp at his injured leg. Stifling a curse, he hopped toward her. "Victoria!" he bellowed as she hiked up her skirts and fled across the hilly terrain. Steven abandoned his wound and followed, catching her and tumbling them both over a rolling hillock. "Damn it, girl," he muttered as they surged, holding on to each other, down the incline and into the center of the plum grove. They spun to a stop on level ground. Victoria lay beneath him. Except for the wild fluttering of her heart, she was absolutely still. Steven's furious gaze impaled her as he rose and brushed at his now stained and rumpled attire. "See where your talk of dignity has gotten us," he ground out. "I do not know why I put up with this. I shall tell you one thing, miss," he said wrathfully, "I will not put up with it again. I am going inside. I refuse to be part of your infantile games any longer." He glared down at her. "You have complicated your life unnecessarily, you know. Simply stated, the facts are these: I love you and you have made it clear that you love me; my father, for dynastic reasons, has negotiated a fine marriage settlement between our family and the Meriams; because of your uncertain lineage your own marital prospects are nil; I am willing to take you under my protection as my mistress. A bargain is struck. What could be simpler? What could be more reasonable?"

Victoria's repressed tears made her voice tight. "You speak a language I do not understand, Steven," she said. "You speak of negotiation and bargaining."

"It is my language," he asserted. "If you do not understand it, there is little hope for us."

"That is the first thing you have said that I agree with," Victoria murmured. She sat up slowly. Looking up at him, she continued. "I, for one, do not appreciate being bargained for as though I were a fine piece of horseflesh or a particularly fertile bit of acreage. If Barbara Meriam is willing to be treated as such, that is her poverty, her narrowness of vision." Victoria's anger was growing. "Dammit to bloody hell, Steven, 'tis you who have complicated things." She stood. "To hell with bargains and negotiations, Steven. Tell that to your bloody father, the bloody viscount. Tell him we are people, that we have brains and hearts and souls. We are not, dammit, negotiable!"

Steven gaped at her for a long, unfocused moment. When at last he was able to speak, his words were barely audible. "My God," he breathed, "where did you ever learn such impolite language?"

Victoria's elegantly winged brow shot up. "Is that really all you can say, Steven?" she asked.

"You *are* common," he stated, his voice hinted at a certain wonder. "A crude source will always tell." His last words were said coldly, but their sting fired Victoria's blood. Her hand swung back, and for the second time that night, Steven's jaw felt the bite of her wrath. Holding his smarting cheek, he snarled, "Bargains are themselves negotiable. Take care you do not negotiate yourself into a lonely old age, Victoria." He spun away from her and made for the house.

"Damn it, Steven," Victoria railed after him. "Stay and fight like a man!" Only the silence of his retreat answered her. She stamped her foot on the damp grasses and could not even manage the satisfaction of a proper thunk. Her mind sputtered indignantly as her pique rose to a towering rage. When the rage could no longer be contained, she took out her frustration on a hyacinth. Kicking violently at a nodding blossom, Victoria watched as the flower bobbed silently and then resignedly divested itself of its petals. Realizing her cruelty, Victoria quickly knelt beside the innocent bush. "Oh," she breathed sorrowfully, "how could I have done such a thing?" She lifted the injured

47

petals and cupped them to her breast. Her tears came with aching slowness now as she raised her gaze to the silvered moon. A tattered, gauzy vapor passed beneath its detached perusal, darkening its luster. How could any of this have happened, she wondered? Only hours ago she had been so certain of everything. Now it was all gone. If Steven had wounded some vital part of her in the cedar forest that afternoon, here in the plum grove he had killed it. What was the thing she had lost, she wondered? What was the thing she had surrendered to Steven Kensington? She raised herself, and as she did so, the petals of the flower floated from her hands. "If I am so common, Steven," she sobbed softly, "why do I feel such uncommon pain?"

"Perhaps," said a voice from behind her, "it is because you are not common." Victoria turned in astonished terror. There was no one there. Her gaze ranged the moon-shadowed expanse of lawn, but she saw no one. "Who is it?" she demanded, summoning all her courage. A faint hope sparked within her. "Steven?" she breathed into the warm night. Her brows drew together as she heard a low chuckle. "You had better make yourself known, sir," she demanded.

"And if I do not," answered the mocking baritone, "will you attack me as you did that innocent flower?"

Victoria's eyes widened. She realized the voice was coming from somewhere high above her and that the person had probably heard every word of her graceless confrontation with Steven Kensington. "Dammit, who are you!" She was only a little frightened.

"More inelegant language," said the voice with maddening dispassion. Victoria's eyes narrowed. She realized that whoever the person was—no doubt an insolent servant, or some puckish neighbor boy deepening his voice to alarm her—he was tucked safely and smugly in the branches of a slender plum tree. She moved cautiously with feigned nonchalance toward the voice as it continued. " 'Tis quite clear that you have lost the affection of the elegant Mr. Kensington, or should I say 'Lord' Kensington. He seems to be quite a catch, but I would not worry overmuch; I think you are better off without him. As a matter of fact, I think—" The monologue was suddenly and unceremoniously cut off as, shaking the slender trunk of one tree, Victoria managed to jerk the branches so that they convulsed wildly. Along with several plums, the tree divested itself almost immediately of the tall, lean figure of a man. He landed on his feet, laughing, and Victoria stepped several paces back. This was no young neighbor boy. She repressed a lurching terror. "Who are you?" she demanded once again. She placed her hands on her hips and planted her feet wide apart. She determined to take an aggressive stance. The man was, after all, trespassing on her property. "There are penalties for invasion of privacy, you know." If nothing else, she would intimidate him with the law.

"Invasion of privacy, madam?" He chuckled. "If anything, my privacy was invaded by your brawl with that pompous ass."

"Watch your tongue," Victoria fumed. "You are speaking to a nobelwoman." In the darkness, she could not see the grin that formed on the man's insolent mouth, but she perceived it. "Whom do you serve?" she demanded, fully prepared to march back into the ball and extract immediate satisfaction from the man's employer.

"I am, madam, my own master," he said. She watched the silhouette bow deeply. "And your ears do not seem to require the diffidence that your apparent nobility might indicate."

Victoria's gaze widened at the affrontery. "How dare you, sir!" she exclaimed. For all Steven's diminishment of her value, she had the self-identity of years behind her. "I am going to demand not only an apology," Victoria asserted, "but some punitive determination as well." At that moment a cloud passed beyond the moon, and the grove was flooded with light. Victoria's widened gaze travelled from the man's broad chest up to the muscular shoulders and beyond. His ruddily bronzed complexion suggested that he was used to the outdoors. His fall from the tree had sent a tumble of rust-colored curls down, in boyish confusion, over his forehead. And his eyes, the color of blue sea glass, sparkled roguishly.

"I can only say, madam," he said softly, "that I am at your service." He bowed again and, in the same gesture, retrieved a somewhat mangled tricorn from the grass. Popping it atop the tangle of burnished curls as he rose, his smile deepened.

Her initial unpreparedness for the man's symmetry of face and form somewhat diminished, Victoria asked, "What business have you here?"

"I am on God's own business," the man assured her. "I am here on the business of survival." Victoria's gaze darkened. The man went on unaffected by her authoritarian display. He regarded, with mocking despair, the tumble of flower petals and the fallen plums that surrounded the two of them. "I came not to destroy nature's magic," he said, "but to benefit by it—as God intended," he finished piously.

"You came to steal plums," Victoria stated flatly.

"That I did, madam," the man agreed with an amiable lack of compunction.

"And you stayed to spy," she added, lifting her chin haughtily.

"Believe me when I tell you that it was not by my choosing that I was witness to the ugly squabble between you and your . . . beau."

"He is not my beau," stated Victoria.

"So it would appear," said the main with an impudently satisfied smile. "And, if I may offer an opinion—"

"You may not," Victoria rejoined.

"You are better off without the blackguard," the man continued as though she had not spoken. "He is not nearly good enough for you."

Victoria regarded the man suspiciously. "Is that your opinion?" she asked.

"It is," he responded confidently. "In my opinion, that fellow deserves a horse whipping. His attitude toward poor Barbara is quite simply unconscionable. The girl probably fancies herself in love with the pompous blighter." He watched for Victoria's affirming nod, and then he went on, pacing in the manner of a court officer. "Of course she does," he said. "I grudgingly admit that he is handsome and, I suppose some might say, charming. Is there any wonder that he has inspired her affection?" He turned to glance at Victoria, and noting that he had her attention, he went on. "The sadder element is," he said, raising an erudite finger, "that—handsome and charming as he is— he has managed to secure your affection as well."

Victoria lowered her gaze. "I hate him," she said quietly.

"No you don't," the man corrected her gently. "You do not hate him one bit. Whose name was it you called before when you first heard me in the tree? Did I not hear you say 'Steven'? Did you not hope, just for the breath of a second, that he had returned?" He studied her as her eyes lifted. In the moonlight, her green gaze sparkled, and the man realized that a glaze of tears had formed there. He moved toward her and placed his arms around her. She stepped into his embrace. For making her—forcing her— to see the truth, he was as much a bastard as Kensington, he chided himself ruefully. He held her for a long moment, and cradling the back of her soft curls in his large hand, he pressed her cheek to his wide shoulder. "Shhh," he crooned softly. "Forgive me," he said after a pause. " 'Tis only that your love for the blighter is such a waste."

"I do not love him," she said, her words muffled in the sea-scented cloth of his coat. "And I am common, you know. I mean I probably am."

The man laughed a rich warm chuckle. "And so am I," he said. "Anyone worth his salt is common."

"But 'tis different for me." Victoria raised her gaze to him. The man drew in his breath. The moonlit halo of her curls captured his imagination. Her emerald gaze, nearly opalescent in the silvered night, enchanted him as, up to this moment, only the swells of the ocean had been able to do. Victoria continued, the gentle music of her voice encloaking him. "I am nobly bred. I do not know how to be common."

"You speak the truth, madam," he murmured. "You are without a doubt the most uncommon woman I have ever met." He lowered his lips to hers, capturing them in a moon-bathed kiss. She responded not as the breathless young girl he had expected but as a woman. Her arms lifted to encircle his neck, and he felt her fingers entwine in the curls that brushed his collar. He drew himself away at last. "Uncommon," he breathed.

" 'Tis my very first kiss," Victoria said, smiling softly. The man regarded with tender appreciation the luminescent vision swimming before him.

"I am most honored." He laughed. "May I have the further honor of claiming your second?"

Victoria's countenance sobered. She drew away from him, but he pulled her back. She had never known the splendor of a man's full and rapt attentions. Oh, she had dreamed of what it would be like to be held in a man's arms. She had known it would be wonderful, but she had not imagined the details. This was her opportunity to discover the mysteries of a world she had only imagined. With a fluttering trepidation, she gave herself to the wonder of his encompassing virility. She allowed the second kiss. She was hesitant but curious as she felt his firm mouth twist over her lips, possessing them with breathtaking authority. His hands roved acquisitively over the tender curves of her body. His lips feathered kisses along the arching column of her throat, and she moaned involuntarily as her body ripened with its own throbbing hunger. She felt herself consumed by a wave of hot unfocused desire. She had no idea what was happening to her . . . or to him. He seemed energized, pulsing with necessity. She arched to him as she felt herself lowered in his strong arms to the grass. At last, she thought, she had discovered the heavenly bliss, the consuming rapture that existed between men and women. If something had died in her this night, something had also been born. She allowed herself to be swept fully into the maelstrom of his need. His heart pounded against her flattened breasts as he pressed her to him.

Mindlessly, he tore at the bodice of her gown, freeing

the mounds of blossoming flesh that he raged to caress. He did not hear the sudden scream, muffled by his own lips, that tore from Victoria's lips. He did not note the gasping struggle going on beneath his exploring hands.

"Let me love you," he breathed in his frenzied passion. "Do not fight me," he commanded. His powerful arms held her tightly; his tongue penetrated the soft, warm recesses of her mouth. The whirling flesh of his desire could not be quelled. His big hand pierced the folds of her gown, tearing at the flimsy lace of her undergarments. It was not until the ragged scream ripped into his consciousness that the ferocity of his advance abated. He glanced down at Victoria, realizing suddenly that she was struggling violently against his aggression. "What is it?" he breathed.

"Stop it," she gasped raggedly. "Let me go!" He drew away from her, and with true disbelief in his eyes, he asked her once again what was wrong. "What is wrong?" she raged breathlessly. "You were about to rape me, you monster!"

His mouth gaped open. "Rape you?" he burst out. "I would never do such a thing."

"Would you not?" Victoria shrieked. "What do you call this?" She held out the tattered edges of her gown and just as quickly tucked them back against her bared breasts. "How dare you!"

The man continued to stare at her as though she had gone insane.

"I may be overzealous," he conceded, "but, love, I was not raping you." A small smile played upon his lips. "I have never felt the need to force any woman." He reached out and ran his fingertips lightly over the luminous flesh that swelled against her ragged bodice. Victoria drew in a quick breath.

"Take your hands off me," she clenched out.

"As you wish," he said softly, but the smile deepened. "Let me understand something. Because I mistook the passion of your response for willingness, you now tell me I was attempting to rape you. Is that it?"

Victoria turned his words over quickly in her mind. "Yes," she said at last.

His brow lifted, doubting her. "Then, your passion did not indicate willingness," he stated, the smile still playing in his eyes.

"No," Victoria answered before she thought on it. She quickly amended her word. "Maybe," she said. "Or . . ." Her lips tightened in confused anger. "You are confusing me," she shot out. "I *was* willing . . . I mean, I . . . I *thought* I was willing. But I never dreamed. . . ." In frustration, Victoria dragged herself up off the ground. She tucked at the tangles of her carefully arranged coif, and when she could not tame it, she merely tore at the pins, allowing the heavy mass its freedom. Curling wisps of moon-frosted hair spun out to frame the soft oval of her face, and the man watched her admiringly from the ground.

"I understand," he said softly.

"Do you really," Victoria ground out. "How noble of you. Do you also understand that you are more the blighter than Steven Kensington could ever be?" She tugged at the tatters of her gown, drawing them more tightly around her. "You deliberately attempted to take advantage of my vulnerability." She shook first one leg and then the other, attempting to rid herself of the scraps of her undergarments that clung to her flesh. "You seduced me into thinking you were consoling me when all you really wanted to do was . . . was . . . Steven Kensington has never attempted anything so uncivilized," she finished triumphantly.

"Oh, I am sure he hasn't," he said, gazing up at her. "Men like Steven Kensington never do. They are bullies, not lovers."

"And you, sir are a lecher." Victoria spun, tatters swirling, and began a hobbled sprint toward the house. "Don't you dare follow me," she flung over her shoulder.

The man chuckled low in his throat. He wondered how the spirited wench would explain away the matter of her appearance to her fashionable friends. Oh, she would no doubt think of something. She was, after all, a *most* spirited wench. And a passionate one as well, he recalled with relish. 'Twas too bad he was leaving India at dawn. He would like to have had another taste of that promising flesh. He must remember on his next trip over to steal his plums from the same grove.

He lifted himself, and brushing idly at his breeches, he allowed himself one more perusal of the girl. As she ran toward the plantation house in the distance, she held on to her torn garments as tightly as she was apparently holding on to her chastity. It was a shame, he sighed, watching her disappear into the moonlit night. He bent down to retrieve his battered hat and began resignedly to fill it with plums.

Victoria hobbled up the steps of the veranda. She would make her way around to the back of the house and enter by the kitchen. She could easily get up the back stairs and return to the ball in time for the leave takings. She stopped short as, pulling herself tighter toward the opened window, she heard the silence of the orchestra. The silence was being filled by the voice of the Viscount Kensington. He was speaking the words that would bind his son Steven forever to another woman.

Chapter Four

The brim of the heavily veiled bonnet swung out in a wide down-swept arch, shadowing the features of the woman who glided up the gangway and onto the ship. She carried a small wicker case while several sailors followed hard behind, trundling the rest of her luggage. She swept onto the spar deck, her flaring cloak catching the sea breezes and snapping out against the riggings as she passed. Disgruntled passengers commented, in her perfumed wake, on the lateness of her arrival and the arrogant manner of her embarkation. But the privileged traveller seemed not to notice, and with a determined distraction, she proceeded directly to her cabin.

"She's the one," hissed a plump woman to her husband.

"Shush," intoned the man beside her. The woman huddled sulkily against the steam of the cold morning.

"She's the airy one," another lady huffed. Her husband nudged her admonishingly. "Well, she is," the second woman sniffed.

"Men," asserted the first lady. "Give them a trim figure, some expensive finery and an exotic scent and they're as content as a pup with a bowlful of milk and marrow." The second woman agreed truculently.

"What makes her so privileged as to imagine she can keep us waiting all these hours?" she demanded.

A neatly attired warrant officer who stood nearby targeted the woman. "She imagines herself privileged because she is privileged," he said flatly.

"Is she now?" the first woman inquired airily.

The seaman nodded. "She is the Lady Noelle Darby—the *Honorable* Lady Darby," he stated. "Believe me, mistresses," he added shaking his head ruefully, " 'twas not the captain's decision to indulge the woman's tardiness. The Gulf of Mannar would have been a memory by this hour had not order been received from Robert Clive, himself, that Lady Darby was to be accommodated. If Captain Tyrrel had his way, the woman—honorable or not—would have been left in the *Spectre*'s wake. The captain's not one to indulge such—"

At that moment, the man's words were interrupted by a shout from the fighting top. "The captain has given the order, Harrt! We're setting sail!" The warrant officer saluted smartly and stepped past the couples. Within seconds, the deck was alive with seamen as preparations were made to shove off.

The capstan groaned mightily as it raised the anchor. Below, bilge pumps clanked as they were set into motion. Hawsers grated as they were heaved on board. Orders were shouted and the sails snapped out against the gray-blue dome of the sky. The lean, high-masted bark, the *Spectre of the Bay*, lurched restively and yawed at long last, beginning its debarkation from the British West Indies to the shores of America.

Below, the Honorable Lady Darby was shown into her small cabin. At her hesitation, the young sailor who attended her smiled apologetically.

"It isn't much, I'll grant your ladyship," he said, "but its a sight better than what the rest of the passengers have. It's the best we got to offer," he added sheepishly. "I mean, unless you want to take over Captain Tyrrel's quarters, milady, it's about all we can manage." A small, nervous chuckle attended his words. "Naturally," the man added hastily, "I wasn't suggestin' anything. The captain's real resentful about complaints, so I wouldn't mention—"

Victoria glanced in his direction, quelling further comment. " 'Twill do," she said tersely. She set her small case on the narrow, spindle-railed platform that she assumed was to become her bed. "How long will the voyage take?" she asked.

"We'll get you there by Christmas," he answered, laughing. At Her Ladyship's lack of response, the man's countenance turned sober. "With the vagaries of the weather, you never really know," he said. "Also, we got the damned British to—" He stopped short, his eyes widening. "Oh, your ladyship," he gasped. "I don't . . . I can't imagine what made me say it."

Victoria waved a dismissive hand. "I am sure 'twill not happen gain."

"Nay, milady," the man said, relieved at the woman's forbearance, " 'twill not happen again, I assure you."

Victoria glanced at the tiny porthole, much boasted upon by her ticket agent. "Can we open that?" she asked.

"That's the *port*hole, milady," the sailor explained patiently. "We only open that when we're in port. If we opened it while we were at sea, we'd have a whale of a time swabbin' the ocean out of the cabin." The sailor laughed once again. Victoria took a deep breath of the thick, musty air and found herself less than amused. The man very quickly stifled his mirth. Clearing his throat, he said, with found solemnity, "Besides that, you'll be wantin' less air and more heat as we head north. If it gets too cold for you, we'll fill up your hot pot with coals." He indicated the round iron pan that swung on a short chain from a ceiling beam. "We'll keep you comfortable, your ladyship," he said with forced cheerfulness as he backed from the low doorway. Gratefully, he stepped from the cabin and swung the door closed, separating himself from the haughty traveller.

Victoria could only imagine his sigh of relief as he was at last acquitted of her company. She had not intended it should be so. With a reflective sigh, she reached up and drew the pins from her bonnet. She breathed relief as she removed the heavy encumbrance and unwound the thick veiling from her face. Shaking out her mass of silver-blond curls, she gratefully tousled them with her fingers. This business of being a patrician was not without its drawbacks. She shrugged out of her travelling cloak and wriggled under the restraints of her stiff corset. She was thankful to note a stand with a ewer and bowl set deeply into it. It could not accommodate a proper bath certainly, but at least she could, once the pitcher was filled, splash her face with water. Above the stand a darkly veined mirror hung crookedly. Victoria bent to inspect her reflected image. She ran her fingertips over the soft planes of her face. Oddly, she looked not very much different than she had looked yesterday. Yesterday, she thought idly. . . . How changed everything was from yesterday.

Yesterday, she was Victoria, unpacking her imported booty with abandoned enthusiasm, listening to David Newton's teatime stories with her friends, riding her favorite Arabian over the lush lands of the plantation, and writing her poetry in the secure cocoon of the cedar forest. And yesterday, she was Victoria, listening to Steven Kensington tell her that he could not marry her, that she was not an appropriate mate for the son of a viscount, that she was not "good" enough for him or any man of their circle. And yesterday she had defied Steven Kensington, the only man she had ever loved, and told him she would not be a part of his life. And she had meant it. Now that the fire of her determination had cooled, however, she could reflect on that decision and its aftermath with some objectivity. Her dispassion did nothing, she realized, to deflect the pain Steven had caused her—and the embarrassment.

Victoria flushed with shame as she recalled her entrance into the ball after her and Steven's terrible confrontation. He had eyed her dispassionately as she entered the room, her chin angled in defiance. She had gazed from person to person—from family to family—challenging them to dismiss what they had always known her to be, challenging them to substantiate Steven's assessment of her prospects. She was, after all, the beloved of this very civilized society. She had regarded her audience expectantly, waiting for their sympathy. But no sympathy had been forthcoming. Again and again, her company had warmly toasted the newly engaged couple. They had, it seemed, forgotten their little favorite. She had suddenly and sinkingly felt the weight of Steven's words, and her defiance had turned to humiliation. And the Victoria she had been—had always known herself to be—had begun to fade.

Yesterday she had met a man and she had discovered passion. She had packed her things—her childhood, really—into four trunks to board a ship bound for America. But that was yesterday. She drew away from the darkly reflected image.

Today she was Lady Darby—the *Honorable* Lady Darby, she thought with a small self-deprecating laugh. What was so damned honorable about being stuffed into a cabin the size of her privy closet at home? Home, she thought wistfully. She missed it already. She wondered in a quick moment of heart-tripping desperation if she'd made the right decision. What was happening there now? The house servants were just rising, Mrs. Jafar corralling them, coercing them, bustling them along in the humid mid-morning heat to their various duties. Would they bring up her breakfast? Find her gone? Would a general alarm be sounded when she was not found in her bed? No, she thought. Katje would have informed them tranquilly that Victoria had left on an extended journey. They would wonder at the bewildering announcement, but they would not question it, at least not until they were alone among themselves. David Newton would be staggered. He would reproach, lecture and berate Katje that she had allowed such a thing to happen. He would scowl darkly about the house and eventually keep to his rooms, silently reprehending both Katje's and Victoria's recklessness. Around teatime, he would lurk at the entrance to Katje's apartments and wait to be invited in to tea, and he would listen grudgingly, disparagingly to her reasons for allowing, and aiding, Victoria's escape. And that is exactly what her decision had been, an escape, she decided now. Katje had seen that. As always, she had understood the true nature of Victoria's need. Katje had listened to the story of Victoria's yesterday, and she had known that Victoria could not stay on in Kolhapur. Her heart had been broken, her spirit badly

60

damaged, her very identity brought into question. If she was to find peace, she must have time to heal. Katje knew all these things, as Victoria had known she would, and so she had appealed to Robert Clive, helped Victoria pack, written a letter of introduction and seen the girl to the only ship leaving for America that day. She had accomplished all this in the period of a few hours because she—Katje d'Aumerle—knew about wounded hearts and about escape . . . and about healing.

Victoria glanced back into the mirror. The emerald sparkle of her darkly-lashed eyes stood out in glittering relief against the murky glass. There was no room for uncertainty. Katje had told her that. Now that she, Victoria, had come to the decision and carried out the first phase of its execution, she could not be thwarted—not by a tiny, airless room, not by a trackless ocean and certainly not by the reservations of her own heart.

A hesitant tap at her cabin door roused her from her reflections and she turned. "Come," she said. As the door swung open, Victoria looked down to find a small boy smiling up at her. "Hello," she greeted him, a question in her voice. What was a lad doing on a seagoing vessel, she wondered.

"I'm Jack," the boy said brightly. "I brought your ladyship her water." The boy held a bucket which seemed far too cumbersome for his little frame. Without further words, he scuttled into the room, climbed up on the only chair and poured the water from the pail into the ewer on the washstand. "I'll be takin' care of you, milady," he said over his skinny shoulder.

"Will you?" said Victoria, uncertainty clear in her tone.

"I'll be gettin' your water and food and such," he affirmed.

"But you're just a little boy," Victoria blurted and instantly realized her mistake.

Jack faced her, his brows pursed. "I ain't so litte," he rejoined, pushing out his narrow chest. "My last birthday made me eight years old."

Victoria hid a smile. "Oh," she answered gently, "I did

not realize you were *that* old. I only meant that you seem rather young to be . . ." her voice trailed off as his scowl darkened.

"I pull my weight, lady." He scrambled down from the chair.

"Is your father a sailor?" Victoria inquired hesitantly.

"Nay, I got no father," the boy said. "Though you might say I got two hundred fathers," he amended with a smile. At Victoria's quizzical look, he continued. "The crew of the *Spectre*'s my father."

"Are you an orphan?" Victoria felt a tug of compassion as she gazed down into his small, upturned, defiant face.

"That bein' the case"—the boy nodded—"the crew took me on." He adopted a confidential tone. "One day I'll be captain of this tub," he said with a mischievous smile. "But if you wouldn't mind," he added hastily, "don't go mentionin' that to Captain Tyrrel. He'd have me flogged for sure." Jack chuckled, and Victoria arched an elegant brow.

"Flogged?" she said tartly.

"You bet," the snippet assured her with manful pluck. "That's the punishment for mutiny. Didn't you know that?"

"I hardly think the fantasy of an imaginative little b—I mean a young man like yourself could be considered even vaguely mutinous, Jack," she said firmly. "In any event," she added, "there shall be no flogging of *anyone* while I am aboard."

"No, ma'am," said the boy uncertainly. "But it seems to me that's only for the captain to decide, so maybe it's just as well you don't mention what I said anyway. I shouldn't like bein' in trouble with Captain Tyrrel."

"Your captain is a strict authoritarian, I take it," said Victoria.

The boy nodded vigorously, then suddenly stopped. "He's a what, your ladyship?" he asked.

"He is a difficult taskmaster," Victoria explained.

"That he is," Jack answered gravely. "Me and the other men ain't lookin' to cross him, if that's what you mean."

"I see," Victoria said thoughtfully. "Well, you need not

fear my indiscretion, Jack," she added kindly.

"You won't be tellin' him what I said?" he asked.

Victoria shook her head vigorously. "I never shall," she answered staunchly.

"Even if he tortures you?" Jack obviously relished the gruesome image. Victoria remained unmoved.

"Even under torture, I shall keep your guilty secret." She smiled at his relief. "Can we be friends now?" she asked.

"If you'd like, milady," the boy said shyly.

"I should like that very much, Jack," she answered.

He beamed up at Victoria. She had no way of knowing it, but she had at that moment planted the seed of undying love in the eight-year-old boy. Any woman who would withstand torture for him deserved his most profound admiration. He moved toward the cabin door. "I'll be back with some food, your ladyship," he said brightly. "I'll see to it cook gives you the best of the fare, too, and some *fresh* bread." He was still smiling happily as he left the tiny room.

Victoria reflected upon the boy's words as she unpacked the few things she had been allowed to keep in her cabin. She reflected, too, on the apparent character of the captain of the *Spectre of the Bay*. Floggings? Torture? She shuddered despite the growing heat in the cabin. 'Twas an ungentle atmosphere in which to raise a young boy, to be sure. This Captain Tyrrel must be a tyrant. She wondered if the child had been taken by force, impressed off the streets of some American town. Oh, Lord, she thought, what had she gotten herself into? Not only was she travelling to the reportedly barbarous wasteland of the American colonies, but she was going there under the authority of a, most assuredly, insane captain. Well, she thought, sighing audibly, she would quite simply have to avoid the man. She was not interested in confronting him, though she would certainly enjoy giving him a piece of her mind concerning the enforced labor of little boys. On the other hand, Jack had seemed happy enough. She would watch that situation carefully. And she would keep to her cabin for the most part. She glanced around the tiny cubicle.

That would not be easy, she reflected soberly. She decided that she would allow herself one turn around the deck every day. For the rest, she would keep to herself. She sat heavily on her bed, bumping herself painfully as the unrelenting rigidity of the mattress met her backside. She pushed herself up and managed to lie full-length on the narrow platform. She felt beneath her the slow rock of the ship, and recalling that she had not slept in over twenty-four hours, she closed her eyes. This might not be such a terrible journey after all, she thought, as the easy roll of the vessel swayed her gently into the arms of slumber.

Chapter Five

Victoria awoke heavily. The languid clanging of the ship's bell, ever occurring hour by hour for the past week, no longer startled her. A moment passed as she unclosed her weighty lids and attempted to recall where she was. She gazed in puzzlement around the chamber as she always did upon awakening. The languorous heat in the tiny space reminded her not only where she was but that since leaving Kolhapur she had been miserable. She plucked at the neckline of her gauzy night rail, hoping the action might stir the melting air. A sharp tap on the door of her cabin roused Victoria. She sat up and swung her legs over the side of her bed. "Come," she said.

The door creaked open, and Jack appeared with her morning tray. "Good mornin', your ladyship," he said brightly.

Victoria managed a tired smile. "Good morning, Jack."

"I got you real rum, today," the boy said proudly. He brought the tray to the bed and placed it on Victoria's lap. "The grog they been servin' won't give a sailor a decent buzz," he pointed out. "But don't you go tellin' Captain Tyrrel," he added with a quick smile.

"I won't tell him, Jack," Victoria said quietly. "But I am afraid you went to the trouble for nothing. I cannot imagine taking rum so early. The grog has served me very well."

Jack gazed at her with an expression of bewilderment. "But everybody takes a little rum in the morning if they can get it."

"All right, Jack." She laughed. She would appease him for the moment she decided and then rid herself of his present later on. She bit into the slice of dark bread he had brought. "I wish you did not have to be so frightened of your captain," she said thoughtfully. "It seems everything you do gives you cause for dread."

Jack settled himself cross-legged on the chair. "Not everything," he said. "Sometimes I behave meself."

"But you're just a little b—" Jack scowled dangerously, and Victoria quickly restated her thought. "Jack," she said, "young men like yourself need a certain outlet for their energies. Don't you ever feel like just . . . playing?"

The boy considered her question carefully. "I do, sometimes," he said thoughtfully. "But then I remember the bodacious 'sponsibilities I got."

"Tell me about your . . ." 'sponsibilities,' " Victoria urged him.

"Well, I got a bell shift, like we all do, and I got my powderin' chores."

"Powdering chores?"

Jack nodded pridefully. "I'm what's called a powder monkey. You know," he explained, "like if we get attacked. If another ship boards us, or tries to, I got to keep the powder comin'."

"You mean powder for the guns," Victoria said.

Again Jack nodded. "With them damned Brits around, you never know when you'll get boarded." Victoria waited for the expected apology but realized that for young Jack these were only words. He went on innocent of any perceived insult. "And then, of course, there's you, milady. That's my biggest 'sponsibility of all. And," he added shyly "the one I like best." He laughed delightedly as Victoria blew him an exaggerated kiss.

A sudden sharp rap on the door interrupted them. Without invitation, a sailor stuck his weathered countenance into the cabin. "Get yourself topside, Jack," he growled without preamble. Without a word the boy scrambled down from the chair and raced from the room. Victoria wondered at his haste but reasoned that one of his "bodacious 'sponsibilities" had called him. She smiled.

Someone had obviously coached the boy—probably the tyrannical captain. Her face sobered. As a matter of fact, Tyrrel probably filled the boy's head with lies about the importance of his responsibilities only to keep cheap labor aboard his ship. There was no excuse for a man who would use an orphan in such a way.

She gulped at her morning stew with anger growing in her heart. Obviously, the captain was also telling the child lies about the British. He had used that word Victoria hated. "Brits," Victoria snarled aloud. How she detested that appellation. Only the very basest of the lowborn used that word in India. Victoria gave in to the rum, gulping it down and feeling a certain perverse satisfaction as the spirited liquid burned her throat. One of these days, she would face the despotic Tyrrel. One of these days, she would tell him exactly what she thought of his oppressive use of that child. She would spare no opprobrium, she thought with spiteful relish as she swung from the bed and began to dress. She splashed her face and neck with tepid water from the ewer and perfumed herself extravagantly. She would tell him loudly and clearly that she knew him to be no gentleman. She stepped into her organza morning dress and fastened the tiny buttons. Fluffing out the light froth of pale green fabric, she realized that this, too, was Tyrrel's fault. The blighter had allowed only two frocks to be kept in her cabin. She'd worn this dress and her lavender muslin all week. Both garments were pitifully limp by this time. When she had asked Jack about the possibility of keeping at least one of her trunks in the cabin, he had told her with frightened eyes that when Captain Tyrrel gave an order, no one disputed it. But this order was unreasonable, Victoria had insisted. Jack had patiently explained that in case of a storm at sea, all personal objects were limited. Everything was stored in the hold, he'd told her and added once again that he hoped she would not make trouble over what the captain would consider a "minor" complaint. Victoria pushed her bonnet onto her head and carefully veiled herself against the harsh, water-reflected sunlight of the Indian Ocean. Perhaps Tyrrel considered her needs minor, but she did not.

Gratefully, she opened the door of her cabin and stepped out onto the gun deck for her daily walk topside. She climbed the stairs leading onto the spar deck and breathed in, through the several light layers of her organdy veiling, the nourishing sea air. Oh, it was heaven after the musky stillness of her cabin. The day was as blazingly bright as her cabin was oppressively dark. The one lamp allowed near her bed shed just barely enough light for her to read the volume of English poetry she had been allowed to retain. And she had to admit, as she strolled idly along the rail, that the tranquil isolation of her cabin had afforded her some much needed privacy in which to write.

Victoria noted with mild curiosity that the deck was not nearly as crowded or raucously noisy as it was on other days. She narrowed her attention to the bow of the ship where, it seemed, all the men had gathered. She strolled toward them only to recoil in horror.

What she saw at the center of the gathered crowd nauseated her. A man was strung, bare-chested to the riggings. Another, holding a short, knotted whip, stood before him. Victoria swallowed hard against the rising bile of her horror. The man with the whip raised his arm.

"Stop!" she screamed. Her horror turning to indignation, she ran toward the gathered seamen. "Don't you dare raise your hand to that gentleman," she commanded.

"I was just about to ring the bell for the captain," the man said, astonished at the interruption.

"The captain?" she demanded. "The captain is aware of this inhumanity?"

"Of course he is," the young sailor said, his bewilderment clear in his voice. "He's got to be a witness."

"A witness to what?" Victoria's voice clenched.

"To the floggin'," the man replied.

"There will be no flogging!" Victoria stated. The men glanced at each other and then back to the woman who held them all at bay. Even the one who was to be punished shrugged a shoulder as best he could in his confined condition, in the direction of his comrades. "Where is your *captain?*" Victoria spat out the last word with virulent disdain.

"He's in his quarters, miss," said one of the men uncertainly. "But I wouldn't—"

"And where are the captain's quarters?" she inquired stiffly.

"They're aft on the gun deck, but you can't—" Victoria pivoted crisply, cutting off any further protestation. A hush fell on the sailors.

"Please don't, your ladyship," called a small, desperate voice. Jack ran and clung to Victoria's skirts. "Please don't do it," he entreated her.

"But I must, Jack," she said, stopping and bending to the boy. "I cannot allow that man to be whipped. I *must* do something. I must reason with the captain." Victoria lifted her gaze as a murmur rose from the men. She looked back down at her small friend.

"This ain't your business," he said in an aching plea. "Captain Tyrrel won't like your botherin' him."

"Nevertheless, I must, Jack." She detached herself from him and continued on her mission.

"Please, don't," Jack called out. Victoria glanced back at him and saw the sag of his thin shoulders as she moved away. Perhaps it was about time she confronted Tyrrel. Perhaps it was just about time.

With determination she climbed back down to the gun deck. She took a deep breath before striding toward the captain's quarters. Once at the door, she stopped, for the first time wondering if her interference in this business was completely wise. Then, as she recalled the man on the sunscorched deck, she knew she could not allow such uncivilized behavior to go unchallenged. She thought, too, of Jack's sweet, trusting eyes imploring her not to face the man. Had Tyrrel inspired that much fear in the lad that he could not bear to think of Victoria even talking to him? This captain had a great deal to answer for. He was nothing more than a bully, besotted by his own authority. Victoria rapped briskly at the door. At the mumbled invitation to enter, she pushed open the door and stepped inside.

The room was at least three times the size of her own, she noted with some contempt. The ceiling was higher, and

69

rather than her one small lamp, it boasted a half dozen. The captain stood with his back to her. He appeared to be studying a map. The desk over which he leaned was a highly polished teak with brass fittings. His stiff woolen waistcoat hung from his broad shoulders with lordly abandon. Victoria drew back her shoulders and lifted her veiled chin.

"Captain Tyrrel," she said, "I am here to speak to you about the situation up on the deck. I shall not leave your quarters until it is resolved. And there is another matter which I strongly feel must be addressed by you. But the immediate problem—"

The man grunted loudly and waved his hand in annoyance as he continued to study his map. He mumbled something that may have been, "Just a minute."

Victoria felt her anger stir. "I will not be dismissed, sir," she rejoined. How dare the arrogant lout wave her off? Who did he imagine himself to be? She quickly reined her indignation. She could not allow emotion to diminish her effectiveness. With renewed determination, Victoria addressed him once again. "There is a man tied to the riggings, Captain Tyrrel," she stated. "I want him removed from there immediately."

"He is to be flogged," the man mumbled dispassionately.

"I am well aware of that," Victoria retorted, "and I want him taken down—now!"

"Are you insane, madam?" the man asked, turning abruptly to face her.

Victoria gasped. Eyes the color of blue sea glass assailed her, and burnished curls fell boyishly over a bronzed forehead.

"Insanity may be your only excuse for this unheard of intrusion. I suggest you claim it immediately before I have *you* strung up to the riggings." He watched her evenly and waited for this meddlesome creature to speak. Instead, he heard only the delicate clearing of a throat behind the veiling. "Speak up or I promise you, madam, I shall make good my threat."

Victoria could manage only small sounds at first. Her

astonishment had rendered her speechless. How could the vagabond cavalier in the plum grove and the cruelly authoritarian Captain Tyrrel be the same man? And why after all they had shared, though their sudden meeting had ended ignominiously, did he not recognize her? But, of course, he did not know who she was! She lifted delicate fingertips to her veiled face. He had no way of discerning her identity. Well, she thought, she would make the most of that for the moment at least. She would deal with other questions at another time. Her concern at the moment was the man up on deck and, of course, young Jack. She took a long calming breath.

"I assure you, Captain Tyrrel, I am not insane," she managed. "And I insist you remove that man on the upper deck from his imprisonment this instant."

"Insist, madam?" inquired the captain with icy calm. His eyes glinted like steely blue fire. Victoria fought the instinct to recoil as the man went on. "You disclaim insanity and yet you dare to make such a demand of the captain of this vessel. The one I assure you is evidence of the other."

"The dispassionate inflicting of pain is the only insanity on this vessel, Captain," Victoria grated.

Tyrrel did not immediately speak. Instead he allowed his gaze to flick over the trim, defiant creature that stood before him. She obviously had no concept of what her little tirade could cost her. "The man is a thief, madam," he explained tolerantly but firmly. "He will be punished."

"What did he steal?" Victoria demanded.

"A pipe, two ounces of tobacco and a pint of rum," the captain answered without apology.

"And for this you would have the man flogged?" Victoria blazed in an orgy of righteousness. "You are a brute, Captain Tyrrel, and a bully and you deserve to go straight to hell."

The captain could not actually see a withering glare, but he knew it was there behind the froth of veiling. For a reason unfathomable to him, he was amused by the woman's wrath. He would have enjoyed seeing for himself her expression of anger. She was, to be sure, a bold little thing and beautiful, too, he would guess. He hid his gentler feelings, however, and merely shrugged a wide shoulder.

"Your assessment of me may be entirely accurate, madam," he said evenly, "but the man's sentence stands. Flogging is the punishment for most offenses on any sea-going vessel. Beyond that," he added with infuriating tranquility, "he is receiving only three lashes—one for each item. On any other ship he would be receiving twenty lashes. His sentence is light and, might I add, the same that I myself would receive for a similar crime."

"I hardly think you would sentence yourself to be humiliated before a shipload of men," Victoria replied stonily.

"But then I know better than to steal," he rejoined coolly.

Victoria almost laughed aloud. Oh, she would enjoy humbling this arrogant rogue. But she must wait. There would be a more perfect time than this. And, it appeared, he was not about to relent on the flogging. She drew back her slender shoulders and lifted her chin. The captain watched her appreciatively.

"You really must excuse me," he said, allowing a small smile to curve his lips. "The day grows warm, and I hate to think of the poor blighter on deck spending any more time than is necessary strapped to the riggings." He plucked his tricorn from a peg and brushed past Victoria. Opening the door, he bowed, ushering her out. "As to the . . . other matter you mentioned about which you feel so strongly, perhaps we could dine together this evening and discuss it." His voice held a mocking deference that both infuriated and intrigued Victoria. From the sanctuary of her heavy veil, she allowed herself a smile. So the egomaniacal swagger was interested in her. This could be used to her advantage. She nodded curtly. "Join me in my cabin at seven, if that is convenient," said her unsuspecting victim.

"I shall do that," Victoria assured him archly. She turned and quickly marched to her own quarters. Once there she breathed deeply, capturing momentary relief. Seconds later, however, her mind whirled with plans. She threw off her bonnet and veil, and her pale curls spun out wildly. She grabbed up the mirror and peered into it. Her eyes flashed emerald fire, reflecting her burning desire to best the strutting cock. She would avenge not only the flogging and Tyrrel's heartless treatment of Jack, but she would avenge his cavalier treatment of her as well. The arrogant bully had met his match.

In the hot silence of her cabin, Victoria heard a bell sound. She looked up and listened. A crack rent the air. A man screamed. Another crack, another scream, then silence resonated in the tiny room. Victoria waited. The air hissed. The final snap pierced the silence. There was no scream. Victoria sat heavily in her chair. As if in a trance, she listened to the din of working sailors begin and grow above her. She could not have stopped this horror, she consoled herself. There was nothing she could have done. She had tried but she had failed. The flogging had taken place. Her fist clenched involuntarily. No, she could not have prevented the cruelty, but perhaps she could prevent other injustices. Perhaps she could cut to the source of the cruelty and smash that vaunting shell from behind which Captain Tyrrel carried out his intimidation. That she might accomplish. The man would not soon forget the humiliation he would suffer at the hands of Victoria Quayle.

Chapter Six

Victoria had called for a bath, and it was with some intricacy that the amenity was arranged. The camboose, or galley stove, was the only open fire allowed on the ship, and it was there, on the wide hearth, that Victoria was to bathe. Jack had hoped to see the large cooking kettle transported to her cabin, but the tiny cubicle, it was decided, would not accommodate the size of the pot. And so, between the dinner hour and the supper hour, heavy canvasses were heaved up and strung around the embrasure. After the pot was filled with sea water (not even Jack's profound adoration of his mistress would justify the use of fresh water for a bath) and the water heated to Jack's exacting specification, Victoria, swathed in blankets, was whisked to the site. Once she had achieved the unheard-of luxury of bathing on a sailing vessel, she was not about to hurry the occasion. She lolled for a long, glorious time in the depths of the soap-scented water. Washing the grime of days from her flesh, she lingered long enough for Jack to assure her, from outside the privacy of the enclosure, that luck was notoriously fickle and, if imposed upon, might vanish altogether. He worried that the captain could appear. If the captain *did* appear, he further asserted, they might all end their days at the bottom of the Indian Ocean.

"Stop nagging, Jack," Victoria soothed. She idled for further long moments as her little benefactor and his cohorts paced the deck, glancing nervously over their shoulders and waiting in dread for the expected, and certainly deserved, retribution. At long last she emerged, and without preamble, she was scuttled back to her cabin as the cordon was hastily disassembled. The whole affair, except for the minor annoyance of Jack's quibbling, was carried out with as little stress to Victoria as possible. She knew, however, that a great deal of bother had been gone to on her account. Fondly, as she dried herself, she imagined the sailors praying that she would decide to remain unwashed for the rest of the voyage.

The bath, however, had been well worth all the trouble it had taken to achieve. Victoria smiled as she smoothed a gardenia-scented cream over her freshly glowing skin. She brushed her hair until it glimmered, nearly translucent in the soft golden light of the tiny cabin. She was about to attend a very important meeting—as important to her as it was to those who had labored so diligently to prepare her for it—and she must have every resource available to her. All her considerable confidence must be brought to bear if she was to conquer the arrogant Tyrrel. If everything went as she planned, the man would have his much deserved comeuppance. After tonight, he would think twice and then a third time about again playing the bully.

Victoria had enjoined Jack to go down into the orlop and rummage through her trunks for her most glorious gown. She slipped into the froth of ivory satin. It rustled down around her slender curves and billowed at her feet in a cloud of point lace. She fluffed the wide tier of the same lace at her bosom, the creamy color of the material matching the tone of her complexion almost exactly. She narrowed her gaze and scrutinized herself in the little mirror. Smoothing at the shimmering length of the long V-shaped bodice, she was satisfied that the gown fit her as perfectly as the day it had been made for her. She lifted her hair and pinned it into a lucent halo atop her head, allowing small, provocative curls to frame her face. She wound a soft curl around a delicate fingertip and allowed it to lie sweetly upon her bare shoulder. A touch of vulnerability never hurt, she reflected studiously, when one was looking to catch someone off guard. And that was what she must do with Tyrrel, she decided. It was not her usual way with men; as a rule, she had dealt with people throughout her life openly and honestly. But then she had never met the likes of this Captain Tyrrel. His arrogance was boundless, his intolerance unforgivable, his lack of morality shameful. He was using dear young Jack more than unjustly. He was exploiting his youth and his lack of adult protection, to be sure, but he was also setting himself up as a kind of hero in the boy's eyes. Tyrrel was molding the lad to be just like himself. And the captain was no model for a child. Tyrrel believed that his cruelty that afternoon had been perfectly justified. He had not even listened to Victoria's protests. A man who would not be reasoned with, who would not compromise, deserved nothing more than to have his arrogance thrown right back into his face. And that was what Victoria intended to do. She had only one weapon at her disposal. She must use it skillfully. Finally, Tyrrel would know what it was to be powerless and perhaps, learning that, he would begin to empathize with the powerlessness that others might feel. He might begin to understand the immorality of using one's privilege as immunity from common decency. Failing that, Victoria decided, Tyrrel would learn, if nothing else, that shameful behavior was never enacted without consequence.

She smiled as she carefully wound a length of light veiling around her head and shoulders, taking care that her face was for the most part hidden. She would reveal her identity only when she deemed that the time was absolutely perfect for such a revelation. Victoria imagined with a quiet relish the reaction of Tyrrel when he discovered that she was the woman he had nearly raped in the plum grove in Kolhapur. The strutting lout would probably never recover from the embarrassment, and Victoria would not ease his abasement. She would carry the humiliation to the limit . . . to the *absolute* limit. And Tyrrel deserved everything he was about to endure. Tonight Captain Tyrrel would meet the impregnable power of Victoria Quayle.

The tiny lantern clock on her washstand told her that it was seven o'clock exactly. She waited several, heart-clenching moments before she opened the door of her cabin and stepped out onto the gun deck. She took a long, calming breath. Her plan was exquisitely mapped out. She needed only to execute it.

The brass of his epaulets shone like dull gold as he answered her light knock. His russet curls had been wetted down and brushed carefully back from his forehead. Victoria would note as the evening wore on that the riot of boyish tangles would slowly and stubbornly make their way from the neatly attempted arrangement. Boots polished, coat brushed, ascot tucked, he looked the perfect figure of authority. His appearance, however, Victoria reminded herself, served only to hide a disreputable abuse of authority.

"May I offer you an aperitif, your ladyship?" he asked ceremoniously. Victoria declined, indicating the veiling that she wore. "Would you mind if I partook?" he inquired.

"Not at all," Victoria murmured. He poured himself a liberal portion of brandy and joined her on a small elegant settee. "I was planning to have a small supper sent in, if that is acceptable," he said politely.

" 'Tis most acceptable, Captain Tyrrel," she answered. "I only wear this"—she indicated her veil with a negligence that belied its essential purpose—"to protect myself against the sun and the night air. I do take it off to eat," she assured him, laughing.

"I am glad." He smiled. " 'Tis not that you are not lovely just as you are, but a man enjoys knowing to whom he is speaking."

"Yes," Victoria agreed. She noted the intensity of his gaze as he attempted to see through the shadowy folds. She guessed that he was a little more than curious as to her appearance. But his time would come. He would know, all too soon, with *exactly* whom he dealt. Victoria felt a certain perverse pleasure at the hindrance of his immediate satisfaction.

"You mentioned that you wished to discuss something with me," he said.

Victoria nodded. "I did, Captain," she answered. He smiled warmly and placed a hand on her forearm.

77

"This is such a special night, your ladyship. Could you not bring yourself to relinquish the use of my title? Call me Greyson," he invited.

Victoria gazed down at his hand, and he removed it good-naturedly. She lifted her regard. "I shall call you anything you wish me to call you, Captain," she said.

"Greyson," he reminded her gently.

"Greyson," she amended. "I shall call you anything you wish me to call you, *Greyson*. However, I do think it important that we talk about Jack."

"Jack?" he asked. His expression sobered. "Has the little rapscallion offended you, milady?"

"The little 'rapscallion' has not offended me, I assure you," she said hastily. "The child is a perfect angel."

Greyson Tyrrel laughed softly. "Jack would crawl out of his skin if he heard himself described as such."

"I doubt that, Cap—Greyson," Victoria said sweetly.

"Then, you don't know Jack," he asserted amiably. "The boy imagines he is Edward Teach himself."

"I suppose in an environment such as this, a black-hearted rogue such as Mr. Teach would be considered a hero by an impressionable child," Victoria rejoined. Then, reining her ire, she went on. "And that is really my point. I wonder, when you speak of Jack as a boy, if you truly understand that he is just that—a little boy? He tells me he is barely eight years old. He also tells me he is required to do a great deal of work on this ship. He is subjected to the horrors of battle, he is allowed to witness the brutality of floggings, and . . . Greyson," she said, softening her tone, "he seems to have a most unfortunate terror of you." From the fortress of her veil, Victoria watched the captain hide a smile. Infuriated, she rose. She must be very careful to gain his trust. Perhaps, she had allowed her disdain of Jack's situation to show too much. She must be more circumspect if the full measure of her plan was to be exacted. She hastily amended her approach. "I simply cannot understand it, Greyson," she went on earnestly. "The boy seems positively certain that you will exact some horrible punishment upon him if he does not behave himself."

"Let me tell you something about Jack," he said, no

longer able to contain his mirth. "That boy is not afraid of anyone."

Victoria recalled the child's unguarded moment of fantasy about someday captaining the *Spectre* and his equally unguarded concern that Captain Tyrrel might discover his dream.

She cocked her head. "He thought you might have him flogged because of a sweet boyish fancy. He bade me that" — she assumed an air of mock solemnity — "even if you tortured me, I must remain silent concerning his confidence."

Greyson Tyrrel allowed himself an expansive smile. "If I were to subject *you* to torture, milady, I should be worthy of nothing more or less than torture myself."

Victoria nodded. "I understand that . . . Greyson," she murmured, "but don't you see, in his fear of you, Jack imagines all sorts of terrible possibilities." She moved toward where he sat, his arm spread over the back of the small settee and one long leg folded comfortably over the other knee. Standing primly before him, she lifted an elegant shoulder. "We — you and I — understand the difference between perception and reality, Greyson, but Jack does not. He sees a man flogged for the smallest offense and — "

Greyson held up the hand that held his brandy and waved away any further discussion. He understood her concern over that circumstance, he asserted, but she, too, must understand the difference between reality and perception. He explained that stealing was a pervasive problem on a seagoing vessel, gone from any port for months at a time. "What if everyone decided to steal?" he asked her. "What if everyone decided to break the rules? Where would discipline be? How could order be kept?" He offered her what, she assumed, he felt was his most winning smile. "As to my own authority in this matter," he insisted, "I am following maritime laws that have existed for hundreds of years. Despite what you may think of me, I am no brute, milady." His eyes hooded, but his smile remained. "You know," he said more softly, "I should like to call you something besides, 'milady.' May I know your given name?"

Victoria held a seething anger. *Isn't it just about time you asked the name of the lady you nearly ravished,* she reflected bitterly. Rather than giving vent to her anger, however she forced a light tinkling laugh. "Of course, Greyson," she said. " 'Tis Victoria." She waited. Had he heard Steven Kensington say her name the night she'd left Kolhapur? If he had, he made no sign of recognition.

"Victoria," he breathed. " 'Tis a lovely name."

" 'Tis quite . . . *common* where I come from." She prodded him with the word.

"Common," he said evenly, his smile evaporating just a bit. His russet brows flickered in what might have been a vague memory, but he shrugged it off. "Won't you join me," he said finally as he stood. "I have had a table set for us." He ushered her to a small, linen-draped table where fine crystal and china glimmered in the golden light of the lamps. He rang a small bell, and almost immediately, a young seaman entered the cabin. Greyson barely took notice of the man. "We shall have our dinner now," he said curtly. He pulled out a chair, and Victoria slid onto it. She smiled secretly as she watched him take his own seat. Oh, the blighter was quite transparent. He was hurrying dinner because he was in a fever of curiosity over her identity. And that was just where Victoria wanted him to be. She would not reveal herself for some time yet. She must make the most of the advantage of her anonymity. The seaman entered the cabin once again, this time carrying a tray. With deferential silence, and not even glancing at the couple, he set several plates before them. Victoria gazed down in near disbelief at what she saw. Plums, peeled and sliced and artfully arranged on small silver fruit plates, were the first course. The man's gall was unbelievable. She shot him a look, but quickly realized that he would have no possible way of knowing that she was the rightful owner of those plums. So much the better, she assured herself, touching the delicate veiling that covered her face.

"Plums," she said softly. "What a pleasant surprise to find such a delicacy in the middle of the ocean."

"I can assure you, Victoria," said Greyson with suave certainty, "we are not totally without the amenities, for all our—as you would have it—brutality."

"Well, you are the captain, after all," Victoria said with a confidential comradery. They laughed together softly. "I suppose you well deserve whatever little gratifications you can manage for yourself."

Greyson nodded. "The mantle of authority is not without its burdens," he sighed.

Beneath her veil, Victoria's gaze darkened. She was about to bring down this pretentious braggart, and she was going to enjoy it enormously. "Still," she demurred, "I find it very difficult to even think of pleasuring myself with food when I imagine that poor man who was flogged today nursing his wounds."

Greyson smiled. "That man is now enjoying a hearty meal himself, Victoria, and swearing to all who will listen that he will never again take to thievery. And his sincerity will be without question, you know." His tone became solemn. "When a man understands that his deeds will be subject to scrutiny—that his *mis*deeds will not go unpunished—he thinks twice, believe me, before he abandons the constraints of morality. Mark my words; that man will not again steal."

Victoria nodded. "I really do understand, Greyson, now that you have taken the time to explain all this to me." The captain nodded in relieved anticipation of her reassurance. "But," she added, diminishing his premature good cheer, "I wonder if Jack understands all this. I think you should tell him exactly what you have told me." She gazed steadily at him.

"I shall do that," he affirmed gravely. "I shall bring him in here very soon and—"

"I think you should do it right now," Victoria said evenly. "I do not think you should wait one more minute to reassure him that everything that is done on this ship is done for a very good reason. He should know that as soon as possible."

"Tomorrow then," Greyson said hastily. "Won't you join me in this delicious—"

"Now," Victoria stated flatly.

"Now, milady?" Greyson asked, unsure of her tone or

her purpose. The bemusement on his face left Victoria with an almost unquenchable desire to giggle. She stifled her mirth very quickly, however. The time had come.

"Now," she repeated softly.

"Well, I hardly think we need disturb the lad's duties just to—"

Her perusal was unwavering, her tone adamant. "The child needs to know that you are no monster, Greyson. The sooner he knows that, the better." She softened perceptibly as she continued. "I am very concerned about this matter, you know. I doubt very much that I can continue the evening in any sort of good spirits unless the problem is cleared up immediately."

She reached across the table and placed delicate fingertips on his bronzed hand. Greyson gazed down at the intimate gesture and then back at Victoria. There was something oddly familiar about this forceful little wench. There was a quality of enchantment about her that made refusal of any request impossible. Oh, he would summon the lad; there was no question of that. The question was, why? Beneath the shadow of her veil he detected the gauzy outline of the perfect oval of her face, the creamy curve of her shoulders. It was not only that alluring promise, however, that bewitched him. There was something else. There was something indefinable and captivating about her. He stood as though mesmerized and rang the little bell. The seaman entered the cabin.

"Get Jack," said Greyson tersely.

"Jack, the powder monkey?" the sailor gaped. "Why would you—"

"Get him and bring him here," Greyson stated.

The man backed from the room without further debate, and Victoria allowed a narrow smile to form on her lips. "This is most kind of you, Greyson," she murmured.

" 'Tis a small thing," he said, his tone warm, though filled with wonder at his own acquiescence. "We shall have this cleared up in no time."

"Yes," said Victoria resolutely, "in no time at all." There was a moment of silence between them, and Victoria wondered if Greyson realized the significance of what was about to happen. She longed to immediately apprise him of what he was about to undergo, but, of course, that was impossible. For her plan to enjoy the most satisfying results, she must wait for just the right moment. Greyson Tyrrel must be unaware, until that moment, of what was happening. If everything worked the way she planned, in fact, his humiliation would be complete before he realized that anything had happened at all. Victoria waited.

After several moments, and a sternly answered rap on the cabin door, Jack entered the room. Victoria's heart melted at the terror she saw barely concealed on the boy's face. She imagined him wondering, in stomach-clenching dread, whether his captain had found out about the bath he'd arranged for Victoria. She smiled beneath her veil as Jack drew back his skinny shoulders and manfully faced whatever retribution he was bound to endure.

"You called for me, Captain," he said, saluting staunchly.

"I did, young sir," Greyson answered. "This lady asked me to summon you because—"

Victoria quickly intervened. She did not want Jack placed in an awkward position—or a position more awkward than the one in which he now found himself, at any rate. She stood amid a rustle of satin. "I had hoped we might have a discussion concerning . . . stealing, Jack."

Jack regarded her quizzically. "Is that you, milady?" he asked.

Victoria could not hide a bubble of laughter. "It is, Jack," she said gently. "And I hoped that we could talk together with the captain about certain . . . moral issues, and the example that is being set for you aboard this ship." Jack stared at her blankly. "I know 'tis hard for you to understand, Jack," she said softly, "but you *will* understand very soon." Victoria intended to make this very quick. Greyson was not sure how he felt about this intrusion into his authority, but he allowed Victoria to continue. "Tell me, Jack," she said, "what do you think of stealing?"

" 'Tis a very bad thing," he answered uncertainly. Perhaps this was some sort of test. He glanced at Captain

Tyrrel and attempted to read his expression. " 'Tis a *very* bad thing," Jack repeated. His eyes darted back to Victoria.

"And how do you feel about people who steal?" she went on.

"They ought to be flogged," said Jack with artless candor.

Perfect, Victoria thought. The boy had been trained very well. Nevermind that his training had been wielded by the insufferably callous Tyrrel, his simple perception of justice would serve her purpose perfectly. She hated exploiting Jack's misguidance this way, but, she consoled herself, he would only benefit from the experience. Before the night was out, Jack would realize Tyrrel's true nature, and the boy would at last know the joy of avenged mistreatment. She continued. "Do you think the rules should apply to everyone, Jack?" she asked.

Jack nodded. "I do," he said with certainty.

Victoria stepped quickly around the table to stand before the lad. On her way, she brushed Greyson's chest with her shoulder. She could almost feel the lout's lack of suspicion as he watched with benign patience the interrogation. He was no doubt feeling a great deal of pride in Jack's unswerving commitment to what the captain considered justice. There was no question that in a very few moments, Tyrrel would get a taste of that justice, Victoria thought derisively as she bent her knees to address Jack at his eye level.

"Do you think the rules ought to be changed if the thief were, for instance, someone of importance?" Once again Jack shook his head. "Let me ask you if the rules should apply to . . . for instance, Captain Tyrrel?"

Jack looked quickly to the captain and then back to Victoria. He knew what the captain would want him to answer; there was no question of that. Jack's discomfort was nevertheless obvious as he spoke. "The rules should apply to everybody, milady," Jack said softly.

"Even Captain Tyrrel?" Jack nodded dully. "Even Captain Tyrrel," Victoria stated flatly. She stood and walked to the table. "Suppose, Jack," she continued, "that Captain

Turrel had stolen something . . . for instance, these plums? Would he be subject to punishment?" For the first time, Victoria noted that Greyson, who had remained expressionless, shifted warily.

Jack eyed them both in abject bemusement. "Of course, milady," he answered.

Victoria lifted her arms and very slowly began to unwrap her veiling. "Well, let me tell you something, Jack," she said quietly, "Captain Tyrrel *did* steal these plums." The boy merely gaped at her. She continued the unveiling, and when it was complete, she stared wordlessly at Greyson Tyrrel. The flash of sea-blue anger registered quickly — after the amazement, after the bewilderment . . . after the sudden, unguarded second of pleased recognition. And, when the anger did come, it was steely in its intensity. Victoria fought a quick moment of apprehension. What had she to be afraid of, she reasoned. She smiled narrowly. "We meet again, Captain," she said softly.

Chapter Seven

The deck of the *Spectre* resonated with a cacophony of unfocused animation. Sailors hustled without looking at one another from duty to duty, making quick work of one chore while nimbly anticipating the next. No man dared the scrutiny of another. Brass was polished, decks swabbed, pinnaces refitted, riggings stretched, recoiled, buckled. Carronades were cleaned, though they had been cleaned only days ago. Every man on board sought with a certain desperate intensity to busy himself, to lose himself in a mindless pandemonium of activity.

Victoria moved among them greeting them, wondering at their remoteness, at the sense of distance she perceived. She had thought she might be a sort of heroine by now. By now everyone had heard that at her instigation, Captain Greyson Tyrrel was to be strung up and flogged for the crime of thievery. As any common seaman might expect to be, the captain of the *Spectre of the Bay* was to be the receiver of maritime justice. Victoria had been certain that she would be roundly applauded for her actions, but instead she had been mainly ignored. Jack had been sullen and uncomfortable with her when he had brought her breakfast and allowed no conversation to pass between them. She had hoped to discuss with the lad the importance of what was to happen, the significance of unseating an abuser of power. Victoria wanted Jack to understand that the humiliation of a bully was true justice—that what he had seen up to now was a travesty of honor. She wanted him to understand that people who use their privileged positions to instill fear were not honorable. And Captain Greyson Tyrrel was not honorable. His punishment would mark the beginning of a new and equitable era on the decks of the *Spectre*. But Jack had not given her the opportunity to tell him those things. He had made quick work of delivering her breakfast tray and had left her cabin immediately, in silence. She wondered at this and speculated that Jack's discomfort and the obvious disquiet among the other seamen might be due to their fear of retribution from the disreputable Tyrrel. His indifference to their opinions, his control of even their innermost thoughts, was well established. Victoria had discerned from the moment she stepped onto the ship that the men's observations were defensively guarded. She knew that once they realized the implication of what she had wrought, they would thank her. They would realize the tyranny of Greyson Tyrrel up to now and would demand the freedom for themselves that they had so long been denied. For the moment, Victoria would endure their detachment from her.

She stood against the gunwhale, gazing out into the sun-sparkled swells of the ocean. The day was clear and blue and hot. It was a perfect time for reckoning and rebirth. She freed her hair and face from the confinement of her netting as she had done so often back home in Kolhapur, and her thick aurora of fleecy curls billowed like a cloud around the oval of her radiant face. She was smiling in reflective joy when Mr. Harrt approached. She nodded genially. The man acknowledged her greeting curtly and began to walk on. He was taken with a sudden thought, however, as he passed and stopped, turning to her. Victoria regarded him almost gratefully as he approached.

"Hello, Mr. Harrt," she said cheerfully. "How are you this fine morning?"

The young warrant officer regarded her thoughtfully. "Hello, Lady Darby," he finally answered. "I am well."

"I am glad to hear it. In truth, I am glad to hear any human voice." She chuckled.

"Really," he stated, lifting a brow.

"Yes," Victoria said. "No one has spoken to me this entire morning, and I was feeling just a bit lonely. But I am much better now," she said as she touched the neatly coated arm that hung at his side. She leaned confidentially near him. "I think everyone is just a little unsettled."

"Do you," the man asked drily.

"I do," said Victoria, nodding with certainty. "I think they find difficulty in interpreting the event to come. 'Tis most unpleasant—the anticipation of a flogging." Her voice held concern and a very real solicitude over the reactions of the men to what they were about to witness, and it was only this sincerity that held Mr. Harrt's vexation in check.

"I find it interesting that you refer to the eventual proceedings as . . . unpleasant," he said softly.

"Oh, but I do think they will be unpleasant," Victoria assured him. "It gives me no pleasure to imagine any man suffering humiliation. Though I take full responsibility for what is about to occur, I must assure you that I anticipate no enjoyment in the spectacle."

"Do you not," said Harrt.

"No," Victoria answered ingenuously. She allowed a small smile to curve her lips. "I will concede a certain . . . satisfaction," she admitted, tilting the young seaman a glance. "After all, Captain Tyrrel has stolen from me, and he must be punished. No man on this ship would expect any less, don't you agree, Mr. Harrt?"

She was a practiced flirt, thought the young officer, and under different circumstances, he might succumb to her wiles but today . . . He forced his glance away from her. "It strikes me, Lady Darby, that you have little concept of what is about to happen," he said quietly.

"The captain is about to be flogged," she responded matter-of-factly. "Is that what you mean?"

"I *mean*," stated Harrt, swinging his gaze back to her, "that Captain Greyson Tyrrel is about to stand before his men and suffer humiliation of the worst sort."

"Exactly," said Victoria brightly. "Isn't that as it should

be?"

"No," the man stated flatly. "That is not as it should be.' Apparently you fail to understand the significance of what you have done."

Victoria regarded him evenly. Undoubtedly this was a case of one officer defending another. "You obviously have not suffered the man's brutality. If you had, you would feel very differently, Mr. Harrt. There is not a man on this ship who will not be grateful to me when this is over."

"Do you really believe that, Lady Darby?" the man asked incredulously.

"Of course," Victoria answered. "These men have suffered too long beneath the yoke of tyranny. They have lived in fear of expressing themselves openly. Why, the first day I boarded this ship I was informed that the captain was 'resentful' about complaints—and Lord knows, I have much about which to complain. I was told that my very real discomfort would be considered 'minor' by Captain Tyrrel. I was also informed by young Jack that he would be flogged for mutinous intent if it was revealed that he had dreams of someday captaining this ship. And yesterday, I witnessed an actual flogging—the most savage assault on another human being that I have ever imagined—and when I spoke to the captain about it, he waved away my protestations as if I were some insipid child. Do not tell me I do not understand the significance of what I have done, Mr. Harrt. I have given expression to the desire of every man on this ship."

"No you have not, Lady Darby," said the man. Victoria arched a pale elegant brow, but the warrant officer continued. "You have certainly not given expression to anything but your own inaccurate perceptions. Everything about which you speak can be easily explained."

"Explained by egotism," Victoria retorted.

"Explained by necessity," the young man countered. "Captain Tyrrel is no monster."

"So he has informed me," Victoria answered drily.

"He is no monster," the officer continued doggedly.

"Captain Tyrrel is a man, Lady Darby. He is a man who happens to have one of the most difficult jobs in the world. This vessel on which we now journey is like a planet in the universe of the sea. Here, miles and miles from civilization, there can be only one rule. Think about it," he said with a passion that made Victoria glance up at him. "Imagine what it would be like to be out here with no strong guiding hand. Imagine what it would be like to be in the middle of this vast universe—two-hundred men, Lady Darby—without leadership. Have you any idea of what life would be aboard this vessel without rules?" He paused briefly, but as Victoria made no response he went on. "Life would be intolerable, madam. You speak so glibly of your 'complaints.' Every man aboard this boat has 'complaints.' And what of the few passengers who have managed to secure passage? Do you imagine they have better accommodations than you? Let me tell you something about how they live—those other passengers and those seamen who serve aboard this vessel. Beneath the deck on which you reside there is another deck. 'Tis called the berthing deck, and 'tis where those men and women sleep and live. 'Tis barely high enough to accommodate a small man's height. The people sit on the floor to eat. There are no beds down there; no *baths* are enjoyed." Victoria offered him a withering glance, but he went on. " 'Tis hot and musty and nearly airless. And that berthing deck houses two-hundred people and more."

"Your captain lives very well, however." Victoria's tone was acidic.

"My captain lives well because I wish him to live well. He must live well—or at least as well as he can, Lady Darby, because, you see, my captain runs this ship. His responsibilities are vast, his obligations matters of life and death. Your own life, Lady Darby, and mine depend upon Greyson Tyrrel making the right decisions. If I misstate an order or make an error in judgement, I run the risk of, at the most, remonstrance. If the captain does so, our very lives could be forfeit. Captain Tyrrel cannot afford the luxury of an uninterrupted sleep. He cannot afford the luxury of a period of respite. He must take his sleep when he can, rest when the opportunity arises, and believe me when I tell you the opportunity does not arise often. While the rest of us take our leisure because it is our turn to take our leisure, Captain Tyrrel is charting our course, keeping us comfortably afloat—on an even keel—guarding our lives. Captain Tyrrel gets no 'turn' at leisure. If I decline to bother my captain with individual complaints, 'tis because I know that his guardianship of me extends far beyond the question of mere creature comforts. His guardianship involves my very life.

"As to young Jack," he continued without pause, "he is the most fortunate of little boys. Greyson Tyrrel found him in the streets of Boston, half dead with hunger, angry at the world, without purpose or position or any reason to live. Now Jack enjoys a very real reason for his existence. He has been given responsibilities aboard this vessel, and he knows the importance of those responsibilities. Oh, believe me, madam, we would do very well without young Jack. The *Spectre of the Bay* would function quite adequately without his services, but without his services our lives would be diminished. And without the sense of direction Jack has received on this ship—from our captain—his life would be so much less, if he had a life at all."

Victoria's own sense of direction had diminished considerably over the past few moments as she listened to Mr. Harrt. Could it be that she had been mistaken in her observations? "Jack said he might be flogged for mutiny if Greyson discovered his desire to captain the *Spectre*," Victoria offered uncertainly.

Mr. Harrt smiled. "Jack has never doubted his importance to this vessel. With that sense of importance has come—most fortunately—a sense of responsibility to the rules. He apparently knows very well the rules concerning mutiny. In his heart, though, Jack knows he is deeply loved by his captain."

"And he loves him in return," Victoria reflected aloud.

The warrant officer nodded. "He does, Lady Darby, as does every man aboard this ship."

It was not for her that Jack pleaded the day of the flogging. It was not for her sake that he begged her not to go to the captain; it was for the captain's sake. Jack could not bear to think of the man being disturbed. And when the boy spoke of mutiny and flogging, he spoke of fantasies — his own fantasies. He needed those fantasies to reinforce his own value as a human being. Victoria lowered her head. She found it difficult to believe that she had been so mistaken. And her mistake would cost a man his dignity. She lifted her gaze.

"Is there no way to stop it?" she asked, her voice clenched with tears.

"No," the man said, lowering his eyes. "Captain Tyrrel has signed the order himself."

Victoria gaped at him. "He has signed an order to have himself flogged?"

"He understood that Jack would be watching this incident very carefully; he would not for all the world set the lad a bad example," Harrt said softly. "Beyond that, the captain would not dream of using the advantage of his position to favor himself."

Victoria's heart tripped desolately. In her mind, she had accused Greyson Tyrrel of exactly that offense. She now knew the truth. She had allowed her personal anger against him for the night in the plum grove to color her attitude toward him as captain of the ship. And, thinking on it — remembering the night she had left Kolhapur — she had to concede that she may have been to some extent at fault for even that circumstance. But that was something she would need to reconcile at another time. For the moment, she needed to think of a way to undo the damage she had done. Perhaps it was too late.

The rumble of men's voices caught her attention as Greyson Tyrrel appeared, bare-chested, on the spar deck. He was accompanied by several of his officers. The contingent of men walked, with unwavering concentration, toward the bow, all of them staring narrowly ahead toward where Greyson was to be secured. The voices of the men died abruptly as Victoria turned to face the approaching

92

cordon. Her eyes widened as they stopped before her. Greyson stepped to her. He stood tall, bronzed against the hot blue of the day, his russet curls falling carelessly over his forehead. The sea blue of his eyes snapped with cold anger. He held out a rolled parchment for her to accept. She stiffened, her green gaze pleading for reprieve.

" 'Tis the order you wished carried out." His tone was unyielding, his lips firm. "Take it," he commanded. She did. She glanced down at the writing and saw only the words—etched beneath her suddenly forming tears—that told her Greyson must endure eight lashes. "Eight plums— eight lashes," he stated curtly. "I do hope this satisfies your sense of . . . justice, milady."

Victoria lifted her gaze. Her eyes were wide, filled with disbelief and sorrow. "I did not think—" she began.

"No, you did not think," answered Greyson. He brushed past her, and with his men, he moved stiffly to where he was to be tied.

"Do it," he said. The seamen obediently secured him between the lines of the bowsprit so that his muscular form loomed large, stretched in a huge cross at the very center of the *Spectre*'s prow. One of the men held in his hand the long, nine-tailed, knotted whip. Another sailor rang the bell three times, but the gesture was unnecessary. Everyone aboard had gathered on the spar deck. Victoria gazed at the solemn and seemingly limitless blanket of humanity that had gathered to watch the spectacle of their captain being flogged. There was no sound. The man who held the whip raised it.

"No!" screamed Victoria. The one word echoed across the vast rolling ocean.

"Do not be a fool, milady," Harrt whispered, grasping her arm. "The sooner this thing is over—"

"No," Victoria repeated raggedly. She broke from Harrt's hold and ran for the bow. "You cannot—" she gasped. "You cannot!"

"Get her below decks," Greyson clenched out.

"No!" she asserted, her voice filled with authority . . . and tears. She raised the parchment. Clutching it against

93

the high ocean winds, she held it above her head. "This is *my* reckoning!" Her voice rang forcefully over the decks. "I will take my own revenge!" The faces staring back at her were filled with wonder and — was there something else? Had she managed to diffuse the solemnity of the occasion? Had she managed to diminish its importance? Facing the man who held the whip, she held out her delicate hand, palm up. "Give that to me," she demanded. The man's eyes darted to Greyson. That man glared at Victoria for a long moment. His glance flicked over her defiantly stiffened little form.

"You will have it this way?" he asked, his words low, for her ears alone.

"I will," she answered. Her emerald gaze flashed against the blue glint of his own.

"So be it," Greyson responded, again softly. He nodded tersely, and the sailor handed Victoria the cat. Pearl-frosted curls wafting out against the clear blue dome of the sky, Victoria turned with the whip and faced the man she was to flog. She raised her weapon. For the breath of a second, she hesitated, noting the glasslike clarity of his regard. She lowered the whip with all her strength. It swung down with a fragile thump against the cording of his broad back.

"One!" the observers shouted. Victoria raised her arm again. Again the muscular back took a flaccid blow. "Two!" the crowd rejoiced. Again the cat was swung, again the proud back accepted the encounter. By this time the gathering was laughing its computation. Word went out among the men as the flogging continued that other items might have been stolen from the same plantation. One man confessed quite openly that he had taken six oranges while another ribaldly admitted to filling his seacap with cashews. "Must have been fifty or sixty nuts in my topper!" he conceded merrily. "I'll take a blow for each." The crowd roared delightedly. By the seventh blow, the audience had become exactly that — an audience. The onlookers might have been watching a holiday spectacle. They cheered raucously as Victoria, arm aching from holding

94

the thick, heavy weapon, brought down the last stroke. A wild chorus of shouts and applause rose from the decks as Greyson was hastily untied. He rubbed at his wrists as he eyed Victoria speculatively. She stood before him, defiance and apology warring in her countenance. At last he turned away. Jerking his head toward his men, he shouldered his way among the onlookers, accepting ribald taunts and hand-shakes and pats on his insignificantly bruised back with good-natured amity. Victoria's gaze did not leave him as, just before he disappeared below decks, he offered her one last contemplative look. And then he was gone.

The crowd dispersed, the laughter dying. The clamor was carried far, over the sparkling billows of the ocean as the vessel moved on, cutting the rolling blue waters keeping its course . . . on an even keel.

Chapter Eight

Days had passed since Victoria had dared show her face on deck. Jack had come into her cabin only to bring food, and when he did, she had felt a sense of uncertainty in him that told her he was still sorting out the events surrounding the flogging of Greyson Tyrrel. Victoria wished desperately that she could speak to him about her feelings, explain to him the complexity of her reasons, but she knew that she must wait until Jack was ready to talk to her and, more importantly, to listen. Jack had hated the confrontation between her and Greyson. He loved them both. The adoration he still felt for Victoria had not diminished. She saw that in his eyes and in the small courtesies he showed her. Shyly, he asked her one day if she needed another bath. Victoria smiled and assured him that she did not.

As they had made their way around the Cape of Good Hope and up into the South Atlantic, the weather had taken a decidedly cooler turn. Some days were almost balmy. Today promised to be one of those days. Victoria peered out of the murky glass of her porthole and eyed the clear azure of the sky. Pinkened puffs of clouds glided cheerily past the opening in the ship's thick side. Victoria reflected for a long moment and then decided that she would chance a stroll on the deck.

She did not bother with the netting to protect her pale skin, but instead decided upon a small parasol. She asked Jack, when he entered to take away her breakfast things, if he would please go down, once again, into the orlop to retrieve it from her trunk. The boy did so with an almost grateful enthusiasm. He longed to do something for her, aside from the necessities, to show his love. Victoria perceived this and was thankful for it. She would hate to have lost Jack's friendship. In truth, he was her only friend, probably the only human being aboard the *Spectre* who did not consider her a fool. She had made herself a laughingstock, but she was not sorry to have done it. The fact was, she would have endured anything to have righted the wrong she had done Greyson Tyrrel. Victoria Quayle, for all her endowments, had always been a generously fair person. Throughout her formative years, Lord Trevor Darby had instilled in her the importance of maintaining her integrity when it came to the judgement of others. She must always, he had tutored her, respond to people with candor, assume their good faith and respect their views. She had allowed her resentment of Greyson to cloud her judgement. The incident in the plum grove in Kolhapur had nothing to do with his ability to command a ship. Victoria realized too late that before judging his worth as captain of the *Spectre,* she should have had all the facts. She should have spoken with him as one concerned human being to another. She should have allowed herself to understand his explanation of the flogging the day she had stormed his quarters. In truth, as she remembered it now, he had attempted to assuage her concern. She had been too caught up in the discovery of who he was to listen. She had been bent on revenge, and once that thought had taken hold, she had allowed it to convolute her entire thinking. One day she must deal with what had happened between them in Kolhapur, but for now she must deal with another sort of problem. She must face the derision of those with whom she must spend a great deal of time during the next weeks, on this little planet in the vast universe of the ocean. She smiled as she thought of Mr. Harrt. She would approach him first. Then she would speak to the sailors one by one, and to the other passengers. At last, if her courage had not deserted her, she would apologize to Greyson Tyrrel. She would not even think beyond that specific gesture to whether or not he would accept the apology. A sudden lurching ache in the middle of her breast told her how much it meant to her that he did accept it. But that thought was for another time. She had yet to ponder her feelings about Greyson. When she took the time to do so, she reminded herself resolutely, she would have a great deal of thinking to do.

An insistent rap on the door roused her from her musings. Jack entered at her invitation, holding the parasol aloft. "I found it," he cried proudly. " 'Twas not easy, your ladyship, but I did it."

Victoria laughed at the lad's enthusiasm, and in an unguarded moment of gratitude for his devotion as well as his little boon, she knelt and embraced him. He responded with the affection he had so long denied himself.

"I love you, mistress," he said, hugging her fiercely.

"Oh, Jack," Victoria breathed into his thin shoulder. "I love you, too." Tears welled in her eyes, and she shut them tightly against the hurt she knew she had caused in the little boy. "I have so much to say to you," she whispered.

"You don't have to say nothin'," Jack answered her. He drew away from her, and his stern little face bespoke his own battle with emotion. "I know you did what you did because you thought it was right," he said staunchly.

"I did, Jack," she said softly. "I really did."

"I know," the lad responded, placing a small hand on her shoulder. "Captain Tyrrel always says—" Jack stopped short and eyed her uncertainly. "You don't mind me talkin' about him, do you?" Victoria shook her head, smiling as she fought her tears. Jack continued. "He says that everybody is mostly always doin' the best they can, mistress. He says even when it don't look like they are, they are."

Victoria nodded gently. "Captain Tyrrel is right, Jack," she replied warmly.

"Well, I *knew* that," answered Jack. "I just wasn't so sure what was goin' on. I ain't asked him about what happened," he said, his tone becoming reflective. "I got some more thinkin' to do," he said softly. "I got to think about lots of things. But the one thing I know is, you was both doin' what you thought was right, 'cause you're both the best people I ever knew." He touched her cheek, and his little hand felt cool on her skin. "Stealin's a bad thing, mistress," he said. "I still believe that, but . . ." He paused, his eyes filled with appeal. "Please don't be too hard on the captain. We depend on him a lot, I mean we all look to him for *everything*. Sometimes we tend to forget that he's only a man, just like the rest of us. That's what Mr. Harrt says, and he's right, you know. Besides, stealin' your plums was wrong, but sometimes it's the only way we get some."

"Did you get some, Jack?" Victoria asked him.

"Four," he said, holding up four fingers shyly. "I suppose I should of taken four of them lashes," he said, ducking his head. Then, as a giggle bubbled to his lips, he raised his eyes. "They didn't look like they hurt all that much anyway."

"That was my intent, Jack," Victoria answered and hugged him once more before allowing him his complete freedom. Wriggling away from her affectionate embrace, he swiped at the spot where she had kissed his cheek. Apparently Jack could take only so much cuddling. Victoria smiled down at him as she stood. "Would you accompany me on deck?" she asked. "I should like to see Mr. Harrt." At Jack's sudden look of skepticism, Victoria splayed a hand. "I only want to apologize, Jack," she said quickly. "There will be no more complaints from me."

"Well, okay," Jack said doubtfully, "if you promise you won't make no more trouble."

Victoria laughed. "My trouble-making days are over," she vowed.

On deck, she approached the neatly attired warrant officer with some diffidence. The man's attention was focused far out to sea, and to gain his attention, Victoria had to touch the carefully creased sleeve of his woolen jacket. He looked abruptly at her as though startled.

"I beg your pardon, Mr. Harrt," she said softly. "I did not mean to frighten you."

"You did not frighten me, your ladyship," Harrt said

ndly. "But you did surprise me. I am glad to see you up from below decks," he said.

" 'Twas my intention to remain in my cabin till we reached the shores of America," she said quietly, "but I could not go another day without apologizing to you."

"To me?" the man asked.

"Yes," Victoria answered solemnly. "I have behaved as badly as a person can behave. I have caused a great deal of angst aboard this ship, and I am deeply sorry." To her amazement, Mr. Harrt merely smiled.

"I do accept your apology, Lady Darby, but let me assure you, you have given the men on this vessel a new perspective. Why, they are still talking about what happened. They have all threatened to go to your cabin to 'confess.' But the captain will not hear of it." His smile deepened. "Whether you know it or not, you have made a great difference in the men, and in the process made my job a great deal easier. It has been a very long time since we had anything about which to laugh. Sometimes we take ourselves entirely too seriously. When that happens, we tend to lose our sense of what is really important, that is, our faith in our fellow human beings. We tend to become too introspective; we lose the desire to communicate." He paused and looked back out to sea. "Do you know how many fights I have broken up in the last few months?" Victoria shook her head, but Harrt did not notice. "There were more than fifteen altercations in the month before you boarded, Lady Darby. 'Tis a sad thing to see men so caught in a web of anger toward one another. Sometimes an incident such as this one is needed to cause people to stop and take a good hard look at themselves." He glanced back at Victoria. "I have never seen such a sense of fellowship among the men. And, if they loved their captain before this, they love him now more than ever. He takes the men's taunts with such equanimity, such good grace, that they begin to see him as one of them. I believe they would do anything for him—and for each other."

Victoria smiled. "If I can begin to believe I have accomplished that, Mr. Harrt," she said softly, "I may one day be

100

able to rid myself of the guilt I feel."

"Do." The young officer laughed. "You are much too pretty to look so sad, especially when there is no need."

"I suppose, before I can be truly liberated, I must do the honorable thing and approach Captain Tyrrel," she sighed.

"You might want to wait on that, your ladyship," said Harrt seriously. He waved away her willingness to chastise herself. " 'Tis not that the captain would not appreciate your apology, I promise you. 'Tis only that"—his gaze swung out to where he had been looking before—"we have been watching carefully since dawn the approach of another ship." He indicated a tiny dot on the horizon. "Do you see it?" he asked. Victoria peered into the mist of the blue distance, but could not make out the figuration of a ship. She saw only a dot. She glanced helplessly at Harrt. "It *is* a ship." He laughed. "You will have to trust me on that."

"Is it American?" Victoria asked.

Harrt shrugged a wide shoulder. "I cannot tell. It approached us from the Gulf of Guinea, so it could be British. It could also be out from the Barbary States. In either case, we need to be extremely wary of it."

"Will it bother us?" Victoria questioned innocently.

" 'Bother,' madam?" laughed Harrt. "Oh, yes. It bothers us now, though we can barely see it."

Victoria smiled. "Then, I shall not 'bother' Captain Tyrrel," she said. "I shall save my apology for another time."

" 'Tis perhaps best."

Victoria turned, then lifting her parasol and peeking around its ruffled edges over her shoulder, she addressed the young officer once again. "Thank you, sir, for your kindness," she said softly.

Harrt tipped his hat. "Thank *you,* your ladyship," he said genially. "And, by the way, Lady Darby, my name is Edmund."

" 'Tis lovely to meet you, Edmund," Victoria answered. "My name is Victoria Quayle." She strolled off, her little umbrella twirling happily.

Throughout the long afternoon, Victoria managed to

101

speak to most of the sailors and many of the passengers. She was greeted with both hearty acceptance and dour condemnation. The men, for the most part, were touched by her simple apology. The women, for the most part, suspected an ulterior motive. Some thought she might have been attempting to garner the attention of the passengers and crew while others surmised she was trying to capture the attention of the handsome captain himself. One woman, however, laughed in dismissal of Victoria's claim that she had brought discomfort to the passengers.

"I've not had that jolly a time in years, milady," the woman answered, patting Victoria's forearm in comradely goodwill. "I'd have paid money to see it!" Victoria could not contain her own mirth as the woman clapped her heavy thigh with a weather-roughened hand. "Sometimes them fellows need a shakin' up, you know. They get too damnable cocky, otherwise."

"I know." Victoria laughed. "Still," she added more seriously, "I hate to think I have diminished the dignity of the office of captain."

"Captain or no captain," the woman rejoined, leaning forward, "they're all alike. They need to get themselves humbled every once in a while. Now don't you go worryin'," she said warmly. "You did okay for yourself. And for the rest of us. My old fellow's been awful quiet since he watched you whippin' the captain." She laughed and swiped at her nose with a thick forearm. "I think maybe the whole thing's got him just a little scared." She raised an eyebrow. "That don't hurt one damn bit, you know—havin' them a little scared. They're a bit nicer to you." She folded her arms across her breast. "No need to apologize to me, dear heart. You did just fine."

Victoria thanked the woman, and as the sun was setting, she decided to go back down into her cabin. She took one last look over the rail to see that the "dot" was still in pursuit. She wondered at it, but put her faith in Greyson Tyrrel that he would not allow it to overtake them.

The *Spectre* swayed easily on the quiet swells of the

South Atlantic. Victoria lay propped in her bed, enjoying the poetry of Mr. Donne. Her lamp flickered silently near. She looked up, closing and resting her eyes for a moment, and listened to the quiet creaking of the oaken boards. She thought of home, of all that she had left, and all that had happened to her since leaving. She had learned a great deal, she realized, in just the few weeks she had spent on board the *Spectre*. She reflected on the words of Edmund Harrt. A seagoing vessel was indeed a very special world unto itself. The ocean was its own universe. It was coming to represent for Victoria a time and place that had been unlike any other in her life. And this day was particularly special. Her brows wrinkled. It *was* very special, she reminded herself. But why? What was special about this *particular* day? Suddenly she sat upright, knocking Mr. Donne onto the light coverlet. Victoria swung her legs over the side of the narrow bed. Today was indeed special. Today was her eighteenth birthday!

She jumped down onto the deck, needing to do something, recalling over the years the ostentatious glitter that had attended this day. Every year of her life, from the time she could remember, and before that she suspected, the entirety of Kolhapur had attended her birthday festivities. No cost was spared, no pageantry was neglected in the celebration of her birth. Victoria longed to tell someone, to share with them the joy and fanfare that had commemorated the event each and every year of her life. But there was no one to tell. This birthday, Victoria would celebrate alone.

She slipped into her nightrobe and stepped outside onto the gun deck. Moving silently, she took the stairs to the upper deck and peered out into the darkness. No one was about. It was just as well, she thought. She moved to the rail, holding her robe tightly around her. Who in this little world really cared that she had been born? Who would think her birth a cause for celebration? Jack would care, she decided, pushing at the wisps of hair that fluttered in the night breezes about her face. And Edmund Harrt might care. But of course neither of them would hold the

103

day in the importance in which it was held by her friends at home.

Last year at this time, she and Lynnie and Marguerite had been together with her other friends on the plantation green. Katje had arranged a lawn party. She had invited jugglers and musicians and a company of troubadours who had composed lyric poetry right on the spot. Their major theme had been courtly love, and they sang and wept and idled about the lawns in fictions of passionate entanglements. Victoria and her friends had laughed — and wept — at the stylized emotions of star-crossed lovers and doting sweethearts. It was a dreamlike evening. Victoria remembered with a sorrowful clenching of her heart that Steven Kensington had just arrived home from Oxford. They had walked in the cedar forest that night, talking of all that had happened during the years in which they had been separated. In her fancies, Victoria made plans for them. She envisioned their future together. It was to be as meltingly romantic as any pastoral interlude improvised by any actors. So many nights she went to sleep dreaming of that future. She had no idea then of the hollow alliance that Steven would propose. She sighed softly.

In the darkness behind her, a presence materialized. She turned, startled. She gazed up into eyes the color of blue sea glass.

" 'Tis late," Greyson said huskily.

"Yes," Victoria answered, as he moved to the rail beside her.

Greyson lit a small cigar, and the light of the tinder flared briefly in the blackness, illuminating the firmly etched bronze of his features, the tousle of his russet curls. Victoria clutched at her fluttering robe. She looked up at him through the veil of her lashes. Sensing her perusal, he glanced down.

"Are you all right?" he asked after a pause.

"I am well," she said unsure of exactly how she felt. "And you . . . Greyson?" He nodded tersely. Victoria took a resigned breath.

"I wanted to—"; "We ought to talk about—" They be-

104

gan their words at the same time and both stopped abruptly. There was silence between them.

Victoria smiled in the darkness and lowered her gaze. "You were very angry with me," she murmured.

"I was," Greyson answered.

"And are you still?" Her regard lifted slowly. She was just a little afraid of what he might answer.

Greyson watched her for a long moment. As he did, a low cloud passed beyond the moon, and her eyes and face became bathed in its pale luster. The sea breezes caught the light ringlets of her hair and curled them around the jewellike oval of her face. How could anyone remain angry, or feel any unkind emotion toward this shimmering creature. One guarded oneself, to be sure, against her obvious allure, but one could not be angry.

"No," he said at last.

"I am glad," Victoria returned. "Then I may apologize without fear of rejection."

Again Greyson regarded her for a long speculative moment. " 'Twas a courageous thing you did, Victoria," he said quietly. "You suffered a great deal of ridicule to insure that the focus of the moment was not my flogging but your vengeance. You made yourself very unsympathetic to the people watching. Was that your intent?"

"Yes." She nodded. "That was my intent."

"Then it is I who must apologize."

Victoria gaze widened. "Oh, no, Greyson. You must not apologize. I was at fault in this. 'Twas my petty certainty that—"

" 'Twas my thievery," Greyson interjected. His eyes glinted a smile. "I've needed flogging for some time now, and so have half the men on board. Whenever we enter a port, we have no compunctions about rifling the orchards thereabouts. We never seem to get our fill of such luxurious fare."

Victoria regarded him woefully. "Had I known that, Greyson," she said earnestly, "you could have had bushels of plums."

"Then the fault for what happened can be divided

105

equally between us," he answered, his smile deepening. "It never occurred to me to ask."

Victoria shook her head. "You do not understand, Greyson," she murmured.

"What do I not understand?" he urged gently.

Victoria allowed her gaze to wander out to the moon-sparkled ocean. "I do not understand it all myself," she said. "How can I explain it to you?" He watched as she struggled with her feelings, and his heart wrenched in sympathy for her. She was so young, so deeply innocent. And yet . . . He recalled with a longing ache her response to his lovemaking the night in Kolhapur. He had damned himself a thousand times since then. Would that he had remembered, that night, the tender innocence with which he had dealt. For all her defiant show of aggression that night, she had been, in truth, a gentle, heartbroken young woman. He had sensed that, and he had sensed that she was in need of the comfort of his arms. And yet, he had allowed his manly passions to overpower his nobler instincts. That would not happen again. He must guard himself. For all her sweet innocence, she was a rare and soul-stirring beauty.

She was suddenly speaking again, and her words came in a breathless rush. "I was angry with you for the night in Kolhapur, and I allowed that anger to distort my attitude toward you. I believed that you were using me for your own pleasure, Greyson. But now I know that I was using you as well." She hurried on. "I wanted someone. I thought it was Steven Kensington, but the truth is I wanted *someone*. I needed to love someone. Steven became the object of all my girlhood fantasies, and when he left me— when I discharged him from my life—I latched on to the first man who was gentle with me, who showed me kindness." She looked up to discover his warm blue gaze upon her. "And you did show me kindness that night, Greyson," she said softly. "You took me in your arms so tenderly, so lovingly. You comforted me, and I sorely needed comforting. 'Twas not your fault alone that the comfort turned to . . . something else. I did not have to allow the first kiss

106

and certainly not the second. But I wanted you to kiss me. I wanted you to make love to me. 'Twas only that I . . . I . . ." her voice trailed off.

"You did not bargain for the intensity of my lust," he said half smiling.

"I did not bargain for the intensity of my own lust, Greyson," she rejoined softly. Caught unguarded by this admission, Greyson eyed her in oblique amazement. Was this marvel of a woman—this wondrous combination of innocence and passion—really standing here next to him, on his own ship? No matter, he remonstrated himself as he hastily shook off his ardor. He would not again attempt seduction of this tender lamb. Better to stick with the experienced wenches. They rarely suffered over their womanly hungers—or his manly ones. And they certainly did not become frightened by them. Still, this virginal young woman intrigued him. Merely standing next to her excited him far beyond what he had known in the arms of any other woman. He did not understand the potency of his response to her. She was a remarkable beauty, it was true, but he had known many beautiful women. His eagerness to feel this particular woman enfolded in his arms, pressed to his thundering heart, bewildered him. When she spoke again, her voice was filled with a soft incredulity, her tone matching his own wonder at the mysterious charm that seemed to magnetize them. "I have only just discovered these things, Greyson," she said, gazing at him. "I am discovering them as I speak. And yet, I knew, even that night in Kolhapur, that I had discovered the 'someone' I was seeking. 'Tis at least part of what drew me away from the plantation . . . to the sea . . . to you." Her green eyes held the shimmer of the moon in their depths, and Greyson felt himself drawn into them. He tossed his cigar down into the swirling depths of the water and turned to her. Taking her slender shoulders in his hands, he drew her gently around to face him.

"We must go slowly in this," he said huskily. "I would give a great deal to be a gentle guide for you, but I am no counselor. I am only a man, Victoria. And, at the moment," he added in self-deprecation, "I am a man who rages to possess you." He held her firmly when she stirred against his grasp. "Listen to me," he intoned. "I am an impatient wooer, not given to courtly games. I am no Steven Kensington, Victoria; I shall not be satisfied with amorous glances and gallant flirtations. I am a seaman, bred in the rough, rude world of sailing ships and wharfside taverns. There is no place in my life for your gentle English traditions of courtship. And," he added sternly, "there is no room in your life for my rock-bound American impatience. I am not the man for you."

"You were that man in Kolhapur," she countered with a gentle resolve. "And you are here on the decks of the *Spectre of the Bay*. What do I care for pale traditions? If I had not lost Steven Kensington—had not met you—I might never have known the joy of my woman's passion. I cannot name what I have come to feel for you, Greyson, but I know it is beyond anything that I have ever felt for anyone. I know it is what I want to feel. Yesterday, I was a girl. Today, because of you, I am a woman. You have taught me not only a woman's passion but a woman's *com*passion. You have given me a woman's heart." With the words, she slipped from his restraint and pressed herself to the lean, muscular length of him, lifting her arms and entwining them around his neck.

"Oh, Greyson," she said softly, "you accepted my cruelty so understandingly; you forgave me so unstintingly. I believed you to be dishonorable, but you are not." She drew him toward her, practically lifting herself off her feet. Her lips taking his in a rapturous kiss, she clung to him. Greyson battled mightily with his vaulting desire and pushed her gently away from him.

"Victoria," he groaned. "You have no idea of what you are arousing in me."

"But I want to arouse you, Greyson," she insisted. "A promise was born between us in Kolhapur, and here on the *Spectre* the promise has been sealed. There can be only one explanation for our meeting again here on your ship. We were predestined to love." Once again her sweet lips took his. The towering ambiguity of his resistance yielded to his hunger and he caught her in a steely embrace. He arched her to him. She complied, aching to feel the hard essence of him against her yearning flesh. He ravished the delicate column of her throat with the heat of throbbing kisses, and the lacy neckline of her fragile gown submitted to the command of his ravening purpose. Victoria whimpered with the agony of her own need. The sound seemed to drag Greyson Tyrrel back to the hard fact of reality.

"Victoria," he gasped raggedly, drawing from her. "For the love of God, woman, I have only so much self-control." He felt her press her womanly curves to him, and he managed a lop-sided smile as he gazed down on her. "What shall I do with you," he groaned hoarsely. "You are every man's dream of fulfillment."

"Then fulfill yourself, Greyson," she offered, her eyes closing, the fans of her dark lashes sweeping the soft curve of her passion-flushed cheeks.

"Victoria," he said after a hesitation. He cupped her delicate chin in his large hand. "Victoria," he repeated sternly. He waited; her eyes popped open, and the liquid bewilderment in her wide green gaze nearly unraveled the control for which he had battled. Neither of them spoke; neither of them moved. The moon-swirled sea air and the fluid cadence of the depthless ocean merged with the thrumming of their hearts as the big ship cut the water. Without further words, Greyson swept her from her feet and strode, carrying her in his strong arms, down into the darkness of the hatchway and across the silent recesses of the lower deck.

Victoria melted against his powerful urgency, her head rolling back over his forearm. Her breast pounded with the heat of her own desire. She entwined her slender arms around the column of his neck, offering herself to perfect fulfillment. "Oh, Greyson," she breathed as he stopped. Her eyes languidly unclosed to find that they were at the door of her cabin. Greyson kicked at it violently, his bared teeth glinting white against the darkness. The door blazed open. The lamp she'd left burning swathed them in the golden aura of its flickering light. Victoria readied herself for surrender. Unimaginably, instead of sweeping her inside, Greyson remained rigid outside the door. Tall, bronzed, battling mightily with some inner conflict, he stood before it, containing her within his embrace. He looked down on her, the tousle of his burnished curls falling over his forehead. The blue glass of his gaze impaled her. Abruptly, he turned away, shaking off some powerful possession. A battle determined, he set her roughly onto her feet.

"Go to bed," he growled. Victoria lifted her unbelieving gaze. Before she could utter a protest, however, he grasped her arm brusquely and walked her just inside the cabin. He turned without further word, slamming the door as he left.

Alone, Victoria stared for long moments at the place from where he had vanished. She felt the heat of his steely embrace leaving her rapidly. She felt cold where once there had been warmth, hollow where once there had been the promise of fulfillment.

At last, her heart agonized, bewildered, she moved to her bed. She realized achingly that once again, she had offered herself, and once again, she had been denied the realization of her dreams. Why? Why was her marriage to Steven denied her? Why was the consummation of her womanly passion with Greyson denied her? Why? Why? Why? What was there about her that kept fulfillment just out of her reach? Was there some unlucky charm that guided her life, some black Circe tearing from her everything she desired? Was some sorcery at work?

She lay down on the hard narrow bunk. If a dark star did hover mystically above her life, she must begin to grapple with its influence, she resolved. She could not allow herself to be hindered at every crucial turning point. She must fight this . . . thing, this demonic source of her misfortune. She gazed out the small port window and watched as the moon glazed a lustrous path over the black sky. Her eyes closed slowly.

One day she would understand; one day she would begin to reckon with the odd turnings of her life. But for now . . . Her confusion had exhausted her. Tomorrow she would begin to unravel all the mysteries. But for now . . . Her breathing evened as, at last, the peace of slumber encloaked her.

Chapter Nine

Bells clanged raucously. Many bells sounded, creating one desperate, frenzied clamor. Victoria lurched to a sitting position, rubbing sleep from her eyes, glancing wildly about at unfamiliar surroundings. Where was she? What was happening? She dragged at the coverlet, clutching it to her breast, and swung her legs over the side of the bed. What bed was this? It was not her own bed — not her bed in Kolhapur. She had dreamed urgently, longingly of Kolhapur. But this was not Kolhapur. She was on a ship . . . the *Spectre of the Bay,* cutting the deathless ocean, heading for the American colonies. Was she still aboard the *Spectre?* Her befuddled senses attempted to sort out what had brought her to this place. The pounding of booted feet above her drew her attention. She placed delicate hands over her ears, shutting out the riot of disonant sound. Shouts, pounding feet, bells, the ship's lurching roll combined to confuse and distract her. She clawed at the coverlet, drawing it more tightly to her. Greyson! she thought wildly. She had offered herself to him — practically forced herself upon him. And now this brawl of noise was proclaiming her transgression!

Victoria bounded to her feet and charged the door. It was locked from the outside. She pounded and slammed herself against its unyielding guardianship. She screamed. No one came. The tumult outside resounded against her pale efforts to be released. She shrieked once again, demanding freedom, but no answering response comforted her. Why had Greyson done this to her? She cried for Jack. A sudden, thunderous roar answered her. Another roar and then a deafening crack resounded, and Victoria was tossed from her feet by a sudden convulsing jolt of the deck. The door burst open. It was Greyson. He filled the entry, and Victoria bolted to her feet, throwing herself against him. Her terrified sobs wracked her body. Greyson swept her up into his strong arms.

"I am taking you down to the lower deck," he grated.

"What is it, Greyson?" she pleaded.

"Enemy fire," he said curtly. He threw her over one broad shoulder and transported her down the rope ladder to the berthing deck.

"What enemy?" was all she could manage.

"Brits," he ground out. He deposited her unceremoniously onto the lower deck. "Stay down here," he commanded, and then he was gone. Victoria attempted to regain her breath after their wild flight below decks. It was not for several moments that she realized she was not alone. She pushed at the tangle of frosted curls that tumbled wildly about her shoulders, blocking her vision, and glanced around. Her eyes widened in the murky darkness as she discovered that she was being watched. She realized at the same moment that the perusal was not a friendly one. She gazed bemusedly into the wary regard of twenty or thirty people.

"What is it?" she asked breathlessly. "What is happening?" She was answered by an unrelenting silence. If the door of her cabin had proven an unyielding barrier, the silence of these people was an even more formidable one. "Please," she said, facing the assembly. "Please, can someone explain? Have we been fired upon by a British vessel?" There was no response. She spotted the woman who had laughed with her the day before over the flogging. "Can you tell me what is going on?" she gasped.

"Lobsterbacks," the woman clenched out.

Victoria flinched. She had never heard the term, but could only assume it referred to the scarlet coats worn by the British military. She maintained what calm she could manage. She must discover what the problem was. "Have the British fired upon us?" she asked desperately.

"Yeah," the woman responded. "The blighters are protectin' their precious tea trade."

Another man joined in. "The red-coated bastards are lookin' for trouble, missy, and they're gonna get it."

Victoria's brows quirked in a puzzled frown.

"I do not understand," she asserted helplessly. "Why, in the Lord's name, would the British fire on this ship?" The crowd eyed her dispassionately.

"The *lord's* name is exactly the problem," a man stated drily. "But it ain't the Lord you're talkin' about."

"Oh, please." Victoria repeated her supplication. "Can someone tell me what is going on?"

One man stepped from the gathering and faced the pleading girl. "Lord North," he stated, "has decided—"

"Are you speaking of the prime minister of England?" Victoria asked.

"I am," the man answered curtly. "He has decided that he is going to ship tea directly from India to the American colonies—without sending it through England."

"He figures us for fools," said the woman who had been Victoria's friend. At once, several people began to speak, adding their own interpretation of the reasoning of Lord North and the reason for the attack on the *Spectre*.

Victoria could make little sense of the explanation, but she gathered that the British were attempting to put a stop to the smuggling of tea by American ships. They apparently had decided that only British tea could be brought into the colonies and that any vessels suspected of carrying the contraband substance were to be boarded.

"But you must understand something," Victoria offered, attempting a desperate rationalization. "Lord North is a friend to the Americans. The explanation for his sending tea directly to the colonies from India could be that he wishes to help you avoid English duties on the tea."

"That's what *he* says," interjected a man irately.

"You Brits stick together, don't you." The crowd moved menacingly forward.

Victoria backed from their advance, splaying her hands before her. "As for this attack," she went on wildly, "there must be some logical explanation."

114

"There is," grated one of the men. "Tyrrel fired first."

"We don't take much to bein' boarded."

"The Brits got no flippin' right!"

Victoria attempted to assimilate the impossibility of what she had heard. "Greyson could not have fired on a British vessel!" she breathed. The assemblage moved threateningly forward, snarling animosity, eyes flashing venom. Victoria felt herself backed to the thick oaken sides of the ship. In a moment, they would be upon her; the faceless, senseless bitterness directed toward her converged viciously, filling the air with condemnation and hate. At that moment a rumbling crack exploded above them. The deck pitched violently, tossing silhouetted figures writhing to the deck. The mob, no longer threatening, grasped at each other for safety as they convulsed in a panic of self-preservation. Women screamed and men dragged them into protective embraces. Victoria was jolted to the deck. She huddled there alone. Another roar seized the sultry air of the berthing deck. Though the noise was muffled in the low confines of the small space, shouts could be heard from above. The pounding of running feet and the clanging of bells could be detected. The deck creaked ominously, jolting first to port and then to starboard. The people clawed at each other, attempting to keep themselves steady, but the spasms of the ship were too severe; the passengers slid across the deck, dragged by the force of the ship's lurching roll. And then, very suddenly, there was silence above — only silence — and the deck rocked slowly to a rolling sway. The people listened intently. No sound could be detected. While the others nursed at their scraped knees and elbows, and sobbed quietly in terror, Victoria crawled stealthily to the rope ladder. Heaving herself upward, she made her way onto the gun deck. She spotted Jack in the writhing mob of seamen, and motioned him to her. Glancing furtively behind him, he shouldered his way through the swarm of men.

"What're you doin' up here, mistress?" he demanded with all the authority his surreptitiousness would allow.

"What has happened, Jack?" she whispered, clutching at his little arm.

115

"They're boardin' us," he answered. Then, detaching him
self from her grasp, he added desperately. "You gotta ge
below. We gotta be on deck to meet the blighters." Victoria
detected his trembling, the anxiety in his voice, but she
could not determine whether the anxiety was for her or be
cause of the British. He had obviously been told terrible
tales of them. The lad was frightened beyond reason.

"Listen to me, Jack," she intoned passionately, "those
sailors boarding this ship are human beings, just like you
are. They are not monsters."

"They're Brits," he shot back.

"Dammit, Jack, I'm a Brit!" she rejoined and then
quickly amended her harsh tone. Aside from her fixed
loathing for the word itself, she realized that Jack had no
thought of this. His countenance blanched. " 'Tis all right
Jack," she consoled him. She knelt before him and took him
in a warm embrace. "Please, Jack" she said softly, "go on to
your duties. Try not to be frightened. 'Twill be all right." He
eyed her uncertainly before he was swept up in the shove of
men heading for the spar deck. Victoria, unnoticed, made
her way to her own cabin. An idea had formed.

She dressed quickly in her ivory satin. Brushing at it and
snapping out the skirts to a regal sheen, she hastily made
herself as imposing a figure of British nobility as possible
She rummaged through her small morroco etui and drew
out her emeralds. She had been allowed to keep her jewels
with her in her cabin, and though she'd brought only a few
pieces from Kolhapur, she had made sure they were some of
her most impressive. She draped the collar of platinum and
green stones around her slender neck and donned the ear
drops. Lifting her hair, she piled it into a lucent tower of
queenly curls. She snapped on her emerald bracelet and
snatched up her frothy parasol. With a long, calming breath
and with one last glance into her little glass, she left her
cabin. Greyson Tyrrel would either kill or bless her for her
interference, but she must take the chance. If he had in fac
fired on an English vessel, he was in very real trouble. And i
he was smuggling tea, he might find himself imprisoned . .
or. . . . She must not even imagine that possibility. She

116

squared her slender shoulders and climbed the steps to the upper deck. Spreading her parasol and lifting it over one shoulder, she began the longest walk of her life. Moving with royal grace, Victoria made her way, her wide skirts swaying hypnotically, toward the prow.

The sailors gathered on the deck formed a hastily cleared aisle. Victoria reached the bow of the ship just as a British officer and several seamen jumped from the gangplank that separated the two vessels onto the deck of the *Spectre*. Greyson stood solemnly before them, his coat and tricorn neatly brushed, his boots polished.

"What in the name of King George is going on here?" demanded Victoria's sweet, musical voice. The regard of the men snapped toward her. She smiled innocently. "I was sleeping and heard all the ruckus. You sailors are always either brawling or merrymaking," she added with a small laugh, "but really, must you display your high spirits so early in the day? A lady must be allowed her beauty sleep, after all." Her British accented tones caught the particular attention of the English officer. He regarded her quizzically. She veiled her gaze. "Oh, my," she said penitantly, "I seem to have interrupted something very serious." She glanced at Greyson. "I hope you will forgive me, Captain, but my curiosity got the better of me. I see you are entertaining a member of the British Royal Navy." She smiled invitingly at the officer and extended her hand. "Won't you allow me to introduce myself," she said. "I am Lady Noelle Darby—the *Honorable* Lady Darby. But please call me Victoria." The man stepped forward, his countenance questioning, and took her hand. Bowing over it, he brushed a courtly kiss on the proffered limb. "Might I know your name?" she inquired sweetly.

The man cleared his throat and answered, barely moving his lips. "Captain Leland Stewart at your service, my lady."

Victoria's tinkling laughter roused the man's attention. "Why, Captain Stewart," she exclaimed. "I know of you. My very dear friend Robert Clive has spoken of you so often and in such glowing terms that I feel we must be old friends. Bobby—I should say, Sir Robert—tells me you are one of

117

our navy's most valuable men."

Captain Stewart quirked an appreciative smile. "Sir Robert has spoken of me?" he asked.

"Oh, yes," Victoria answered, her eyes wide and serious in her pale face. "He was at my home the night before I left Kolhapur, and he mentioned that you were in the Gulf of Guinea." Victoria had recalled the indication of Edmund Hartt as to the English ship's direction of approach. She hoped she had remembered his words correctly and guessed she had as the captain smiled broadly. Victoria continued, touching his sleeve as she leaned to him. "Sir Robert seemed quite concerned that so many of our men were unnecessarily patrolling these foreign environs."

"Unnecessarily patrolling?" the man inquired.

"Of course," Victoria answered brightly. "Sir Robert contends that no intelligent American captain would carry tea these days." She glanced at Greyson through the veil of her lashes and offered him a seductive smile. His reaction to her bold display was unreadable in the hooded glint of his regard. Victoria went on brazenly. "And Sir Robert would certainly not have arranged passage for me on a vessel smuggling contraband." She laughed again, the light musical sound drifting over the tight cordon of perspiring men. The sailors behind her seemed to relax, and the men facing her glanced at each other warily. Her gaze quickly settled back on Captain Stewart. "I am assuming that is why you are visiting the *Spectre* . . . Leland, to ask Captain Tyrrel if he is carrying tea." Her tone was confidential and dripping with comradely understanding. "We must be ever watchful of these American colonists," she said in gentle communion with the man's undoubted burden. "I can assure you, however, that there is no tea aboard this ship."

"We were fired upon, my lady," he said quietly, eyeing her uncertainly. "Why would Captain Tyrrel have done that had he nothing to hide?"

Victoria laughed brightly. "Oh, I am sure there is some logical explanation, Leland. Perhaps your ship was mistaken for one of those Barbary vessels," she said, again recalling Mr. Harrt's speculation on the identity of the ship.

"In any event, you would not even question the presence of tea on this ship if you knew what I have been offered to drink. Every morning, I am enjoined to take a dollop of the most ungodly concoction. 'Tis called grog," she derided, "but I know it to be a combination of cheap rum and water. What a ghastly way to begin one's day." She laughed. "I think I should give a million pounds sterling for a cup of decent British tea." She eyed the captain expectantly and was rewarded with his invitation to join him on board his own ship. Waving brightly to the crew of the *Spectre,* Victoria was aided aboard the English ship.

A heart-gripping few moments passed while the British sailors faced the American crew. Victoria had insisted that Captain Tyrrel join her and Leland Stewart so that Greyson might put forth his own explanation of the attack on the English ship, and to "show him what the Americans are missing by eliminating British tea from their diets," she intoned with sly gaiety. Without their captains, the men began, finally, a collaborative retelling of the morning's battle. What began as a taunting thrust by one of the *Spectre*'s crew became a jolly recital.

"If your bowsprit hadn't fouled in the rigging of the *Spectre,*" called one man, "you never would've gotten near enough to board us."

"A whole broadside raked you fellows," returned a British sailor. "You never had a chance."

"We got your foremast, though," said another fellow.

"But your mizzen don't look too flippin' healthy!" the men laughed in good-natured agreement that both ships had put up a perfectly respectable fight.

As the raucous laughter filtered down to the lower decks, the passengers began to emerge to see what the apparent fun was about. They were quickly and avidly informed of the events that had taken place. They voiced diverse opinions of the role in all this of Victoria Quayle. One woman, a particularly dour lady, expressed the belief that though Lady Darby may have been responsible for the abatement of the hostilities between the two ships, she was, nevertheless, a British subject and, therefore, responsible for much of the initial concern.

"But we are British subjects, too," another lady said hesitantly in the face of the other woman's ire.

"We are Americans," that woman was informed with categorical certainty.

"She's on that English ship, drinkin' tea, while we're here scared out of our wits!" a man accused. "Beyond that," the man continued doggedly, "she's headin' for the colonies. What's she goin' to do when she gets there, bein' so friendly with the Brits. We got enough of them in Boston. We don't need any more." The passengers gathered to listen to the man. With a determined hostility, their opinions swayed further and further in Victoria's disfavor. One woman felt Victoria should be isolated from the rest of the passengers while a man suggested she be dropped at the nearest port and left there to fend for herself. It was even observed that she might be tried as a spy and forced to walk the plank, but the group speculated bitterly that it would be difficult to force that issue considering the fact that the captain might frown on such an outmoded form of vigilante justice.

"If he opposes us," snarled one man, "maybe we'll discover where his loyalties really lie."

The group was not aware of the fact that they had a most curious listener. Jack stood apart, but close enough that he could hear the dangerous tide of swelling antagonism toward his beloved mistress and his captain. Once Victoria and Greyson had reboarded the *Spectre,* and the British sailors were dismissed, the couple retired *together,* it was bitingly noted, to the captain's quarters while both crews attempted to untangle the two ships. Jack noted with growing anxiety the sullen faces of the passengers.

"I say we get rid of her," a man growled as the couple passed.

"Those God-haters have got to be shown!" another agreed. "We'll make her an example."

"If the captain won't agree to it, we'll take matters into our own hands," stated a man through clenched teeth. The others concurred, their voices lowering conspiratorially.

Once inside Greyson's cabin, Victoria breathed a long,

relieved sigh as she collapsed onto the small settee. She eyed Greyson's stern expression resignedly. "Strangle me if you must, Captain," she said tiredly, "but I did what I believed was right." She lowered her gaze against his perusal and was immediately bemused to hear low laughter rumble from his throat. She glanced up to find him standing above her, hands on hips, his head thrown back in pure unbridled mirth.

"Oh, Victoria," he said at last, "what shall I do with you?" She arched a questioning brow. "You are as unmanageable as—'tis said—we colonists have become." He reached out and raised her from the sofa, pulling her roughly into his embrace. He gazed down on her, tenderness in the clear depths of his regard. "Just about an hour ago," he said huskily, "I was ready to toss you over my knee. When I saw you saunter onto the deck, parading all your aristocratic affectations, I might have cuffed you soundly. I had no idea at the time that you were rendering one of the most magnificent performances I have ever had the pleasure to witness."

Victoria tilted him a smile. "When I put my mind to it, Captain Tyrrel, I am a most convincing patrician."

Greyson laughed. He looked down into the glittering mischief of her green gaze. Slowly his perusal sobered. "Most convincing," he said huskily.

Before Victoria could respond archly that apparently her powers of persuasion had some limit at least where he was concerned, Jack erupted into the room.

"We got trouble," he asserted, forgetting even to salute.

Both Greyson and Victoria regarded him in astonishment. "What is it, Jack?" they asked him. "What is the trouble?"

"There's dangerous talk topside," he declared. "The passengers is makin' threats against you, mistress. And they been talkin' about you protectin' a redcoat, Captain," he said to Greyson. "I ain't usually scared of such stuff, but today I got a real bad feelin'. People are so mad about the Brits boardin' an' all, that I'm feelin' like we ought to take them serious."

"But I don't understand, Jack," Victoria breathed. "I thought everyone would thank me for keeping their captain out of the brig and helping to avert a search of the ship."

"They ain't thankin' you, mistress," he said solemnly. "There's too many of them who are rousin' up the others. I'm awful worried." He pulled off his seacap and swiped at his perspiration-sheened face. "They've all gone down onto the berthin' deck, an' I got a feelin' they're plannin' somethin' against you."

"But this is unbelievable," Victoria exclaimed.

"I am afraid it is not," Greyson answered. He considered her for a long moment as he brushed a roughened fingertip over her distress-pinkened cheek. " 'Tis an unfortunate fact that feelings run high in the colonies, Victoria. The British aristocracy is less than well-favored I fear. I myself hold no love for that particular class of people." He allowed a rakish half-smile to curve his firm lips. "Except for one rather remarkable exception." His expression hardened quickly, however. "I am sorry to say it, love, but we have our reasons."

"Well, thank you very much, Captain," Victoria huffed, turning from him and crossing her arms over her breast. "Why don't you just toss me to the wolves, then?"

Greyson took her shoulders in his large hands and turned her to face him. "Forgive me, Victoria—I know this does not set well with your long-held ideas of civilized behavior—but I am telling you the truth."

"That he is," Jack interjected. "It ain't against you particularly, mistress," he hastily assured her. "But, you know . . . you're on the other side."

"Our point is, Victoria, these people have been sorely tested today," Greyson said gently, "and for a very long time before this. You must try to understand their point of view."

"I understand nothing, Greyson," she wailed softly. "I thought I was helping them—and you. You fired on one of His Majesty's vessels; you could be hanged for such a crime. As to this tea business, I have no idea whether or not you are carrying smuggled tea, but if you are—and I do not wish to know one way or the other—I have kept you all out of the

122

gaol."

"Sshhh," he crooned, as he drew her toward him, realizing that tears were welling in her uncomprehending gaze. "We shall think of something."

"We will, mistress," assured Jack worriedly. "We'll get you outta this."

Victoria sniffed loudly, and Greyson offered her a kerchief. "Have the English untangled from our bowsprit, Jack?" he asked over his wide shoulder.

"I'll go see, Captain." Jack darted from the room.

"It just doesn't make any sense, Greyson," Victoria said, drawing away from him.

"I know that, love. Sometimes I think none of this makes any sense." He raked his long fingers through the tumble of his russet curls. "I will be perfectly honest with you and tell you that I am damned tired of this wrangling between the English and the colonists. Something needs to happen, and very soon."

Victoria eyed him uncertainly as she wiped at her nose. "Uncle David said the same thing," she offered. "And Sir Geoff, Lynnie Franklyn's father, is positive there will be a war." Greyson looked quickly at her. "But Uncle David says 'twill never come to that," she assured him.

"Tell 'Uncle David' not to be so sure," he rejoined abruptly. "If what happened today keeps up—and it will, I fear—the colonials will be hard pressed to resist striking back. As it was, I could only plead an error in judgment to Captain Stewart for firing upon him today." He smiled briefly. "I do not think he would have accepted my explanation had it not been for your wicked charms." He moved to her and took her into a casual embrace. "Stewart was bound to see me nailed to the yardarm until your sweetly innocent remark about Mr. Harrt's unfortunate eyesight and your observation that the sun might have been in his eyes." Greyson laughed. "Once again, my love, you managed to diffuse a most explosive situation."

Victoria looked up at him, her green gaze liquid and yielding. Greyson caught himself being drawn by that emerald seduction. He reached up and the roughness of his fingertips touched the pale silk of her cheek. Then immediately he seemed to will his hand back to his side. Victoria realized his discomfort and drew hastily away.

"I had no hope that Captain Stewart would believe me," she murmured by way of breaching her own embarrassment and Greyson's.

"You will find that most people are prone to believe what they want to believe," he answered shortly. "But the fact is, love," he added more gently after a pause, "I managed to get two shots off at the blighter. Had I not been reined by your Mr. Harrt, I would have sunk the tub."

"*My* Mr. Harrt?" she asked.

Greyson arched an ironic gaze. "Yes, love, *your* Mr. Harrt. I think the gentleman is in love with you."

A sudden flush pinkened her cheeks. "That is silly, Greyson," she asserted shyly.

"Is it?" he asked. "Then tell me why he mentioned you at least fifteen times between the hours of dawn and eight this morn. And this when we were under siege. 'Twas because of his certainty that you ought to be with the others that I finally came below decks to get you down there. My assumption was that you would be safer locked in your cabin, but Harrt nagged me until I transferred you below decks."

"I am not so sure your own judgement was not the correct one in this case," Victoria said sadly. "Those people were bent on taking out their frustrations against the British on me." She gazed up at him, her expression clouded with bewilderment. "I have never done anything to them. Why do they hate me so?" She seated herself heavily on the settee. "I would have been better off if I had stayed in Kolhapur, or at least if I had taken another ship," she added.

Greyson eyed her thoughtfully. He was about to respond when Jack exploded into the cabin.

"They got the bow lines untangled, Captain," he informed Greyson with a sharp salute. "They're pullin' off now."

Victoria rose suddenly in a rustle of satin. "Are any of the passengers on deck?" she asked.

"No, mistress," Jack answered. "I just told you, they've

gone down to—"

"What about the sailors?"

"What about them?" the lad questioned.

"What are they doing?"

"Well," Jack began slowly, attempting to answer the odd inquisition with as much accuracy as possible, "Mr. Curry's checkin' the mizzenmast with Mr. Bailey and Mr. Cheever. Mr. Longdon and Mr. Sharp are both on the foredeck riggin', and Mr.—"

"They are all busy then," Victoria stated. Jack nodded with certainty. "Then," said Victoria in triumph, "they might not have noted the exchange of one female aristocrat for one lad from Stewart's crew."

"What are you talking about, Victoria?" asked Greyson.

"I have a plan that might solve both our problems, at least for the duration of this voyage. We will put it out that Lady Darby, realizing her untenable circumstance aboard this ship, decided to join Captain Stewart. And, we could say that aboard the English ship there was a lad who longed to sail to the American colonies. You—in your wisdom, Captain Tyrrel—offered to make the trade." She smiled perkily. "That will solve everything. The passengers will be rid of me, and they will soon realize you had no intention of protecting the English Lady who was nothing but a troublemaker anyway. Beyond that, they will have a second powder monkey to see to the filling of the guns should another ship attack. What do you think?"

She looked from Greyson to Jack. Both males regarded her skeptically. "First of all, Victoria," said Greyson with a wry smile playing about his firm lips, "if you board Stewart's ship, 'twill put quite a crimp in your plans to voyage to America."

"And how's this new powder monkey supposed to fit into the picture?" Jack demanded. "What happens to old Jack when he does?"

"Listen to me, both of you," Victoria soothed quickly. "*I* will be your new powder monkey." She eyed them both expectantly, but neither seemed to comprehend the excellence of her plan. "I shall not really go with Stewart," she explained patiently. "That is only what we will tell the passengers. I shall simply dress the part of a lad and blend in with the crew."

Jack's immediate smile echoed Greyson's own acceptance of at least the possibility of such a plan. He glanced down at the shapely form, now hidden for the most part beneath the voluminous folds of her gown, and savored in his mind a most appetizing image of Victoria in breeches. "Yes," he intoned, lifting his gaze. "It just might work." His firm lips quirked into a mischievous smile. "I must warn you, though, love," he said, brushing his rough fingertips along her cheek, "I am a most demanding captain. Your pay aboard the *Spectre* will be meagre and your . . . duties many."

Victoria's face reddened beneath his distinctly uncaptainlike perusal. "I shall perform every one of my duties with zeal . . . Captain," she said softly.

Jack eyed the two of them in disgust. Here they had just come up with a gleefully rousing adventure, and now it was being spoiled with all this cow-eyed simpering. "Are we goin' to do it or not," he grumbled.

"Of course we are, Jack," Victoria consoled him. "We just have to think about the best way to proceed."

"Just a minute," Greyson interjected, sobering. "I said the plan *might* work. There are many things that could go wrong." He eyed Jack. " 'Tis an enormous responsibility we shall be given, lad. We shall be the only two on board, except of course for Mr. Harrt, who will know Victoria's secret."

Jack nodded somberly. "I know that, Captain," he declared, only a little annoyed at Greyson's unnecessary admonishment.

"We could put her very life in jeopardy if we were to reveal — even for an instant — her identity. People would be angry then, not only that she was an Englishwoman but that she had deceived them. People do not like to be deceived."

"I got you, Captain," he asserted.

"Jack is mature beyond his years, Captain Tyrrel," Victoria said. "You should know that by now."

"I do know it. My caution is due to the fact that I am not

126

entirely comfortable with the plan," he admitted. Before Victoria had the opportunity to respond, a sharp rapping at the door interrupted their conversation. "What is it?" Greyson called, looking guardedly at the other two.

" 'Tis Solomon MacFee, Captain Tyrrel. Some of us wish to see you topside."

"This, I fear, is the moment we have awaited." He moved quickly to the door. "I shall be up presently," he called tersely. He turned to Victoria and Jack. "Wait for me here," he whispered. "I shall be back as quickly as possible. Lock this door the moment I leave. I am about to test our unfortunately necessary deception."

"Good luck to all of us," Victoria said with gentle encouragement. She and Jack secured the door after he had left. "Well, Jack," she sighed, "I suppose the next step is to get me some clothes."

Jack smiled devilishly. "Did you ever know me to fall down on a job for you, mistress?" he asked. "I been thinkin' already about Mr. Longdon. He's the youngest and smallest man aboard—'cept for me—and I'll bet he's got an extra set of clothes."

"You are the most resourceful of lads." She cupped his chin in her hand.

Jack smiled up at her. Then his face became sober. "I got one question, mistress," he said.

Victoria quirked a brow. "What is it, Jack?"

"What's re . . . re . . . sourceful?"

"To my best information," Victoria responded with a small laugh, "it means, the ability to arrange a bath for someone desperately in need of a bath in the middle of the Indian Ocean."

"I did that," Jack said excitedly. "So I guess I really am . . . re . . . re—What you said."

"You are, indeed, Jack."

"Does it mean I got to steal Mr. Longdon's clothes for you?"

"It means you *will* steal Mr. Longdon's clothes, Jack," Victoria said sadly.

"Yeah," Jack agreed, shaking his head, "but it ain't goin'

to be easy."

"Well, just look at it this way," Victoria said in gentle resignation, "you only have to steal the clothes, Jack; I shall have to wear them." They laughed together. Then, immediately recalling their guarded condition and stifling their mirth, they settled themselves at the small table to play a game of cards and await Greyson's return.

Chapter Ten

The ruse was barely working. It might have worked perfectly except for Greyson's interference. There had been the minor upheaval over Mr. Longdon's missing breeches, shirt and doublet, and the questioning of the crew and passengers by Mr. Harrt as to where the garments might be — who might have "accidentally" purloined them — but, more threatening to the plan, were Greyson's constant attempts to protect Victoria from the notice of the others aboard. With her face grimed, her voice lowered to a hoarse murmur, a seacap covering her curls and her stolen clothes hanging large and bulky over her slender frame, Victoria blended well with the crew. Many of the men were not over eighteen, and she — as a "younger man," though not so young as Jack — adapted to the good-natured taunts and off-color ribaldry that were accepted products of long months at sea with a shyness that might have been the natural result of her newness on board an American ship. No one suspected that the young English seaman was, in fact, a British aristocrat named Victoria Quayle. If it were not for Greyson's insistence that she become his cabin boy, the ruse may have worked perfectly.

Her long absences from the deck, and from work details, made the crew suspicious of her, and of the captain. Whenever she appeared among the crew, she was greeted with oblique glances and unconcealed intimations that she was being unfairly favored. Greyson had insisted that she accept the accommodation of his big bed at night as he took solace in a nearby hammock. Though she was not completely comfortable with the arrangement, she could not argue him

129

down concerning it. No one would ever know the difference, he asserted. As his cabin boy, she could enjoy a few hours of comfort, eat a hearty meal and be back among the other sailors before dawn. He refused to budge on this command. He had even asserted his authority as captain of the ship to sway her reluctance to accept the luxury. What Greyson did not realize was that nights for Victoria, lying so near him, inhaling the sea and tobacco scent of him, hearing his even breath, imagining it hot against the delicate flesh of her neck and shoulders as it had been the night of her birthday, was little better than torture for Victoria. It was only when Greyson's duties interrupted the night — and that was mercifully often — that Victoria realized the intended benefits of this enforced accommodation. Before dawn — rested on those occasions, at any rate — she would scuttle to her duties for the day, only to be called back to the captain's quarters by an arbitrary command from her captain. How else, he demanded of her, could he keep her from being too visible, at least fairly comfortable and safe from the unfocused infuriation of the other passengers?

Greyson had returned from his meeting with them the day of the boarding by the British vessel and had informed Jack and Victoria that retaliation had been planned. He would not relate the details of what Victoria's fate might have been and remained grimly silent at Jack's pleas for the gruesome particulars. Victoria had asserted that she was happier not to know. She preferred to concentrate on whether or not the passengers had believed the unlikely story of the exchange of a young seaman for the troublesome English lady. The passengers had indeed believed him, Greyson assured her, when he informed them that Victoria had been placed aboard the English ship under the protection of Captain Stewart and that a young seaman had been exchanged for her. One lady seemed particularly relieved that Victoria was no longer aboard. That woman's husband, she privately informed Greyson, was bent on his own special revenge. He had been whetting his longknife with unusual concentration since the moment Victoria had boarded, she worried, and so it was just as well the English woman had been transferred off the *Spectre*. Though she felt little sympathy toward Victoria, the woman did not wish to see her husband involved in a criminal act against her. Greyson thanked the woman gravely for her confidence and realized because of it that there would be no way to protect Victoria — short of locking her in his cabin and posting a twenty-four hour guard — from the vengeance of the passengers. Victoria roundly pooh-poohed that thought, arguing that it was impractical for a months' long voyage at sea, and there was no guarantee that some fanatical passenger might not overpower the guard and reek his revenge on her for her imagined British "crimes" in any event. She insisted that only as a member of the crew and a working-class lad devoid of any political loyalties would she be safe aboard an American vessel. At Greyson's protests that the passengers might be reasoned with, she stamped her small satin-clad foot and maintained that he was naive to imagine that there was an area for negotiation in the thinking of the colonials in this case. Greyson reluctantly conceded at least that. Their anger was unfocused but very real. Too much had passed between the American colonists and the British for anyone to truly understand the problems that existed between them, much less to try to solve them in the space of time it took to make a sea voyage. Victoria was perceived as a loyal member of the British aristocracy, reflected Greyson resignedly, and because of her English breeding, in league with the arrogant and unlawful domination of George Hanover and his taxation-obsessed parliament. Victoria Quayle — the Honorable Lady Noelle Darby — was, according to the Americans, their enemy.

In the end, Victoria had prevailed. Greyson had, because of her unrelenting logic and her tenacious presentation of that logic, allowed the masquerade. And though he remained uncomfortable with it, he watched with a certain admiration, and — if he admitted the truth — lust-filled appreciation, his new powder monkey go, breech-clad, about her duties. She scrambled with the riggings, her shapely backside temptingly obvious to anyone bothering to inspect that part of a ragtag powder monkey's anatomy beneath Mr. Longdon's britches, and drew and hauled as aggressively as any man on board. She did not allow for lapses in her strength; in truth, there seemed to be amazingly few lapses in her strength. This was no fragile English lady, thought

131

Greyson, as he regarded her appreciatively one day. This was no spoiled child of wealth and position; Victoria Quayle was a woman of rare and admirable duplicities. She was soft — so soft, so yielding and tender in his arms — and yet there was a toughness about her, a sinewy energy that belied her womanly bounty and diminished Greyson's own long-held opinions concerning the deficiencies of finely-bred, tea-drinking English ladies. And yet she was that, too. He laughed inwardly when he recalled her lilting performance for Captain Stewart. Watching her, his arms folded over his broad chest, an admiring smile grazing his lips, he became enraptured in the variety that was Victoria. And yet, there were moments — more and more moments these days — when his discontent with the plan overpowered him. He flinched involuntarily as he watched her heave a thick coil of running rig over her shoulder and deposit it, heavily, at another location.

"Your expressions display a most uncaptainlike ardor, Captain," warned a low voice from behind him. He turned abruptly to find Mr. Harrt watching him. Greyson sobered quickly.

"Oh, Lord, Edmund," he confided, "more and more, I find myself dreading each day's dawn." He sighed as their attention returned to the struggling Victoria. "Look at her," Greyson said softly. Some main hatch planking had needed to be refurbished, and most hands had been put on that assignment several days before. The job required the tearing up of timbers, the sanding and planing of them, and their replacement. "Did you really have to order her onto this job?" he asked the young warrant officer. "She is, after all, my cabin boy."

Mr. Harrt lifted a wide shoulder. "What would you have me do, Captain?" he responded quietly. "As it is, I keep her as sheltered as I can. 'Tis not easy to protect her, though. Even as a cabin boy, she is expected to be part of the crew. These scalawags have no sympathy for an able-bodied man who, for whatever reasons, does not pull his own weight."

"She is supposed to be only fourteen; we agreed she could not possibly look older than that. Does her tender age make no difference to them?" Suddenly, Greyson's teeth bared angrily, and a hard glint flashed in his eyes as he noted the

132

roughness of a shove inflicted on Victoria by a big seaman. He grabbed the hilt of his sword and would have called the man on it, but Mr. Harrt's quick, cautioning hand on his girded shoulder stopped his interference.

" 'Tis not worth it, Captain Tyrrel," Harrt reasoned hastily. "What satisfaction you would gain in thrashing the lubber would be lost in the derision of the men—for both you and the lady." He felt Greyson relent beneath his restraint. "I know 'tis hard," he added. "Do you think I enjoy watching this?" Greyson shot him a glance. "Listen to me," Harrt said earnestly, "I know 'tis not acceptable seamanship to speak to one's captain this way, but we knew there would be sacrifices involved in this charade. We spoke of them—considered them all. If we go about defending her against every bully, every ungentle circumstance, we will undo all our efforts up to now. We may even risk exposing her to terrible, life-threatening danger. She will survive this, Captain Tyrrel, believe me," the man finished.

Victoria winced at the possibility of confrontation. She had expected it for some time. She had watched Greyson worriedly each time she was treated roughly or given a job which his glinting eyes told her he felt was too arduous for her to handle. She glanced nervously in his direction as she was prodded rudely by Mr. Curry.

"Them boards is pilin' up, boy," he snarled. "Let's have 'em."

"Quit shovin'," Victoria snarled back. She hastily bent to her task, however, and dragged a rough oaken board across the deck to receive the man's expert skills at carpentry. As Mr. Curry concentrated on his assignment, with Victoria's woefully insufficient weight holding down the thick planking, she lifted her gaze cautiously. Thank heaven for Mr. Harrt's moderation, she reflected as she watched in relief the hard won abatement of Greyson's anger. She sighed inaudibly. His anger never truly abated, she thought resignedly. He had agreed to this pretense most reluctantly, and every day of it had brought his reluctance roiling to the surface of their relationship. Unfortunately, his grumbling discontent was, when they were together, transferred from the sailors and Mr. Harrt to her. He railed and growled at her for their offenses. He kicked at innocent chairs and sent

133

guiltless charts and maps flying about his quarters. Tonight, again, she would face his sulky humor because of Mr. Curry's incivility.

"Drop them knees, boy," the very uncivil Mr. Curry groused. "You got barely enough weight to flatten a fog-bow." Victoria shot him a dangerous glare but quickly obeyed his command lest she invite further abuse. She managed a grumbled curse in the process. Grumbled curses had become for her a practiced skill by now. They were expected of all the men and especially the boys. Victoria had come to the conclusion that males somehow revelled in their own ability to make other males curse them. What had begun as a natural response to discourtesy had become something of a contest in her eyes. Perhaps it only seemed so, but the more vulgar her responses became, the more she seemed to be accepted by the sailors. She was slowly included in their jokes, in their scuttlebutt. The more peevish and crusty she appeared, the less brusque they seemed. Mr. Curry glanced up at her. "Get it outta here, lad," he said almost gently. Her surliness must have softened his temper, she reflected with satisfaction. She, therefore, mumbled another quickly improvised curse and hauled the plank away.

"Outch!" Victoria wailed as Greyson daubed the stinging salve onto her blistered palms. "Please, no more nursing, Greyson!" She attempted to drag her bruised fingers from his grasp, but he held her wrist firmly, and gravely continued his unwelcome ministrations.

"Stop wriggling," he admonished.

"The cure is far more painful than the affliction," she rejoined tartly. "I should hesitate to inflict such a lamentable remedy on my bloody horse. Just let me be."

He lifted a hooded gaze to her, and Victoria immediately realized her error. "I shall let you be when you are out of harm's way," he clenched. "Until that time, Lady Darby, you will accept what little comfort I can offer you or I shall end this ridiculous masquerade here and now."

She reached out and with her free hand she caressed the bronzed planes of his unsmiling countenance. "I am sorry, Greyson," she said soothingly, hoping to avert the tide of his

134

biting anger. She brushed at the tousle of his russet curls and smiled. "I do appreciate your tender care of me," she said softly.

" 'Tis little enough comfort I can offer," he rejoined. Taking the hand with which she touched him, he scowled down on it. "Look at your sweet flesh," he observed. "That this abuse should happen—" He let go of her hands and stood abruptly, raking his lean fingers through his thick hair. Rolling his head back in exasperation, he sighed, turning from her. "I do not approve of this, Victoria," he said brusquely. "I cannot bear seeing you handled this way. You were born to be petted and cossetted, for God's sake, you were not born for this ill-use. 'Tis an insult to your breeding."

She laughed softly and raised herself from the bed. She moved to him, playfully entwining her arms around his middle, and rested her head in weary tenderness against his muscular back. "I thought you detested my breeding, Greyson," she reminded him quietly.

He turned to her and held her shoulders in his large hands. "Your breeding, perhaps, but never you," he answered. His blue gaze glinted over her. The fine gauze of his best cambric shirt that covered her from shoulder to creamy thigh served not to conceal but to accentuate the shadowed curves of the glorious form beneath it. Above the wide collar, the slim column of her neck rose, touchingly vulnerable beneath the pile of pearlescent curls atop her head. The oval cameo of her face radiated perfect innocence, perfect trust, perfect—His thought went unfinished as he wrestled with a growing awareness of her feelings toward him.

He was attempting to ignore that which he was finding it difficult to confront. Victoria seemed to have surrendered, without a second thought, to the strength of her feelings toward him. The rapturous moments they had shared on the deck came crashing back to him each time she yielded to a tender impulse. And their long hours of enforced intimacy had given voice to those impulses with more and more frequency as the days went on. Greyson was aware of something—a certain unfathomable sensation—growing within him as well. He could not name the thing he felt. The power of his hunger for Victoria was understandable. Her remarkable beauty, her winsome flirtatiousness would drive a man

135

to lunacy. But there was something else. He longed to protect her in some inexplicable way. He wanted her near him. He yearned for a gentle word, a sweet touch. Greyson manfully fought these soul-weakening ardors and battled against himself each night when Victoria came into his cabin to enjoy her few unencumbered hours of relaxation. He was reluctant to relinquish a long-held and carefully tended guardianship over his emotions. He liked women well enough, he had reflected during long, restless moments when the scent of her filled his soul and the sound of her soft breath encloaked his passion-driven senses. He adored women, he reminded himself. Had he not taken it upon himself to personally see to the pleasure of half the women in Boston? He had soothed the disconsolate, cheered the sullen, oiled the reluctant and generally upgraded the quality of female life wherever he perceived a necessary upgrading. Greyson Tyrrel was a widely-known defender of and participator in the happiness of women. No one could accuse him of not liking them; why, he doted on them. But this new and inexplicable feeling bewildered him. Victoria roused in him what the other women he'd known had managed to rouse, but with her there was something more. With her, there was an indefinable other feeling. He could not explain it to himself, could not begin to examine it, for it had no precedent. There was nothing by which to compare the soaring warmth he felt in her presence. And he wished her presence always. The others he had come to know were part and then not part of his life. It was expected and indifferently accepted that they meandered in and out of his day to day existence. In truth, he would not have had it any other way. But now, with Victoria, there was a tearing when she left his side before dawn. There was a frustrating rush of anger and longing when he watched her from afar and could not possess her, could not muscle her away from other circumstances and take her in his arms. Greyson had no idea what was happening to him.

He found himself unable to understand or to cope with the sweet power of her conflicting postures. She adored him and yet she would defy him, argue with him, confront him. She seemed to make her own rules concerning their relationship.

Greyson smiled inwardly. "You tempt me far too power-fully, love," he said huskily.

Victoria tilted a coy gaze. "Do I?" she asked innocently.

Greyson nodded. What was he to do with this adorable little seductress. He knew that he could take her now. He knew that he could impale her upon the hot thrust of his passion and that she would submit joyously with a womanly passion of her own. Her tender flesh would yield to him as a delicate bird would succumb to his knife . . . and that was what he feared. He had told her that they must go slowly. He must at all costs remember that. This little bird was to be handled carefully, and Greyson would not yield to a cage. There must be perfect understanding between them as to what the outcome would be of a union between them. He turned abruptly away from her. How in hell was he to explain all this to her when he did not himself understand any of it.

With a ragged breath, he mumbled that he was going topside to smoke, and he made for the door, slamming from it with remarkable brusqueness. Victoria sighed. She moved slowly to the great bed and sank into it. She wondered if Greyson would always be a mystery to her. But perhaps his behavior was no mystery. Perhaps, once again, it was her unfortunate star that drew him from her. Perhaps it was that mystical preeminence that repelled him. Would it haunt her forever? Would she never know the fulfillment of her dreams? She glanced around the room, and her gaze lingered on the empty hammock where Greyson slept these nights. At least tonight, she reflected with resignation, she would not be tormented by his presence. She let her lids fall. Tonight, at least, she would receive a much deserved respite from her duties as a much-abused young English seaman.

Chapter Eleven

A cool, lucent mist had begun to penetrate the air as the *Spectre of the Bay* began its passage through the mid-Atlantic. Hot sapphire days were giving way more and more frequently to days of breezy opalescent aquamarine. As the climate cooled, however, Greyson's temper had heated. The proprietary grate of his tone when he ordered Victoria — or as she was now known, Rod Sutcliff — to his cabin for special orders, was the reigning subject of scuttlebutt. No man aboard questioned the captain outright, but his familiar beckoning of the lad whenever strenuous work was at hand, his assigning of him to the more moderate tasks, against the orders of Mr. Harrt, was ever a source of irritation to the other sailors. The boy was being coddled, and there was no excuse for it. He was in perfect health, of sound body. There was no reason on earth why he should not be given the same tasks expected of any other man on aboard. The open taunting that Victoria suffered of late had stretched her tolerance of Greyson's ill-humor to the limit. Her patience, strained to the snap, she finally assailed him one day in his quarters.

"Lower your voice, Victoria," he hissed, "lest you bring about your own retribution."

"Retribution!" she gaped. "Do you know what you have put me through, Greyson? Sometimes I think 'twould be better to suffer the fate — whatever it may be — the passengers have in mind than to endure your 'protection.' The men are no longer shy about their derision of me. You may have noticed I am last at the drinking fountain —"

"The scuttlebutt," he corrected her.

"The bloody *drinking fountain*," she persevered angrily,

138

"where they gather to gossip about the 'unnatural' alliance between you and me. They wonder—and rightfully so—why you pamper me. I heard one fellow remark that perhaps you enjoyed the affections of little boys, for heaven's sake. This attention you are showering upon me, Greyson, does neither of us any good. We conjured this plan so that you would be safe from suspicion of secret British loyalty and so that I might have a safe and relatively comfortable passage to the colonies. Well, neither purpose is being served. They still suspect you; if you are not given to perversion, they reason, then your attitude toward me may lie in your political loyalties. As for me, my passage has been far from comfortable. The men deny me water when I am thirsty, they pinch, poke and shove me at their will, they oil my pannikin so my food tastes like mud—if they allow me any food at all—"

"You have plenty to eat right here, Victoria," he stated.

"But that is not the point, Greyson. Those men abhor me! Don't you understand? I have worked long and hard to earn their trust, and now they hate me."

"I will not have you cleaning the goddamned bilge pumps, Victoria," he grated. " 'Tis beneath you."

" 'Tis not beneath Rod Sutcliff," she shot back. "You are being unreasonable, Greyson." The azalea of her lips formed a quick pout, and she folded her arms across her breast. "Edmund is doing his best to—"

" 'Edmund,' is it," Greyson interjected, his brow lifting acidly.

"Yes, *Edmund,* dammit!" she retorted. "Warrant Officer Hart, *Mr.* Harrt—what you will—the man is doing his best to help me blend in with the crew. He cannot have me ringing bells all day or polishing the brass on the Charley Noble for the rest of the voyage. We agreed to this plan to protect my very life, Greyson, and now your illogical behavior is threatening both the plan *and* my life."

"It was a bad plan," he rejoined. "Look at you." He raked her with a derisive gaze. "You look like a street urchin." He ignored the fact that the sun and sea air had turned her creamy complexion to a light honey. He did not note the fact that her cheeks had pinkened to a rose flush and her rounded figure had blossomed with a taut womanly

139

strength. He reached out and flicked the tatters of Mr. Longdon's sea jacket. He jogged her sea cap, knocking it askew, and tugged at the luminescent curls his gesture revealed. He fingered the tresses disapprovingly. "Your hair is like straw," he intoned, ignoring the radiant silk sliding over his roughened fingertips. Greyson failed to notice that Victoria stiffened. He also failed to note the darkening of her perusal. "We shall have some cleaning up to do when we get you to Boston," he said with a despairing sigh.

"Shall we," Victoria clenched.

"Yes," Greyson assured her coolly. " 'Twill take a miracle to turn you back into the finely bred English lady you were when we met."

She tilted her steady gaze. "May I ask you this, Captain Tyrrel? What is it you suggest I do to discourage this unholy tide of ruin that seems to have overtaken me?"

He looked at her sharply. "You are mocking my concern, Victoria," he said.

"And you are acting just as insufferably as Steven Kensington." She jerked off the sea cap and her sun-bleached mane spun out wildly, giving her an untamed, fiercely challenging look. "Dammit to bloody hell, Greyson, you are every bit the snob Steven ever was about women. We are talking here about my life, dammit. I will not suffer your ungovernable male pride one more moment. And that is what this is about, you know. You have some barbaric notion that you must protect me from all discomfort. Well, I warn you, Greyson, I will not be treated this way." She paused as he gaped at her in confusion. "Do not look so surprised," she shot at him. "I do not seek your damned 'protection.' If I had wanted that of a man, I could have stayed in Kolhapur. I want your respect. If you respect me — if you respect my life — you will stop this bloody, ridiculous male posturing over the bloody bilge pumps. You will allow Mr. Harrt to do his job, and you will let me do mine. My job right now, incidentally, is the preservation of my life." She pulled on the woolen cap once again and stuffed her fleecy tresses beneath it. "If you have no interest in that, Captain Tyrrel, then we have nothing further to say to each other." She spun away from him and started for the door, but he reached out to grasp her arm. She turned abruptly, slapping away his attempt to restrain her. Her wide green gaze flashed a dazzling emerald storm. "Take your hands off of me," she ground out. "When I wish you to touch me, I shall let you know." She snapped away from him and slammed from the room.

In the sudden glaring silence of her exit, Greyson remained slack-jawed with disbelief. His arms hung weightless at his sides. He had never felt so powerless in his life, and this before the wrath of a tiny slip of a lass. He could not believe it. It was many moments before anger began to take hold. So, the wench wanted respect, did she? So, she demanded liberation from his protective male instincts? Well, that she would have. Victoria may have flinched at the feral glint that flared roguishly in the sea-glass blue of his gaze. Greyson Tyrrel was rightfully proud of his ability to handle women, and no stripling would get away with referring to his attentions as "ridiculous male posturing." From this moment on, she would be responsible for her own protection. They would both discover whether his instincts had been ridiculous or not. He brushed at the fine wool of his coat and the cool brass of his epaulets, then straightened his cummerbund. The very independent Lady Darby would soon discover what independence on a seagoing vessel really meant. With a satisfied half-smile and a jaunty spring to his step, the captain strode from his cabin to inspect his crew — his entire crew. He had been very uncaptainlike where Victoria was concerned. But that was over; she was as much a part of the crew as any other man, and she had damned well better pull her weight, he resolved, or he would know the reason why.

The damage had already been done. If Victoria had managed for a time to gain the fellowship of the other sailors, she had lost that same fellowship irrevocably under the careful and lamentable patronage of her captain. She now sidled about her chores, furtively glancing about her, wondering when the next blow would fall, when the next taunt would wound her. She was not all that thin-skinned; but she had

141

enjoyed the men's favor, and their disparagement broke her heart, especially after her painstaking efforts to gain their good will. She missed the ribald geniality of the men, the risqué jokes they told, the mischievous tricks they played on each other and of which she had for a short time been a part. Now her appearance anywhere on the ship was greeted with wary silence or mumbled derision. Jack's best efforts to draw her back into the brotherhood were roundly disparaged. Even Victoria's own practiced grumbled curses could not regain the favor she had lost.

"Get your butt workin', boy," a sailor ordered as he strode by her and poked her soundly in the shoulder.

She grumbled a curse pointedly—hopefully—but received no chuckled response, and resignedly, as the man had passed her by anyway, she went back to scrubbing the grog tub. Would this voyage never end, she thought wearily. The days stretched endlessly with empty, aching slowness. She had not only lost the favor of the men, but she had lost the few hours of solace she had known in Greyson's cabin each night, for she would not go back to him. He would more than likely never forgive her for her attack on his masculinity, and she was little inclined to apologize. Not this time, she resolved grimly. In fact, she would wait for an apology from him. Tonight, she had no doubt, they would both once again sleep alone. Victoria Quayle was used to getting her own way—her obstinacy was what had brought her here in the first place—and, though she really knew very little about Greyson, she suspected a stubborn tendency beneath that roguishly schoolboy exterior. Most men were proud. She thought, with a bitter-sweet pang, of Uncle David and his continual retellings of his martial triumphs. She laughed inwardly when she recalled his stories of his soldierhood in the colonies, and she remembered her fascination with those stories. Teatime was invariably story time in Kolhapur.

A low clearing of a throat behind her roused her attention, and she glanced over her shoulder to find Edmund Harrt regarding her. His expression was unreadable, and Victoria straightened and offered him an excessively jaunty salute.

"You work goes well, boy?" he inquired sharply.

"Aye, sir," Victoria answered.

"At ease, lad," said the man. He regarded her steadily. "Are you all right?" he intoned.

"Aye, sir," she said softly.

Once again the young officer cleared his throat. "It strikes me, Rod, that you've not had a period of rest in some time."

"Just got off one, sir." Victoria hid a twinkling amusement at Mr. Harrt's concern.

"I see," he fumbled. "Well, then, I suppose I should allow you to get back to your work." He paused. "Assigned to the grog tub, I see."

"Yes, sir, and the food kettles."

Edmund's brown eyes shifted uncomfortably. No one was about. He looked at her, an aching worry shadowing his gaze. "I am sorry," he said very quietly. They both glanced unhappily down into the musky, rusted depths of the big pot. Except for the cleaning of the bilge pumps, this was the most unfriendly job on the ship.

"I can bear it, Mr. Harrt," Victoria said gently.

He regarded her reddened hands and the thick rough stone which she held. With that stone, she had scoured the morning long the tainted depths of all the metal pots on board the *Spectre*. He lifted his regard. "You ought to be taking baths in those pots, not scrubbing them," he said with a small rueful smile.

"My bath taking days are over, I fear," she responded with as much good humor as she could manage.

"Nevertheless," answered Edmund Harrt, "I insist you take a break from it. 'Twas never my intention that you should scar yourself." He glanced once again at the split and roughened skin of her delicate hands. "Please," he added quietly. "I would feel so much better about all this. Find yourself a secure little place and hide yourself from time to time."

Victoria cocked her gaze at the tall young man. "Where would you suggest I go, Edmund?" she chided him. " 'Tis one fact of an ocean voyage that I have managed to accept. There are no private places for a powder monkey."

"But you are not a powder monkey," he answered and then immediately reined his ire. He glanced quickly over his shoulder and then back to Victoria. "You are a member of the aristocracy," he intoned urgently. "You have a right to expect certain accommodations. That is why we placed you in a cabin when you boarded. We could not just dump you onto the berthing deck with the others." A sudden light came into his eyes. "Your cabin is empty!" he reminded her.

"But I could not go there," she responded, not completely convinced.

"And why not," Harrt encouraged her softly. " 'Tis your cabin; you paid for it. No one goes in there." He paused and dared to place his hand on her slender shoulder. "You need to be reminded of who you are," he said gently.

Victoria managed a small smile. "We will see," she answered. Her voice was warm. She realized that she had not thought of who she was in a very long time. She wondered, however, if she would have the courage to steal away to her cabin. Mr. Harrt was correct, she reminded herself. She had paid for the accommodation; why should she deny herself its use?

Harrt turned his gentle touch into a gruff pat of encouragement as they both noted the appearance of Mr. Curry nearby. "You are doing a commendable job, Rod," Mr. Harrt said curtly. "Keep it up." He turned as Victoria offered him a salute and moved away. Curry sneered audibly and went on to his own assignment.

Once again, Victoria reflected with a resigned sigh, she had managed to garner the disapproval of one of the sailors. She went back to her work, thinking about Edmund's words. He had recalled for her images of her past life. How she missed that gentle existence, that lyrical time. She emerged surreptitiously from the metal depths of the big pot and glanced around her. No one was near. No one would notice if . . .

Her cabin looked much the same as when she'd left it weeks before to assume the disguise of a young powder monkey. Stealing inside, she peered once more into the quiet regions of the gun deck. The sailors were either topside or taking assigned rests on the berthing deck. At this time of the day all was quiet. She closed the door with a stealthy click and moved to the drawer beneath the washstand. There inside she found both the small Moroccan case where she kept her jewels, and her parchment and charcoal just as she had left them. She had little use for the jewels these days, she reminded herself with a rueful smile, but lifting them from the case and lovingly examining their ever-glittering sparkle gave her a sense of continuity that she had not experienced in a very long time. They recalled for her, her glorious youth in Kolhapur. That foundation on which her whole life was based would always be there just as these emeralds she now held would always glitter, offering ocular proof of her identity. No matter how far she strayed from her true self, these gems would always remind her of who she was. She felt a certain comforting warmth as she snuggled onto her bed — the bed she had once coldly derided as narrow and hard — with her jewels, the emeralds clutched and twined in her fingers, and her parchment and charcoal. Her poetry, too, was a reminder that Victoria Quayle still existed in this hard unyielding world she had chosen to inhabit. Closing her eyes, she held the charcoal above the paper. At last, she opened her eyes and began to write:

I lie awake in the shadows of the greens
Which rest upon my soul the peace I've prized
These years —
And yet I know
I must not remain the same
Where life has no more sky for me to reach
Or hills to climb
Beyond the leaves so green
That cover me
From myself that longs to grow.
A voyage to the colonies,
Where my father's pride rides the rocks and waves
Of the seas that have saved his strength for me.
I must run to unknown arms
Stronger and longer than this forest, I know.
He'll hold me firm against the womb
I tear and bear my own rebirth —
Which I must earn
And burn the old cord

That has bound me to my cradle
Of greens from which I've sucked —
And from which now I've grown beyond . . .

She had longed so for possibilities. The possibilities had
appeared, had offered themselves, were yet offering themselves. She must make the most of them. She must not lose
hope. Her dream of seeing the colonies would very soon
become a reality. She must endure whatever was necessary
to preserve that dream, to make it a reality. If this voyage
was less than she had hoped it would be, if her affection for
Greyson Tyrrel was to be shattered on the jagged rocks of
their mutual obstinacy, then so be it. Her purpose was, finally, not to secure Greyson's love. Her purpose was to
know the land of her parents' birth. She must remember
that, just as she must remember the wounds she had received at the hands of Steven Kensington. She had thought
him the only man she would ever love, she reminded herself.
She had trusted that he would marry her and that together
they would share a symmetric future of love, care and shar-
ing. But that had not happened. Steven had broken the unspoken vow between them just as Greyson had broken his
vow to help her deliver herself from the wrath of the American colonials. Greyson's betrayal was so much worse than
Steven's, she thought bitterly, because he had known from
the beginning their mutual purpose. If Steven had known
anything at all about her design, he had never indicated his
knowledge. He had listened patiently to her meandering
plans and remained silent. He had never given her false
hope. Greyson had. He had led her to believe that he would
guard their secret, had lectured Jack and Edmund Harrt
extensively on the necessity of maintaining their silence. He
had pridefully promised his own.
Victoria allowed that her wounds at the hands of these
two men had been much her own fault, if not the fault of the
pervasive contingency of some dark force. She must face the
truth about herself. She tended to go too fast, assume too
much, trust too unstintingly. That would not happen again.
Victoria Quayle would guard her heart from this moment
on. Never again would she allow a man to invade that for-

tress. Her naivete—her eagerness to put her faith in dreams, the imperfections of her life in the random power of an evil guiding charm—was a thing of the past. On this voyage, she had become a woman, and women took responsibility for their own imperfections, put their faith in realities.

The ship's planking creaked lazily. Victoria felt herself at ease with her newfound resolve. Her heightened sense of her own power over her life and her relief at her decision caused a lightening of her spirit. Her lids slowly dropped, a small smile formed upon her lips and her shoulders slackened in serenity. She leaned back against the even oaken sides of the *Spectre* and felt herself dozing.

An odd squeak roused her. Her eyes popped open, and she realized that someone was turning the handle of her cabin door. Before she could react, the door unclosed. She sat up straight and faced the hard scrutiny of Mr. Curry.

"What are you doin', boy" he demanded.

"I was . . . I was just lookin' for . . . for . . ." Victoria grappled wildly for an explanation for her presence in the cabin of the British woman who had left the *Spectre* in disgrace. Curry lurched forward and grabbed her arm. Her papers and charcoal scattered as he dragged her from the bed. The outraged seaman shook her soundly.

"I always thought you was a little too sure of yourself boy," he grated as he hauled her through the doorway and along the deck. "It does my heart good to hear you fumblin' for a bloody answer."

Victoria strained against him, attempting to jerk away from his grasp, but Curry had the power of righteous anger on his side. He tugged at her, pulling her up the steps to the spar deck. "I wasn't doin' anything," she railed in her hoarse, adolescent-boy voice.

"We'll just see if the captain agrees," Curry retorted. "He's been so flippin' protective of you, afraid you might have to get them delicate hands of yours dirty; let's just see how he feels about you now." He dragged Victoria, tripping and stumbling over her own feet, to the foredeck and threw her unceremoniously to the deck before Greyson's large uniformed presence. The captain loomed high above her, hands on his hips, feet spread wide apart. Victoria looked up wide-eyed as Greyson gazed down, astonishment in his sea-glass gaze. He targeted Curry.

"What's amiss here, man?" he demanded.

"Kid's been snoopin' in the lady's cabin, sir," Curry answered with a sharp salute. "Thought you'd want to question him." Greyson looked quickly to Mr. Harrt, and that man guardedly communicated only incomprehension. Greyson returned his hooded appraisal to Mr. Curry, noting also the arrival of many of the crew and most of the passengers at the site of the anticipated confrontation.

"Has he an explanation, Mr. Curry?" asked Greyson.

"No, Captain," the seaman answered. Greyson glanced down at Victoria. Concern and triumph jostled for position in his stern countenance. The lass had demanded freedom from his protection and look where it had gotten her, he reflected smugly. Almost immediately, however, his glinting perusal lifted and scanned the weathered faces of the angry sailors, and he realized that Victoria had not bargained for outright censure. "If you want my opinion, Captain," Mr. Curry was saying, "I'd say the lad was huntin' for the lady's jewels." He held out the Moroccan case. "He had this next to 'im when I grabbed 'im." The implication was clear. A rumble of menacing disapproval rose from the gathering. Victoria glanced around wildly and drew herself up to face the onslaught of insinuation.

"Look!" shouted one of the sailors. "Look what he's got in his hand!" All attention was riveted on Victoria, and she suddenly remembered something. She lifted her left hand almost without comprehension and realized that her emeralds were still entwined in her fingers. Her eyes widened; her glance darted to Greyson.

"He was stealin' them jewels!" a man roared, and the others joined him in a terrible ejaculation of rage.

"That snotty little pup!" shrieked Mr. Longdon. "That's what coddlin'll do to a boy!" The others agreed in a surging crest of righteousness. Greyson stiffened above her, his face a mask of bronzed planes, his expression unreadable. His glinting sea-glass gaze quelled the rolling tide of outraged denunciation. An uneasy silence blanketed the deck.

"In the absence of Lady Darby to make a formal accusation," Greyson began, his voice clear and strong on the blue sea winds, "I cannot sentence this lad." Mr. Harrt glanced quickly at him and then at Victoria. He noted the relieved sag of her small shoulders.

"I accuse him." Mr. Curry stepped forward. Behind him others began to do the same. Mr. Longdon stepped forth. Mr. Cheever joined them as did Mr. Bailey and Mr. Sharp. Slowly, unrelentingly the crew gathered one by one in a viniculum of malice against the young pampered English seaman. "We accuse Rod Sutcliff of thievery, Captain Tyrrel," they exhorted, "and we demand the sentence of flogging."

Greyson glanced down at Victoria. Her widened gaze glittered with terror. He slowly lifted his eyes. They both knew what he must — as captain of the *Spectre* — command. The tousle of his curls was riffled by the breezes. Victoria watched him mesmerized. In his hardened countenance she saw the image of her own flogging. She was strung between the prow lines. Naked, she would be known to all as the Honorable Lady Noelle Darby. The unveiling would not save her. The crowd would take a horrid delight in her punishment. The knotted instrument of barbarous justice would be raised, the horrible scarring torture executed. A scream raged inside her. She would not survive! The world dimmed, darkened. The sky swam beneath her. A frenzied, thunderous roar cracked. Silence reigned.

Chapter Twelve

Victoria's eyes fluttered open. She was being jerked rudely to her feet. She fought against the hands that clawed and dragged at her. One hand, a strong hand, grasped her arm and propelled her through the maddened throng. She screamed. The sound was a woman's sound. The pawing, jostling hands hesitated. Victoria felt herself clasped against a hard familiar presence.

"Stop!" a ringing baritone commanded.

"What the bloody hell is going on here," a man asserted.

"Do we flog a thief or don't we?" demanded another.

"I said stop. That is an order." The first voice towered above the confusion. The seamen backed, snarling away from their quarry. "I command you to stand at attention!" The men did so, though they watched warily as Greyson and the other officers, swords drawn, stepped between them and the young English seaman. Victoria saw only their broad backs, but realized that a dangerous confrontation was taking place. Jack was suddenly beside her.

"Get back with the others, Jack," she whispered urgently, "lest they think you in cahoots with me."

"I ain't movin'," the little boy intoned. "And you ain't makin' me. If there's gonna be a mutiny, I'm with you and the captain."

"A mutiny," Victoria gaped. Jack nodded shortly. "No," she breathed. "I will not have it; not because of me." Despite Jack's restraining hand, she burst through the cordon of strong backs, past Greyson, and faced her accusers. Greyson captured her arm in his big hand.

"Get back," he grated, his teeth bared white against the

150

bronzed granite of his countenance.

"I will not," she shot back defiantly. She turned to the violently angry mass of humanity before her. She tore from Greyson's restraint, and before he could re-seize her, she burst out, "You cannot accuse me of stealing!" Her voice rang clearly over the aggressively narrowed regard of the sailors. "You cannot accuse a woman of stealing her own jewels!" With the words, she grabbed her sea cap and snatched it from her head. The removal of its tight sheathing exposed to the ocean winds the spun-sugar swirl of her hair.

The crowd roared its amazement. Angry mutterings were heard beneath the sonorous din.

"You have saved yourself from a flogging," Greyson ground out as he once again seized her arm, "but you forgot about the wrath of the colonials."

Victoria targeted him with a reckless glare. "Did you imagine I was going to allow mutiny on this vessel?" she challenged. "Let the narrow-thinking bounders kill me, if that is their plan. At least I shall die with a clear conscience."

For a long moment sapphire locked with emerald in a diamond-hard clash of wills. Around Victoria and Greyson, anger swelled. Epithets flew. They felt Jack's tugging urgency at their side.

"You gotta do somethin', Captain," he prodded desperately. Both people became suddenly aware of the maelstrom of rage that surged up from the gathered passengers. Greyson faced them, raising his sword perceptibly. The other officers stood very close to him, their own weapons at the ready.

"Back away," Greyson commanded the converging crowd.

"We ain't sailors," shouted one of the men. "You can't order us."

"I can and shall," Greyson challenged. "Now back away." His tone held a steely rigidity, and his eyes narrowed, glinting blue-silver fire. Nearly three-hundred people registered reluctant awe at the captain's courage. With half a dozen men behind him, a woman and a little boy, he faced their

151

numbers and challenged them. No one dared question his authority, not even anonymously. To misjudge his courage or his strength might prove a fatal underestimation. There was no sound. Even the ocean seemed to silence itself beneath the cut of the proud vessel.

"This situation has gone far enough," Greyson charged. "As you see," he continued, "this is, in fact, Lady Noelle Darby. She disguised herself as a young English seaman to protect herself from your unreasoning anger." His hard gaze targeted the passengers. They responded with surreptitious mutters. "Quiet!" Greyson commanded them. "As a powder monkey," he said, scanning the faces of his crew, "she attempted to gain your favor by diligent hard work. But you shunned her because of my concern for her." The men, recalling the captain's favoritism, grumbled dully. "Again — I demand quiet!" Greyson shot out. "I do not expect any of you to be reasonable, but I tell you this," he clenched, "none of what has happened is this woman's fault. She is as courageous a human being as I have ever met, and I will not have such a woman intimidated aboard my vessel — and *it is my vessel*," he added, his broad shoulders expanding threateningly, daring denial of his words. No one spoke, but he saw the menace in their glowering countenances. Intimidation alone was not his answer. He eyed them thoughtfully for a long moment. "Victoria Quayle has refused my protection up to now," he said, his voice carrying on the sea winds, "but I shall now disregard her wishes and inform you that before this hour is out, she will no longer be at will to refuse my aid. She shall be under my protection not only as my passenger but as my wife." Victoria shot him a look of disbelief. Jack's brows lifted as a broad smile creased his face. Edmund Harrt's gaze narrowed. Greyson turned to glance at the young officer. "Mr. Harrt will perform the marriage under my sanction." He looked back at the crowd as he gathered Victoria to his chest. He quelled the clatter of their amazement with his own silence. "You shall — every one of you — be witness to this union," he said at last. "Once it is accomplished, there shall be no question of this woman's place aboard the *Spectre of the Bay*." He scanned the gathering and was satisfied with their collective acceptance of the significance of his words. Turning, he placed his attention on Mr. Harrt. The officer watched him as he verbally endowed him with the authority to perform a marriage. The three people stepped forward. In less time than it took to drop a kedge anchor, Victoria and Greyson had become husband and wife.

Greyson turned, once the wedding was over, to the crowd. "Let me present," he said a roguish glint in his sea-glass blue eyes, "*Mrs.* Greyson Tyrrel."

The crowd roared its approval. Victoria gazed out at those who had so very recently condemned her. What was it, she wondered dazedly, that now made her their friend? Standing before them, her light, sun-sparkled hair blowing wildly about the pale oval of her face, the tatters of Mr. Longdon's grimy apparel hanging too large about her small frame, a translucent bewilderment in her uncomprehending regard, she knew only that she must appear a very unbride-like bride. She smiled faintly. She felt Greyson's hard embrace as he drew her forward, shouldering them through the cheering assemblage. She glanced up at him, wondering what had prompted this, still disbelieving it had happened, wondering what would happen next.

Greyson swept them both into his cabin and closed the door. The two people faced each other. In the sudden silence—for no one, not even Jack or Mr. Harrt would dare to disturb them in what they knew would be a difficult moment for both—Victoria and Greyson watched each other for reaction. Neither wanted to be first to voice a response to this most unusual turn of fortune. The deck rolled cautiously beneath them as though it, too, knew the intricacy of emotion that must be faced by the newly bound husband and wife. Victoria felt her chin lift. Her chin often lifted in answer to tension—though, in the whole of her young life, Victoria Quayle had not known many moments as rivetingly precarious as this one. She eyed Greyson, her moist lips budding in question. She would let him speak first, she decided. He was always so roguishly, schoolboyishly sure of himself—cocksure—she thought irreverently. She would wait—allow him to make the first analysis of what had happened between them.

153

Greyson shifted. Tall, bronzed, draped in the raiments of his authority, he at last began to divest himself of at least that defense. His sword and gunbelt went first, then his blue woolen waistcoat and doublet. Victoria folded her arms across her breast and lifted a pale brow. She wondered if it was his intent to strip himself naked before her and demand his husbandly rights as they stood there. Booted, tightly breeched, cambric-shirted, he stood before her at last. He seemed about to speak. Then he turned, placing his hands on the slanted teak map table, and leaned over it.

"Have you nothing to say?" he asked.

"What would you have me say?" she rejoined softly. "You know," she added reflectively, "you might have asked me that question before you passed down your most recent injunction."

He turned to her abruptly, but reined whatever words he was about to speak. She tilted her glance expectantly. "I suppose," he conceded after a pause, "I might have fallen to my knee and proposed formally." He allowed a small smile to etch his lips. "What would you have done, Victoria, had I done that?"

She lifted a slim shoulder. "I suppose," she answered negligently, hiding a smile, "I would have accused you of insanity."

He arched a russet brow and placed his hands on his lean hips. "Do you believe that?" he asked, his blue perusal glinting amusement.

Victoria regarded him coolly. "I am not sure what I believe, Captain Tyrrel. I shall tell you this, though, you are certainly consistent."

He crossed his forearms over his chest and widened his stance. "How so?" he inquired.

"You told me once that you were not given to gentle traditions of courtship," she reminded him. "You informed me that you had no time for 'gallant flirtations.' "

"And you told me that you cared nothing for 'pale traditions,' " he responded without pause.

Victoria lowered her gaze, her lashes fanning a dark fringe over the gentle curves of her cheekbones. "I did say that," she answered. She lifted a liquid regard, and her green eyes revealed opalescent approval of what he had done. "There is one tradition, however, of which I approve . . ." Her voice, lyrical with promise, trailed off. Greyson moved to her slowly and reached out a roughened fingertip to brush a wispy curl from her cheek.

"Your hair is not like straw," he said huskily, " 'tis like silk."

"Perhaps," she breathed, "you would like to 'clean me up' before you touch me so that I more resemble that 'finely bred English lady' of your memory."

He winced a half-smile. "You torture me with my own words," he said. "May I remind you that you warned me against touching you? You informed me that when you wished me to touch you, you would let me know."

"I remember," Victoria answered, nodding solemnly. " 'Twould be difficult to enjoy the fullest pleasures of the traditional wedding night without . . . touching."

"Yes . . . 'twould be . . . difficult." They gazed at each other for a long moment. Memory clouded. The present was all they knew. They moved toward each other—she, dainty, sun-kissed, yielding, he, strong, weather-bronzed, hungry. He lifted her from her feet and held her for a breath of a moment in his arms before sweeping her to his great bed. He laid her down there and stretched himself alongside of her. His lean length pressed against her, he watched as she began to respond, with small writhing gestures, to his light caresses. Her eyes closed as he removed Mr. Longdon's tattered garments from her creamy flesh. With agonizing slowness, he drew off first the doublet and then the soft, weathered shirt. His big hands unloosed the lacings at her belly, and he trailed the breeches down her thighs, his fingertips languidly following, abrading her tingling senses. He feathered hot kisses where his fingertips had been. His lips and tongue took small bits of her flesh in moist, possessive nibbles. Arching her to him, laying bare the delicate unguarded tenderness of her virginal breasts, he took full pleasure in his advantage and feasted ravenously on his succulent quarry.

Victoria felt hot tides of pleasure course through her. Her heart pounded, sending liquid fire swarming through her veins. She was submerged beneath the frenzied power of Greyson. He caressed and stroked and suckled, attentive to her every response for all his growing urgency. She was bathed in fluid hunger. She tore at his clothing, needing to feel the hot abrasion of his manly fur upon her. He ripped at the constraints of his garments with equal rapacity, and when he was freed from them, he drew himself over her. She gazed up at him, her eyes lucent with desire. He checked himself for the breath of a second.

"Are you very sure," he rasped.

"I am," she breathed. She drew his lips down to hers, and he lingered over the melting flower of her submission, urging her to sun-heated heights of necessity. He placed his large hand beneath her buttocks and lifted her to the virile throb of his need. She arched further, her innocent impatience firing his voracious hunger. He entered the sweet realm where primal rapture was to be found. The smoothness of the invasion, however, was cut short as Victoria felt the first searing pain. Her amazement became fear, and the fear erupted into a cry, ripped from the bewilderment of her heart.

"What are you doing, Greyson?" she shrieked.

His mouth came down on hers as much to quiet her as to reassure her. " 'Tis only momentary," he breathed hoarsely, his lips still on hers. "I promise you. 'Twill last only seconds." He thrust once again, tearing through the barrier of Victoria's innocence. He held her beneath him as she writhed, attempting to free herself from the unexpected and unimagined agony. Why was he doing this to her? Her mind raged with possibility. Was this Greyson's revenge? Had he entrapped her, planned this all along? She struggled in a frenzy of terror as again, he drove himself into her.

"Stop, Greyson," she cried. "Stop hurting me, please!"

The savagery done, he paused inside her. Crooning tender words, he brushed at her perspiration sheened face and hair. He looked down into her tear-stung gaze.

" 'Tis all right," he said softly. " 'Tis over." Listening to the caress of his words, his gentling tones, seeing the tender concern in his eyes, Victoria at last ceased her struggles. "Let me love you," he said gently. Victoria girded herself against further pain. She nodded. In her sweet countenance Greyson observed a mixture of disappointment and devotion. He smiled. "Oh, love," he breathed, "I am the most fortunate of men. But, I promise you," he added, "the hurting is over." He eased himself back from her, and she felt her heart trip. "Trust me, love," he said.

Reluctantly, she lifted her arms, entwining them around his neck. She tunneled her fingertips into the thick fringe of russet curls she found there and grasped them for assurance. She wanted to trust him. She listened to his tender words and allowed him entrance once again. He fondled and petted her, stroking her anguish away with his touch. Victoria realized a rekindling of her desire almost at once. She felt little rills of pleasure tremble beneath her flesh. Fluid sparks of reawakened need shot through her as he tenderly lingered where he seemed to know he would pleasure her most. A golden aura of tingling warmth spread up from the bud of her passion as she felt his powerful essence inside her. Moving slowly, languorously, he thawed whatever resistance was left in her. She melted in harmony to the burning enchantment of his sun-touched magic. They basked together in a glowing rapture. As they explored and enticed each other, pulsing fires began to grow, flaring into molten desire. In seething unity, they throbbed together to the blazing purity of completion. They shuddered together at the peak of ecstasy. Together they held the enchantment between them, exulting in its trembling perfection. Victoria longed to contain the moment forever. She held Greyson tightly, breathing raggedly against him. He stroked and soothed her trembling pulses until at last he felt her soften beneath him, her breath become even. He looked down on her, and in her repletion, she seemed to shimmer, pearllike in the encompassing bronze of his embrace.

"I cannot believe you are real," he breathed in wonder. "You might be a dream."

"I am no dream, Greyson," she whispered, gazing up at him. "I am real. I am every bit as real as my love for you."

A small supper had been decorously left outside the cabin

door, and Greyson and Victoria had satisfied at least that part of their hunger very quickly—in bed, draped in a rumpled coverlet. They laughed together as they ate the last of the plums—no doubt supplied by Jack from his private stock—and drank from the jug of wine that had been donated to their honeymoon festivities. Greyson brushed at a crumb of bread that had snuggled itself into the silken fleece of her hair.

Eyeing her with irreverent amusement, he assured her that he would indeed need to "clean her up" before presenting her in Boston as his wife. This was the first moment of niggling doubt Victoria had felt since their hastily contrived marriage. She shifted in discomfort beneath his amorous playfulness. Noting the clouding of her expression he inquired what was wrong.

"Nothing, Greyson," she responded a bit too hastily.

He offered a knowing smile. "We are an old married couple now, Victoria," he chided her. "You cannot glibly hide your feelings from your husband, you know. You answer nothing, but I know there is a very big something beneath that word."

"Yes," she answered penitently, "there is . . . something." She paused and lowered her gaze. Lifting it slowly, she said, "We have been so caught up in this moment, Greyson, we have not even begun to explore the possible difficulties we might have to face in the colonies."

Greyson lay back, his hands folded comfortably behind his head. "There shall be no difficulties, Victoria," he said with certainty. "You are my wife now. No one will question your political loyalties." The burnished curls falling in a boyish tousle over his forehead, the roguish assurance in the amused blue of his gaze, checked Victoria's immediate response.

She would have told him that her own convictions might be the ones to cause them difficulty. She might have reminded him that whatever the problems between the British and the Americans, she was bound by certain loyalties, bred on certain ideologies. She knew she would find it impossible to blithely abandon the concepts of human behavior with which she had grown up. She reminded herself, however, that she really knew nothing of the content of the American culture. She had only the word of Uncle David and the wealthy planters of Kolhapur on which to base her opinion of the people. And she understood that that opinion was a biased one. She reminded herself also that she knew nearly nothing of the problems besetting the relationship between England and her American colonies. Before she could begin to make any decisions concerning her behavior toward them, she must discover the nature of the people and their attitudes toward the Mother Country.

Victoria reposed in the curve of Greyson's muscled shoulder. "Tell me about these people—the passengers on the *Spectre*," she said. "Where do they come from, why are they aboard?"

"Most of them are from Boston," Greyson told her. "After the long war with the French, many found it necessary to leave the town. They travelled to other colonies, to foreign shores, to different places to seek financial respite from that hard war." He glanced down at her and arched a brow. "What exactly did you wish to know?" he asked.

"Well," she said thoughtfully, running delicate fingertips over the muscled hollows and hills of his lightly furred chest, "I suppose I am curious as to the presence of so many Americans on a vessel journeying from India."

"They sought jobs there," he said. "Many of them worked for a time for the British East India Company. They have chosen to leave at this time because policies toward the shipping of tea to the colonies has changed and those policies threaten our very way of life."

"I do not understand," said Victoria.

Greyson raised himself up on one elbow. "Do you really want to hear this, love?" he asked her. She nodded and Greyson lay back, cradling her in one strong arm. "The whole story is complicated, but I shall tell you briefly that the East India Company began about three years ago to buy up great quantities of tea." Victoria knew that to be true. Her own plantation had yielded enormous profits from that market. She listened carefully as Greyson went on. "The company did not bargain for the effectiveness of an American boycott of heavily-taxed English tea and found itself suddenly with an overabundance of the product. It has been decided, therefore, that the East India tea should be sent directly to America; that it should not be sent to England first." Victoria listened patiently. She had heard as much from the passengers. Greyson continued. "The reasoning is that import and export duties will be avoided and that the Americans may buy the tea directly from the company at rock-bottom prices."

"That seems reasonable," Victoria offered.

"It may seem reasonable, love, but it is really only a diversionary measure by the British government to save the East India Company from bankruptcy. Beyond that, the idea poses a serious economic threat to American merchants. If the English are allowed to set up government stores selling tea, what is to stop them from creating similar monopolies with products such as salt, tobacco, soap? It could mean the destruction of the American middle class. In Boston we depend upon trade for our livelihood. Where would we be if the British were allowed to destroy that trade? America would become a small farming country controlled by England. And that circumstance would leave very few options for the Town of Boston. We have no farmland; we might cease to exist. Believe me, love," he said solemnly, "not one case of East India tea can be allowed to land on American shores."

Victoria's brows quirked. She felt herself beginning to understand the point of view of the American colonials, but the question remaining was why the people so avidly renounced British intervention in their affairs. America was after all a British colony. She hesitantly voiced her question. Greyson smiled ruefully.

"Isn't it obvious, love?" he said gently. Victoria attempted to discern just *what* was obvious.

"Is it that the Americans no longer wish to be a colony?" she ventured.

"You have your answer," he responded grimly.

"But why?" Victoria gaped, sitting up.

Greyson regarded her for a long moment. His gaze flickered over her. She watched him, waiting for his answer, innocently unaware of the fact that her action had caused the

160

coverlet to fall away. The truth was, he had no desire to continue this political treatise. He smiled lazily. Lifting a muscled arm, he reached for the wild tousle of her curls and entwined a silken handful in his fingers. He drew her firmly down to him. Apparently, her lesson in colonial polity was at an end.

"Do you know how beautiful you are?" he asked. "Do you know how you drive me to lunacy with wanting you?"

"Have you not had enough of me?" she inquired saucily. In answer, Greyson drew her lips to his. Her breasts, tender with Greyson's often over zealous ministrations, tingled with the abrasion of his coarsely downed chest. His big hands roved her ripened flesh. He rolled her onto her back and regarded her. In his blue-misted gaze there was reluctant wonder.

"I never thought it would happen to me," he rumbled.

"What would happen?" she asked gently.

"That I would fall in love," he answered. "And I do love you, Victoria." He had not said the words before. Victoria felt a swelling in her heart at his admission. She drew his lips to hers, and once again, as they had many times in the past few hours, they lingered long in the sensate aura of their devotion.

The days and nights — especially the nights — of the *Spectre*'s voyage would pass all too quickly, Victoria reflected as she took her breakfast alone the next morning. She munched appreciatively on the corncakes and sausages Jack had brought to the cabin for her. She had seen in his suppressed grin, and in the twinkling happiness that lit his eyes, all the joy that he felt at the uniting of his two favorite people.

"You and the captain are kind of like the mum and the daddy of the boat now," he'd said with a barely contained giggle.

"I suppose you could say that, Jack." Victoria smiled, for it occurred to her that Jack might truly crave at least the fantasy of that sort of familial structure in his young life, though he would no doubt fiercely deny such a need. For all his firmly guarded independence, Jack was no different than any other child. He was no different than Victoria herself had been. Even once she had known the shadowed truth of her origin, she had delighted in the spousal image presented to her by Lord Trevor and Katje. In her imaginings, when she was young, she had even called herself Victoria Darby. It was not until later, once Uncle David and she had begun to invent a past for her, that she had finally accepted Quayle as her surname and had begun to feel a certain pride in that name. At least she'd had a name to cling to. Jack had none, had even boasted of that fact. But Victoria knew that as she had when she was a child, Jack enjoyed very frankly the notion that at the heart of this random and difficult universe in which they all existed, there was at least the illusion of order. And wasn't that what everyone was seeking really? Even fantasies of order were welcome where no order existed. The thought sobered her.

She slowly passed a napkin over her lips and pushed away her breakfast tray. A fantasy of order . . . where no order existed. The words tumbled over each other in her mind. That is exactly what Greyson had created with their marriage—a fantasy of order, not only for Jack but for the passengers and crew. The tumult caused by her presence on the ship had left him no choice. Her lips parted in sudden comprehension. Greyson had married her in order to bring peace to his little universe. And his gesture *had* brought peace for all of them. Jack had told Victoria that everyone aboard was happily anticipating her arrival on deck that morning. They wanted to make their amends to her for all the hardships they had caused her, for all the insults and ill feelings they had inflicted upon her. Jack had informed her with a rather forced gravity that she might want to wear her prettiest dress that day in case—just in case—a party had been planned in her honor. Apologies, parties, good-will— all the trappings of peace, all the benefactions of order— were present where once there had been anger and black looks and suspicion. Order had been restored to the decks of the *Spectre of the Bay*. Greyson had done what needed doing. He had sacrificed himself for the benefit of those over whom he held absolute ordinance. He'd brought peace to his world—but at what price.

Nevermind that their wedding night had been a splendorous awakening of their mutual and long-suppressed passion. What would become of the rest of their lives? How long would that quick-silver moment of crystalline perfection last? Surely such sudden and rapturous ecstasy would burn itself out over time. And what would be left? Victoria stood, a shudder passing through her. She drew Greyson's shirt more tightly around her as if it might bring him nearer to her. *Oh, Greyson,* she thought fearfully, *will you blame me? Will you hate me one day for being the instrument of your entrapment? This journey will be over soon, and when it is we shall both have to face the reality of our marriage. In this idyllic little world, it is the perfect arrangement—the only option. But what will become of our relationship when we must finally live in the real world?*

Victoria sat heavily on the little sofa. She and Greyson must have some time. They must begin to sort out their feelings for each other. They must discover if this enforced marriage—this fantasy of marriage—would endure the arena of everyday life. Would she and Greyson be able to remain friends through emotional stress, through physical adversity, through disagreements and mood swings and individual growth? These were the substantive elements of life in the real world. Could their marriage survive such realities? There was no way of knowing such a thing—not now, not under the existing circumstances. Before their marriage could really begin, she and Greyson must get to know each other. They must discover who they would become when reality invaded their lives. Victoria was not about to make the same mistake she'd made with Steven Kensington. She had allowed herself to believe in an illusion of Steven that had overridden who he really was. She had never bothered to discover him in all his ancestral snobbery. She'd fallen hopelessly in love with a dream of Steven that simply did not exist. And now there was Greyson. Victoria determined that this time there would be no illusions. She knew that the only way she could insure their future together was to separate herself from Greyson when they arrived in Boston. It would not be easy, but she would suggest to Greyson that she live,

163

as she originally planned, with Katje's friends the Frankland-Fosters. That way she and Greyson could court, they could begin to discover hidden expectations and suppressed obliquities in each other. They could begin to discover whether or not they liked each other. There was no question of their love, Victoria reflected with a small smile. An abrupt knock on the cabin door interrupted her musings. Victoria quickly laced up Greyson's shirt and, opening the door a crack, peeked outside.

Edmund Harrt offered her a measuring look. "Have you finished your breakfast?" he asked.

"Oh, yes, Edmund," Victoria said, a question in her voice.

The young man smiled. "I am instructed to escort you topside within the next few minutes."

Victoria nodded, a knowing smile pursing her lips. She lowered her gaze. "Jack mentioned that I might wish to dress with some particular care this morn," she murmured.

Edmund nodded. "I shall wait out here, your ladyship," he said.

Victoria closed the door and turned to her toilette. Once she had donned her gown and felt suitably presentable, she invited the young warrant officer inside.

"I just need to dress my hair, Edmund," she said. "If you do not mind watching, you can wait in here." She felt strangely at ease with this man. He had offered so much in the way of support and friendship that Victoria felt she could share with him even her most intimate perspectives. She plumped down onto the bed and began to brush her tangled mass of curls. "Sit anywhere, Edmund," she said as he moved into the room. He watched her as he lowered himself onto the sofa.

"I haven't had the opportunity to wish you happiness, Victoria," he said softly.

She lowered her gaze. "Thank you, Edmund," she responded, her tone subdued. The young man looked mildly startled.

"Is everything all right?" he asked.

"Oh, yes," she said, perhaps too quickly, "why do you ask?"

Edmund shrugged a wide shoulder. "It only seemed to me that your voice held a certain . . . well, irresolution, I suppose. I just wondered . . ." His words trailed off, and he busied himself with his immaculately manicured fingernails. "The marriage happened awfully quick," he added quietly.

"I know that," Victoria said. She stood and walked to the glass. She lifted the heavy mass of her opalescent curls and pinned them atop her head. "I have wondered myself about what the future holds for the Greyson Tyrrels." She turned to find Edmund watching her. The intensity of his gaze disconcerted her, and she moved hastily to find her parasol. Edmund was as concerned as she about her and Greyson's hasty marriage. He seemed to be scrutinizing her for answers, and Victoria had no answers. At last she faced him and smiled ruefully. "I know you are probably worried, Edmund," she said, "but I promise you that everything will work out between Greyson and me. We just need some time to get to know each other," she assured him with a confidence she did not feel. Edmund seemed to sense her forced optimism.

"I shall tell you something, Victoria," he said, looking up into her eyes. "I feel very close to you. Look to me for protection if you need to. Greyson is a good man — but you know that. He is also a rather . . . stubborn fellow and quite fixed in his beliefs. You and he are entering a difficult time. You may find problems arising that might seem insurmountable. Your family is very far away, and —"

"I have no family, Edmund," Victoria said softly. "I have no idea who my parents are or anything else about my past."

Edmund stood and moved to her, placing his arm around her slender shoulders.

"I thought as much," he said. Victoria looked up quizzically. Edmund merely smiled warmly. "I know more about you than you might imagine, Victoria. We are kindred spirits, you and I, and that is all the more reason for you to lean on me. Boston is a cold and lonely town, and right now it is a profoundly divided place. Greyson Tyrrel is very much a part of that unstable atmosphere. I am not. As an outsider, you may need someone sometime. I should like to be that

165

someone. I should like to offer a kind of refuge to you. Think of me as your family. If ever you face anything that seems so deeply impossible that you cannot imagine how it can be overcome, call on me. I will help. I, too, am an outsider. I shall always be with you, even when it seems I am far away."

Victoria gazed up into the warmth of his regard. How grateful she was for a friend such as Edmund Harrt. In the maelstrom of difficulties she was about to face, she took comfort in at least that relationship. She once again realized an intensity in his scrutiny and guessed that Greyson had been correct in his assessment of Edmund's feelings for her. Perhaps secretly Edmund was just a little bit in love with her. Well, so be it, she thought contentedly. Maybe she even shared a certain part of his feeling. Nothing could come of an innocent and unrequited secret love except an affectionate friendship. If Edmund Harrt felt he knew Victoria, then she felt she understood him. He offered his arm, and together they made their way up onto the spar deck for Victoria's "surprise" party.

Edmund Harrt was more than attentive for the rest of the day and for the rest of the voyage. Victoria knew that in him she had found a friend. She confided to him what she knew of her past, she spoke of her love of poetry, and she talked openly of her uncertainty about her marriage to Greyson. Through it all, Edmund Harrt listened with the quiet interest of a deeply concerned counselor. About her past, he seemed thoughtful and sympathetic. About her poetry, he seemed enthusiastic. Most importantly, he agreed with her that she should not jump into marriage with Greyson, that she should give herself and the captain the grace of time and distance before bounding into that most confining and unyielding of all human promises.

Edmund told Victoria something of his own past — of his home in Salem, of his mother who still lived there. He spoke, too, of his ambivalence about the political situation in Boston. He told Victoria that he was concerned with different and, to him, larger issues. Victoria attempted to question him on what he considered more important than the problems now dividing the American colonists, but Edmund seemed distant and uncommunicative on the subject. Whatever haunted Edmund Harrt, whatever in his past concerned him more deeply than the controversy that now divided the entire population of the colonies, was something he seemed unable to discuss. One day, when he was ready, Victoria decided, he would talk about it. She would not pursue the mystery, though it aroused her curiosity. In truth, her concern for Edmund Harrt paled in the face of her anxiety over her marriage. She must come to a decision, and she must do it very soon.

Chapter Thirteen

Before dawn, in the quiet rose-gray darkness, Victoria leaned against the taffrail of the *Spectre*. She watched where she had been disappear beyond the lacy flux of the ship's wake. Today was the day they were to reach Boston; even now, if one looked beyond the foredeck, a gray configuration of rock could be detected along the horizon. Their voyage had carried them thousands of miles, from the steamy inlets of the cerulean Arabian Sea to the surging billows of the silvered Atlantic. The wind blew white and icy here, and the sky, when the sun came up, lacked luster, beginning and ending its appearance barely discernible from the sea on which it shone.

Victoria drew Greyson's heavy woolen cloak more tightly around her shoulders, snuggling into it for warmth and for his scent, reminding her of his prior presence within its folds. Wearing it made her feel close to him. And she needed to feel close to him just now. Greyson, always awake before dawn, was at the helm. Even apart, they shared a quiet, knowing harmony of communication. Soon he would join her. They would go below decks into the warmth of the captain's cabin where they would speak again of why she felt she could not stay with him once they had reached Boston. She would remind him that she needed time to understand the temper of the American colonials before she could begin to live among them as his wife. She would refute his assertion that they—the two of them—could live in harmony even with their very different ideological persuasions. She would tell him, as she had told him again and again, that she could not remain submissively beside him while he joined the cause for the separation of the American colonies from the Sovereign Rule. She did not understand that cause, and until she did understand it — she doubted she would ever agree it was right — she must learn all she could about its source. It would not take long, she had assured him, she was a most eager student. Beyond that, and much more importantly, Greyson had married her under incredible duress, she had reminded him. They had had no moments of gentle courtship — they had had no courtship at all. Victoria and Greyson did not know each other in the way that married couples ought to know each other. Husbands and wives ought to be each other's best friends. In order for such a relationship to form, two people must take the time to acquaint themselves with every nuance of the other's character. Victoria had not realized how important the "gentle traditions" of her life in Kolhapur had been to her, especially where they concerned courtship. She smiled wryly. She'd certainly had the advantage of those traditions in her relationship with Steven Kensington, and look where they'd gotten her. Steven had insisted, even after all their early courting days, that she become his mistress. He had felt, he said, it was the best arrangement for both of them. For all their long acquaintance, Victoria had not known Steven Kensington at all — and he had not known her. Her chin angled upward into the misting air of the coming dawn. Victoria had loved Steven Kensington, or thought she did. She had invested years of her life in that fruitless pursuit. She would not make the same mistake with Greyson Tyrrel. She must be sure of her feelings for him. She must be sure of his feelings for her. She wanted their relationship to be forever. All the more reason, she resolved, that she must endeavor to make their foundations strong. Greyson believed her unreasonable, but she knew that she was being practical. Greyson and she had battled out the question of her decision across oceans. She had been firm. He had been intractable. He had called her mutinous. She had called him obstinate. Through it all, her resolve — mutinous though it may be — had not wavered; his determination had not faltered. And through it all, the two very assertive people had

169

known the splendor of unfailing desire. The tempest of their battles rarely matched the temptestuousness of their love-making. For all her certainty that her decision was correct on grounds of logic, Victoria knew—her heart told her—that she must not lose Greyson Tyrrel. She loved him. She must have him, and she must have him forever even if it meant that they must live apart for a time. They must give their budding love an opportunity to blossom fully. One day, when the roots of their love were strong, they would be together completely, forming the center of a perfect, ever-growing bouquet. In the meantime, she sighed inwardly, the battle would continue even on this their last day aboard the *Spectre*.

Greyson would brawl and rail that a wife ought to be with her husband. Victoria would gently remind him that she would be with him . . . always. They shared a love that no ideological distance could breach and no amount of separation could dissolve. If their love was as strong as Victoria believed it to be, there was no question that one day—and very soon, too—they would begin a life together. And that life would be founded on the fullest knowledge of each other that any couple had ever shared.

She felt him near her. Glancing over her shoulder, she smiled through the fading darkness into the sea-glass luster of his eyes. Unspoken, explicit, their correspondence led them to each other's arms and down the hatchway into the milky darkness of the captain's quarters. Oh, they would have their battle before the sun was high, but first . . .

Victoria shrugged off the heavy cloak and hung it on a hook near the door. Slowly she began to unfasten the lacings of her gown, turning to him, tempting him with her languor. A velvet heat began to flow through him as she allowed the garment to slide down the delicate curvings of her form to fall in a frothy heap at her ankles. She lifted her chin, defiance glittering darkly in her wide gaze. She was daring him to ignore the upthrusting of her young breasts beneath the fragile lace of her chemise.

She reached out, and with enticing fingertips, she divested his broad shoulders of his coat and then his shirt.

Drawing and stretching the fabric tautly down his muscular arms, she leaned to him, caressing his furred, bronzed chest with her tongue and teeth. Nipping lovingly at the sinewed flesh, she held him captive against the sweet torture of her lips. His head rolled back in a delirium of passion, and she took the more vulnerable new territory in stunning hot little bites. Seething hunger flared, blood quickened, tolerance exploded. In an agonized fever of need, he galvanized himself against her restraint, enchained her in the throbbing steel of his embrace. He lifted her, sweeping her from her feet and onto the great bed. Lowering himself over her, tearing at the lacy chemise, he filled the rapacious hunger of his soul with the succulence of her tender flesh. She writhed beneath him in an ecstasy of maddened pleasure. She entwined her legs around the lean, muscular column of his middle as he lifted the moist flowering core of her need to his powerful command. He thrust in a towering rage of desire. Victoria received the flaming charge rapturously, with breathless charges of her own. The sudden turbulence of their passion crested, swirling them to dizzying, heartgripping heights. Together, in the fiery dazzle of their joy, together, in the darkness of the cabin, Greyson and Victoria touched the sun.

Soul-melting pleasure undulated through them, bathing them in a golden ecstasy. Liquid rills of wonder cooled the wild fires of their pulsing need. They lay together in the curling vapor of their repletion, breathless with the unexpected sublimity of their union. They marvelled that they could attain such heights, such soaring perfection.

Victoria snuggled pearllike in the firm bronze of Greyson's muscled arms. She felt, against her passion-flushed cheek, the furring of his chest, the rhythmic pounding of his heart, the rumbling, hoarse whisper of his words of love. His hot breath stirred the lucent ringlets of her hair.

How could she envision living without this man who loved her so well? And yet, even now as she lay with him in the snug, secure nest of his embrace, as the dawn cast its sallow fingers through the port window, she did envision it and knew it must be so. She held him hard against the cold that seeped beneath the thick counterpane. Cradled in his hard arms, in the growing cold, her tenderness for him grew.

No words could ever express to him her devotion. No mere articulations could tell him how deeply she loved him. She reveled in the silence, in the unspoken splendor of their ardor as they lay together in the dawning light. And yet, she thought resignedly, there would be words between them before the sun was high, and they would not be words of love.

Victoria watched the shoreline close in around her. This gray presence then was to be her new home. She studied closely every physical feature that came into view. The most significant and obvious was a configuration of three high hills. Collectively the rugged mass was called the Trimountain. In the center, the highest peak rose majestically, a tall tower at its top. This would be the Beacon Hill of which Greyson had spoken, the tower having been built more than a hundred years ago as the first line of defense against a French invasion from Canada. Other peaks dotted the peninsula—once called Shawmut—and Greyson had named them all. There was Bunker or Breed's Hill to the north and Fort Hill to the south, Windmill Hill, West Hill—so many hills; it was no wonder the Puritan fathers had referred to Boston as the "Citty upon a hill."

As the *Spectre of the Bay* cut the choppy waters of Boston Harbor, tiers of peak-roofed houses covered with weatherboarding or clapboards became more distinct. They occupied the descending slope of land that reached to the cove the ship was now entering. Wharves jutted out from every angle of the beaches. One wharf, longer than the others, cut through the inland waters and out into the harbor. Ships of every description rode high on the roiling silvery breakers. As the *Spectre* neared the wharf, Victoria could see the tangle of humanity bustling about the busy seaport.

" 'Tis a pretty sight," rhapsodized a woman who stood near Victoria. "This Boston Town of mine is heaven here on earth."

"I did not dream 'twas so big and . . . and . . . hurried,"

172

Victoria breathed, fear edging her voice.

The woman eyed her in amusement. "Have you never seen a port town before?"

"Not one that is quite so impressive," Victoria answered with a small smile of her own. She thought briefly of the port at Kolhapur, its languid little bursts of animation on days when ships yawed into the steamy harbor. She glanced at the woman. "The place I come from is not nearly so energized."

"There are not many places as energized as Boston," said the woman pridefully.

" 'Tis so crowded," Victoria said, scanning the brisk and nimble efforts of the people, animals, carts and coaches to avoid slamming into each other.

"Ah, 'tis only crowded down here at the Town Cove." The woman explained. "Up northerly, up near the common land, there's lots of space." She indicated, with a wave of her hand, the area near the Beacon Hill. "Your upper crust don't think too much of the hill area, but my old fellow and me like it just fine. We got clean air, lots of space, good grazin'." The woman laughed. "Let the rich folks have their precious Town Cove. I hope they never find out what they're missin'."

"I wonder where I shall live." Victoria mused aloud.

"Why, you'll live where the captain lives," the woman said.

"I am afraid not," Victoria responded with a rueful smile. At the woman's questioning look, she explained. "I plan to stay with friends for a while." She did not go on, for she felt the woman's disapproval. Victoria could not explain to her the reasons. Even if the woman understood, she would not approve of Victoria's complex thinking on the issue. For one thing, there was a zealous allegiance to this land in the woman's tone; she would never accept Victoria's reticence toward anything concerning Boston or the Bay Colony. In many ways, Victoria admired this parochial pride. "Wherever I live," she said gently, "I am sure 'twill be lovely."

The woman eyed her speculatively. "You'll probably be up by the Faneuil Market place," she said shortly. "What's the name of your people?"

"The family I'm staying with are the Frankland-Fosters," answered Victoria.

"Oh, them," the woman intoned in disapproval. "They got the biggest, grandest house on Hanover Street."

"Have they," Victoria responded with interest.

The woman nodded tersely and moved away. Obviously Vivien Frankland-Foster and her husband Lord Neville were not among the favorite of the people who lived up "northerly", in the area of the common land, at the foot of the Beacon Hill. Victoria watched the woman trundle off. It was painfully clear that a gap existed between two very distinct worlds here in the town of Boston. She wondered where she and Greyson would fit in.

She turned slightly and noted that Greyson was watching her. He leaned against the helmsrail as she glanced his way and offered him a small wave. As the ship yawed, the bay breezes caught his burnished hair, lifting and sweeping dark curls over his tanned forehead. Between his glinting white teeth, he held a cheroot. His regard was stony. Victoria turned away. Her cloak whipped around her in the snapping, off-shore wind. She had not been warm in a very long time, she reflected.

Beneath the heavy veiling of Victoria's traveling outfit, Greyson had seen the glint of crystalline curls, the lucence of ivory flesh, the flash of emerald eyes. He eyed the trim figure beneath the fluid agitation of her cloak. Memories of that trim figure unbound, abandoned in his arms heated his blood. But now Victoria was determined to defy him. Once again the chit's contentious nature had reared itself, and the confrontation between them had hovered over their relationship from the Tropic of Cancer to the Boston Harbor. She would not be swayed. With teeth-clenching reluctance he had earlier in the day sent out a small pinnace with a messenger carrying Victoria's letter of introduction to see that the Frankland-Fosters were apprised of the *Spectre*'s arrival in Boston; their coach would be awaiting Victoria at the pier. But his compliance with that sweetly-requested demand in no way indicated a compliance on his part they they should not live as man and wife. At long last, he had unraveled his feelings for Victoria. At long last, he had discovered that he loved her. At long last, he had built for himself a most luxurious cage; he'd married the girl. He was determined to enjoy the benefits of that long-avoided circumstance.

Greyson Tyrrel watched as Victoria's chin lifted, her shoulders drawn back defiantly, as though she knew exactly what he was thinking. She was no ordinary woman. But then, he reminded himself, he was no ordinary man.

The *Spectre of the Bay* shuddered as it neared the long wharf, hard to the vessel's port side. Orders were shouted, running rigs unbound. The mighty sails luffed on the sprightly winds, the capstan groaned.

Victoria turned suddenly as she felt an urgent tugging on her cloak. She looked down to find Jack gazing up at her. Bending her knees, she faced him. This would be the hardest parting of all.

"Oh, Jack," she said softly, "you came to say good-bye."

His grim little face, grimy with the work of landing, set in a stern denial. He swallowed with some difficulty. "I ain't sayin' good-bye, your ladyship. I only wanted to tell you . . . to tell you that while you're in Boston Town, I'll be here on the *Spectre* and . . . well, don't you go forgettin' ole Jack."

"I won't," Victoria answered. "And you must promise not to forget me." Her throat was tight with emotion. Jack turned away abruptly and strode rapidly, his shoulders rigid, back to his work. Victoria watched him go. She stood slowly, and slowly she faced the salient, salty gray world that was to be her new home.

Beneath a cloud-pillowed sky, Victoria was led by Greyson down the gangway and onto the hustling dock area. She stepped carefully over the wide, wooden planking, attempting to avoid the sloshing swells of the icy harbor water. Spirits heightened despite the cold wintery air, Victoria moved through the masses of people that jostled her. She recalled a tract she had read. It was written by a Mr. Josselyn and described the thriving town as " . . . the Metropolis of this Colony . . . furnished with many fair Gardens and Orchards." Victoria, remembering the words, felt the promise of growth and purpose that seemed to emanate from the very pores of the seaport city.

She treaded awkwardly but excitedly among the swarms of humanity and searched for some sign of the Frankland-Foster carriage. Tripping once, she felt Greyson's strong arm catch her and lift her onto the pebbled roadway that met the dock. Her bonnet falling, the thick veiling grabbed at the pearly tendrils of her coif and sent them swirling in the December winds. She had so wanted to make a good impression on Katje's friends. She made a hasty effort to pat the errant tresses into place, but before she could, she felt Greyson pulling her along. Her disorientation was immediately interrupted by a low, musical laugh. She looked up to find herself facing the most beautiful woman she had ever seen.

"Welcome to Boston, my dear," said the lady. "I am Vivien." She held out a gloved hand, and Victoria hesitantly returned the greeting.

"Lady Frankland-Foster?" she inquired uncertainly.

Vivien Frankland-Foster nodded, her large, rose-plumed bonnet dipping elegantly. The woman was tall, her delicate shoulders higher than Victoria's own. She had a mane of coral-colored waves which were swept high above the white column of her long neck. Her eyes, however, were the magnets that drew Victoria's astonished gaze. They were a velvety gray with flecks of green that flashed warmly in the white winter sunlight. "And you are Victoria," the woman said. "My darling Katje has written so much about you, I would have known you anywhere." She laughed quietly. "And this gentleman is, I take it, Captain Tyrrel." She lifted a questioning cinnamon-colored brow.

"And Victoria's husband," he said, his gaze hooding.

Vivien merely nodded. "I see," she said smoothly. "Will you both be staying with us?" she asked.

"N-no," Victoria responded hastily, her gaze darting first to Greyson and then to the astonishingly beautiful woman who stood so serenely before them. "Just me, Lady Frankland-Foster."

176

"Call me Vivien," the woman said warmly. She looked up into Greyson's stern visage. "Naturally, Captain Tyrrel, we shall expect you to dinner tonight. You shall be most welcome in our home at any time, in fact." She took Victoria's elbow in her gloved hand and swept the girl into a waiting chaise. Once they were both positioned comfortably, she offered Greyson a luxurious nod of her plumed head and signalled her driver to be off. "Eight o'clock, Captain," she called back with a small, elegant wave of her hand. She turned then to Victoria and offered an empirical smile. "A most well-favored gentleman, that captain," she said knowingly. "Katje did not write me of him."

"We were married aboard his ship," Victoria replied uncertainly. " 'Twas really a gesture on his part to save my life. But now . . ." She lowered her gaze, studying her fingers. "Well, it all happened so quickly."

Vivien patted Victoria's hand, assuring her that no further explanation was needed. "For now," she said gently, " 'tis enough." She regarded the girl thoughtfully. Victoria knitted her brows beneath the older woman's scrutiny and lifted her gaze.

"I do love him," she said softly.

"Really," stated Vivien Frankland-Foster.

"Oh, yes," Victoria replied quickly.

Vivien laughed a low languid murmur. "I believe I knew that," she said softly. "I have not reached my thirty-ninth year without some ability to judge the temper of human relationships." She watched Victoria serenely. "I do love a romantic drama," she said, "even at my age." Victoria quickly averted her astonished gaze. She had not suspected that Vivien Frankland-Foster was *middle-aged*. She even seemed proud of the fact. In many ways, Victoria reflected, she was very much like Katje — mature, confident, tranquil. Perhaps, she thought hopefully, she would not be as lonely without Greyson as she had feared. Perhaps, she had found a friend.

The chaise lurched to a rolling stop before a spacious gambrel-roofed house. A carriage gate in a ten-foot high fence was opened and led into a paved courtyard. Victoria

177

gazed out at the main front. Nine lofty windows lined the first floor, which was at least one hundred feet long. The second floor was graced with several balconies, while a third floor lofted above that. A carriage house stood at the opposite end of the house from the street, and beyond that stables, sheds and fruit rooms could be seen. The gardens, viewed from that vantage, contained four large square beds. Trellises and many fruit trees promised a springtime fragrant with green new life. This was truly — as the woman on the ship had said — "the biggest, grandest house on Hanover Street."

The brawny driver helped them down, and Vivien led them from the carriage and to one of the two main doorways. They were ushered inside, their cloaks and bonnets taken by a young woman whom Vivien introduced as Dory.

"Is Lord Frankland-Foster at home?" she asked the girl as they swept through the carpeted hallway. Dory shook her head. "Well," said Vivien, "we shall have our tea anyway. Bring it into the small parlor." She led Victoria into a grandly furnished room and indicated a chair. She chuckled at her young guest's look of wonderment.

"We were told you lived like barbarians," Victoria breathed. She could not keep her awe in check as she studied the room. The walls were covered in a rich, black silk that had been appliqued with small pink flowers. Along the bottom half of the walls, the wainscoting and wood panelling were painted a deep mulberry pink which Vivien explained was, in fact, made with mulberries. The wide brick hearth was fitted with brass fixtures that glinted in the glow of the warming fire. On either side of the fireplace there stood two curved settees of rose-colored velvet. Chairs and tables of richly polished oak dotted the thick Turkish carpet which covered the wide-planked, highly lacquered flooring. Victoria moved to a wall lined with leather-bound books.

"My husband's hobby," said Vivien. "He believes a man should own great books." She laughed. "Of course they are all English . . . and I don't believe Neville has ever read one."

"We were led to believe there was great poverty here in

178

America," said Victoria.

"There is," Vivien answered. "There is a great deal of individual wealth here, but very little municipal wealth. The streets of this town teem with poverty-stricken women and children." She glanced away. "I know it seems immodest of us to live this way, but we do what we can." She looked back at Victoria, and a smile lightened her lovely face. "I am a member of a women's organization, Victoria. We quilt and sew and try to raise money for the poor. You must join us, you know. You shall meet all sorts of wonderful ladies. Mrs. Higginson and Mrs. Otis and Mrs. Hamilton and Mrs. Adams. My husband is not all that approving of association with them but—"

Vivien's words were cut off as the little maid entered, carrying a huge silver tray. Vivien nodded a thank-you and remained silent as she watched the girl leave the room. "She is ever so devoted to Neville," she said as she poured. Victoria moved to a small tapestry-upholstered chair and accepted a delicately patterned porcelain cup. "We have sugar, too," Vivien said brightly. It had not passed Victoria's notice that Vivien Frankland-Foster spoke with a veiled alteration in her voice when she spoke of her husband. Victoria wondered about their relationship.

"Do you have children?" Victoria asked her.

"Oh, yes," said Vivien, her face becoming animated with love and a certain sadness. "Derrick is at Jesus College and my little one, Thomas, is at Harrow. My husband, you see, believes in a good *English* education. There are many fine schools in the colonies, but Neville has no use for any of them. Harvard College is not very far from here. 'Tis a magnificent school. It was built nearly a hundred-fifty years ago. Imagine it, Victoria, the early settlers of this land were still living in thatch-roofed mud huts, yet they had such respect for the value of education that they built that magnificent college." She lowered her eyes abruptly and stared into her cup. Her tone altered perceptibly. "That," she said softly, "is my regular speech to Neville. I have told him that nearly every day since we left England. But he will have none of it." Her manner had become subdued. Indeed, since they

179

had entered the house, the effervescence of Vivien Frankland-Foster had slowly, but inexorably waned. She seemed a quite different woman than the one who had, with all the playful instincts of a true romantic, invited Greyson Tyrrel to dinner.

"How do you come to be in America?" Victoria asked.

Vivien glanced up. "My husband is a very influential man, Victoria," she said almost bitterly. "He is an agent of the king himself, a magistrate. Governor Hutchinson depends upon my husband for all sorts of important business." Her gaze was hard. "Governor Hutchinson would be at a complete loss without my husband's intervention in all manner of colonial affairs. You might say that next to the governor, my husband is the most important man in the Massachusetts Bay colony." Unbelievably, the woman's eyes filled with tears, and they ran unchecked down her cheeks as she continued. "If my husband were any less important to the king's dealings with the American colonists, I might have remained in my lovely house in Ipswich, England and visited my sons every Tuesday and every Saturday." Her voice had taken on a hysterical note. "As it is, I am bound to this ugly tract of desolation in the middle of the Atlantic Ocean, and I may *never* see my sons."

At last, Vivien's emotions came to a peak. Her proud shoulders slumped and the cup slipped from her hand to roll onto the carpet at her feet. Victoria rose quickly from her chair and knelt at the woman's side. Taking Vivien in her arms, she waited for her sobs to subside. Slowly the older woman controlled herself. "I am sorry, Victoria," she said finally. With a last trembling, she drew away from the girl and straightened herself. Using a napkin to wipe her tears, she added wearily, "I rarely allow myself the indulgence of tears. If I did not maintain my composure"—she laughed ruefully—"we should all have to move to higher ground. 'Twill not happen again."

"But 'tis all right, Vivien," Victoria said gently. "You have a great deal to be sad about. It must be horrible to be separated from your children and your home."

" 'Tis that," said Vivien, wiping away the last of her tears.

180

She gazed down at Victoria and smiled. "Poor little thing," she said. "I was supposed to be taking care of you."

"Perhaps," said Victoria, "we might take care of each other."

Vivien nodded and took Victoria's hand. "Let this be the beginning of a perfect friendship, Victoria," she said.

"I think the friendship has already begun," Victoria answered, smiling. She took a napkin and began sopping up the spilled tea. Above her, she felt Vivien rise and move to the center of the room. Victoria glanced up to realize she was being watched. From her position on her hands and knees, she saw a man's neatly booted feet and calves. She looked up further to see immaculate buff breeches and a plum waistcoat of fine satin. The stern face above that, encased in a pristine white wig, told her that from her lowly perspective, she was meeting for the first time the master of the house. She scrambled to her feet, tripping on her gown in the process.

"Lady Darby, I presume," said the man humorlessly.

" 'Tis Victoria, darling." Vivien, now completely composed, moved to her husband's side. "This is my husband Neville."

Victoria offered her most deferential curtsy and then, with what she felt was her most disarming smile, extended her hand to Lord Frankland-Foster. "I am very pleased to meet you, sir."

The man bowed stiffly, taking Victoria's hand in a terse greeting. "I hope we shall not often find you hunkering on the carpet, Lady Darby," he said sternly.

"Oh, no, Lord Frankland-Foster," Victoria hastened to assure him. " 'Twas only . . . only that I . . . "

"I spilled some tea, dear," said Vivien easily. "Victoria was kind enough to wipe it up before it spotted the carpet."

"We have servants for such things," Neville replied, lifting a disdainful brow. He glanced back at Victoria. "Now, Lady Darby—"

"Please call me Victoria," she said brightly.

"Lady Darby," returned Lord Frankland-Foster stonily, "Vivien and I welcome you to our home, of course. I must

181

warn you, however, that I do not quite approve of your visit and said so to Lady Frankland-Foster. These are troubled times, your ladyship."

"I have heard as much, sir," said Victoria seriously.

Neville lifted a disdainful brow. "Have you indeed. Then you have heard as well that the Bay colony is a particularly unsuitable place for a young lady of your apparent breeding. Mrs. d'Aumerle should have known better than to send you here." His regard slowly swung to Vivien. "I hope you have written Katje a letter apprising her of my disapproval," he said. Vivien nodded. Victoria caught the sadness in her acquiescence. "Good," said Neville. He turned back to face Victoria. "Now that you are here, miss," he said contemptuously, "your welfare is my responsibility. I take that responsibility very seriously. I shall brook no hanky-panky from you."

Hanky-panky? Victoria thought with a sudden burst of amusement. She hastily repressed her mirth, however, and merely nodded. "Naturally not, sir," she murmured.

"There will be no time for 'hanky-panky,' Neville dear," said Vivien lightly. She moved to the table to pour her husband's tea. "We shall keep our little guest busy with all sorts of parties and teas. And do not forget our Christmas ball on the sixteenth."

"Yes," said the master of the house as he accepted his tea. His attention was riveted on Victoria. "Is everything in order for that eventuality?"

Vivien laughed. "Neville is the only person I know who refers to a Christmas ball as an 'eventuality.' " She turned to her husband and graced his cheek with a light kiss. "Yes," she said with assurance, "everything is in order. There are a few details to be worked out within the next week, but our dear Victoria can help me now she is here." The three people seated themselves about the room. As they conversed — or, rather, as Vivien attempted to keep the conversation alive — Victoria noted that Neville Frankland-Foster's glare remained steadily upon her. She could not rid herself of the notion that for some reason, he disliked her intensely. She attempted pretty smiles and modest glances, but the man remained unmoved. At last she contented herself with staring down into her cup and occasionally swirling its contents to divert herself. Her head swung up sharply as a familiar name was mentioned.

"Greyson Tyrrel?" thundered her host. "I cannot abide the man. Whatever made you invite him?"

" 'Twas a courtesy, Neville," Vivien was explaining. "Victoria and he—"

"Colonel Everett is coming over," Neville glowered. He stood and strode to the hearth. "Dammit, woman, you have made a lovely mess for me."

"Is there a problem?" Victoria asked in a small voice.

"Not at all, dear," said Vivien hastily.

"Of course there is a problem," Neville interjected harshly. "Colonel Jared Everett is the second in command of our British forces in this colony. Greyson Tyrrel's name has been linked with that bloody band of rapscallions who call themselves the Sons of Liberty. I would call that a problem."

"But, Neville," Vivien soothed, "no one knows the identity of any of those boys. How can you be sure Captain Tyrrel is one of them?"

"Who are the Sons of Liberty?" Victoria asked.

Vivien hastily turned to her. "They are just some local young ruffians, Victoria. They have caused a bit of trouble hereabouts."

Neville Frankland-Foster's nostrils flared. "You call them 'young ruffians,' Vivien?" he demanded. "Those blasted 'liberty' devils have made more problems for our soldiers than either of you can possibly imagine. They've instigated riots, stoned and looted the homes of local tax agents and customs collectors—"

"I was only trying to be polite, Neville," Vivien said quietly.

"Your attempt to be polite may cost me a powerful friend, Vivien. In future please do check with me before you go about turning my home into a retreat for colonial rabble."

Vivien cocked her head. "I was under the impression that this was my home, too, Neville," she said with a small smile.

183

"Oh, yes, yes," the man replied in exasperation. " 'Tis your home too, Vivien, but dammit, woman, I cannot have this sort of disorder in my household. First this bloody chit decides to —" He blanched suddenly, turning to face Victoria. "I beg your pardon, Lady Darby," he blustered. Victoria acknowledged him curtly, but she now knew exactly where she stood in the opinion of Neville Frankland-Foster. He went on. "You know my position in this colony, Vivien. If nothing else, Tyrrel is known for a bloody womanizer. He is a scoundrel of the first order. I should imagine you would think twice and then again about offering your hospitality to such a man." Vivien hid a grimace and looked worriedly toward Victoria. An unspoken agreement was born between them that they would, for a time at least, refrain from mentioning Victoria's marriage to Greyson Tyrrel. Neville continued. "Such people belong up north with that Godless Harvard ruck. They do not belong in respectable homes." He moved to the table and set his cup down with a decided click. "Dinner tonight will be a disaster," he proclaimed. He shot a look at Victoria. "You shall, nevertheless, be expected to dress for it, young lady." With a sniff and a last disdainful glower at his wife, he left the room.

Chapter Fourteen

Victoria was ushered into her third floor bedroom by the little maid. The girl was just barely Victoria's own age, and for all her deference, there was an underlying defiance in the girl's attitude.

"Lady Frankland-Foster says you'll be wanting a bath," the girl said as she showed Victoria where her clothes had been placed. "I'll be coming up later."

Victoria smiled and thanked the girl. "What was your name?" she asked.

"It was and is Dory," stated the girl. She stared with open challenge at Victoria who turned away in puzzlement. She had never encountered such insolence in a servant in her life. Naturally, the problem was not hers, and Victoria — a stranger in the house — would not take the initiative to reprimand her. But she wondered that the girl dared such an attitude in this household that was run by the rigid Lord Neville Frankland-Foster.

"Thank you, Dory," she murmured as she unpacked her toilette articles. She watched peripherally as the girl flipped her skirts impertinently and sauntered from the room. Victoria's gaze wandered about her as she took in her surroundings.

The bedchamber, not nearly as grand as her own in Kolhapur, was nevertheless charming. It reflected, to a great extent, the rock-cold, coastal world outside. There was a certain austere sapience about that world, a certain lack of ornamentation that was both reassuring and chilling. This new land, void of affectation, offered no steamy, tranquil forests in which to hide, no opulent lushness in which to shroud oneself. This Boston Town was barren as glass, uncompromising as pewter, artless as a raw pearl. Victoria's room reflected that artlessness.

The walls and moldings had been whitewashed from the wide-planked flooring to the low ceilings. Across the bottom half of the several small-paned windows, curtains, white and opaque, were hung. Their tiny print of pale pink and green wild flowers was repeated on both the thick quilted bed cover and on the slope of the ceiling beneath which the bed was nestled. A fire purled on the hearth and cast its pale aura over randomly placed braided rugs.

Victoria sat in a high-backed rocker near one window. Parting the curtain, she looked out at a low sun paling through the empty branches of a maple tree. She rocked quietly and thought of all that had brought her to this bleak and unsheltered world. Her mind wandered to her last few hours in Kolhapur.

Steven had glanced at her balefully as she had finally entered the ballroom of the plantation house. Barbara Meriam had held on to his arm with proprietary smugness. Her greeting to Victoria was uncharacteristically bold. "You missed the announcement of the season," Barbara boasted. "But then you might have missed it on purpose. There is no sense in rubbing one's own nose in one's defeat." She had laughed cruelly and led Steven onto the dance floor for their first dance together as an engaged couple. Steven, usually so confident and assured, seemed, beneath Barbara's haughty control, dubious, apprehensive and even despondent. "He will grow old very quickly," Katje had intoned softly, sadly as she watched the two. What forces could have commanded such a change in the listless Barbara, she wondered darkly. What forces, indeed, thought Victoria with contemptuous satisfaction, had turned this so perfect coupling into what promised to be a very one-sided effusion of blood. The "blooded" Barbara was a singularly appropriate penalty for the self-important Steven Kensington.

Victoria's anger had diminished rapidly, however, as she watched the once robust Steven cower beneath his fiancée's, newly-ascended aggression. Steven had represented to Victoria all that was golden, all that was vital and promising

186

about a relationship with a man. Now, however, he had become a pale shadow of that representation. Everything that Kolhapur had once guaranteed to her—optimistic expectation, a confident assumption of security—had, in fact, vanished that night in the plum grove. That night she had met Greyson Tyrrel. That night she had realized that her future lay not in the lush fantasy of green opulence, but in some gray, salt-misted world across the sea—a world she'd only imagined. And now she was here. Her future was in the present.

She thought of Greyson, of what Lord Frankland-Foster had inadvertently revealed about the character of her husband. She was having difficulty in reconciling the picture of her tall, scrupulously attentive lover as a vagabond roué. She found it hard to imagine him loving then abandoning all manner of women. And yet . . . an image conjured itself before her. She closed her eyes, but the image flared brighter. Laughing sea-glass blue eyes flicked roguishly over her. Strong white teeth glinted against the bronzed planes of an arrogant smile. A tousle of russet curls fell boyishly over a forehead beneath a cocked tricorn. Oh yes, she thought resolutely, Greyson Tyrrel was capable of honey-tongued persuasion. For all his conscientious captaining of the *Spectre,* he was no doubt a rogue where women were concerned. Had he not nearly taken her—a stranger to him—that night in Kolhapur? Had he not made the assumption that she would receive his attentions passively, perhaps even thankfully? And, to an extent, she had received his attentions, if not passively then at least enthusiastically. She had opened herself to a complete stranger. If she, not knowing him, had been willing to accommodate his passion, had responded with a passion of her own, imagine what he was capable of given the opportunity of seduction.

Seduction! The word jolted her. She stood, knocking the little rocker into a convulsion of jerking, back and forth spasms. Had he seduced her? The possibility was not unthinkable. A man like Greyson—virile, hungry, powerful in his passions—might very well have devised a way in which to force her willingness. He might have planned to heighten her sensitivities to him. He might have purposely left no choice to her but to accept that hastily contrived shipboard marriage. And he might have done it all for one purpose only. He might have done it all to satisfy his towering lust. How did a man like Greyson Tyrrel manage to abstain for months at sea from the satisfaction of his appetites, after all? He probably did not abstain—that was the answer. He probably seduced a woman on every voyage. And now he was back in Boston where, undoubtedly, he had women thrusting themselves at him, falling over themselves to accommodate him.

The door swung open. Victoria turned abruptly, stunning the several servants who stepped inside with her challenging glare. Dory swaggered into the room.

"We brought your tub and water, your ladyship," she said mildly. She directed the other servants and watched as the noblewoman attempted to compose herself.

"From now on," Victoria said curtly, "you will knock before you enter this room." She took a calming breath. She had not intended such harshness toward the girl.

Dory merely smiled narrowly. "I shall remember that," she said. Once the other servants had left the room, Victoria allowed the girl to undress her and ready her bath. She stepped into the blessedly hot water and languished in its scented depths for some moments.

"I have not had a bath in months," she breathed. The girl, Dory, began to soap her hair. For all her insolence, she was discerned by Victoria to be a most accomplished lady's maid. Once Victoria was out of the tub and had been patted dry and wrapped in a thick dressing gown, Dory began brushing at the wet, clinging fleece of Victoria's curls. She sat near the fire on a low, cushioned stool and allowed the girl to work magic on the defiant tresses. She lifted and pinned Victoria's hair into an aureate of opalescent waves and curls, allowing a few wispy ringlets to fall sweetly about her neck and shoulders. Impressed with the girl's talent as a coiffeuse, she allowed her to choose her gown for the evening. As she was dressing her, Victoria wondered aloud about Dory's private life.

The girl merely shrugged. "I only get Tuesdays off," she said.

"Do you have a beau?" Victoria asked, hoping to diffuse her former harshness.

Dory smiled slyly. "I have one," she answered, but said no more.

"I bet he is the handsomest of lads," Victoria urged. Dory smiled enigmatically. "What is his name?" asked Victoria. The girl shrugged a saucy shoulder. She was not about to relate anything of her private life. Victoria wondered if this girl was acquainted with Greyson Tyrrel—she must know something of him, he being so apparently well-known about town. She drew a hesitant breath and questioned Dory on the subject. Dory sighed.

"Captain Tyrrel . . . " she repeated the name almost dreamily. "Now, he's a bloody stallion if ever there was one. There's not a lady in Boston who wouldn't lift her petticoat to that proud swain—who, in truth, has *not* lifted her petticoat in salute of him," she added with a bawdy flip of her skirt. She paused at Victoria's lack of response. "Pardon me, your ladyship," she said hiding a distinctly impertinent smile.

" 'Tis all right, Dory," said Victoria. She meant to keep the bitterness out of her tone, but it crept to the surface, and the girl lifted a questioning brow.

"Do you know him?" she queried.

"Oh, I know him," Victoria answered resentfully.

"Well, it doesn't surprise me any." She laughed.

Victoria wanted to correct any false impressions the girl's sly attitude suggested. "Greyson and I—" she said abruptly and then halted. It suddenly occurred to her that to mention their marriage might open her to a battery of ridicule. "Captain Tyrrel is my . . . captain . . . " she finished lamely.

"You came over on the *Spectre of the Bay*," the girl responded.

"Yes," Victoria answered.

"*Spectre*'s a fine ship—one of Boston Town's finest," Dory said conversationally. "Thirty-ton, eighteen guns, fifteen knots sailing to windward. She's as proud and lean a vessel as any we have."

"You know a great deal about the *Spectre*," Victoria said.

"Everyone in this town knows about ships, my lady. Ships

189

is all we've got. 'Tis our life's blood, those mighty vessels."
She narrowed her perusal and concentrated fiercely on the
fastenings of Victoria's gown. "Our captains are the finest
anywhere," she added. "But none so fine as our glorious
Tyrrel." She spun Victoria around and surveyed her work.
"Will you take the fichu, my lady?" she asked. Victoria's
head swirled with questions of her own. *What about Greyson's private life?* she wanted to demand. What do you
know about that proud "stallion"? Instead, she merely nodded. The girl draped the lacy length of netting over Victoria's shoulders and tucked it into the bosom of her gown.
"Will that be all?" she asked. Again, Victoria nodded. Dory
dipped a quick curtsy and left the room.

In many ways the conversation with the maid had been
enlightening and confounding. Victoria had learned that
Lord Frankland-Foster's evaluation of Greyson was not one
based merely on his own disapproval of the captain's political views. He was speaking from a well-grounded and probably widely-held knowledge of Greyson's reputation.
Victoria's cheeks flared with embarrassment. How could
she have allowed herself to be taken in by such a man? And
now she must live among these people, in the glare of their
knowledge of Greyson's ribald and ungentlemanly attitude
toward women. Victoria would be nothing but another of
his conquests.

He was probably already trying to figure out how to free
himself from the messy entanglement of their marriage. She
would make it clear to him that he was under no obligation
to her. He was free to live his own life . . . and she, free to
live hers.

Her lantern clock told her that it was after eight. She
stepped from her room and traversed the long hallway down
to the second-floor landing. The great staircase loomed
down into the darkened entry hall. No one was about. From
a room below, she heard voices. She began her descent
slowly, dreading to face her husband, knowing that once
again the future she had envisioned was not to be. That she
loved him, would sadly always love him, she thought with
aching resolve, was very much beside the point. Victoria
must harden her heart against that soul-weakening emo-

tion. To want what she could not have was unproductive, and so she would once again make herself a fortress of not wanting. She would gird herself against Greyson's charms, disallow his powerful appeal to tempt its way into her senses. She would make a great show of gaiety this night, she decided. Greyson Tyrrel was in her territory now. The sodden decks of a seagoing vessel might prove a fertile hunting ground for him, at least where she was concerned, but the drawing room of an elegant home would present an obstacle for which even the "glorious Tyrrel" was no match. Let the scoundrel attempt a seduction here in the house of Lord Neville Frankland-Foster. He would discover resources in Victoria Quayle that his powerful seas and equally powerful abilities of seduction had managed to submerge.

Victoria stopped before a tall mirror in the shadowed hallway. She surveyed herself critically. Her hair glowed luminescent, its opaline curls arranged in an enchanting halo around the perfect oval of her face. Her eyes were shaded with just a touch of kohl and her natural ivory-gold glow was augmented by the palest flush of rouge. Her gown of crystalline aqua satin dipped to a deep rounded neckline. The puffed, elbow-length sleeves dripped pristine point lace — the same lace which also made up the fichu. In a hasty moment of defiance, she tore off the little accoutrement and allowed the ripeness of her bosom to show, lustrously white above the neckline of the gown. Let Greyson Tyrrel see what he had so casually tossed away, she thought as she threw down the airy froth of lace. Let him see, and let him damn himself for his carelessness in love. She ran her tongue over the soft, pink bow of her lips, giving herself one more critical perusal, and turned from the glass to meet her challenge.

To her astonishment, she charged as she turned straight into the vested and waistcoated chest of Greyson Tyrrel. Her eyes shot up to his laughing blue ones. Her fingers flew up to cover her bumped and throbbing nose. Tears of mortification and pain came to her eyes.

"You detestable oaf," she railed. "Haven't you learned to make your presence known?"

Greyson had a difficult time hiding his amusement. "I am so very sorry, my lady," he apologized.

Victoria noting the twitch at one corner of his lips and the devilish glint in his eyes decided that he was not sorry at all. The rogue was, in fact, laughing at her. The clearing of his throat several times did nothing to conceal the fact that he was nearly doubling over with mirth. Embarrassment became rage as her tear-glazed eyes widened with the discovery.

"Have you no shame, Greyson Tyrrel?" she demanded. Greyson's humor was immediately quelled as he noted with a sudden horror the rivulets of blood that were tracking their way down Victoria's upraised hand.

"My God, girl," he ejaculated. "I've bloodied your nose." He grabbed her shoulders in one strong arm, arching her back. With his other hand he drew out his handkerchief and, wrestling her hand away from her nose, shoved the cloth against it. Pushing her down into a prone position on the floor, he bent over her, holding her shoulders aloft while keeping her head back and angled downward. Victoria's muffled shrieks at the rough treatment brought the people scrambling from the room off the hallway. They stared in amazement at the incredible scene—Victoria struggling and protesting wildly beneath the unrelenting ministrations of her captor.

"What in the bloody hell is going on here," thundered Lord Frankland-Foster. "What are you doing to the girl?"

Gasping against Victoria's frenzied struggle, Greyson dared not look up. "Get water," he commanded. "Bloody nose!"

"Oh, my God," Vivien cried. "Dory! Dory!" she shouted as she charged down the hallway. "Get water!"

"Dammit to hell," Greyson exploded as Victoria wriggled desperately.

Vivien reappeared. She knelt beside the fallen Victoria and attempted to soothe her. At last Dory appeared carrying a pot of sloshing water. Applying wet cloths to Victoria's nose, Vivien managed to reassure her that she was not being violently assaulted, but only helped. "Keep her shoulders up, Greyson," she scolded. Then to Victoria she said gently, " 'Tis all right, darling. Calm yourself."

When finally the bleeding abated, Victoria was allowed to

lie flat for a while. A much chastened Greyson Tyrrel leaned solicitously over her. "I am so sorry, Victoria," he groaned remorsefully as he wiped away the blood that had dried on her cheeks and chin. "Will you ever forgive me?"

Victoria merely scowled at him and maintained an unrelenting silence.

Vivien raised herself with the assistance of the men and lifted a fallen tress of her flame-colored hair. "Well, the crisis seems to be over," she said on a breath. "There will be time enough for forgiveness later, Captain. In the meantime, Victoria, you ought to meet our other dinner guest." A young soldier stepped forward and leaned down to be introduced. "This is Colonel Jared Everett," Vivien said brightly. "May I present Victoria Quayle, Lady Darby." Victoria lifted her hand, and the gentleman took it reverently.

"How do you do, Lady Darby," he said quietly. " 'Tis a pleasure indeed to meet you." His smile was warm.

"The pleasure is mine, Colonel Everett," said Victoria politely.

Neville Frankland-Foster stepped forward and leaned over, glowering into the scene. "I want an explanation of this, young woman," he humphed. "And it had better be a good one. Every time I enter a room, I find you lying about on the floor." He straightened massaging at his back. Casting a dour glance at Vivien he said, "I am deeply sorry for this, Jared."

"Not at all, sir," said the man. He eyed Vivien and then Greyson and a touch of amusement lilted across his handsome countenance. "Let us go back into the parlor and have ourselves a brandy." He led the older man away.

Vivien sighed relief and directed Dory back to the kitchen with the pot of water. Once the girl was gone, the three of them alone together in the hallway, she glanced toward Greyson and smiled. "Let us help Victoria into the other room," she said softly. "I think we could all do with a brandy."

Dinner that evening, compared to its unlikely prelude, was a mild affair. The meal proceeded pleasantly enough with Vivien, Jared and Victoria exchanging quips and banter while Neville grumped about the lack of decorum shown

193

by young people during these ungracious times. While Victoria was not in the least impressed by Lord Frankland-Foster's diatribe, she was deeply satisfied at Greyson's guilty solicitude and, more importantly, by his apparent jealousy of the gracious young colonel. That gentleman spoke easily, laughed quietly and complimented the women shyly. Greyson, on the other hand, after several glasses of wine, was comparatively loud, immodestly boastful and, finally, before the evening ended, proceeded to get quietly drunk while regarding Victoria through hooded lids from a dark corner of the room. Victoria, noting this, decided that she had made the right decision about their relationship. Let Greyson have his triumphs; she would not spend the rest of her life clinging to an infatuation that was surely beneath the prospects of a well-bred English lady.

At shortly after eleven o'clock, Victoria excused herself, claiming extreme fatigue. In her bedroom, she exulted in a flush of triumph. Her first day in America had surely been a success. She slipped into her nightclothes and nestled comfortably beneath her cozy bed coverings. If there were any small doubts lingering, she would think about them at another time. For now, she would rest in the assurance that she had made the right decision to live apart from Greyson. That was apparently what his lifestyle demanded and what she must do to preserve her dignity. She fell, in a short time, into an exhausted slumber.

The crack of the low fire roused her briefly. She snuggled more deeply into her roseate sleep. Another sound . . . another brief awakening. The waves whispered against the solid oak of the hull. Crystalline breezes embraced her flesh. Her filmy nightdress wafted, in the ocean wind, above her. Its stricturing confinement was carried away on salty breezes. Victoria floated with it on undulating zephyrs of tangent pleasure. She touched the fine, graceful hills and hollows of manly flesh, heard the pure exhalation of manly ardor, inhaled the scent of manly passion. She tasted the pungent flavors of sweet ecstasy. Her heart pounded with the rapturous abandonment of earthly constraint. She was lifted, rejuvenated, luxuriously liberated. Demanding lips grazed her yielding flesh in a hungering frenzy. An agony of need began to build inside her. It pulsated, pitching itself against her heart. She drew herself nearer the source of her need, pushed against the hard, muscular walls that kept her outside the soft, inner core of repletion. She arched urgently to her desire, becoming one with its seductive mastery, its sublime transcendence. She could not think, she could only feel, only demand. Mindlessly, she opened herself like a budded flower to the glory of the ripening sun.

She unclosed her eyes. In an anguish of realization, Victoria knew this was no dream. Greyson was above her, his sea-glass gaze impaling her with his desire. A scream rose in her throat, but his hand, rough and savage, silenced her. Her mind reeled. Her eyes widened in horror, she breathed "no" into the rose-gold darkness, but his lips came down on hers, commanding her to silence. His words against her lips, whispered on hot breaths, became the anchor to which she clung.

"Victoria." The word was soft, enchaining as the steel of his embrace. "Victoria. Victoria. You are mine." Hands, large and warm and gentle for all their roughness roved her bruised consciousness. Lips, moist, caressing, hungry awakened her passion. Greyson was holding her, loving her, carrying her to the seascape of her deepest desire. She loved him. Oh, yes, she loved him. There could be no question of that. There should never have been a question. Once outer garments were stripped away, once accommodations and additions and protections were lifted, there was left only the love. She had known it and knew it now. His name tore from her lips.

"Greyson," she breathed, "I do love you."

He lifted her to the throbbing summit of their mutual need. She yielded, blossoming fully to his mastery. He pierced the soft vortex of her womanhood, thrusting power-fully again and again, filling her with pulsating tongues of liquid fire. Volcanic eruptions shuddered beneath the force of his driving savagery. Victoria was impelled to a pagan hunger. She clutched at him, clawed the hard sinews that held her captive, reeled in a desperate craving for relief. Holding each other in a coursing deluge of throbbing reple-tion, they surged together in the flux and flow of tempestuous rapture. They washed together onto the shores of reality, breathless with the ebbing torrent of their desire. He held himself above her, taking his weight on his muscled arms, watching the lucent mist of her surfeited hunger fill her wondering gaze.

He breathed in, savoring the delicate scent of her passion. He drew her to his chest and rolled to his side, cradling her close. "Never leave me," he groaned. "Oh, God, Victoria, never leave me again." With her drawn to his lean length, the succulent, soft flesh of her breasts and belly flattened against him, he threw his muscular thigh possessively over her hips, imprisoned the delicate flesh of her buttocks in one big hand and held her there until they fell at last into a dreamless slumber.

A pre-dawn glow glossed the small room with a milky light. Greyson's dawning consciousness unnerved him. He did not want to be awake. The delicate air where he now reposed was savory. He breathed in, drawing the silken scent closer. Surely he had died and was in heaven with an angel. The angel sighed. Greyson's eyes flew open. He was not in heaven! Reality struck him like a boulder. He was in bed, in the Frankland-Foster house, in Boston, Massachusetts. He had ravished the household's titled guest. In his amorously drunken state, he had entered her room and taken by force the Honorable Lady Darby. His eyes flew to the window. That was how he had gotten in. He ought to be thrown from that same window, he groaned inwardly. His befuddled mind reeled. That "Lady" was his wife he reminded himself hotly. He had every right to be here. Then, why was he feeling so damned guilty? Was it because he had sensed throughout the evening that Victoria would not want him to enter her room, would not want his attentions? But he had a right, he reminded himself once again. Then, why had he climbed a Maple tree outside her window, stealthily made his way onto a second floor balcony and climbed from there into her bedroom through a window? He tried to recall why he'd thought it was the right thing to do at the time. He glanced over at Victoria, peacefully wriggling against him.

Oh, he knew why he did it. He rested his head on one large hand, and with the other he reached out and stroked the creamy luminescence of her skin. Tiny curls, the color of opals, wreathed her upturned face. What husband would not covet such beauty in his own wife? Her mouth budded at his touch, and her pale brows drew together in a sleeping question. He smoothed at her forehead with his thumb. He could not bear it that he was the cause of her disturbed peace. Her disturbed peace, he chided himself wrathfully. He had indeed disturbed her peace. Like a thief in the night, he had seized her woman's treasure and used it for his own drunken pleasure. But, oh, drunken or not, the pleasure had been his . . . and hers. He smiled down at her innocent slumber and brushed the silken flesh of her shoulder with his lips. This lady, this most womanly of wives, had wanted him as lustily as he had wanted her. He recalled the sublime moment when she had called out his name. In the sweetness of her passion, she had cried out her enduring love. His smile deepened. She was testing a certain independence. For the moment he would endure her coolness toward him; he knew her devotion to him was boundless. He had proof of that devotion. He was glad he'd taken the chance. She could not fight the power of her love for him.

Carefully, he eased himself from the warm bed. He stepped into his breeches and boots. 'Twould not be in either his or Victoria's best interests for him to be found here. Apparently, Lord Frankland-Foster did not know they were married, and Greyson had not had the opportunity to make it known. The man's unrelenting — and, quite frankly, well-founded — hostility toward him would make future encounters difficult. And there had been that damned bloody nose incident. Looking down ruefully at the sleeping Victoria, Greyson shook his head. He must get her out of this house. That was the only hope for the survival of their marriage. He would get her out of here; her confidence in him and their love would overcome all obstacles. Grabbing his shirt and waistcoat, he shrugged them onto his broad shoulders, and after a last, lingering kiss, he made his way from the window and down to the muddy ground outside.

In the pre-dawn quiet of the day, he whistled a saucy old

197

sea chanty as he began his walk back to the *Spectre*. He looked up to the milky sky; it was a snow sky. The air was cold and heavy with promise. Greyson felt the promise of the future. Optimism abounded in him. This little wife of his had always found him more than passing gifted in the art of pleasuring her. She would welcome the remembrance of his invasion of her bedchamber. She would come to him, he reflected confidently. This nonsense about living with the Frankland-Fosters until she realized an understanding of the colonial temper toward England would be washed away in the tide of her passion for him. She would come to him, he mused with satisfaction, and it would not be long before she did.

Chapter Fifteen

Victoria awakened softly, remembering. She smiled in her half-sleep and reached out. She was not entirely surprised when she did not find Greyson next to her. She had a vague recollection of their parting, of adoring caresses, of a feathery kiss. Her eyes still closed, she reached for the pillow where his head had lain. She hugged it to her. It still smelled of him. Breathing deeply, she allowed his manly scent to fill her with remembered tenderness. The rapture of the night encloaked her. She slowly opened her eyes. The morning's dull chill might have been, for Victoria, the invigorating ether of a paradisiacal dawn. She would never again view this little room in the same way. It was her eden — hers and Greyson's.

She stretched luxuriously. Her husband certainly had a way with women, she thought with a contented smile. *A way with women.* She sat up suddenly, hugging her coverlet and his pillow to her breast. Looking down on the soft creases where his burnished curls had rested, she envisioned the laughter in his sea-blue gaze. She flung the pillow away from her. How quickly her resolve had vanished beneath his practiced skill. How adroitly he had mastered her, how dexterously he had bent her to his will. Her husband was a most gifted seducer.

Victoria swung from her bed and grabbed up her dressing gown. Clutching it around her against the chill, she went to the hearth and stirred at the low fire, watching sparks fly up into the chimney. She threw down the poker and moved to the window. She viewed the lusterless yet portentous sky. As she watched, huge snowflakes began to materialize, drifting and pristine against the mist-cold sky. Victoria caught her breath. Her eyes widened. Never in her life had she seen such fragile beauty. Her heart quickened. She might have been a part of a wondrous dream. But the dream was real; the snowflakes, delicate and crystalline, were real. She watched as, very slowly, their numbers thickened, swirling, to cradle the world in a frosty, translucent cloud. Today was a new day, she decided. She would start from here with her first sight of snow — her second day in the American colonies. Ringing for Dory, Victoria began an arduous toilette.

"You have recovered from your ordeal," Vivien said with a smile as Victoria entered the family dining room.

Victoria eyed her hesitantly. "My ordeal?" she asked.

"I mean your bloodied nose," Vivien replied.

"Oh, I have," Victoria answered with what could only be described as rampant relief.

"I am glad to hear it," Vivien said, pouring them each a cup of coffee. A servant set a breakfast of eggs and corncakes before Victoria, and the younger woman ate hungrily, though her mood remained preoccupied. "I am not so sure 'twas a good idea to invite Captain Tyrrel," Vivien mused, leaving a distinct opening for Victoria.

"Why not?" asked the girl. At the arch of Vivien's elegant brow, Victoria managed a small smile. "I am glad you invited him, Vivien," she said. "It gave me the opportunity to confront some questions between us. Naturally," Victoria added, her brows knitting, "some questions are just too complicated for immediate resolution."

"My husband's evaluation of Greyson's character, for instance." At Victoria's reluctant nod, Vivien continued. "The Captain Tyrrels of this world do present a dilemma, do they not." Vivien lit a small cigar — a habit she and many women had rebelliously acquired since James I had decried the use of tobacco, especially for females, calling it "ye foul weed." A gently vaporous curl of smoke drifted on the quiet morning air. "Do you know what attracted me to Neville?" Vivien asked in a seemingly abrupt change of subject. "About him there was the suggestion—just the suggestion, mind you—of danger. Oh, I know you will find that difficult to believe now, but then it was true. All those years ago . . ." Vivien's low, musical voice trailed off. Exquisitely beautiful in the pale morning light, her gray-green eyes held a delicate sadness. "I recall that I was always just a little bit afraid of him." She tilted an eloquent gaze. "I still am, Victoria. And do you know why?" At Victoria's questioning interest, Vivien smiled sorrowfully. "I am afraid of him because I do not know him. Oh, I know what Neville Frankland-Foster represents; I know *what* he is. But I do not know *who* he is. There is a fine distinction between the two. And, sadly, Neville has been satisfied that our relationship should remain on that basis. Men *will* be satisfied, you know." She arched a ginger-colored brow. "They would rather not answer questions. But—" she added pointedly, "that should not stop us from asking." She sipped at her coffee and eyed the younger woman over the rim of her cup. Victoria's smooth brow puckered in a frown of puzzlement. She twined delicate fingertips into the luminescent curls that fell sweetly about her face in innocent tangles.

"Do you think I should ask Greyson about his . . . reputation?" she asked.

Vivien lifted an elegant shoulder. "He may not tell you the truth, but his answer may reveal a great deal about him." She paused. "I only wish that I had been more forceful in my relationship with Neville. Over twenty years have gone by now, Victoria, and for me there is little hope. Neville is perfectly satisfied with what we have. And, in many ways, I am too . . . I suppose. What we have is not perfect and it is not beautiful, but it is predictable. 'Tis only when circumstances change that one realizes just how predictable one's marriage has become.

"You have the opportunity to make something beautiful with Greyson, if you think it worth your while, if you love him. Think about that, Victoria," she said softly. "Think about what you really want. And then think about what you must do to get it." She understood Victoria's bewilderment, saw it in the clouding of her emerald gaze. "I know 'tis confusing," she said warmly. "We must protect ourselves. One day one approach seems logical, and then another possibility arises that seems more logical yet." Vivien chuckled. "When you refuse to settle for the security and comfort of a predictable relationship, you discover what vacillation really is. Men are difficult to deal with," she allowed. "They are like benevolent tyrants. They decide how things *ought* to be. They describe our behavior as pouty or difficult when their decisions differ from our expectations. On his ship, Greyson Tyrrel was king. You had little choice in the matter of his charms. Let us see if his powers of mastery are quite so potent on dry land."

Victoria sighed audibly. "What if they are?" she asked, recalling with resignation the previous night.

Vivien laughed. " 'Twould not surprise me if that is the case," she said knowingly. She waved long aristocratic fingers as Victoria suddenly paled. "But I would not worry overmuch," she said, eyeing the younger woman keenly. "I have a feeling you are every bit the match for that lusty rogue. For all your fragile appearance, your reputation precedes you. Katje and I have corresponded for all the years of your life, and she has written in glowing terms of your spirit and determination. Do not allow a few months on a vessel with a charming but — by all reports — persuasive rake deplete your confidence. For heaven's sake, girl, remember yourself. And remember—" she added, taking Victoria's hand in hers, "remember, above all, what you really want. Ask your questions." She smiled a warning. "Do not be satisfied with the first answer you receive, either," she said gently.

Victoria had just now been reminded of something of which she had not thought in a very long time. She was no puling victim of a doting infatuation. She was not like Greyson's other women. On the contrary, she was a woman with a mission. She was Greyson's wife, and she was not about to abandon her marriage or her husband to the charms of others. Had she not uprooted herself, left the comfort of her childhood home because she would not accept the pale imitation of marriage that Steven Kensington had offered her?

She had forgotten, in the face of Greyson's overpowering virility, that Victoria Quayle was not a woman to be toyed with. She had her own power. She suddenly sat straighter. Yesterday, she had been willing to yield the man she loved, but today she had learned from her exquisitely candid and elegant friend that she must not yield. She must fight for what she wanted. And Greyson Tyrrel was what she wanted.

Vivien sat back comfortably, enjoying the urbane comfort of her "foul weed." She watched Victoria's reaction to her words. This was the Victoria she'd learned, from Katje's letters, to admire. A glitter of determination shown in the girl's piquant smile. Her cheeks pinkened with the love of challenge. Vivien had made no mistake. This young woman was, indeed, a match for the handsome Tyrrel.

A sudden rap on the door startled both women. Dory entered without invitation. "The florist is here, Lady Frankland-Foster," she said with a fearful desperation in her tone, "and he's got himself into a terrible fight with the chandler."

Vivien lifted herself resignedly from the table. "I suppose I shall have to intervene," she said. She and Victoria left their quiet morning communion to repair to the kitchen and arbitrate the noisy confrontation between the florist and the chandler.

Throughout the day, Victoria became entangled in the jubilant and maddening labyrinth of preparations for the Christmas ball. Vivien explained to her that she began the preparations each day by making up a hundred — "at *least* a hundred" — lists. There were lists for the drapers, lists for the silversmith, lists for the pie-seller, the vendor of produce at the public market and the codfish merchant down on Milk Street. The annual Frankland-Foster ball could always be counted upon to breathe new financial life into the town of Boston. The fact that the citizens would go back to their former poverty when the spending was over, did not dim their holiday joy. Prosperity — even temporary prosperity — was always exhilarating.

There were lists of invited — and disinvited — guests to be reappraised as well. Victoria suggested, hesitantly, that she would like to send an invitation to her husband. Vivien laughingly agreed, reminding Victoria that they would both be in grave trouble with Neville once he discovered their base and foul treachery. Lord Frankland-Foster had been less than impressed with Greyson upon their meeting, and had blustered to Vivien that the man's reputation as a rascal was indeed well-founded. A message was, nevertheless, dispatched to the *Spectre of the Bay.* Victoria waited throughout the long, snowy afternoon for his response. Glancing expectantly from windows, inquiring nonchalantly of the servants as to whether callers had come leaving messages or cards, running down hallways and assailing visiting tradesmen as they knocked on one door or another, Victoria spent the day in a frenzy of expectation. By the time the family had gathered for supper, Vivien noted ruefully that the girl was positively despondent. Her spirits had slowly but relentlessly sagged as she realized that Greyson was apparently not intending to respond to the invitation.

Vivien's lips tightened as she sipped at her evening brandy. She could have happily strangled the scapegrace Tyrrel and dumped him without compunction into the Charles. For all Victoria's previous resolve where he was concerned, she had fallen victim because of his careless treatment of her to a prevailing bewilderment about their relationship. Victoria was as confused as ever about their future. It would take some doing to restore her confidence of the morning. *Men,* Vivien reflected derisively, they never ceased to bedevil the female population with their thoughtlessness. Vivien hoped upon further reflection that Greyson's neglect was only thoughtlessness. If he was toying with Victoria, she would, in fact, strangle him.

Victoria excused herself listlessly and made her way to bed before ten o'clock. She was exhausted and defeated as she nestled beneath her covers that night. Greyson did not appear, as she had half expected him to, and it was just as well. When next they met, she had a great deal to say to him, and what she had to say needed distance from her cozy sheets. She was not about to be swayed by the soaring power of his masculine charms. She must guard herself from that potent influence.

Victoria wanted a relationship with her husband that transcended physical gratification. When she was young—before she'd left Kolhapur—the quenching of her adolescent necessities had been all she'd considered. And then Steven Kensington had made his repugnant proposal. In his way, he had taught her how shallow such arrangements were. Victoria wanted a relationship for all time, a relationship that would not fade as her youthful urges faded—as her husband's ravening hunger faded. She wondered, as her eyes yielded to her exhaustion, if Greyson's cravings would ever diminish. She thought not. Involuntarily, a smile crossed her lips. Nevertheless, she thought idly as she drifted into slumber, she must see to it that their union was founded on love not lust.

The next morning Victoria found herself returned once again to the laughter and quickly dissipated quarrels among the artisans in the kitchen of the Frankland-Foster house. The day had dawned sunny and snow-sparkled. Even the usually sullen and insolent Dory seemed carried along on the sprightly tide of gaiety that accompanied the unusually bright morning and the cheery preparations for the ball. It was readily obvious that she appreciated seeing her friends among the tradespeople leaving the house with smiles and pocketsful of shiny coin. With their newly-found affluence these people would be able to feed their families for weeks.

"That one," Dory said to Victoria as they stood together over heaps of unbaked cookie dough, "has a wife, six children, a mother-in-law and a fat dog to feed." She saluted the happy upholsterer as he charged through the kitchen and out the back door. "He shall be a hero in his house tonight," she added laughing. She, too, seemed happy that the household was providing the local families with a much needed respite from their poverty.

"Ribbons!" exclaimed a voice from behind the ever-swinging kitchen door. Vivien burst into the room. "Ribbons!" she repeated frantically. Victoria glanced up, through the flour-hazed air.

"Did you say "ribbons"?" she asked.

"I did," stated the usually placid Vivien. "I forgot to order ribbons."

Victoria wiped her hands on her apron. She and Dory had been busy all morning helping the cook bake and decorate Christmas cookies. She looked down at the list that Vivien was flourishing and to the specific item her elegant hostess was indicating with a fluttering fingertip. "For heaven's sake, Vivien, let me look," she said. She grasped Vivien's wrist gently and took the list from her hand. "Now what is this about ribbons," she inquired soothingly.

"We agreed," Vivien began, attempting to compose herself, "quite emphatically, that the entrance hall should be decorated with red and green ribbons."

Victoria nodded. "That was what we decided. Is there a problem?"

"The only problem is, we have no ribbons!"

"Maybe we could get some," Victoria answered calmly, trying not to get caught up in Vivien's agitation.

"The market might have them," offered Dory helpfully.

"I am sure they have," Victoria responded. "One of us can find the time to run the errand." She glanced around at the chaos of the kitchen. On every surface doughy forms were spread and waiting to be sugared. The cookies that had come out of the tin kitchen were cooling on wooden racks that dotted the tables and cutting blocks.

"I can't go," Dory said sullenly as she began laboriously stirring cranberries into a bread batter. Her cheerfulness extended just so far. "And Clough's got the chaise out for repair."

"I would go myself," wailed Vivien, "but Mr. Kent is coming to inspect every tapestry in the house for repair."

Victoria looked once again over the pale dusting of sugar that coated everything, including the floor, and sighed. "I shall go," she said finally.

"But, Victoria," Vivien protested, "you cannot. You've no idea where you are going and—"

"How difficult could it be to find the market, Vivien?" Victoria said with assurance. She drew off her apron and hung it on a wall hook. Pouring water from a jug into the cast iron sink, she rinsed off her floury hands and dried them. "I have been wanting to see the market hall anyway." She laughed. " 'Twill be an adventure." She fairly pushed Vivien through the swinging door and into the dining room. "The importance of red and green ribbons cannot be overstated," she said. "Let me get into my walking suit," she added as she started up the staircase, "and I shall be on my way."

"The least I can do is help you," called Vivien, following her. The two women made their way up the narrow third floor staircase and into Victoria's room. Victoria went about, with Vivien's assistance, preparing for her adventure.

"I shall enjoy this little jaunt, Vivien," she said. "I've not been out and about since I arrived in Boston."

Vivien gazed out of the window. "It looks very pleasant outside," she observed. "You should have a lovely walk." She pursed her lips. "Are you sure you do not mind going?"

Victoria shook her head firmly. "I am looking forward to it," she answered. She was standing before the glass, arranging her mane of fleecy curls beneath a green bonnet. "I need an adventure, Vivien," she explained. Her last words were said softly but with intensity. "Everything has been so . . . so . . . " she twirled listlessly at an errant wisp that curled onto her cheek. "Everything has been lovely here, but. . ." her voice trailed off.

"Do you like your woolen cloak?" Vivien said into the silence that followed. The garment had been a gift from her to Victoria.

The girl looked down at the sweeping soft folds and brushed at it with her gloved hands. "The color is lovely," she murmured.

"It matches your eyes," Vivien assured her.

Their talk was rambling and unfocused. At last Victoria looked directly into Vivien's warm gaze. "I have no idea what to do about Greyson," she said in a rush. "I love him, but right at this moment I do not like him very much."

Vivien took the girl's face in her hands. "It might help you to know that you are not alone," she said gently. "We women

207

are not so much fools, Victoria, as we are trusting. We believe every man to be basically honest. The assumption of goodness in all men is both our virtue and our curse." She smiled sadly. " 'Tis a basic flaw, I suppose, but one I like in us. It marks the difference between men and women. They look for hidden motives, we assume sincerity. Even knowing that basic truth about us, I firmly believe that Greyson was being merely careless about not accepting your invitation to the ball. I cannot believe that he is being false to you."

"How can I be sure?" Victoria asked.

"I suppose you must ask him." Vivien led her to the door. "But wait until you are ready for such things," she added firmly. "You must pick your own time." She brushed at the pearlescent curls that fringed Victoria's forehead. "Plan your strategy," she instructed gently, "devise your approach, and then pray that destiny cooperates." Both women laughed. Arm in arm they descended the stairs, and with final instructions, Victoria was sent on her way.

Chapter Sixteen

Victoria felt almost cozy as she ambled the three blocks from the house to the Faneuil Market hall. The spun-sugar world of winter encloaked her as snugly as the woolen muffler she'd tucked around her chin and neck. Stepping carefully, looking everywhere, she made her way along the narrow, snowy streets. The day was softly bright. Her cloak brushed against the low bows of fir trees that were festively dressed in their winter greenery and heavy with pine cones. The sky, blue and clear, was dotted with a few powdery puffs of clouds, and the sun glistened brilliantly on the world.

Victoria stopped and watched as a pair of squirrels frolicked on the snow. They chased each other up the branches of trees that hung low and were laden with the white cloak of winter. She laughed and took walnuts—purloined from Vivien's Christmas kitchen—from her reticule and held them out for the skittish creatures. Their furry tails jerked nervously as they approached and snatched the proffered treats, then skittered away leaving tiny tracks in the powdered snow. Victoria glanced up, a smile still curving her lips, as a shadow crossed between herself and the sun. She stiffened as she realized that above her loomed the tall figure of Greyson Tyrrel. She stood hastily and brushed at the sweeping folds of her cloak.

"Hello, love," he said seductively. His tricorn held in his large fist was pressed to his chest as he bowed in his most courtly fashion. He might have been a pattern for chivalry.

"Greyson," she said on a breath. Not ready to see him, not knowing what to say, she attempted to pass by. He stepped easily into her path and then stepped once again, blocking her as she corrected her course. She stopped and looked up into the glacial blue of his eyes. "I am on my way to market," she murmured. "Would you mind allowing me to pass?"

"Mind?" he asked, his voice dripping tranquility. "Of course I mind."

Victoria's gaze darkened. "I am in a great hurry," she said.

"Are you?" he responded silkily. He placed his hat onto his rumpled curls, pushing a burnished tousle down onto his forehead. "I'd hoped we might talk."

Victoria sighed. "I do not know what to say to you Greyson," she replied earnestly.

"You are my wife, love. Surely words do not come so hard between us."

"I am afraid they do," Victoria answered, lowering her eyes. "And I am afraid," she said softly, "that I must sort out my feelings about you before we discuss our future."

"If it is about that damned bloody nose, I am sorry," he said ruefully.

"Oh, for heaven's sake, Greyson—" she began. "That is not the problem."

"What then?" he asked. "Is it because I came into your bedchamber?"

She avoided his scrutiny. "Partly that," she said softly. "And other things. . . ."

His gaze hooded. "When you said you wanted to live apart from me, I did understand. But I will not be denied my husbandly rights." He paused. "If that was your intention, you may forget it, Victoria. If you are uncomfortable meeting in the Frankland-Foster house, in the future, we can meet on the *Spectre*. I warn you, though, if you do not come to me, I shall come to you." He smiled lazily and cupped her chin in his big hand. " 'Twas never my intention that we should not enjoy that very special dividend of the marriage bond; I assume your intentions were the same."

Victoria drew away from his touch. She could not trust herself to be near him, to feel the overpowering influence of his warm presence. She took a few steps away. "You do not understand, Greyson."

He eyed her in puzzlement. "You have accused me of not understanding before, love," he said. "I cannot begin to understand what I do not know about. Won't you explain to me what I do not understand?"

" 'Tis something I have heard . . . about you," she said, looking up into the warm blue gaze.

Greyson laughed. "From that pompous colonel," he suggested.

"You know nothing about Colonel Everett," she retorted.

"I know you took a shine to him," Greyson said, his smile vanishing. "Is this dark 'problem' we have related to him?"

"It is not," Victoria stated.

"You seem defensive on the subject," Greyson said evenly.

"I am not defensive!" she rejoined . . . defensively. Victoria immediately amended her attitude. "This has nothing to do with Colonel Everett," she said, regaining her composure. "This has to do with you, with my feelings about you, with your feelings about me, with the very foundation of our marriage." Her eyes took on a woeful appeal. "It has to do with everything, Greyson, don't you understand?"

"Do you love me?" he asked.

Victoria quickly lifted her regard. "Of course I love you. How could you doubt it?"

"Then, what is the problem?" he asked. His eyes glinted in amusement.

Victoria turned from that roguish self-assurance. "The problem," she stated, "is that I am not the only woman who feels that way about you, Captain Tyrrel." She pushed by him. Her crisp steps were matched by his long stride as he ambled along beside her. To Victoria's consternation, she realized it was his intention to accompany her.

"Captain Tyrrel, is it?" he said amiably.

"Greyson," she sighed, recalling Vivien's admonition, "you are apparently going to press me on this, knowing I am not prepared to discuss it, and so I shall ask you a question. Simply put, my question to you must be, do *you* love *me?*"

"Of course I do," he answered as they walked.

Victoria stopped abruptly and turned to him, setting him off-balance in the powdery snow. "Do you love me, Greyson," she repeated, "not as you love every other woman in the town of Boston, but as a wife?"

"Yes," he said in honest confusion.

Victoria scrutinized him carefully as though she might discern the truth of what he said in his eyes. "Such a declaration might not come so easily to a more sincere gentleman," she intoned. "Think about my question, Captain."

"I do not have to think about your question, Victoria," he said easily. "I love you."

"Would you give up all your former conquests for me?" she asked pointedly.

"Yes," he answered.

"Would you make me the only woman in your life . . . *forever*?"

Greyson rolled back his head in exasperation. "Yes, Victoria. I would give up all my former conquests. I would swim the oceans, climb the mountains, tame the forests of Canada *and* the Ohio Valley. I would fly to the stars on pigeon wings and—"

"There is no need to be condescending, Greyson," she shot back. She spun away from him and began her walk once again. "If you will excuse me, I must go and buy some ribbons."

"Ribbons?" he asked in confusion. This was a most bewildering lady, Greyson reflected as he strode to catch up with her spirited escape.

"Ribbons," she retorted.

"For milady's hair?" he chuckled.

"For the hallway." Victoria stopped once again and rounded on him. "For the hallway, Captain Tyrrel. For the bloody hallway. The Frankland-Fosters are giving a ball," she said, looking straight into his eyes. With each word, her anger grew. "You were sent an invitation to that ball and you—very uncordially—refused to respond to that invitation. I suppose," she added, "that your social calendar is full and that is the reason you have apparently declined."

"Victoria," he said wryly, "it may just be that my social secretary neglected to inform me of the invitation. For some of us, the pursuit of amusement is just not a priority."

"You seemed ready enough to pursue your own amusements the other night, Greyson," she ground out. "Let me tell you something," she rushed on, "there will be some very eligible young men at that ball. And do you know something? I shall bet you that not one of those young men — no matter how irresistible they find me — will make their way into my bedchamber and gratify their disgusting cravings between my sheets." As she turned from him, she felt herself jerked ungently back to face him.

"Disgusting cravings?" he said with a satiric grin. "You did not find my cravings quite so disgusting when you shared them, lady."

Victoria's hand swung back, but before it could connect with Greyson's smug jaw, he grasped her wrist with lightninglike dispatch. The astounding force of the blow and counter blow sent them both skidding and tumbling into the soft snow. As Victoria strained to regain her footing, she found herself restrained by Greyson. His muscled arm capturing her waist, he plumped them both deeper into the pillowed snow. Victoria made an effort to right herself; but Greyson held her fast, and her struggles were to no avail. She was a prisoner. She glared at him icily.

"Let me go, Greyson," she demanded.

Greyson threw back his head, and his laughter only served to enrage her. Her wriggling increased mightily, and they were both sucked farther down into the heavy drift. At last, Greyson rolled atop her, stretching his full lean form above her. Capturing her wrists and pinning them above her head, he surveyed his pugnacious captive.

"My little wife is a feisty wench," he observed drily.

"Dammit, Greyson," she spat, "I shall scream rape if you continue to restrain me!"

Greyson merely gazed down at her. " 'Tis a bit late for such an accusation," he murmured, his mirth apparent in the sparkle of his sea-glass regard. A moment of knowing silence passed between them. "Now what is all this about, love," he said huskily.

Victoria watched him warily. Her breasts heaved with her ragged breath. She felt that terrible glowing warmth swelling between them. In this circumstance, they could discuss nothing intelligently, she decided.

"Let me go, Greyson," she clenched and once again resumed her exertions.

"Wait," he said almost gently, though he continued to restrain her. "Listen to me for one moment, Victoria." She felt her resolve turn to water at his seductive tone.

"What is it," she snapped, attempting to ignore the effect on her of his overpowering masculinity.

He smiled knowingly. "We obviously have some unfinished business between us," he purred. He increased the tension of his grasp on her wrists only long enough to restrain her sudden struggle. "You are angry about something," he said solicitously. "Can we not talk about it?"

"I shall talk with you," she replied coldly, battling the response of her treacherous body, "but I insist we be on neutral ground."

He laughed low in his throat. "The lady is requesting a truce," he said. "And a truce she shall have." He rose and offered his assistance to Victoria. Clinging to his hand, she climbed from the snow bank and back onto the hardened surface of the narrow street. She brushed out her skirts, snapping them smartly as Greyson continued. " 'Tis a lovely day, Victoria. We are going for a sleigh ride." He grabbed at her hand and started off, but she held herself firmly back.

"Just a minute, Greyson," she said coolly. She must be very careful now. She quickly lowered her gaze. That shock of sunset-colored curls falling over his forehead, those laughing aqua eyes framed by curling, russet lashes, that boyishly etched mouth might cause her to weaken, might call up that instinct in her that never failed to diffuse rational thought. She must not, under any circumstance, allow her guard to fall. She straightened her heavy bonnet.

"I shall go with you, Greyson," she said stiffly, "but I must warn you that if you truly intend to discuss our problems, I shall not be party to any . . . hanky-panky." She startled herself and Greyson with the use of Lord Frankland-Foster's prosaic phrase. Victoria shifted uncomfortably and then girded herself against the amusement she saw in his eyes. "When one is truly interested in building an honest relationship, one does not allow emotionalism to interfere with one's thinking." Her voice remained even, as though she were discussing a point of semantics with a particularly dense child. She did not notice the darkening of Greyson's countenance. "One expects the person one marries to respect one, to offer kindness and support and understanding. One must choose a person who will not take advantage of one's vulnerabilities." The smile vanished from Greyson's lips. His gaze iced over. "One should be able to expect that from whomever one marries. And I shall expect that from you today."

At once Greyson advanced on her. Before she could follow her instinct to recoil, she felt her shoulders taken in an unrelenting grip. She felt herself arched and nearly lifted from her feet as he snapped her to his hard chest.

"Does 'one' ignore an honest appeal?" he growled. His eyes had become a startling shade of slate. "I was not aware, Mrs. Tyrrel, or Lady Darby, or whatever the hell you are calling yourself these days, that I have been taking advantage of your 'vulnerabilities.' Is it too much to ask that a husband be allowed to talk to his wife? Is it too much to ask that he be allowed to share her bed? Goddammit, woman, I love you. Whatever the problems between us, we can solve them. We do not need all this bloody banter." He shook her soundly.

"Is brute force your only response to this serious matter, Greyson?" she clenched derisively as she pushed against him.

"Brute force!" he thundered. "Would you like to see brute force? I will show you *brute force,* lady." Without preamble his lips came down on hers. She twisted, attempting to free herself from his savage assault, but his arms were like steel bands constraining her. She struggled wildly as he pressed her, molding her into his hard length. She felt her heartbeat quicken, pounding fiercely beneath her flattened breasts. The bright world darkened as his tongue demanded and gained entrance between her clenched teeth. The abyss of his mastery threatened to overtake her. She squirmed,

215

moaning beneath the bruising demand of Greyson's power. At last he pulled away and, with cold dispatch, released her. "That, Mrs. Tyrrel, is brute force," he grated. "Does 'one' distinguish the difference, or does 'one' desire another illustration?"

Her knees weakened, Victoria backed from him through the impediment of the heavy snow. "One—I . . . understand the difference," she gasped.

"Good," he growled, "then let us have no more discussion of this force business. Whatever problems you imagine us to have will be discussed rationally, between two rational people." He paused, regaining his control. He saw the fear and bewilderment in her wide gaze. He had known many women—this was, he had ascertained, one of their "problems"—and he had dealt with many moods, but none of those had affected him quite so powerfully. This little green-eyed, sugar-haired sprite was making him feel the most unaccomplished of brutes. He longed to take her in his arms and comfort her. "Victoria," he said huskily, " 'twas not my intention to frighten you. I do not want to brutalize you. I only want to love you."

"You have done a fine job of that today, Greyson," she shot back, all fear dissipated. Greyson smiled, but her next words sobered him. "I shall accept a truce for this day. And we shall have a rational discussion. But you must promise not to touch me." His brows lifted. She cut off any rejoinder. "You must *promise* not to touch me, Greyson, or I shall not go on your sleigh ride or anywhere else with you." How easily the command had slipped from her lips. She'd said the words almost carelessly, as though she had not experienced every moment of their lovemaking again and again in her mind as well as in her heart; as though she did not tremble with longing for his muscled arms to take her in his commanding embrace even as she spoke. She hoped he would comply, for she knew they could never accomplish anything if he did not. Noting with some consternation the mischief in his gaze, she decided that he might be taking her admonition lightly. So be it, she reflected. She would simply have to discourage him. Nevermind that he was irritatingly overconfident of his masculine charms, she must force herself to be strong. She lifted her chin. "Do we have an agreement?"

Greyson nodded dutifully. "We have," he said softly. He ventured another small smile. "Shall we be on our way?" Victoria nodded curtly.

Taking her arm firmly in his large hand, he led her down toward the river. Victoria did not even think to protest as he dragged her toward a waiting sleigh. Realizing, however, that he was in fact touching her just after he had vowed not to, he lifted his hands in a gesture of submission. "Forgive me, love," he said, his eyes sparkling with devilment. " 'Twill not happen again." Victoria eyed him warily.

"What can I do for y', Captain," said a little man who stood by with his hat squashed deferentially in his grimy hands.

"You can fire up those nags of yours, Bouchard," replied Greyson. "I am taking the lady for a ride."

The driver chortled and scrambled into the seat. "Where we goin', Captain?" he asked with overweening servility.

" 'We' are not going anywhere, Bouchard," Greyson replied laughing. He tossed a coin to the cramp-shouldered menial and indicated with a jerk of his thumb that the owner of the sleigh was to vanish. The scrawny chap nodded, flashing a toothless grin, and scuttled down to the ground. "I think you would sell your mother for a coin," Greyson chuckled at the driver as he tossed another coin. The man nodded, chortling as he caught the silver.

"That I would, Captain," he said as he ambled off, testing the validity of the money with his toughened gums.

Greyson turned back to Victoria. "After you, my lady," he said lightly, indicating the sleigh, but making no move to assist her. Victoria looked quickly up at the height of the sleigh and then just as quickly back at Greyson. Her gaze narrowed. So that was his game, she determined. Well, she would play it. She grasped on to the fittings and attempted to heave herself up. Failing, she stepped back and made another try. She shot a withering glare at her husband, daring him to laugh. He managed not to.

217

"Will you help me," she said flatly.

He arched a russet brow. "Are you sure?" he asked solemnly.

"Yes," she hissed.

With what may have seemed an almost mocking gravity, Greyson bent to his task. "As long as you insist," he sighed.

"Oh, really, Greyson," Victoria said in exasperation as she settled into her seat and watched him bound with easy grace into his. He offered her a roguish smile as he slapped the reigns. The sleigh lurched to a start, bells jangling joyously in the crisp air.

"May I ask where we are going?" Victoria inquired after some moments.

"We are going on a holiday errand, Mrs. Tyrrel," he said cheerfully. He glanced over at her. "If I recall, there was a matter of ribbons to be settled." He laughed. "I think red and green would be most appropriate, don't you?"

Victoria kept her gaze on the iced-over river Charles. "It may not seem important to you, Greyson—"

"On the contrary," he interrupted jovially, "one cannot overstate the importance of red and green ribbons at this time of year." His words echoed her own earlier. She looked at him in surprise, fully expecting to find mockery in his eyes, but she found only a sincere expression of exhilaration in his smile. "You will naturally be wanting *silk* ribbons," he added with a wink. Victoria narrowed her gaze. Greyson's smile deepened. "I would not think of attending a Christmas ball if I could not be assured the presence of silk ribbons."

"You will be attending, then," Victoria said archly.

"Of course." Greyson laughed. "We have quite a ride ahead of us, love," he said gently. "Enjoy it."

"If we are going to be gone a long time, Greyson, I really should stop and tell Vivien."

Greyson laughed. "Ever the gently bred lady of manners," he said and swung the horses down the next street. Once they had told a startled Vivien and an obviously envious Dory that they would be gone for the day, they once again took their seats in the sleigh. Victoria settled into the nest of furs that surrounded her and decided that she might as well take Greyson's advice and try to enjoy the ride. The sweet frosty air breezed by them as they rode. Salty smells blew up from the Charles. Beneath them, the sleigh runners made a soft shushing sound that mingled with the muffled clop of the horses' hooves in the packed snow. As they left the city and travelled onto the narrow neck of land that separated the town from the mainland, houses and shops disappeared, and the world was silent and serenely snowbound. The snow-laden branches of fur trees formed a wintery canopy over the narrow road. The sun sparkled on the pillowy softness, and the sleigh bells jingled merrily in the quiet depth of the little town Greyson identified as Cambridge. The horses slowed as Greyson pointed out the two, copper-vaulted brick buildings that made up the Harvard College campus.

"That building to the north," Greyson said, drawing in the reigns, "is called Harvard Hall." He leaned toward Victoria, sliding his arm over the top of her seat. "I shall tell you a little story about that building," he said, chuckling, "for I know you like stories. That building is really the second Harvard Hall." His eyes twinkled with merriment. "In '64 a fire broke out and destroyed Harvard Hall and all its contents, including the John Harvard book collection given to the College in 1638. On the night of the blaze," he continued, "a student removed one of the books from that collection, entitled *CHRISTIAN WARFARE AGAINST THE DEVIL, WORLD AND FLESH,* by John Downame. Now, the next day, when the student realized that he possessed the only remaining book of the collection, he went to President Holyoke and presented the book to him. The president thanked him graciously, took the book, then expelled the lad for taking the book without permission."

Victoria found the story charming, and the couple laughed together in joyous appreciation of it. As she looked up into his clear blue eyes, she found there a sweet gratitude for their momentary closeness. His hand slid to her shoulder, but he hastily drew it away. Victoria wondered as he took the reigns once more if her prerequisite for the day's ride had not been a mistake. She nestled more snugly into the furs and sighed as the sleigh jogged merrily on. After a time, they approached a small clapboard cottage, and the horses slowed.

"Where are we?" Victoria asked quietly for she did not wish to intrude on the peaceful scene.

Greyson smiled and pointed up to a wooden sign that swung cheerily on a hinge above the door. "Misty Molly's," the sign proclaimed. "Ribbons," Greyson said, stepping down onto the packed snow and assisting Victoria from the high seat. The couple moved to the little front door and pushed it open. The scent of woodsmoke and spices filled Victoria's senses. Inside, Greyson seated her at one of several small tables that dotted the earthen floor.

"What a charming place," Victoria said, smiling. Her attention was taken by a fireplace that reached to the low, raftered ceiling and dominated one end of the room. Within its huge depths, a colorful fire purled and snapped. Victoria noted that the room was pleasantly overheated, and she unwrapped herself from her cloak and muffler and removed her hat. Within moments, a plumply attractive woman entered from an inside door.

"Ahoy, Captain Tyrrel," she called brightly. "How are you, you old seahorse?"

Greyson moved to the woman and took her in a bearlike embrace. "I am fine, Moll," he said. "How about yourself?" His tone was distinctly affectionate. Victoria eyed them both. Moll was a handsome woman—if somewhat flaunting in her appearance—tall, big-boned and voluptuously curved. She might be a bit too old to inspire a romantic interest in Greyson, Victoria reflected with a vague disdain. Still . . . one never knew about such things where Greyson Tyrrel was concerned. Victoria managed a sweet smile as the woman advanced.

"How do you do?" she offered politely.

"I'm fine, mistress," Moll answered. She placed a hand on her well-rounded hip. "Havin' a day out with the captain, I see," she said with only a hint of derision.

"I am enjoying a day out with my husband," Victoria

responded still sweetly.

"Husband, is it?" The woman swung Greyson an arch-browed look.

He smiled weakly. "Meet Victoria Tyrrel, Moll," he said.

Molly leaned back, crossing her arms over her heavy breast. "Now what did you go and do that for, Grey?" she asked.

Greyson cleared his throat. "Well, I . . . we . . . " He glanced at Victoria who offered no assistance. Instead, she folded her arms as well and regarded him with placid interest. She, too, waited for his answer.

Molly poked at him with an elbow and laughed. "There's a lot of hearts gonna be broken over this bit of news," she said bawdily. She glanced at Victoria. "I hope you got yourself a good stout ball and chain, my girl. Believe me," she said, indicating Greyson with a jerk of her mobcapped head, "you'll be needin' it." She laughed once more as she swung away from them. "I'll get you some dinner." Glancing once more over her shoulder, she offered a knowing wink and left the room.

Greyson seated himself uncomfortably and made an awkward attempt at conversation. Victoria merely glared. When at last she spoke, her tone was clenched and disparaging.

"Well, 'Grey,' " she said, "is this what I can expect each time we appear in public together?"

Greyson splayed his large hands. "I do not know why she said that, love," he answered. " 'Tis not as if Moll and I were ever *that* close."

"How close do you consider close, Greyson," she railed in a whisper. Her restraint had been strained to the snap. Greyson merely shrugged and made a feeble attempt to jolly her out of her wrath. But his countenance soon sobered. "Dammit, Greyson, this is exactly what I was speaking of before. According to my sources, you are a very well-known Lothario in these parts. How do I know your powers of indifferent seduction do not extend to me?" It was out before Victoria had an opportunity to couch her accusation. She regarded him in resignation. "I wanted to be much more circumspect on this subject, Greyson," she said softly, "but I

221

suppose 'tis best that my feelings are out in the open." She paused briefly, wondering if he would respond. He did not. She relinquished her desire for diplomacy and went on. "I know you love me, in your way, Greyson, but I am seeking something that means a great deal to me. I left Kolhapur all those months ago because I had lost something very important to me. I lost the ability to trust. Vivien reminded me today that that ability is one of a woman's greatest virtues. And," she said, lowering her gaze, "it is also one of our greatest burdens. Nevertheless, I want to be able to trust again. I want to trust you."

Greyson regarded her thoughtfully. There was no hint of devilment in his voice as he finally spoke. "Let me tell you something about me, Victoria," he said softly. "I am what you say I am. More accurately, I was that. When we met, I kept myself in check where you were concerned because I realized that with you I was very different than I'd been before. I did not understand it myself until recently. I wanted you, 'tis true." He reached out and cupped her chin in his large hand. He offered her a lop-sided smile of self-deprecation. "Oh, love, I wanted you. I still want you, every moment of every day. Beyond that, though, with you I knew a fullness that I never dreamed was possible. You are everything to me. You," he said seriously, "are everything I need or want in this world. If every other thing in my life vanished tomorrow, I would go on happily if only I could have you by my side. If that is not love, Victoria, then you tell me what is." Before she could respond, he rose and moved around the table to her side. Lifting her from her chair, he gazed into the firelit verdancy of her eyes. He took her in a tender embrace. "Oh, love," he breathed, "please do trust me. I shall never give you reason not to."

Victoria felt herself enchanted by the warmth of his embrace, by the sweetness of his words. She melted into the encloaking security of his arms. Never would she doubt him. She lifted her gaze and saw the sincerity, the love in his azure eyes. The firelight glinted in the space that separated them and then vanished as the space was closed. They kissed long and rapturously, knowing that what was between them would last forever.

A gusty laugh interrupted them as Molly erupted into the room. "Hope you folks are hungry," she stated, offering a bawdy wink. She set on the table a bowl of steaming fish stew for each. "Start with that," she said. "I'll be back." Greyson and Victoria followed her with their gazes as she left the room and smiled softly.

"Are you . . . hungry, madam?" he asked.

"Oh, yes," Victoria answered. Laughing together, they took their seats at the round wooden table. They enjoyed the stew, and then Moll returned with more food.

" 'Twas a parlous young codfish gave up his life for that dainty bit of provender," Greyson complimented her.

The woman gave him an appreciative poke as she set before them a succulent concoction of beef, beets, potatoes and onions which she pridefully identified as red-flannel hash. Its accompaniment was a delicate-tasting casserole of white peas, corn and beans, called succotash. Victoria had never enjoyed such exotic fare, and she complimented Moll extravagantly over that and over the Indian pudding glazed with hard sauce that the woman served as dessert. Each mouth-watering flavor was a treat to be savored, she told the woman. When the meal had ended, Moll set before them mugs of hot spiced cider and took a mug herself. She had engaged her pot boy to help her serve, and the lad at last sat down at a rickety piano near the front door and began to play. He obviously favored this employment over the other, for while his serving skills were, at best, awkward and apologetic, his playing had the true authority of the truly talented. His music was lilting, extravagantly touching and masterfully played.

"How old are you?" Victoria asked the boy when he paused between melodies.

"Fifteen, mistress," the lad said shyly.

"Never had a lesson in his life," stated Moll with pride. "His parents think music is sinful," she added with an arch of a penciled brow. "Now to me," she philosophised, " 'tis the greater sin to deprive such talent from bein' tended to. If ever a boy deserved music lessons . . . " She shook her head gravely.

"He has a rare gift," Victoria agreed. "Why are his parents so reluctant to nurture it?"

"Puritan," said Moll, as if there was no need to explain any further. "You should have heard his old man when I got me that piano. He threatened to force the lad to quit his job here, but I vowed I'd not let the boy play it." She grinned impishly. "I guess I got a sin on my soul," she said. "But what the hell, I ain't one of the 'saved' anyway, so what's the difference." She chuckled resignedly and placed her elbows contentedly on the table.

The three adults listened to the boy in awed rapture as he continued to play far into the afternoon. The crackling fire danced merrily and was built up each time it began to waver. The raftered room was alight with its golden glow and the sweetly soft music. Victoria would have been content to stay there forever. As the sky outside the small windows darkened, Molly nudged Greyson knowingly.

"You want your little wife to have a look at my private stock?" she asked with uncharacteristic softness.

Greyson nodded and smiled. "You are a generous piece of work, old girl," he told her as he affectionately patted her ample rump as she rose.

Molly jerked a thumb in his direction and offered Victoria a wink. "Ain't he the rascal, though?" She laughed. She placed a kiss on his cheek. "Time was I'd of tamed this rakehell," she assured them both.

"Your old fellow, James, would have stripped my hide had I made improper advances," Greyson said, his smile deepening. As Molly swung from the room, Greyson stopped her with a thought. "We need some holiday ribbons Moll, if you'd be so generous."

"You got them, Grey," she said as she exited.

Victoria and Greyson moved to the side of the old wooden piano and stood by the boy as he continued to play. His tunes had taken on a melancholy shading as the day wore on. The tinkle of the keys now had a lingering coloration. Victoria hummed the simple tune the boy was playing, and seeing her enjoyment, he drew out the song. Greyson's sin-

FREE

BOOK CERTIFICATE

ZEBRA HOME SUBSCRIPTION SERVICE, INC.

YES! Please start my subscription to Zebra Historical Romances and send me my free Zebra Novel along with my first month's Romances. I understand that I may preview these four new Zebra Historical Romances Free for 10 days. If I'm not satisfied with them I may return the four books within 10 days and owe nothing. Otherwise I will pay just $3.50 each; a total of $14.00 (a $15.80 value—I save $1.80). Then each month I will receive the 4 newest titles as soon as they come off the press for the same 10 day Free preview and low price. I may return any shipment and I may cancel this arrangement at any time. There is no minimum number of books to buy and there are no shipping, handling or postage charges. Regardless of what I do, the **FREE** book is mine to keep.

Name _____
(Please Print)

Address _____ Apt. # _____

City _____ State _____ Zip _____

Telephone ( ) _____

Signature _____
(if under 18, parent or guardian must sign)

Terms and offer subject to change without notice.

MAIL IN THE COUPON
BELOW TODAY

GET FREE GIFT

To get your Free your **ZEBRA HISTORICAL ROMANCE** fill out the coupon below and send it in today. As soon as we receive the coupon, we'll send your first month's books to preview Free for 10 days along with your **FREE NOVEL**.

cere baritone joined her, and they smiled together as the melody reached a delicately chorded close.

Victoria smiled down at the young pianist. "You are a very talented young man," she murmured.

The boy nodded a thank you and began to play again. His long agile fingers caressed the keyboard with a tenderness that most people reserved for animate objects. But then, to this boy, thought Victoria admiringly, the instrument had a life of its own. He coaxed it and plied it with loving attention. For his efforts, the old instrument offered its most appealing harmonies and tones, as though its rough exterior needed only loving attention to reveal its deeper grandeur.

Victoria lay her head against Greyson's wide shoulder as the drifting melody carried her on a golden mist to some lyrical liminal place and time. She forgot the feel of her feet on the earthen floor and was lifted, in Greyson's arms, away from mundane realities and to a world that swayed gently to gentle rhythms. They lingered there in delicate harmony. They applauded the boy as he finished the song.

Molly came into the room and moved to their side. She patted the boy's shoulder and brushed his cheek with affection. The four people shared a quiet moment of deep attachment. For them, the cold world outside might not have existed. Their newly found friendship, heartened by the soul-touching music, framed their final moments together.

Victoria was led to a sea chest which had been trundled into the room. She was invited to peruse its contents. Layers of silks and organdies greeted her. Beneath the fabrics, brass boxes glinted in the firelight.

"Open one," Molly invited. Victoria lifted one of the little boxes which were in themselves a treasure. She gasped as she saw revealed a tumble of rings — silver and gold rounds, some encrusted with gems — twinkling up at her. "Take one," said Molly softly.

"Oh, I could not," Victoria gaped. Molly scooped out a handful of the little jewels and held them out. As Victoria gazed down at them, an idea seemed to strike her. She glanced at the boy. "Is it all right?" she asked Moll. The woman smiled. Victoria picked out several rings, and mov-

225

ing to the boy, she held his hand in her own and placed one on each of his fingers. "Talented hands should be graced," she said warmly. The boy gazed down at his newly adorned fingers, and then, taking Victoria's hand in his, he kissed it.

"Thank you," he said softly, looking into her eyes. "I shall play something special for you." He turned back to the piano and began a tender folk tune. The glint of the rings as they danced over the keys lent a tangible dimension—a visual poetry—to the young man's music.

"You've made a friend today," said Molly.

"I think I have," Victoria said, eyeing the older woman with a gentle smile.

"Look, love," said Greyson. He held up a basket for Victoria's inspection. "Ribbons," he exulted. Victoria gaped at the deluge of richly-colored strands.

"Oh, Moll," she breathed, "thank you! They are perfect. She reached into the basket and pulled out an armful. Freed from their confinement, yards of silken ribbons tumbled to the floor at her feet. Everyone laughed as Victoria and Molly attempted to gather up the slippery tendrils. Victoria laughed, too, and with a sprightly accompaniment on the tinkling piano, the two women bundled up the kaleidoscopic array and plunked it back into the container. Catching various errant wisps of color, they finally got the writhing, radiantly gelatinous collection organized.

"You might have helped, you know," Victoria said, tilting a glance at Greyson, who was laughing hardest of all.

"I might have," he answered, attempting to contain his mirth, "but 'twas so much more fun just watching."

Molly and Victoria exchanged a resigned glance. "They are little boys at heart," said the older woman, "every honey-tongued one of them." Shaking her head tolerantly, she bundled Victoria into her cloak. " 'Tis gettin' on to dark now, you two." She eyed Greyson. "You'd better get this sweet thing out of here before my old James gets home with his pals. This is no fit place for a lady or anyone else once they start their nightly carousin'." She bustled the two people toward the door. Good-byes were quick and sentimental as Victoria and Greyson nestled themselves into the furs that warmed the sleigh's front seat. The horses had been fed and watered and were eager to begin the journey home. They wickered in the cold, silent twilit air, and bells jangling merrily, they began a sprightly trot toward Boston.

Chapter Seventeen

Victoria watched from the sleigh as the small, weather-boarded cottage disappeared behind them. Smoke drifted from the chimney to hang mistily against the thickening twilight. She offered a final wave to Molly, who stood just outside the door and then, at last, driven by the December cold, went back inside. Victoria turned and straightened herself among the furs. As the sleigh entered the deep woods on the way back to Boston, the moon rose to light the snow-pillowed path with a pearly light. No sounds greeted them in the forest. There was only the light tinkle of the sleigh bells, the quiet clop of the horses' hooves and the soft abrasion of the runners against the packed snow. Those whispers of sound were the only evidence of any life in this interior and private world. Drawing the warmth of the furs over her, Victoria knew a contentment she had never even imagined. She felt as one, in complete harmony with this wondrous universe of hushed, silvered softness.

The reins hung slack in Greyson's big hands, for the horses knew exactly where they were headed. They needed little guidance. Victoria snuggled next to him. He put his arm around her and drew her closer. As the sleigh entered a small hollow, Greyson pulled to the side of the road. He turned to her and lifted her chin with one gloved fingertip. A question lurked in the sea blue of his eyes. Her liquid gaze in the moon-washed dark told him she was glad he'd stopped.

"I do not think I can wait until we reach Boston," he said with a roguish smile.

"I would not want you to," she whispered. Greyson caught his breath. She lifted her hand and brushed at the tousled curls that grazed his forehead.

"You are every man's dream," he breathed huskily.

"I only want to be yours, Greyson," she answered, as he reached out and brushed an iridescent curl from her cheek.

"Oh, you are mine," he said. "You are like an angel — so soft, so warm, so lustrous. I long to feel the sweet curve of your flesh against me, love. 'Tis all I live for." He encircled her in his embrace; she swept off her bonnet, and her radiant curls fell in an opalescent cascade about her shoulders. Her head fell back. Greyson's lips explored the tender flesh of her arched throat. He radiated heat and hunger, and she molded herself to him as he wrapped them both beneath the tangle of thick furs.

"Greyson," she whispered. "I don't think we should —"

"Don't think, my angel," he whispered hoarsely. He unclasped the fastenings of her cloak and, with agonizing slowness, those of her gown. She had no resistance. His kisses ravishing her bared breasts and belly were whispered fire. She felt consumed. He cherished her yielding flesh, and she, naked beneath the furs, opened to him like a winter blossom opens to the power of the sun. Beneath the furs, his sea-scented essence became the very air she breathed. There was for her no separate ordinance of man and nature. Greyson was all. He was the sky and the sea and the moon-bathed universe. With his caresses, he warmed her. With his mouth, he fired her passion. With his tongue, he penetrated the boundaries of her soul. He lingered long and hungrily in that ripely fertile garden. She felt herself lifted on crests of liquid rapture to heights beyond the stars. He breathed her name as he entered her. His breath, the word, the pounding ecstasy of deliverance from all earthly bounds came together in one rapturous epiphany. A shudder resonated between them as they lingered, holding on to that throbbing moment of heated bliss. Victoria arched herself to his lean form, feeling the quickness of his heart, the tight pulses of his repletion.

"Greyson," she breathed, as his embrace overwhelmed her with its tender power. "I love you."

"And I love you," he answered. He lifted her to him and they shared a lingering kiss.

Outside the furs, the reality of hooves pounding on the

snow pricked at their absorption in the lambent flow of their still-fiery hunger. Greyson suddenly twisted above her and turned his attention to the dark roadway. In the moonlit shadows, a figure charged toward them. Victoria drew up the furs to cover herself.

"What is it," she whispered.

Greyson said nothing but reached beneath the seat and drew out a musket. Keeping it hidden in the camouflaging furs, he watched with grim patience the approach of horse and rider. At last, the lone man revealed himself.

He called out, his voice husky in his attempt to be heard but not discovered. "Greyson Tyrrel, is that you, sir?"

"Who approaches?" Greyson called back.

" 'Tis Paul" came the hoarse reply.

"Paul!" Greyson relaxed immediately, shoving the gun back beneath the seat. He assisted Victoria in making herself hastily presentable. " 'Tis a friend," he assured her. "What news, Paul?" he inquired as the man skidded to a stop before the sleigh.

"Sorry for the intrusion, mistress," the rider said amiably, touching the brim of his tricorn. "My name is Paul Revere." Victoria's eyes widened. This was the troublesome engraver that Uncle David had so roundly disparaged.

"To the point, Paul," said Greyson, disallowing further amenities with impatience.

"Governor Hutchinson has flatly refused to order the tea ships out of the harbor," said the young intruder.

"He must be mad," stated Greyson.

The rider nodded grimly. "Adams has ordered everyone to the Old South Meeting House. He wants you there."

"Has our next move been decided, Paul?" asked Greyson.

"Nay," the man answered, shaking his head. " 'Tis what they hope to discuss tonight."

"We cannot allow the ships to be unloaded," Greyson said resolutely.

" 'Twould be a tragedy," Paul agreed. "Some of the men have suggested that we attempt to negotiate directly with the captain of the *Dartmouth*. That is where you come in, Grey. We are hoping to avoid any violence. Adams feels you would be the best one to speak for us."

"Ride ahead, Paul, and tell them I shall be there as quickly as possible," Greyson said.

"I shall," said the man, "but do hurry, Grey, there have already been several fights broken up by the Brits." With a last friendly nod to Victoria, Paul Revere wheeled his horse and took off at a pounding gallop.

"What is the problem?" Victoria asked as Greyson let out the reins and snapped them, spurring the sleigh to a lurching start.

"Tea," Greyson answered tersely.

"Tea?" she inquired. Wordlessly Greyson urged the horses to a run. With more speed than Victoria thought necessary, they charged along the narrow road toward Boston. "Is this the same problem you spoke of on the *Spectre*?" she asked.

"It is," he said.

"Oh, Greyson," she sighed. "Why don't you just let the British land their bloody tea. If you don't want it, throw it into the Boston Harbor."

Greyson arched her a glance. "We just might do that, love," he said.

Golden patches of light dotted the landscape as the sleigh travelled past houses and inns. Twinkling with inviting warmth, the houses became more and more numerous as they made their way toward the Town Cove. Suddenly a disturbance up ahead caught their attention. Greyson pulled back on the reins, slowing the horses as they cautiously approached a knot of boisterous men. Halting the vehicle a few feet from the fracas, Greyson jumped from the seat. He indicated to Victoria that she should stay where she was. He purposefully strode toward the skirmish. Two men were in the center, arguing heatedly while others gathered around them encouraging one or the other.

"Grey!" shouted one of the men. "Grey Tyrrel is here," he said to his compatriots. "Perhaps he can talk some sense into this bloody fool."

"Bloody fool, sir?" rejoined another man. "I shall give you *bloody* you lantern-faced numskull!" The man lunged, and immediately all those gathered joined one side or the other in a jabbing, punching brawl.

"Stop!" commanded another voice. "Let Captain Tyrrel

speak." The man shouldered his way through the heaving spree of male bodies as they formed a reluctant aisle for him. "Greyson," he said, extending his hand. "Speak to these lubbers." Greyson stepped into the center of the tension-filled morass. He recognized several of his men from the *Spectre,* including Edmund Harrt.

"What is the problem here," he demanded.

"The problem," panted a perspiring gentleman, identifying himself as Captain Hall, "is that these men are insisting I take the *Dartmouth* back to India. This I cannot do! I've explained as much, but the blighters are determined to make a bloody fight of it with *me.* For God's sake, I have no control over this business. I just drive the bloody boat."

"We thought by appealing directly to the captain, we might be able to avoid some nasty business," another man explained, as he swiped at his blood-stained lower lip.

"What these 'gentlemen' " — Captain Hall eyed the other men caustically — "do not understand, Captain Tyrrel, is that I have little choice in this matter. You know yourself that under the law, I was forced to make entry of my ship and cargo at the custom house upon landing."

"To fail to do so," Greyson said, nodding, "would have subjected you to a fine."

"The *Captain,* the *Eleanor,* the *Beaver* and the *William* are also docked at Griffin's Wharf, and their masters came under the same legal strictures as I. We were given twenty days to unload our cargo. That deadline is upon us. We *will* unload within the next twenty-four hours. We've got no flippin' choice, Captain Tyrrel, can't you explain that to these contentious bastards?"

"You forget, Captain Hall," said Greyson, his gaze hooding, "I am one of these contentious bastards."

The man recoiled perceptibly. He splayed his hands in a gesture of helplessness. "I have no quarrel with you, Captain, or with any of these men," he said hastily, "but I tell you this, your threats and your protests are futile."

Another man, a Captain Bruce, affirmed Captain Hall's words. "If I could sail the *Eleanor* out of the Boston Harbor tonight, I would. But I am as much a victim of the law as you."

The crowd surged angrily forward. "Let's bush fight 'em!" came the cry. And, "They need tarrin' and featherin', is what they need!"

"No!" Greyson commanded, and the men hesitated, some halting others and encouraging them to listen to a calmer head.

Victoria, curious, left the sleigh and moved cautiously to Greyson's side. Greyson eyed her sternly, but a voice from the crowd caught his attention.

"If we cut off their captains, we can subdue their seamen with very little loss!" Greyson felt the character of the assembly take on a feral posture. He placed himself in front of Victoria.

"No!" he repeated, and this time his tone brooked no controversy. The men backed off beligerently. "We have twenty-four hours to fight this, men," Greyson said. We must not resort to violence toward these captains. They are not our enemies." He surveyed the group warily. He could not permit action against the two captains, and yet he knew that the crowd lusted for some sort of satisfaction. "Our enemy," he continued, "is the accursed tea they carry."

The men murmured demands for harsh justice. Their rumbling declarations built to a surging anger.

"What revenge can we inflict on the bloody tea?" one man raged. "I say we—"

"I say we take stock of what we are about," Greyson rejoined. "We must consider our interest, not merely our position. Think, gentlemen; will doing violence to these captains really solve our problems with the Brits? Tarring and feathering these men will only slake our thirst for some kind of vengeance. Our frustrations will be satisfied for the moment, but what will violence toward Captain Hall and Captain Bruce really solve? 'Twill solve nothing. Think, gentlemen; what do we really want?"

"We want to be rid of the bloody tea!" shouted a voice. Others joined his declaration. Greyson was again enjoined to play the mediator.

"And will violence to these two men accomplish that?" he thundered over their roiling belligerence. He was forced to shout his next words, and Victoria found herself cowering in

233

the din of the men's acrimony. "I say," Greyson went on, "we let these men go their way. I say we leave them in peace, and I say we meet like civilized men to discuss our next move."

Before the gathering could respond, a small legation of British soldiers charged toward them. Their horses wheeled and pranced before the crowd.

"What in the hell is going on here!" demanded a stentorious voice. The men paused and the red-coated soldier repeated his question. Anger and hatred seethed in the cold air of the dark Boston street. Mumbled expressions of bitterness and long suppressed hostility roiled within the gathering of men. At last, Captain Hall spoke.

"We were . . . uh . . . planning a card game, sir," he said genially. "These boys got a bit upset when Captain Bruce and I suggested whist." The two captains laughed and nudged their tormentors into at least a pretended show of good-natured rambunctiousness. Tapping at each other with open palms, the men resembled hearty school boys just released for recess rather than men engaged in a potentially deadly clash.

Greyson, forcing a smile, stepped between two of the "card players" who were beginning to take their frisky rollick just a bit too seriously. "Easy, men," he intoned. He looked up at the British officer, recognizing for the first time the countenance of Jared Everett.

"Well, Colonel, we meet again," he said, his manner grandly jovial. "How are you this evening?"

Colonel Everett eyed Greyson and those surrounding him narrowly. "What is this all about, Tyrrel?" he asked pointedly.

"Exactly what Captain Hall said, Colonel."

"I find that difficult to believe," he said drily.

"But it is true," a small female voice offered. Jared Everett's eyes widened. He immediately displaced his tricorn as he spotted Victoria among the men.

"Lady Darby," he gaped. "What in the bloody h— What are you doing here?"

"I was shopping for ribbons." She pointed back toward the sleigh where the basket sat nestled in the back seat among a pile of blankets. "Captain Tyrrel and I just stopped to greet

234

some of these gentlemen. We thought they might be interested in a game of cards."

Jared Everett's gaze slid back to Greyson. "You were shopping for . . . ribbons?" he asked.

"I needed an escort, Colonel," Victoria called up to the young officer, "and Captain Tyrrel was kind enough to aid me." She flirted her lashes at the young officer and dimpled prettily. Twirling a long, frosted curl on her gloved finger, she managed a tinkling laugh. "A lady cannot be too careful in these troubled times."

Jared Everett cleared his throat. "Yes, I agree," he managed. He eyed his men, and with a curt salute, he dismissed them. He offered a small smile to the assembly. "You gentlemen will be more careful in future not to let your little . . . disagreements get out of hand, I trust?" He offered Greyson a cordial wink, then wheeling his horse, he rode off.

A collective relief was sighed as the men turned their awestruck gazes to Victoria. She smiled and modestly lowered her lashes. Offering a small curtsy, she spun, and her cloak flaring, she made her way back to the sleigh. The men shook hands all around, their tensions alleviated, and Captains Hall and Bruce hastily made their way from the group with a genial admonishment.

"Whatever action you decide to take, gentlemen," said Captain Hall, "I do hope you will remember that we are working blokes just like yourselves."

"We mean you no harm, and we profoundly hope you feel the same about us," added Captain Bruce. Both men hurried off.

"They have a point," said Edmund Harrt, at last approaching Greyson. He turned a grim attention to the men. "You were all too willing to take out your frustrations toward Parliament upon two innocent sea captains. I hope we have all learned a lesson this night."

"What are you doing here, Edmund?" Greyson inquired.

The young warrant officer shrugged a wide shoulder. "I was about the town, Captain," he said. "I got embroiled in this little mix-up purely by accident."

Greyson glanced over toward the sleigh. "Now you are here, Edmund, you could do me a favor." The seaman nodded. "Would you escort Victoria home?"

Edmund Harrt grinned broadly, and Greyson knew a moment of hesitation. " 'Tis rather an emergency, Mr. Harrt," he grumbled. "You needn't make an issue of it."

The man saluted smartly. "As you say, Captain Tyrrel," he said solemnly. He ambled off with a jaunty step, and Greyson narrowed his gaze at the departing younger man.

"Shall we get to the meeting, Grey?" demanded one of the men. Greyson's attention was immediately drawn to the gathering.

He eyed the men. "Aye," he said reluctantly. With one last glance toward Victoria and the sleigh . . . and the lean young fellow bounding up into the driver's seat, he started off toward the Old South Meeting House.

Chapter Eighteen

Victoria eyed Edmund Harrt in puzzlement. He smiled sheepishly. "The captain asked me to escort you home, my lady," he said.

"Why couldn't 'the captain' take me home himself?" she asked.

"He has business to attend," Edmund answered vaguely.

"Business?" Victoria questioned. Edmund merely nodded. "Is it over this tea problem?"

"I am afraid so," the young man answered. His manner was resigned. He took up the reins and snapped them out. The old horses lurched to a start. "I hope you do not mind, my lady," he said glancing at her. "I am a poor substitution for Greyson Tyrrel."

Victoria turned away with a small smile. " 'Tis perfectly all right, Edmund," she said. "I suppose," she added after a pause, "I just do not understand Greyson's involvement in all this." She looked straight into the eyes of the young officer. "Does Greyson favor separation from the Sovereign Rule?"

Edmund Harrt laughed. "You shall have to ask him yourself. I try not to get involved in these political wranglings."

" 'Twould seem," said Victoria stiffly, "that one cannot live in this Boston Town without getting involved in at least a very apparent class and cultural distinction. I have been here a mere three days, and already I have seen it — been a part of it. The Frankland-Fosters live very well."

"Most friends to the king live well," stated the young man.

"Are you — ?"

"I do not get involved," Edmund said shortly. He glanced quickly at Victoria. "I was born here, in Salem," he said. "I do understand the colonial temper; but most of my life has been spent on the sea, and that is the way I prefer to keep it. The sea is a separate world, Victoria. 'Tis an existence unto itself. 'Tis the only place I know where a man is free to chart his own course. Naturally," he added with a genial wink, "one must follow one's captain when one is a mere warrant officer. But one day I shall have my own ship. One day, I shall sail the seas, and I shall be a rule unto myself." He laughed in self-deprecation. "That day is far, I fear, but 'twill happen. I am often a very lucky man," he added quietly.

Victoria watched this capable and apparently spirited fellow. She had found him on the *Spectre* to be most fairminded, devoted to his circumstance and now determined to keep an open mind.

The sleigh came to a jerking stop before the Frankland-Foster house. Edmund turned to her. His eyes glinted in the cold moonlit air. " 'Twas a brave thing you did tonight, Victoria. The captain is a lucky man to have such a one as you by his side."

"Thank you, Edmund," Victoria answered shyly. "I suppose I am only brave because I do not know any better."

"Still," Edmund insisted, " 'twas courageous of you to aline yourself with a band of rabble the way you did."

"Quite honestly," she said, "I know nothing of the politics here. I do not really understand the ideological differences between the rabble and the gentry, so it makes little difference to me with whom I aline myself."

Edmund threw back his head and laughed. "Except where it concerns my captain," he said.

"Your captain," agreed Victoria, "and mine." She smiled mischievously. "I shall tell you another thing. If Lord Neville Frankland-Foster represents the gentry, I should rather be associated with the rabble." The two young people laughed together as Victoria detailed the admonishment the older gentleman had handed down to her concerning the question of "hanky-panky." "I suppose," Victoria conceded as Edmund assisted her down from the sleigh, "that the fellow is just looking after my best interests, but honestly, Edmund, he does present a most didactic picture of propriety. I don't know how, with him holding jurisdiction over me, I can expect to have any *fun*. He looks so mean all the time. Well," she said at last, "Vivien is a love, and I suppose I shall just have to look to her to intercede for me in the future." Her face became troubled. "I must say, though, Vivien seems ill-equipped to handle the old poop, though she handles everything else with style." She looked up into the admiring gaze of Edmund Harrt. Her cheeks pinkened at his perusal.

"I have a feeling you can handle your own affairs, Victoria," he said seriously. "You seem to be a most capable lady."

"Thank you, Edmund," she said. "And thank you for escorting me home. I hope to see you again."

The young man smiled broadly as Victoria turned to make her way into the house. "You may count on that, my lady," he said, half to himself.

Dismissed. That was the only way Victoria could describe her feelings as she made her way into the darkly lit hallway of the Frankland-Foster mansion. Greyson was apparently caught up in this problem that seemed to divide the American colony, and he was not about to allow even her presence to interfere. She slipped out of her cloak and bonnet and lifted the basket of ribbons so that she might take them into the dining room to sort them on the long table.

"Where have you been, young woman?"

Victoria's startled gaze shot up to find Sir Neville standing very near. She had not suspected his presence. From his pristine wig to his lime satin waistcoat to his buckled and polished patens, he was the picture of righteous authority. "I have been out shopping for ribbons," she answered, "for the ball." She attempted a brightness she did not feel. "Is there a problem?"

"The problem," stated the man in a stentorian tone, "is that our house guest — a young lady we have been enjoined to chaperone — has been out gallivanting all day, and no one knew where she was."

Victoria faced him squarely. She was in no temper to fence with this querulous prig. Affecting a lofty attitude of her own, she said, "On the contrary, sir, both Vivien and Dory knew where I was. And I might add that the necessity you have imposed upon yourself as my chaperone is most uncalled for and, believe me, unwelcome. It is not my intention to be rude, sir, but I promise you I am quite grown up and have developed the ability to care for myself."

"Vivien went out searching for you. Did you see her?"

"No," Victoria answered tersely.

"Who were you with?" Sir Neville asked with lordly certainty of his right to know.

"A friend," Victoria answered curtly. "In fact, several friends." She stepped away from the man to make her way to the dining room. Sir Neville's hand shot out, grasping at her arm and spilling the contents of her basket onto the carpeted floor. She gaped up at him. "I beg your pardon, Lord Frankland-Foster," she breathed. She looked quickly down at the basket and the scattered ribbons and then back at the man who held her. Her green gaze narrowed. "Unhand me," she clenched.

"I asked you a question, young lady," he rejoined imperiously.

"And I answered your question." Victoria jerked herself from his grip.

"You did not answer to my satisfaction. Who was this friend?" he asked with authority.

Victoria took a deep, calming breath. She needed the moment to check her rising anger. She remembered Lord Frankland-Foster's senseless fury when Greyson's name had been mentioned the day she arrived. She wanted no repeat of that scene. She knew that Sir Neville's ire would spark her own. She must live for some time in this household, and there was no point in getting into a snit with the master of the house before the first week was out.

"I really do appreciate your concern for me," she said with exaggerated cordiality. There was no hint of animosity in her voice. "I assure you I was perfectly safe. I am sorry Vivien found it necessary to go looking for me. I shall make it my business, in the future, to inform you of my whereabouts at all times." Naturally, Victoria had no intention of keeping such a commitment, but she thought it best for the moment to humor her tyrannical host. At some later time, she would take the matter to Vivien and hope that she could abate this unnecessary show of guardianship. Victoria, assuming the matter was ended, knelt to gather up the tousle of ribbons. It was some time before she felt the unrelenting perusal of Lord Frankland-Foster. She glanced up and was startled to find an overweening benevolence in his gaze.

"My wife was at the market this evening, Lady Darby," he said, his voice silky. "I thought she might have returned with you."

"N-no, Sir Neville, I did not see Vivien," Victoria replied uncertainly. She bent once again to her task. As she rose, Neville assisted her with courtly solicitude. "Th-thank you, sir," she said warily.

"I thought dear Viv might be outside seeing to the horses," he said slyly. "We would not want her popping in at an inopportune moment, now would we?" Victoria, bemused at the sudden alteration of his attitude and his reference to Vivien, stared dumbly at him. He continued as he assisted her into the dining room. "If I seem pettish, 'tis only because I feel responsible for the welfare of our relationship — Viv being such a vulnerable old thing." He took her elbow as they entered the room. "Is that so hard to understand? Can you appreciate how I feel?"

"Of course," Victoria answered. She attempted to sort out what this new approach could possibly mean. Was it his intention to atone for his rudeness of the past? Why did he keep making reference to Vivien? Victoria had no idea. It was only a moment, however, before she began to sense the dawning of a horrible awareness. The carnal glint in Sir Neville's eyes was difficult to misinterpret as he began to help her with the sorting.

"Such pretty colors," he purred. Victoria stiffened. He stood just to her left, and his arm kept sliding nonchalantly against her shoulder as he reached across the table. She moved slightly, but he followed her down the table, doggedly repeating his attentions. This could not possibly be happening, Victoria thought wildly. Her mind raced in denial. This man was the husband of her friend, Vivien — an elegant and exquisitely beautiful woman. He was a British nobleman, a respected gentleman, at least the age of Lord Trevor Darby. He could not possibly be intending to compromise both her and himself. And yet, here in his own house, having just expounded on the importance to him of her welfare, Lord Frankland-Foster was, with the insistence of a lascivious adolescent, pursuing her. If his persistent chaperonage had been unwelcome, this new behavior was even less desired. She must think. She must find a way to discourage this. She glanced up at the man and discovered him smiling meaningfully down at her. She looked quickly away. Perhaps she could remind him of his obligation to his wife.

"Vivien will be so pleased with the decorations," Victoria said with forced brightness. She backed away from her host and held up two shades of silk — one purple and one orange. "I think these will look very well wrapped around the columns in the front hall, don't you," she went on rapidly. In a frenzy, she realized that Sir Neville was rounding on her, backing her toward the table. "Please, Sir Neville," she gasped, fending him off with splayed hands, "I think 'twould be best if I continued the sorting alone . . . or you could do it!" she asserted. "That is a wonderful idea! I shall go up to my room — or perhaps 'twould be better if I went out to the kitchen, or — "

Sir Neville cut her off, encompassing her waist in one arm. He was surprisingly strong for an earl, she thought senselessly. She turned, attempted to free herself, but he merely grasped her with his other arm and turned her back to face him, arching her over the table's edge. No matter which way she twisted, she only abetted his intent.

"Do not fight what has been between us since the moment we met," he insisted as his lips came down to brush her ear.

"I do not know what you mean!" she gasped.

"Oh, yes you do, Victoria. You felt as I did. I could tell the moment we were introduced that — "

"The moment we were introduced," she interrupted him, "you began a tirade against me."

"That was only to put Vivien off the scent," he groaned huskily.

"The scent!" Victoria blurted. "What are you talking

about?"

"I did not want her to suspect what was between us," he replied, his breath ragged.

"There is nothing between us," Victoria asserted. She shoved at the amorous nobleman, and caught off-balance, he stumbled backwards. "If you come near me again, Sir Neville," she cried shrilly, "I shall have to use force against you." The man merely smiled, devilment snapping in his eyes.

Victoria swung back her arm and stunned him with a slap. He held on to his jaw, and amazingly, his gaze became liquid with desire. "Lady Darby," he breathed. "You are so fiery!" Victoria blanched as he lunged for her. She scrambled backward to avoid his advance, but realized too late that she had landed in a sitting position on the table. Neville quickly took advantage of her momentary disability and pushed her onto her back. His lips charged over hers, and to avoid contact, she twisted, slipping among the tangle of ribbons. She arched her way, in her prone position, across the table. Sir Neville hiked himself up and slid to her side. "This is the way I like it, my dear," he said rhapsodically. "Spontaneity is so exciting!" His lips came down once again, and Victoria wriggled away, struggling wildly. He followed her, sliding along the polished surface, and, in the process, wreathing both of them in the parti-colored strands of silk.

"Please, Sir Neville," Victoria screamed, "try to remember yourself!" He merely laughed, seeming to enjoy her struggle, apparently regarding it as play. At last capturing her, he rolled her onto him. As she thrashed against her captivity, she raised a glossy spume of ribbons. "If you do not let me go," she railed, "I shall tell Vivien!"

"No you won't." He chuckled. "You wouldn't hurt the dear thing. You are much too enamoured of her." Victoria scrambled off of him, but he lunged onto her back. She lay facedown, the ribbons heaped around her and Sir Neville atop her. She was finding it difficult to breathe beneath his weight. "Besides," he went on, "if you do tell her, I shall deny it and say *you* attempted to seduce *me*. Whom do you suppose she will believe, my feisty wench, you or me?" He laughed. With all her strength, Victoria bucked him off. He flopped, sprawling and laughing, onto his back beside her. In the tussle, he'd managed to entangle them both in cascades of silk. He lay, breathing raggedly, thoroughly enjoying himself, while Victoria sat up and attempted to disencumber herself from the gelatinous mass.

"You are the most depraved of men, Sir Neville," she grated.

He grabbed her and pulled her down to him. "Am I depraved because I enjoy a healthy bounce with a frosty little piece of baggage?" he breathed.

"A healthy bounce?" Victoria rejoined. "On the bloody dining room table? And what in the bloody hell do you mean calling me frosty?" she demanded.

Sir Neville bellowed appreciative laughter. "You *are* frosty, my dear. As tight and as cold as a bonny glacier—not like that ragamuffin Dory. That grimy little bird would do anything for me, and quite frankly, she is getting to be a bore. Once I defrost you, missy—and I shall defrost you—I see for us a most agreeable future." Victoria felt his hold on her slacken as his confidence grew. She wrenched herself away from him and charged from the table, dragging ribbons. She jumped to the floor and rounded on Sir Neville. He lunged after her, intending another series of playful romps, but Victoria obstructed his pursuit, grabbing the basket from the table and with it barricading his access to her.

"You stay away from me," she grated. "If you come one step nearer, I shall . . . I shall . . ."

"What will you do, little rebel?" he inquired with a placid smile.

Victoria had no idea of what she would do. She considered that she might grab a dining chair and break it over the coxcomb's head. He well deserved whatever retribution on which she finally decided. He had not only compromised her, but he openly admitted to dallying with a servant. He was the beau Dory had so proudly and so guardedly admitted to, Victoria recalled with disgust. "Believe me, Sir Neville," she ground out, "if you take one more step, I shall do something."

244

Before Victoria had an opportunity to carry out her threat, the front door burst open. The couple, staring each other down, suddenly turned to the arched entrance of the dining room. In a matter of seconds, Vivien appeared there, swinging her cloak from her shoulders smiling brightly.

"Hello, you two," she greeted them. Her cheeks were flushed pink, and her eyes sparkled in exhilaration. "I have just come up from the market," she told them. "I managed to get some lovely Scrod for supper." Vivien looked very young and glowing with the pleasure of exertion. The little maid, Dory, appeared behind her with a thickly wrapped package. "Get that to the kitchen," Vivien said, addressing the girl. "And have cook see to it immediately." She went back into the hallway to hang up her cloak, and Victoria noted that before the maid turned to her errand, she regarded Sir Neville and then Victoria with a puckered frown. Victoria lowered her gaze. Sir Neville, standing by her side, seemed to puff up perceptibly, and Victoria's ire rose. The old hound seemed positively filled with pride. At that moment Vivien breezed back into the room, and Dory disappeared. "What have you two been up to?" Vivien inquired as she slipped off her gloves. She eyed the pair expectantly, and then her brow wrinkled. She gazed directly at Victoria, and the girl felt herself cringe beneath her friend's perusal. When she spoke again, Vivien's voice was heavy with irony. " 'Twould seem you have decided to decorate yourself for the holiday instead of the front hall." She laughed and stepped toward Victoria. Lifting a silk strand from the girl's shoulder, she held it up for a humorous inspection. Victoria reached up and realized that her hair and shoulders were festooned with ribbons. She began pulling them off with sheepish haste and, at the same time, attempted to straighten her tousled hair. Lord Frankland-Foster drew a ribbon from his own shoulder and straightened his stock. He regarded his wife coolly.

"We were sorting these ribbons, my dear Viv," he said easily. Victoria shot him a glare.

"I am so glad you found them," Vivien said. She handed the ribbon back to Victoria and eyed the glossy mess on the dining table. Victoria turned hastily and began to gather it

245

up and stuff it into the basket. Spotting a strand which had latched itself onto Sir Neville's breeches, she seized it away with what she hoped the man would notice was unnecessary force. He merely lifted a brow and smiled thinly. His expression held an intimate promise, and Victoria winced inwardly. How dared the old bastard place her in this position? she railed inwardly. The worst part of it was, he showed absolutely no remorse for what he had done. In fact, he seemed flushed with pride. Victoria was angered to the depths of her moral consciousness. Why, she wondered, should she be feeling all the guilt? She had done nothing to encourage him . . . or had she? Her face warmed and reddened as she attempted to recall any gesture she may have made, any signal that might have led Sir Neville to believe she would welcome his advances. She could think of nothing. She glanced at Vivien and found her watching them both quizzically. What a picture they must have made, standing there side by side, Victoria bedecked with her shame and her newly acquired ribbons and Lord Frankland-Foster, tall, haughty, icily indifferent to the proceedings of a moment ago. Victoria attempted a smile for Vivien. She could never allow the woman to suspect her husband's degeneracy. The revelation would be too painful. And Victoria intended to see to it that the incident — whatever its cause — would never be repeated.

"I shall take the ribbons into the kitchen," she mumbled.

"Let me help you finish your sorting," said Sir Neville as he placed his hand on the small of Victoria's back. She graced him with a stony regard.

"I can manage," she said curtly. She marched, her shoulders stiffened, from the room. Victoria noted angrily, as she made her exit, that Sir Neville had turned his solicitous attention to his wife.

"Let me take your gloves and hat, darling," he was saying as he led her into the parlor. "You look positively *flushed*." And, "We had better fix you a large brandy and put you right to bed. A woman your age should not be taking so liberally of the night air."

"But you sent me out, Neville." Vivien laughed. "You said you could not live another day without Scrod."

Victoria's stomach lurched and tightened. Her fists clenched as she strangled the basket she held. What she would not give to pummel that old lecher and puncture his high-flown shamelessness. As it was, she fully intended to have a few threatening words — and more than a few, if necessary — with the insolent Dory. At least where that situation was concerned, Vivien would not again be made the brunt of her husband's audacious behavior.

As she entered the kitchen, Victoria eyed the girl speculatively. She wondered what Dory's reaction to the incident would be. She did not have long to wait.

"You lookin' to have the master all to yourself?" asked Dory. The cook, working at the butcher's block, lifted a brow.

"Watch your blathering tongue, girl," she said to Dory. She offered Victoria an apologetic glance. Victoria set the basket down decisively.

"I shall need help dressing for supper," she said and exited the room. Dory, eyeing the cook in triumph, followed.

"Let me tell you something," Victoria said, rounding on the little maid as she entered the bedchamber. "What I do — or do not do — with Lord Neville is my business. But for you, my girl, the game is up. Your *relationship*," she spat the word, "has ended. As of this moment, you are to have nothing more to do with Lord Neville Frankland-Foster. Is that understood?"

Dory met Victoria's stormy gaze with an astonished gape. "What the master does in his own house is his business," the girl rejoined. " 'Tis none of yours."

" 'Tis all of mine," Victoria snapped. "His wife happens to be a very dear friend of mine, and I shall not allow her to be hurt."

"What was it *you* were intendin' to do, give her a Christmas present?" the girl retorted, lifting her chin. Victoria's emerald eyes narrowed and Dory cringed.

"You mind your own business concerning that, girl. I shall handle Lord Neville on my own and with no help from you."

The smile that — amazingly — formed on Dory's lips was challenging and triumphant. "I shall be most anxious to see

247

you handlin' Lord Neville," she said languidly. She spun with a flip of her skirts and left the room. Victoria plumped down heavily into her little rocker.

Whatever the outcome of her confrontation with the impertinent Dory, she had a feeling her troubles with Neville Frankland-Foster had just begun.

Chapter Nineteen

The entryway of the Frankland-Foster house was festively adorned with ribbons. As guests circulated among the rooms, they were greeted in each by a glittery array of Christmas sparkle. Two fir trees had been decorated with candles and cut-glass ornaments and stood twinkling on either side of the hearth in the main parlor. Other smaller trees throughout the house were garnished with lacquered fruit and candies. Silver sconces held long elegant tapers which flickered aureoles of glowing light. Evergreen wreaths adorned with cinnamon sticks and small spice bags hung on every freshly painted wall. The guests, dressed in shimmering taffetas and satins, might have been part of the planned decorations. The small parlor and the adjoining library had been cleared for dancing. Victoria, wearing a gown of deep rose velvet with lace on the bodice and full sleeves, stood amid the brilliantine splendor, enjoying the nutty scents of spiced cider and burning pine logs and the lilting strains of a small consort. She happily anticipated Greyson's arrival and might have been completely content had it not been for her disgust at Lord Frankland-Foster's display of overweening vigilance toward his wife. He appeared to be the perfect husband as well as the perfect host.

Victoria had passed many fretful hours thinking over the incident in the dining room and her subsequent confrontation with the arrogant Dory. She had decided absolutely against informing Vivien of her husband's perfidy. But she wondered just how long the man's licentious nature could be hidden. As it was, Lord Neville had approached Victoria many times during the past day, attempting to lure her, on one pretense or other, into dark corners and uninhabited rooms. Victoria had managed to repulse his advances and had even directed several weighty insults at the man. But he persisted with the confidence of a person absolutely convinced of his own charms. Lurking in hallways and outside of doors, he had pounced upon her, assuring her that given the opportunity, he could prove a most talented paramour. Dory had added her own brand of insolence to Victoria's frustration. The girl offered saucy glances and snide smiles each time Victoria and she encountered one another. With all this intrigue, how was she to keep Vivien from discovering the truth?

Victoria glanced up as the woman in question, gowned magnificently in emerald velvet, danced by partnered with the compact and impeccably attired Colonel Jared Everett. The golden ornamentation on his crimson coat seemed festively appropriate for the evening. He and Vivien made a striking couple — he, tawny-eyed, elegantly virile, a roguishly irreverent smile gracing his conversation and she, flame-haired, delicately pale and blithely and willingly charmed by the young officer. Why could Vivien not have found someone like Jared Everett? Why had she been yoked with the depraved Lord Frankland-Foster? Vivien, so strong and yet so vulnerable, deserved someone caring, intelligent, honest, Victoria reflected. She deserved someone whose vitality and love of life matched her own. At nearly forty years of age, she still retained the happy glow of radiant womanhood. Why had the fates decreed she should be saddled with a faithless husband? She could no doubt entrance any man in the room with her beauty and her complete lack of guile. Jared offered a smile and a nod of his head as they danced by.

After responding with a nod and a warm smile of her own, Victoria shot a glare in the direction of Lord Frankland-Foster. To her immediate horror, she realized that he had been looking at her. He seemed to take her regard as invitation, and in the company of another gentleman, he moved toward her. With both men nearly upon her, there was, quite simply, no escape. She managed a weak smile for the benefit of the other man and awaited their approach.

"Good evening, my dear," said Neville Frankland-Foster,

his demeanor grandly expansive and oily. "How lovely you look tonight." His survey slid down to the tiny holes in her lace decolletage. His smile was narrow as he at last met her eyes. "You never fail to honor my house," he purred. Victoria scowled darkly as he lifted her hand and placed a proprietary kiss upon it. "Let me introduce our guest," he said to the gentleman who stood nearby. "Lady Darby, may I present General Thomas Gage."

The general bowed over her hand. " 'Tis a pleasure to meet you, Lady Darby," said the man stiffly. His regard seemed oblique and wary, as though he was studying her.

"Victoria," she murmured uncertainly.

"Lady Darby is just over from India," blustered Sir Neville. "She shall be gracing our land for a time." He chortled gleefully. "We must keep her here as long as possible—find her a proper Englishman to enhance her visit. There is nothing like a romance to encourage a young lady's nesting instincts." Victoria offered him a withering stare and turned her attention back to the general.

"I hope you are enjoying the festivities, General Gage," she said.

"Please call me Thomas." Again, Victoria noted the intensity with which the man studied her.

"Thomas," she responded with a smile. "Lady Frankland-Foster has worked so tirelessly to provide a festive atmosphere. I think she has done a remarkable job of it, don't you?" She offered Sir Neville an arch-browed glare.

"Vivien is a perfect hostess," said Thomas Gage.

"Oh, indeed she is," Neville interjected with an overabundance of generosity in his tone. He nearly giggled in his attempt to impress the general with his delight in his wife's talents. "The dear woman never ceases to amaze me."

Not waiting for a response from their host, Victoria turned to the general. Her radiant smile encloaked him. "Won't you accompany me to the supper table, Thomas?" she asked.

The man nodded. "I should be honored, Lady Darby." He smiled, his caution somewhat diminished. Victoria offered Lord Frankland-Foster a peremptory curtsy and moved off with the general toward the dining room.

Pristine linens and services of silver covered every surface in that elegantly glittering room. The dining table had been festooned with garlands of evergreen, and a sumptuous banquet had been laid. Victoria flinched inwardly as she thought of what had occurred there only the night before. She held on to her composure though, and she and General Gage looked over the savory fare. A plump roasted goose in cherry sauce nestled in a deep platter at one end of the expanse of food. Plates of spiced beef and ham were available as well as bowls of steaming corn and onions. A large pot of beans in a dark and bubbly syrup graced the center of the table. Victoria glanced up at the general as they passed with several other guests along the table, deciding on just what delectables to choose for their own plates.

"I hear those savory beans are a product of a marvelous trading practice," said Victoria, attempting light conversation with this most austere gentleman. "Apparently, molasses is brought from the West Indies and distilled into rum here in America—in Cambridge, I am told, and in Medford. What is left of the molasses is combined en casserole with these delectable little vegetables, and the combination produces the most delightful taste treat. My uncle David— David Newton of the British armed forces in America—" she added solemnly, for she knew David would be happy to have himself mentioned in that context, "tells me they are available nowhere else in the world." She smiled ingenuously, prideful of her bit of knowledge, and several seconds passed before she realized that Thomas Gage was not smiling back. "Am I not correct in my information?" she asked artlessly.

"You are correct, Lady Darby," said the man. He glanced around, and Victoria noted that the other guests had inexplicably vanished. "This . . . trading practice you mention has caused something of a problem between the colonists and the British."

"Really?" said Victoria.

"Well, yes," the general said. "Before the war with the French, the American traders were involved in a triangular trade with the West Indies and Britain. 'Twas a lucrative enterprise, and the Americans had been keeping the profits to themselves. Naturally, King George was somewhat aston-

252

ished when he heard of the money that was being made here by the Americans and none of it coming back into the coffers of the Mother Country. Believe me," he said solemnly, "England needed money at the time. The war with the French lasted over seven years, and there were two years of localized fighting with their Indian allies before that." He led Victoria to a seat in the main parlor. "In '63, when the fighting finally ended," he continued, "England was without funds. To alleviate that problem, Parliament passed a series of laws, one of which was known as the Sugar Act, and it applied to the molasses trade," he said indicating his plate. "This very taste treat you mentioned caused a great deal of trouble for our good Sovereign. You see, under the new law, the colonials were enjoined to pay a tariff on their trade with the West Indies. I am afraid," he said tightly, "they resented it."

"In many ways," Victoria responded conversationally, "one can understand their resentment. As I understand it, that trade had been going on for over half a century. I suppose the colonists had begun to depend on that income."

General Gage eyed her sternly. "What they failed to consider, of course, is that any revenue enjoyed by a colony must also be extended to its Motherland. What would be the point of colonization if a country could not expect to share in the wealth of its colonies? There would be no advantage at all to sponsorship of a colony if that were not the case."

Victoria nodded bleakly. Of course Thomas Gage was correct. His logic was impeccable. And yet, she could not fail to understand the very real frustration of the colonists over what they must have considered an injustice. This was undoubtedly the "contention over sugar" that had been mentioned by Katje and Uncle David. Victoria was not sure she would ever understand the tangle of issues that existed between the two countries. That reflection raised the question in her mind of Greyson's whereabouts. She wondered if his absence had anything to do with the tea situation. She eyed General Gage. Intuitively, she knew she could not question him directly about it, but she wondered if a circumspect inquiry might not lead to an answer that would shed some light on the matter.

"The problems between the Americans and the British

have been going on for some time," she ventured finally.

The general nodded grimly. "That they have, my lady, and they are not about to end in the near future, I fear."

"When I arrived here, I got the distinct impression there was some problem over . . . tea," she said.

Thomas Gage stiffened perceptibly. His eyes glinted suspiciously, and his brow plowed a dark frown into his forehead. "What do you know about tea, Lady Darby?" he demanded.

Victoria flinched at the outburst. "Nothing," she said hastily. A few others in the room had turned to the couple and eyed them curiously. Victoria smiled weakly and shrugged a dismissive shoulder. She never should have mentioned the apparently forbidden word. General Gage glared at her as though he believed she was hiding something.

"Why did you mention it, then?" he questioned. His expression contained the threat of martial justice if she did not come up with an answer satisfactory to him.

"I . . . I honestly do not know," she replied. " 'Tis only that tea seems to be a pressing source of concern here." She attempted a smile. " 'Tis obviously a sensitive area. Perhaps we should not speak of it further." Her smile sweetened, but the general was unmoved.

"I do not think you understand just how sensitive the matter is, Lady Darby. Your reluctance to continue our discussion leads me to believe that you are aware of some information not known to me. You seem all too willing to defend these scurvy rebels in any event." Victoria's temper began to rise as she considered the unnecessary harshness of his reaction. The general eyed her keenly. "You have obviously heard rumors about His Majesty's tea ships," he admonished. "You had better tell me what you know, Lady Darby."

"I know nothing, General," she said, rising from the sofa. "I may add that I resent your intimations."

Thomas Gage stood as well. "Forgive me, Lady Darby," he said evenly, " 'tis only that the ships have been threatened, and if, by some chance, you have heard something, if you are privy to some information—"

"For heaven's sake, General Gage, I have been here less than a week," she retorted. "I have no vested interests in the political wranglings I have observed." She arched a brow furiously. Unmindful of the stares she was receiving from the other guests, she went on. "If I seem defensive of the colonists' point of view, 'tis only that I am attempting to sort out the questions involved and come to my own conclusions. That *is* still an option open to a British subject, I presume." The assembled guests had crowded into the room. A collective gasp rose at the girl's temerity.

"How dare you say this to me," General Gage clenched. "The British Empire does not 'wrangle' with anyone, my girl."

Victoria's emerald gaze glinted. "The problem here," she said narrowly, "does not seem to be British tea so much as it is British arrogance."

In the moment of terrible silence that followed, Vivien swept into the room in a cloud of velvet. Sitting down at the rosewood grand piano, she plumbed a chord. "I have just learned the prettiest new piece. I shall play it for you while the consort rests," she announced brightly. "Won't you turn pages, Victoria?" she asked smoothly. Victoria glared for one last defiant moment at General Gage and then moved toward the piano. "Thank you, dear," Vivien said as she began the trills of a lively Christmas song. When the tune had ended, Vivien quickly rose and received the approbation of her guests. Then, smiling serenely, she made her way from the room, Victoria clutched firmly at her side.

"Victoria," she said, her eyes woeful and worried, "what happened in there?" Vivien had dragged the younger woman into a dark corner of the entry hall.

"I wish I knew," Victoria answered ruefully. "The man was questioning me about tea, and—"

"What do you know about that?" asked Vivien.

"Nothing," Victoria wailed in a whisper. "Why does everyone assume—"

"If you know anything at all, Victoria, you'd better tell me." Vivien's tone was almost as harsh as the general's had been.

"Is something wrong?" the girl asked, her tone becoming deadly serious.

"Jared has told me that something is amiss—or expected

to be. I should hate to think of Greyson being involved in anything unlawful." Vivien took Victoria's arm in an imperative grip. "The soldiers are afraid for the lives of those captains on the British ships."

Victoria nodded. "We were involved in an altercation last night," she acknowledged.

"Oh, God, 'tis true, then," Vivien moaned.

"What is true?" Victoria questioned desperately. She felt a thrill of fear tremble beneath her flesh.

"Word is out that you were seen among the rebels last night, Victoria," Vivien whispered. "That is why Gage was so severe with you. No one believed the gossip, of course, but when you mentioned the tea business, Thomas must have surmised that the rumor was at least possible."

"I must ask you this," said Victoria. "Was it Jared who mentioned that I was seen with the rebels?"

Vivien looked astonished. "How would Jared know such a thing?"

"He broke up the dispute between the captains and the patriots," explained Victoria.

Vivien's eyes became liquid. "Jared is too much the gentleman to mention such a thing," she said.

"But don't you see? If Jared did not mention it, then I have an enemy out there."

"You have made a powerful enemy right here — in General Thomas Gage, Victoria," said Vivien bluntly. She regarded the girl keenly. "There is no time for lectures or recriminations, but if you know where Greyson is, you had better get to him. If he and his men are planning any violence against the captains, they had better abandon their plans. The soldiers have been ordered to shoot to kill."

Victoria's eyes widened. Her voice when she spoke was a hoarse whisper. "I promise you, Vivien, I am not involved in any rebel activities. The only thing I know for certain is that Greyson was supposed to be here tonight," she nearly sobbed. "They *must* be planning something. 'Tis the only thing that would have kept him away."

"You had better find him, then," Vivien urged. "His very life could be in danger." Before either of them could react, the front door burst open. Several red-coated men exploded into the hall.

"Where is General Gage," they demanded. Vivien drew back her shoulders and faced them.

"Is there a problem?" she asked with as much tranquility as she could muster. "This is a party after all." She smiled.

One of the soldiers stepped forward and bowed deferentially. "We must see the general, madam," he said.

"But, I do not—"

"What is it?" General Gage stepped from the parlor.

The man saluted smartly. A small, grimy fellow was produced from the midst of the assembled soldiers. The guests collected behind the general and eyed the skinny tattered man.

"Tell your story, Bouchard," ordered the soldier.

The man twisted a threadbare cap in his bony hands. "Do I get me coin, like usual?" he asked. Assured that his reward would be forthcoming, he cleared his throat. "I think 'twas Sammy Adams got the boys stirred up. They're all meetin' at the Old South Meetin' House. They been meetin' there for two solid nights now." He eyed the general suspiciously. "You sure I'll get me coin?" he said narrowly.

"Yes, you smarmy, mole-eyed imbecile," Thomas Gage thundered, "now what do you know?"

The little informer flinched, cocking his head and drawing it down into his shoulders as though he was expecting a blow. He swiped at his nose with a tattered sleeve, and tears popped into his eyes. "Tonight they was talkin' about Indians."

"Indians!" Gage bellowed. "What about Indians?"

"I don't know," the hunch-shouldered Bouchard sobbed pitifully. "I only heard about Indians."

"Get him out of here," the general said in disgust. "As an informer, this pea-brained skunk is as good as nothing."

Bouchard cowered in his place. "What about me coin, Gen'ral?" he whined, tears streaming down his weasellike features.

The general stepped to him and cuffed him soundly. "You deserve nothing," he said. He nodded curtly to a soldier, and that man tossed the little man his reward. "We are too soft with you, Bouchard. 'Tis not as if we seek your information." The skinny creature smiled his gratitude and scuttled away.

257

Victoria watched the man go. She recognized him as the owner of the sleigh she and Greyson had hired to take them to Cambridge. She wondered if Greyson knew he was a British informer. Sir Neville had said that Greyson was involved with a group of patriots — or hooligans, as David Newton had called them — and, though she had no idea of exactly what his political activities involved, she knew this would be valuable information for him to have. This was information she must tuck away and relate to Greyson in the not-too-distant future. Victoria looked up to find Lord Frankland-Foster just entering the room. His stock was badly wrinkled and his wig askew. Dory stood, wild-eyed, behind him. Victoria glanced quickly at Vivien, but she seemed unaware that anything was amiss.

"What is going on here?" Sir Neville demanded.

"I am not sure as yet," said General Gage, "but those colonial scalawags are apparently planning something." He charged down the hallway. "Everett, get the horses. We will take ourselves to the Old South Meeting House and see what all this is about." Jared Everett moved to the door, and offering Victoria and Vivien a surreptitious wink, he exited. Gage stopped briefly to glower at Victoria. She eyed him innocently. "These bounders are just looking for trouble," he said harshly. He turned abruptly to Neville as that man opened the front door to accommodate the general's exit. "They have done everything in their power to rankle me. We shall patrol these streets until there isn't a manjack among them who is not afraid to step out of his door at night." His horse was brought around to the front steps, and General Gage mounted in one sweeping bound. His face looked grim as he regarded the assemblage of people with angry resolve. "These Bostonians are absolutely unmanageable," he said. The crowd nodded and murmured their agreement. Victoria and Vivien remained quietly wary. The general wheeled his horse. "If the blighters dare to make a mockery of my command, they shall deal not only with me but with the wrath of all England!" He and his men rode off in a thunder of righteous resolve. The company was left to go inside and speculate on what might be the outcome of this terrible night.

"The king has been entirely too liberal," grated one gentleman.

"That brand of outlaws that call themselves the Sons of Liberty ought to be tarred and feathered," asserted another.

Victoria turned frightened eyes on Vivien. That woman urged, with her own assertive regard, that Victoria must take some action. What could she do, she thought wildly. She must get to Greyson; that was the first thing.

Dammit, Greyson Tyrrel, she reflected angrily as she made her unobtrusive way through the crowd and up the staircase, *why couldn't you have just come to the ball tonight?*

Chapter Twenty

Outside the Frankland-Foster mansion, Victoria, in the guise of Rod Sutcliff, slipped through the garden. The chill night breezes stirred the air. The sky was blackened with wintery clouds. The trellises that in the summer would be veiled with bowers of foliage stood starkly skeletal above her. Victoria shuddered involuntarily against the cold and against the terror that clutched her heart.

In the distance she heard the rumble of hooves — evidence of the vigilance of the British soldiers. Victoria thought briefly of running back into the house where she could be warm and safe. Glancing over her shoulder, she left a longing to be secure in the comfort of that impregnable fortress. Her mission was far too important, however. Resolutely, she turned from the house. She lifted her chin, challenging the dark and the cold to daunt her. She moved stealthily to the street. A twig snapped. She recoiled in terror. Her heart pounded, racing wildly. Only a twig, she told herself determinedly. She took long calming breaths and went on, past the iron gate into the darkened street.

She traversed the quiet, snow-covered roadway with rapid steps. She must find Greyson. She must warn him that the British were alert to every potentiality. They had been ordered to shoot to kill. An owl hooted. Victoria's heart fluttered. Along her way, she glanced into tangled winter gardens that lined the streets. The British soldiers could be anywhere. Stark branches of trees shuddered above her in the night winds. Overhead, the clouds raced, suddenly baring a stark-white winter moon. Victoria looked up. A click resonated in the darkness behind her. She turned.

"Stand still," ordered a voice. "State your name."

Her hands lifted immediately, splayed in a gesture of surrender. Her mind whirled. " 'Tis Rod," she said, remembering to adopt her hoarse young man voice. "Rod Sutcliff."

Before her a man dressed in a red jacket stepped out from the shadows. He held a musket. "State your business."

"I am walking home," she said, inventing rapidly. "I was helping out with a party at the Frankland-Foster house." Her words came in a rush. When she thought of this later, she was not to remember what she had said. "I thought I might have me an ale at the Bull and Crown."

"The Bull and Crown's the other way," the man stated dispassionately.

Victoria managed a hoarse chuckle. "I suppose I nipped a bit too freely of the cider at the party. I guess I lost me way, sir."

" 'Tis not a night to be out, lad," said the soldier. He lowered his weapon. "Get to the Bull and Crown if you must," he admonished, "but don't go wandering." Victoria lowered her hands and offered the soldier a nod. "And do not be surprised if you are stopped again before you get there, boy. We're trusting no one tonight."

Victoria touched the brim of her battered sea cap. "Thanks for the advice, sir," she said, striding past the man toward the Bull and Crown.

The hairs on the back of her neck prickled as she thought of the man watching her retreat. Once she was well on her way, she finally allowed breath to enter her lungs. Taking in air as she attempted to walk calmly, she found herself shuddering involuntarily. She continued on the main street, hoping that the soldier behind her had turned his attention to other distractions.

A warm yellow light and bawdy music greeted Victoria as she stepped across Milk Street to enter the Bull and Crown. Her feet crunched quietly in the snow. She had decided after her detainment by the British officer that perhaps this was the best place to go. She had no idea of the location of the Old South Meeting House. It occurred to her that she might be able to obtain some information here. She had no trouble finding the notorious tavern. It was situated directly in her

261

path on the main street that led from Hanover to the Long Wharf. Its swinging sign, creaking in the winter winds above the door, displayed a bull and a crown.

Pushing at the narrow entrance, she found herself on the threshold of what might have been a sybaritic vision of hell. The low-raftered room was washed in flickering golden lamplight. Garishly painted bawds threw back their heads in ribald laughter, their plump shoulders and bosoms carelessly bared. Men fondled them freely and dragged them onto grime-crusted laps. Long shadows fingered the walls and ceiling, promising dark niches where Satan's business could be well-attended. The fiddle wound to a squalling terminus, and the laughter and conversation died as a particularly tawdry woman approached Victoria. She slung her wide hips boldly as she moved to the front of the tavern. Fingering the tattered lace at the neckline of her tinsel-colored gown, she smiled snidely.

"What can we do for y', lad," she asked in a mockery of seduction. Her extravagantly kohl-shadowed eyes held a malevolent mirth, and her red mouth twitched in anticipation of the newcomer's response. The bawd was not disappointed.

"I . . . I am lookin' for someone," Victoria murmured. Her heart fluttered wildly as the collection of incorrigibles burst into gales of laughing profanities.

"Ain't we all," shouted a raspy voice from the dim interior of the room.

Victoria attempted to concentrate on the woman before her. "I'm lookin' for Captain Tyrrel."

"So is everybody else in this town," the woman shrieked in a coarse parody of laughter. "Listen, little fella," the woman said, advancing on Victoria, "I got a better idea for y'." She plucked at Victoria's grimy sleeve. "I'll take y' into the corner and show y' somethin'."

As the woman relentlessly followed, Victoria backed toward the door. "Th-thanks anyway," she muttered.

The woman bared a mouthful of yellowed teeth and reached out her chubby hand. "What're y' scared of, boy?" She grinned, urged on by the others. "Y' needn't be scared of ole Bonny, y' know. She'd be real nice to y'. I bet y'r a pretty lad." Finding the latch, Victoria lifted it carefully. "C'mon, laddie, let's have a look at y'." The woman suddenly snatched at Victoria's cap. Wresting it from her head, she gaped as a wild mane of fleecy curls spun out. With a breathless lunge, Victoria turned and fled from the tavern. She ran wildly, desperately, to escape the terrible howling of laughter that followed her and diminished only with distance.

Out on the street again, Victoria pounded away from the Bull and Crown. She had no idea where she was. The moon hovered above her, lighting her way relentlessly. There seemed nowhere to hide. If she were discovered now, she would be vulnerable to terrible danger. She might even be accused as a spy. She darted behind a low building as she realized that she was nearing a wharf.

Suddenly in the dark distance, she spotted what appeared to be a black configuration. She peered against the thickening night as the moon was shrouded by low-scudding clouds. The thing was long and seemed to crawl along the ground. It moved, creeping, toward the wharf.

Onward it inched along, silently, stealthily. Victoria's eyes widened. She hid in the shadows of buildings as, mesmerized, she followed the thing. At last it reached the end of the pier. It broke up into individual segments, small scuttering scraps of one huge mass. Victoria saw with a shudder of horror that portions of the thing were scaling the side of an idling ship. Quickly, the shapes scurried up the planking. Other shapes scuttled about the dock.

A splash broke the silence. A roar of men's voices resounded on the cold air. Another splash, another roar. Again, the two sounds pierced the dark and then again. Minutes passed as the ritual continued. A shout came from behind Victoria, and a new sound—the sound of thundering hooves—sent vibrations up from the snow-packed ground. Victoria huddled in the shadows of the building. The figures down on the dock began to scatter. The figures that had ascended the sides of the ship descended, swarming away from the scene. Horses roared past her; shouts resonated in the chilled darkness.

Suddenly, unbelievably, a huge Indian stood, towering over her. Victoria's last remembered image was that of a red blanket, a feathered headdress and sea-glass blue eyes.

The image faded rapidly as an empty swirling blackness overwhelmed her.

"Won't you at least try to swallow a little more broth, darling?" It was Vivien's voice, soothing, smooth and warm. Victoria's eyelids fluttered open. She gazed into a misting liquid dimness. A cup was held to her lips. A tepid liquid was sliding down her throat. She swallowed obediently.

"Vivien?" she asked. "Is it you?"

"Yes, darling," the gentle voice answered. Victoria closed and then reopened her eyes, attempting to clear her vision. Vivien appeared in a wavery image over her.

"Where . . . where am I?"

"You are home, in bed," Vivien answered. She smiled. "You have drifted in and out of sleep all night and most of the morning."

"How did I get here?"

Vivien laughed her low, musical murmur of sound. "A very handsome young man brought you here," she said.

"Greyson?" Vivien nodded. "But . . . what happened?"

" 'Tis hard to say . . . exactly . . . " Vivien's voice trailed off, and she rose, moving to the porcelain ewer on the washstand. She swished a cloth into the water bowl and wrung it out. Returning to the bed, she placed the cool, wet cloth on Victoria's forehead. "Greyson gave no information. He delivered you to the servants in the kitchen, ordering them to summon me. As soon as I appeared he vanished."

"He is all right, then?" Victoria asked, sitting up abruptly, spilling the cloth from her head.

Vivien gently urged her to lie down and tried to replace the moist cloth. "He is fine," she answered, patting Victoria's arm. "Apparently, though, there has been some . . . trouble—"

Victoria popped up. "What trouble?" she questioned.

"As nearly as I can understand it, a band of Indians boarded His Majesty's tea ships last night and threw the tea overboard." She breathed a sigh before Victoria could question her. "I do not know if Greyson was involved," she said. "Apparently, no one knows who the culprits were."

264

Victoria lay back. Vivien watched relief wash over her. "I must see him," the girl said softly.

Vivien hesitated. "Greyson did leave a message for you, before he disappeared last night," she said. Victoria looked up quickly. Vivien splayed a calming hand. "He said . . . under no circumstances were you to try to contact him. His advice should be well-considered, Victoria. He is—as is every young colonist—under suspicion. The British are questioning everyone. 'Twould not be in your best interest to be seen with him." She reached out and laid a cool hand on Victoria's forehead. "I know how difficult this must be for you," she said gently.

At that moment, Neville shoved open the door. His keen gaze glittered righteously as he surveyed the pair. "Where were you last night, miss?" he demanded, targeting Victoria.

"Neville, please," said Vivien as she stood and hastily moved to his side.

Lord Frankland-Foster eyed his wife disdainfully. "Leave us," he commanded. For the first time, Victoria saw defiance in Vivien's attitude toward her husband.

"I will not leave, Neville," she said, lifting her delicate chin. Neville's eyes widened and then immediately narrowed.

"Stay then," he grated. He shoved past his wife. Glowering over Victoria, he repeated his question.

When Victoria hesitated, Vivien moved again to her husband's side. "Victoria took some fresh air," she said. "Is that what you mean?"

"I *mean*," Neville said pointedly, "that this young woman was absent from the party last evening and was not to be found anywhere for several hours." He rounded on his wife. "I have just had word that she was seen at the Bull and Crown at just about the time those rebel degenerates were down at Griffin's Wharf doing their ungodly mischief."

Vivien shot a look at Victoria then slowly swung her gaze back to Neville. "You must be mad to believe such nonsense," she intoned.

Neville stiffened, his face mottled with rage. "How dare you," he grated.

Vivien retained a tranquil demeanor. "I dare, Neville," she said softly, "because no one in his right mind would believe

265

that Victoria would leave an elegant party and make her way to a notorious dock-side tavern. Why would she do such a thing? Think about it," she added, attempting a small laugh. "What could be more ludicrous?"

Neville took a calming breath. His doubleted shoulders and chest expanded autocratically. "I could agree with you on that," he clenched. "What I do not understand is why she was brought into our kitchen after midnight, dressed as a ragamuffin, by a known miscreant. Explain that to me, dear wife." It was obvious that Dory had had Sir Neville's ear.

Victoria swung her legs over the side of the bed and stood up. She swayed whoozily, but Vivien caught her and helped her to regain her balance. "I was feeling ill, Sir Neville," she said. "I needed some fresh air."

"And well you should have been ill, Lady Darby," Lord Frankland-Foster grated. "From what I understand, you made a spectacle of yourself."

Victoria eyed him narrowly. "And how would you have known such a thing?" she asked. "From what I could see, you, too, made yourself inexplicably absent from the festivities, Sir Neville." Her glance darted to Vivien. Victoria knew a pang of regret at having made such a reference, but she quickly decided that the man had forced the issue. He hastily backed away from the confrontation.

"I was—As host, you see, I," he sputtered. He hooded his gaze as he riveted Victoria with a reproving glower. His incertitude was apparently momentary. "I had duties to attend, young woman," he stated. "Beyond that, my absence is not the issue here. *I* am not the one who was seen at the Bull and Crown. *I* am not the one who was unceremoniously dumped, like so much laundry, in the kitchen of this house by Greyson Tyrrel. And," he added significantly, "I am not the one who got into a brawl with the commander-in-chief of the British armed forces in the colony of Massachusetts." He regarded both women with a challenging glare. "I cannot have these goings on in my house." He raised a triumphant brow at Vivien. "And this *is my house*," he stated. "Whatever little generosities I have afforded you, Vivien, are over. These are desperate times, and they call for desperate measures." His gaze darted to Victoria. "You, miss, are now under surveillance. Take that as a threat, if you wish to. I tell you this," he added, his teeth clenching, "I shall protect you—for now. I shall protect you not because you deserve protection but because I want no member of my household involved in a scandal. I also say to you that if one breath of misdeed where you are concerned reaches my ears, I shall toss you out of my house on your shapely behind. You see, I happen to know there is a reason why you might have been seen at the Bull and Crown. I happen to know you are not above *any* suspicion, and I shall have no qualm about bringing the wrath of the law down on your head. Not only that," he added slyly, "but I shall see to it that your Captain Greyson Tyrrel—" he spat the name derisively, "is accused of sedition in the proselytization of a loyal British subject." He smiled thinly. "I do not think the charge will be difficult to prove, your ladyship. I have it on excellent authority that as you crossed the ocean, on board the *Spectre of the Bay,* you and Greyson Tyrrel—a known enemy of the crown—were married."

" 'Tis no secret, Neville," Vivien hastily responded, glancing at Victoria. "The issue never arose. The first day Victoria arrived . . . we meant to tell you, but the time never seemed right. And after you accused Captain Tyrrel of spurious behavior, we thought it best to—"

"Captain Tyrrel's . . . *behavior*," the man rejoined, "is exactly the issue, Vivien. He and his band of infamous brutes are being questioned at this moment about the business last night. They had better be able to come up with some answers, because this time there will be no mercy for those responsible. They have laid hands on His Majesty's property, destroyed His Majesty's cargo. They are no longer dealing with local officials and weary soldiers; they are now dealing with King George himself. And if they are accused they shall hang." His lips twisted in a parody of mirth. "Their reputation precedes them, you see. Every one of them had better come up with a plausible alibi, for if one fails to convince his inquisitor, they shall all die. Treason *is* punishable by death—according to the law," he finished.

"As I hear it," Vivien ventured, "Indians committed the crime."

"Indians," Neville retorted in derision. "No one believes

267

for a moment that Indians perpetrated this foul depravity. 'Twas that notorious gang of vicious rebels that did the deed; everyone knows it." Vivien lifted a cinnamon-colored brow. "If they do not yet *know* it," Neville ground out, "they soon will." He spun on his thickly heeled paten and exited the room.

Both women sighed, relieved at his departure. Victoria sat down heavily on the bed. She eyed Vivien cautiously. "Last night," the girl began slowly, "I saw Greyson down by Griffin's Wharf." She hesitated as Vivien's regard darkened. Victoria went on. "I think," she said resignedly, "he was dressed as an Indian."

Chapter Twenty-one

Victoria waited until the Frankland-Foster household was asleep before she made her way down to the *Spectre of the Bay*. She braved the cold and dangerous night for one reason—to warn Greyson that the British suspected him and other known rebels of laying hands on His Majesty's property and destroying it. Dressed once again as a young man, she dared to leave her bed and the security of the mansion to traverse the unfamiliar tangle of darkened streets and find Greyson. She spotted him now walking the wharf near the boat, a cheroot held in his teeth. The glowing tip of the cigar shed just enough light so that Victoria could make out the familiar jawline, the etched lips and the golden stubble of beard on the strong chin.

"Greyson," she hissed into the darkness. He turned abruptly, warily. This was a night to be wary.

He moved toward the sound, silently. "Who is it?" he said, peering into the dark.

Victoria stepped from the shadows. Before she could speak, Greyson lunged for her. "Wait!" she cried hoarsely as he wrestled her to the dock. " 'Tis me!" she whispered. His eyes widened. The cigar still in his teeth, he gaped down at her.

"For the love of God, Victoria," he exclaimed, and then, glancing into the darkness around them, he quickly lifted her and carried her onto the deck of the *Spectre*. "What the hell are you doing out again," he demanded, once they were safely in the captain's quarters.

"I had no choice, Greyson," she explained, her tone desperate. "Lord Frankland-Foster said—"

269

Greyson grasped her arms and pulled her to his chest. "Dammit it, woman," he growled, "when will you remember your place!" Victoria reminded him calmly that her place was with him. He set her roughly away from him and then, just as quickly, rounded on her, drawing her into his arms. "Don't you understand what has happened tonight? 'Tis not a time to be gallivanting. I cannot bear to think of your being in danger," he said. He cradled the back of her head in one large hand and gazed down fiercely into her widened eyes. "You must go back to the house and remain there until I say otherwise. Do you understand?" Victoria's countenance became rigid.

"Dammit to bloody hell, Greyson," she challenged, "I came to warn you about what you have done—"

"I know *exactly* what I have done!" he grated. "Now I want you to get back to Vivien's house, woman, and I shall not tell you again."

Victoria's emerald gaze clouded with tears." I wanted to help you, Greyson," she whispered. "I love you." The simple declaration warmed Greyson's heart and stirred his soul. He looked down at her for a long moment, then at last he drew her to his chest, holding her, lifting his eyes to the Deity.

"What shall I do with my little rebel," he groaned.

"You might at least listen to her," she said softly, her voice muffled by the hard expanse of his chest. The strong throbbing of his heart infused her with a sudden stirring awareness of the life and need that pulsated within her. She tried to pull herself from him, but he held her, cradling her in the protection of his embrace.

"Oh, Victoria," he breathed into her hair, "I do not deserve such a woman."

The tears that had begun to form vanished in the melting happiness that Victoria always experienced in Greyson's embrace. Her arms slid around his lean middle, and she drew herself closer to him. She could not get him close enough. She longed to make them one—one being, one thought, one soul. Perhaps, if she held him hard enough, close enough, he might abandon this foolhardy cause of his. Perhaps he would take himself out of harm's way. She hoped it was not too late. She suddenly remembered her mission. She struggled away from him. Her thickly-lashed gaze met his.

"Listen to me, Greyson," she said desperately, for she

could see in his eyes that her need had fired his own. "You must listen to me. I came out tonight because I wanted to tell you something." It was at that moment that she knew she must fight a determined battle with her ripening passion.

"You have disobeyed me once again, love," Greyson whispered into her ear. The hot hunger of his embrace encloaked her, and Victoria knew only that she must convince him that what he was doing might endanger his very life.

"I disobeyed you," she moaned between kisses, "because I had to see you." Her own swelling passion would surely diffuse the importance of her mission. She attempted to draw herself away from the mastery of his need and the betrayal of her own body. "I had to warn you, Greyson," she breathed. "Oh, please, let me speak." Instead of that, Greyson pulled her onto the wide bed where they had shared so many glorious nights. Victoria gasped as he tugged at the constraints of her clothing. He took her breast in his big hand and lowered his lips to tease the responding bud of passion. "No, Greyson . . . let me tell you," she exclaimed. But his desire had carried them both too far.

The battle was not going well. Victoria struggled beneath Greyson, but he would not be deterred. As she tried to speak, his lips came down on hers, bruising in their primal hunger. His hands pleasured themselves and her as they tore relentlessly at her clothing, as they stroked her quivering nakedness. She felt herself dashed against the hard heat of his hunger. She felt herself enchained by the melting ache of her own need. She arched herself to his fiery power, opening her womanhood to the life-giving thrusts, the pulsing sword of his manly strength. The universe shattered. Victoria and Greyson were one—one being, one thought, one soul.

It was always this way for them. They lingered long in the rapture of their oneness, in the lambent embers of their love. Kisses, tender and consuming, warmed their cooling passion.

Victoria sighed as they trembled, holding one another, knowing that they were once again two people—two very different people. She must tell him what she had come to tell him, and yet this moment was so sweet. She did not wish to disturb its softness with harsh words. But Victoria girded herself. The harsh words needed to be said. She had to communicate to Greyson what Neville Frankland-Foster had told

271

her. She raised herself on one arm, taking slow breaths, looking down into Greyson's love-softened gaze. Her silken curls fell about her face and shoulders and teased them both with fleecy tendrils. She flicked them back impatiently.

"You are in grave danger," she said. "Sir Neville told me that you might be accused of treason."

"I know, love," he said gently, placing a roughened fingertip over her lips. "I know." He paused. "I have already been questioned. I could be arrested at any moment. 'Tis all part of the plan," he said. His tone held resolve and resignation.

Tears shimmered her gaze for the second time that night. "Won't you give up this rash ideal?" she asked.

A soft smile formed on his lips and he drew her down into the hills and hollows of his muscled embrace. "I cannot, Victoria. If I could — for you — I would, but — " At that moment the pounding of boots could be heard above them. Abrasive shouts filled the night. Greyson bounded from the bed and hastily stepped into his breeches and boots. "Stay there," he commanded as he lunged for the door. Victoria's eyes widened with horror as she saw the cabin door explode. Redcoated soldiers erupted into the room. Victoria could not count them, she only saw that they were surrounding Greyson and enmeshing him in a scarlet deluge. He was not even fighting. Standing proud and tall as a powerful red deer, he allowed them to surround him.

"You will allow me one last word with my wife," he said, and the nobility in his tone and his demeanor halted the work of the determined soldier who was binding Greyson's wrists. The man looked up, hesitating, but completing his task. The soldier in charge nodded after a pause as his gaze swung to Victoria, who was now huddled in the tumbled mass of bedsheets. Her pale countenance and widened eyes bespoke the unspeakable horror she was witnessing. Greyson moved to her slowly. "Try not to be afraid, love," he said softly. "Try to be strong, and try — as you have never tried before — to do as I say. Go back to Vivien. Stay there until I send for you. Do you understand?"

Victoria nodded mutely, lifting herself, pulling up the sheets to cover her nakedness. "Oh, Greyson," she breathed, taking him in her arms, barely able to speak. Kneeling before him amid the rumpled evidence of their passion, she gazed up into his eyes. "I shall do as you say," she managed. He longed to embrace her, but the British bonds were tight. He leaned down and kissed her lips. Cruelly, he was jerked from her.

Wordlessly, the soldiers led him from the cabin. As they disappeared into the darkness of the gun deck, Victoria heard only the dying cadence of their boots. Her tears came hot on her cheeks. Suddenly, Edmund Harrt was there. He sat beside Victoria on the bed, cradling her in a comforting embrace.

"I shall take you home, Victoria," he said gently.

The long nights of the coastal winter were achingly cold for Victoria. There was some consolation, however, as she nestled at last beneath her covers in the privacy of her room. The depravity of Lord Frankland-Foster slithered through her days like an evil thing. He stung her daily with sly innuendos and cutting allusions to her tenuous position in his household, but so far, he had not invaded her bedchamber. He hinted at threats against her husband. Though Greyson and his men had been cleared of any charges concerning what was now being termed "The Boston Tea Party," they were still very much under careful scrutiny by the authorities. Victoria knew intuitively that she must not approach him. Of course, she had the order from his own lips, but beyond that, she understood that it would be dangerous for them to be seen together. Her own reputation had been profoundly damaged. Rumors whirled about the town. Unfocused and certainly inconclusive, the gossip, nevertheless, kept her inside the house and away from the possibility of public inquiry — and official censure.

She busied herself writing letters to Katje and David. They may have heard of the trouble over here, she wrote, but she assured them it affected her life not at all. She couched her responses to their questions about the political issues in a carefully projected optimism. They asked her about the swift and retributive action taken by the British government against the colonists — about a series of laws called the "Coercive Acts" designed to coerce the obedience of the Americans. Victoria explained her interpretation of the new laws, but attempted to downplay the reaction of the colonists. It was not easy, for each law had shocked and infuriated the

273

American colonials. Public protests were not uncommon. Many Americans were calling the laws "The Intolerable Acts." British officials accused of crimes were, under the new laws, tried not in the colonies but in England or in Halifax, Nova Scotia. These "loyal" citizens would be protected, therefore, from any trumped up charges or so-called patriot juries. The capital of the colony had been moved from Boston to Salem. General Gage had been installed as a military governor, replacing Thomas Hutchinson. Under the law, the military reinforcements sent by the king to enforce these new and startling restraints were housed either in barracks built by the Bostonians, or, worse in the eyes of the colonists, they were quartered in private homes. Most restrictive — and damaging — of all the punitive actions was the planned closing of the Boston Harbor. For the town of Boston, at least, this was the most destructive of the new measures. It was aimed directly at the trade and mercantilism that kept the town alive. And once the law was enacted — in June of that year it was anticipated — it would remain extant until the culprits who perpetrated the destruction of His Majesty's tea were found and restitution made for its loss. Victoria did not mention this, of course, in her letters to India. In truth, no one believed that King George would actually close the Port of Boston — one of the most generative and vigorous ports in the world. Victoria told them that. She did not remind them that at least two of the laws violated English Common Laws in existence for centuries: that a man must be tried in the location of his crime, and that every British subject enjoyed the inalienable right to call his home his castle. The Americans denounced the laws, calling them tyrannical and unreasonable. But Victoria did not speak of that. Instead she wrote of British solidarity in support of the king. And she wrote of friendships she had made among certain of the more discerning colonial women, calling them delightful and friendly. In fact, Victoria had attended Vivien's sewing circle. She had met several of Boston's most prominent women, including Mrs. Otis and Mrs. Higginson and Mrs. Gannett, and the absolutely fascinating Mrs. Adams. With humorous impiety, Victoria reminded Uncle David that Abby Adams was the wife of the town's *only* gentleman — John Adams. Victoria wrote of teas and entertainments that Vivien had arranged at the Frankland-Foster mansion. In fact, such social functions were becoming fewer by the week. The population of the town was dropping rapidly as angry and disheartened citizens travelled to South Dorchester, Weymouth and other towns to find work. It was even rumored that many men had left to join a recently formed militia — but Victoria did not speak of that.

She read Katje's letter concerning the now year-old marriage of Steven Kensington and Barbara Meriam. Barbara, pregnant with the couple's first child, Katje wrote, was more deeply and scandalously imperious than ever. Her domination of her husband was the talk of the district. She had forced Steven to quit his card night *and* his polo. She had even — with the threat of terrible retribution if he did not comply — ordered him to his own bedchamber for the duration of her confinement. Steven seemed to accept this with surprising alacrity, wrote Katje. However, she added, he had — with the threat of a colonial uprising — joined the military. Victoria read this last information over. Steven had joined the military and was expected, within the next year, to be sent to America with his own command.

Victoria lowered the letter slowly into her lap. The golden image of Steven appeared and lingered before her. She closed her eyes against the image, but it only glimmered more intensely. So much time had passed, she reflected, remembering their last night together in Kolhapur. Steven may even be a father by now. What would have happened if he had not been so eager to succumb to his father's dictates, if he had married her instead of Barbara? How different their lives might have been.

Victoria shook herself firmly. She must not question what life had offered her. Whatever star had guided her destiny, it had led her to the wondrous Greyson. It was his laughing image, his roguish presence, that filled her mind and heart and overshadowed every other thought now. She recalled those idyllic days aboard the *Spectre* after she and Greyson had been married. She recalled his gentle care of her, his responsiveness to her every need. Balmy days were spent in agonies of hunger, cool nights were enjoyed in raptures of splendrous commemorations of their love. These were the things she had to remember about Greyson. She could not think of the terrible weeks they had been apart. She could not blame him for his dedication to a cause she could not embrace. She had to retain a belief in him, in what he was doing. He must have suffered greatly at the hands of the British, she shuddered. He had been incarcerated for several weeks now. The British excused their illegal action, saying that he was being questioned and held "for his own protection" against those who might attempt to influence him. Greyson along with Samuel Adams and several other men were the chief suspects in the tea affair. Victoria wondered tearfully every day if Greyson had been beaten or in other ways tortured to force him to admit to his guilt. And Victoria knew he was guilty. She wanted, nevertheless, to hear it from his own lips. For, once she heard him say the words, she could begin to sort out her feelings about what he had done. For now, she merely waited.

Her terrible frustration was not aided by the lecherous Lord Frankland-Foster. His menacing advances were becoming a serious threat to her composure. For Vivien's sake, she remained silent, rebuffing him with stolid looks and sullen refusals. She wondered how long it would be before he stormed the privacy of her bedchamber and demanded her compliance. His threats included denouncing her as a spy, but, so far, she was able to thwart him with nonchalantly lifted shoulders and irreverent challenges. "I dare you," she seemed to communicate with her unperturbed demeanor. In any event, Victoria thought bitterly, he still had the little drudge, Dory, on which to slake his lust. The girl, for all Victoria's threats to her, was still very much about — and extremely sure of herself. Worse, she had taken to baiting Victoria. She told her that Greyson had been released from British custody. She said that he was once again a man of the town and very much in demand by the female population.

The girl alleged often and with rapacious glee that Greyson was seeing not only several young acquaintances of hers but that he was consorting with the notorious tart, Bonny Bowdoin. Victoria's brows furrowed at that bit of information. If this was the same "Bonny" she had met at the Bull and Crown, Greyson's taste had changed radically since they had been together. Still, she reflected, she knew very little about Greyson's taste. What she did know was that he was a man of deep and galvanic hungers. And, he was not without reputation as both a fighter *and* a lover.

Victoria's musings were interrupted by the appearance in

the parlor of the little maid Dory. The girl curtsied flippantly, a triumphant smirk curling her lips. Victoria regarded her tiredly. What new information had the girl with which to torture her today?

"What is it, Dory," she asked disinterestedly.

"She's here," Dory answered smugly.

Victoria's interest kindled. "Who is here?" she asked.

"Who do you think?" Dory's face was alight with the glow of conquest. " 'Tis that woman I was tellin' you about that's romancin' the captain, that Bonny Bowdoin. She's at the front door." Victoria paled. She stood slowly, the letter from home drifting unnoticed to the floor.

"What does she want?" Victoria asked.

"How should I know," Dory answered, lifting a thin shoulder. "Shall I send her in?"

Victoria nodded mutely. She watched Dory exit the room and brushed hastily at her skirts as she awaited the appearance of the woman who was apparently her rival for Greyson's affections. Within seconds, the woman appeared. Tall and thick bosomed, Bonny Bowdoin stood at the arched entrance to the parlor. Her head, beneath her profusely flowered bonnet, tilted as she offered a greeting.

Victoria, eyes widened, surveyed the woman. Her gown, a brilliant amethyst satin with puffed undersleeves of heliotrope lace, rustled majestically as she stepped forward and leaned toward Victoria. That woman recoiled perceptibly. "I got a message for you from the captain," Bonny said, undaunted. "He wants you to know the Brits have released him." She glanced over her shoulder then continued in a cautious, quiet tone. "He's back on the *Spectre,* but he don't want you tryin' to see him. He says as soon as it's safe, he'll contact you." She eyed Victoria speculatively. "You got that?" she asked, for the younger woman seemed not to comprehend her words. Victoria only nodded hesitantly. Bonny Bowdoin pursed her lips, and her brow furrowed. "It's real important, Lady Darby, that you do what the captain says. He wanted me to remind you of that, 'cause he says you're kind of rebellious and he can't ever be sure what you might do . . ." Bonny's voice trailed off, and she smiled sheepishly. "I think he meant it in a nicer way than it sounds — you know what I mean," the woman added. Victoria only stared. Bonny arched a blond brow and drew back her shoulders.

"The Brits is arrestin' everybody," she stated, "and Grey wanted me to tell you to stick close to your friends." When, once again, Victoria did not respond, Bonny regarded her sardonically. "You don't say much, do you?" she observed. Then, lifting her shoulders in a dispassionate shrug, the woman turned, and snuggling her hands into her fur muff, she ambled, swaying from the room, mumbling, "Well, I done my part. What can you do with somebody who insists on goin' about dressed up like a lad?"

Victoria sat heavily. She did not hear the front door slam, nor did she note Dory as the girl poked her head into the room to survey Victoria's reaction to Bonny's visit.

In fact, Victoria had paid scant attention to Bonny's warning. She knew only that the rumors Dory had gleefully related must be true. At the very least it was true that Greyson had confided in Bonny Bowdoin about his release and not in her. Victoria regraded the doorway from which that woman had exited. The look of the woman registered in her mind as she recalled the fashionable gown — meretricious though it may have been — and the regal way she carried herself. She was being kept very well by someone. Was that someone Greyson Tyrrel? Victoria's emerald gaze narrowed, glittering dangerously. So Greyson was out of jail, and he was ordering his wife — through a notorious lady of ill-repute — to stay away from him. Victoria stood and made what some might have considered a rash decision. She went to the writing desk and composed a note, demanding to meet with Greyson. She knew how dangerous such a meeting could be. She realized that under the present circumstances, she and Greyson ought not to be seen together, but she also knew that she could not go on doubting, wondering, allowing Greyson to grow farther and farther away from her. She would talk to him, dammit. She would discover his true feelings for her. If he wanted Bonny, that was one thing. Victoria could not, and would not fight the tart for Greyson's affections.

She gazed down at the note she had written. It was nothing short of vitriol. She crumpled it slowly. It was not at all what she wanted to say to her husband. She loved Greyson deeply, she had faith that ultimately he loved her. She composed another note. She needed to see him, to understand the present circumstances. If only she could talk to him, she might be able to endure the sacrifices she was apparently expected to make. If only she could fully understand his great cause, she might be able to allow his absence from her with more generosity of spirit. She might even encourage that absence in the name of a greater good.

As she dressed for her meeting with her husband, she pondered what good at all could come of his activities. He had done nothing really but make the British violently angry. This tea business had aggravated an already tension-filled situation. He and his cohorts had succeeded in getting themselves arrested, forcing the suspension of civilian law and seeing to it that the entirety of Boston Town was under the siege of martial law. In the bargain, he had threatened the very foundation of their marriage. But, of course, that was something she must give Greyson an opportunity to explain. She could not take the word of a brazen kitchen wench whose own shamelessness was no doubt the spur of her accusations.

Victoria made her way from the house stealthily, avoiding the interference of Sir Neville. She hoped to meet Greyson at a little cent shop that she and Vivien had discovered at the base of King Street on the corner of Union, and had advised him of that location in her note. She had felt that the district there was crowded enough that they would not be noticed, and yet the shop, itself, was secluded in an alley behind a large house.

She hurried along in a misting rain. It had rained for many days now. Victoria sighed as she drew her cloak more tightly around her shoulders and wriggled uncomfortably beneath the chilly dampness of the day. She had decided against taking the chaise. The fewer people who knew of her errand, the safer she and Greyson would be. There were only three people privy to her plan. There were she and Greyson, of course, and the little boy she'd hired to take her message to the *Spectre,* and even he did not realize exactly what the message contained. The lad had reminded her in so many ways of Jack. She smiled, thinking of him, wondering how he was faring through all of this. He had no doubt been devastated to hear of Greyson's arrest. If she had dared, she would have suggested to Vivien that they take him in. Naturally, Victoria thought bleakly, Neville Frankland-Foster would never have agreed to such an arrangement. Beyond that, Victoria had not even dared go near the *Spectre*. It really wouldn't have mattered, though. She chuckled aloud, imagining Jack's reaction at being forced to leave his beloved captain. Once she and Greyson had their own house, she would welcome the piquant young Jack into her heart once again. She would care for him in the way a boy of his spirit and vitality and loyalty ought to be taken care of. Someday, perhaps, she would even take him back to Kolhapur to be spoiled by Katje and Uncle David and Mrs. Jafar. He would enjoy robust rides over the rolling green hills and hollows of the plantation. He could swim in the sparkling blue pools. He could enjoy the resplendent childhood that Victoria had enjoyed. That was the life for Jack. She would be sure to ask Greyson about him. It was with a lightened heart that she stepped into the little shop. The tinkling of the bell announced her entrance, and she looked around to find, among the three or four other customers, the smiling figure of Edmund Harrt.

He lifted his tricorn and held it before him as he bowed. "Lady Darby," he proclaimed.

Victoria was disappointed, but she smiled at his formality. "I am Mrs. Tyrrel now, Edmund," she said, offering her hand.

Edmund quirked a sandy brow. "I suppose that would depend these days upon whom you are speaking to."

Victoria nodded sadly. "You are so right," she said. Glancing around the store, she swung her gaze back to the young warrant officer. He noted her anticipation and offered his own sad smile.

"He could not come, Victoria," he said, leading her to a quiet corner.

She eyed him worriedly. "Has he been released from prison?" she asked, needing to confirm what she already knew. Edmund nodded. Victoria's heart twisted painfully. "When?"

"A week ago," he said softly. Victoria wondered how could Edmund have known of her message to Greyson? He seemed to read her question. "He asked me to come in his stead; he bade me tell you that he was . . . indisposed."

"Indisposed, Edmund," she wailed softly. "I need to see him. Why hasn't he contacted me?"

The young man hesitated. "The fact is, Victoria, he wondered whether it was wise for you to have suggested this meeting at all." Victoria's displeasure was clear, and Edmund Harrt continued hastily. "You must consider that the two of you are on shaky ground right now," he said. "Neither of you is above suspicion. Greyson's culpability is, naturally, much greater than your own, but . . . well, the truth is, Victoria, your name has been bandied about in a most . . . uncomplimentary context."

"You mean because of my little breach of British etiquette with General Gage," she stated. "I tell you this, Edmund, I am not in the least penitent about the things I said to him. He was arrogant and totally parochial. One would think there was only one point of view to be considered in all this—the British point of view. I do not agree with the colonists on many points, including this tea party they staged, Lord knows, but I acknowledge that they may have their reasons for their bitterness. I believe I am within my rights as a British citizen to—"

"You are well within your rights, Victoria," Edmund said soothingly. His eyes darted around the room, and Victoria realized she may have been speaking entirely too freely in these awkward times. Edmund went on in a more fitting tone, his voice gently hushed. "You do know"—he smiled—"there is that very dogmatic British tradition of absolute loyalty to the Crown." He laughed softly. Victoria, too, managed a smile. "I suppose Gage, in his provincialism, expected you to take the British side, no matter the issue." He paused, then continued pointedly. "If that were the only problem you faced, I believe you would not be in trouble. The real problem is that your confrontation with the general came on the heels of your being seen in the company of a group of troublemakers. Then, after that, you were spotted at the Bull and Crown." He sighed. "And to make matters worse for you, if they can get worse, I am afraid everyone now knows that you are Mrs. Greyson Tyrrel."

"But how did that get out, Edmund? Lady Frankland-Foster and I were the only ones that knew the truth, except of course for Greyson."

"And every man and woman aboard the *Spectre*," Edmund reminded her. "A marriage witnessed by nearly three hundred people is not something that can be kept secret for long," he said cheerlessly. "It was bound to come out."

"I was not even *trying* to keep it a secret," Victoria said earnestly. "I was perfectly ready to acknowledge our marriage. Vivien and I just thought that for the moment, as long as Lord Frankland-Foster was so intolerant of Greyson's reputation, we had best not mention it. That really was the only reason the fact of our marriage never came out."

"Some would have it that you hid the fact deliberately. Because of that there are many among the British who believe that you and Greyson Tyrrel are in collusion for some deceitful purpose," Edmund responded quietly. "I am so sorry, Victoria, but I am afraid you simply got off on the wrong foot in this town. The British gentry mistrust you for your marriage to Greyson, and the colonists mistrust you because you are a member of the British gentry. The times engender suspicion; everyone seems to be looking for hidden motives."

"Yes," Victoria agreed. "Despite Sir Neville's warning, I seem to have gotten myself involved in all sorts of hanky-panky." She smiled, but her face immediately sobered. She looked up into the brown lucence of Edmund's eyes. "Do you think I have an enemy here?" she asked in a small voice.

Edmund quirked a brow. "An enemy?" he asked.

"I know it sounds odd, but I have the distinct feeling that someone wants to see me discredited." She lifted a slim shoulder and smiled ruefully. "Perhaps it is only the temper of the times that stimulates my paranoia, but I cannot ignore certain facts. Someone has been spreading the news of my indiscretions. I just wonder who dislikes me that much. I thought the passengers and crew had been mollified by my marriage to Greyson," she said, "but apparently there is at least one among them who was not mollified—who intends to see me sacrificed in the bedlam of this cause."

Edmund placed a comforting arm around her shoulders. "If I thought there was anyone like that in this town, I would personally strangle him, Victoria," he said. "I think it is as you first pointed out. These are confusing times for all of us. You are being singled out right now. Tomorrow someone else will catch the public scrutiny. You must try not to take all this personally." He smiled down at her. "I know 'tis hard," he said, "but I have always known you were a woman of spirit and determination. You will surmount this momentary obstacle to your happiness."

"I could surmount it much easier if my husband were by my side," she said, her face woeful. She paused and looked up at Edmund Harrt. "If I could believe that Greyson still loved me, I think I could face anything."

"Of course he loves you, Victoria," Edmund said, turning her to face him. He lifted her chin with a gloved forefinger. "Whatever made you think he did not?"

"He did not come today," she offered. Tears popped into her wide gaze.

"He could not come, Victoria," Edmund assured her. "You must know how occupied he is these days."

Victoria nodded. "I do understand that," she responded softly, "but there is something else. I have heard that he . . . dallies with other women. I cannot bear to think of that. It breaks my heart."

"If Greyson dallies with others, sweet, I do not know about it." His smile was warm. "Besides, are you going to listen to the same type of innuendo of which you, yourself, have been a victim, or are you gong to have faith in the man you love?" He laughed and pulled her gently to his chest. "Even if our captain is . . . dallying," he said, "and I do not believe he is, 'twould never change the fact that he adores you. You must not dwell on such treacherous thoughts, sweet." He held her for several moments. Victoria clung to him, her tears abating. So like a loving brother was this Edmund Harrt—this most gentle of gentle men.

Victoria drew away from him so that she could look up into the velvet brown of his eyes. "You do know that Greyson loves me, then?"

"I do," he said kindly. He led her to the door. "Let me see you home." As they walked together in the misty chill, Edmund kept his arm snugly around her shoulders. "This is getting to be quite a habit for us"—he laughed—"me seeing you home, I mean. If Captain Tyrrel doesn't keep a better eye on you, I might just decide to take you home—to my home." They laughed together, softly, securely, like the two old friends they had become.

Another of Dory's sly insinuations as she built up the evening fire in Victoria's room both aggravated and aggrieved Victoria. She, as was her custom, did not respond to the jibe, but it left her discouraged. If Greyson were here with her, the impudent girl would not be able to make such allu-

283

sions. If they had a normal marriage, Victoria would know her husband's whereabouts. Edmund Harrt had done nothing, really, to assuage her distress. Oh, she believed him when he told her that Greyson loved her. The question was, of course, could Greyson be faithful to her?

She sat tiredly in her rocker. Next to her on a table were her writing materials: her parchment and her charcoal. She had not written a poem in months, and poetry, as always, became her solace. She held the charcoal above the paper as her eyes closed. At last her lids lifted, and she began to write.

When in existence to sleep is your test;
Even though you have tossed and thought all night.
The brain rejects peace and the heart cannot rest;
Better to live to death or die in life?
To drink wine with her or breakfast with me;
We wait for your decision to take place.
She knows your flesh; your soul is mine to see
How lines of time have strained and changed your face.
She knows your taste for wine; I know your breath.
She feels your pulses; I can read your palm.
She stirs your glass; your sense soars at my breast.
When you've had too much, you reach to me for calm.
    To live and die in restless resistance;
    When sleep is the test of life's existence.

She smiled as she regarded what she had written. One day she would show it to her husband.

Victoria prepared for bed. It had been a long day. She snuggled gratefully beneath her covers. Outside, she heard the spatter of the now freezing rain against her window. She watched as the crackling fire grew dim. She fell wearily, warmly, dreamily into slumber.

In her dreams, she felt Greyson's presence. She felt his weight next to her in the darkness. He lifted her in his strong arms, drawing her to him. He held her, hovering above her like a bronze star. His russet curls brushed her cheek as his lips feathered her face and neck with tender, hungering kisses. "Oh, love," he whispered.

His warm breath radiated desire, and Victoria felt an urgency grow beneath her ripening flesh. From her breasts to her belly, she felt hunger take hold. She arched to his masterful caress. Buds of ecstasy erupted in tiny liquid blossoms of flowering need. She opened her eyes. It was no dream.

Greyson was there, his glinting presence above her in the golden firelight filled the depths of her vision. No question passed her lips, no breath of doubt. She raised her arms, entwining them around the strong column of his neck. As his big hands roved her body, she yielded to his towering essence. She tunneled her fingertips into his thick curls and pressed him to her. Their lips met in a fiery caress.

In a fever of seething need, too long repressed, they stirred each other, exploring lambent hungers, igniting smoldering passions. Hot, pulsing geysers licked at Victoria's innermost core, heating her desire, melting her soul. She opened herself to the mercy of Greyson's voracious power, laid herself bare to his mastery. He slaked his thirst for her at the fountain of her woman's bounty.

Lifting her to him, possessing her in the storm of his passion, he consumed her. She writhed beneath his ravenous appetite. The flux of her rapture pulsed life into his manly veins. He took her with the force of a lightning bolt, his power generated by the surge of her need. She was hurled upward, upward beyond stars and suns. The universe exploded inside of her, shattering her will, filling her with a pumping, pungent repletion.

She held a long breath, feeling only the throbbing of her heart, the dark heat of Greyson's surfeited ardor. She felt his muscled arms tighten around her as he sought to capture that moment of their mutual ecstasy. Eternity echoed in the tiny hollows of their embrace. They pressed it closer, not wanting it to escape. Their breathing melded in a hushed symphony of fulfillment.

Greyson lifted himself, taking his weight on his arms. He gazed down on her. "Oh, love," he breathed. "How long it has been."

A smile curved the flower of her lips. "I could not have waited another second," she whispered. Their eyes, shimmering fluidly in the dark, held each other. Now, there was no misgiving, no uncertainty, no distrust. Victoria believed in the full measure of Greyson's love. She gave herself in full measure in a silent communication. They had no need of words.

But the words came, suddenly, terrifyingly. The door of

her room crashed open; Sir Neville boiled into the room. Fury glazing his eyes, he stood before the bed holding a candle. In a rage, he hurled the candle at them.

"Bitch!" he shrieked. "You slattern bitch!"

Greyson leapt from the bed, charging the intruder and tumbling them both to the floor. Victoria pounded out the fire the candle had started on the counterpane. Greyson and Neville roiled in a writhing frenzy in the center of the room. With sudden dispatch, Greyson rammed a powerful blow into Neville's belly and sent the older man careening to the floor. The battle was over before it had begun.

"What the bloody hell is going on here?" Greyson ejaculated. He threw Victoria her dressing gown and stepped into his breeches. "Who in the name of satan are you?" he demanded of the gasping gagging man who writhed beneath him in the center of the room. Victoria rose and hastened, with shaking fingers, to light a lamp.

"He is Lord Frankland-Foster," she breathed, clutching at her cursorily donned gown.

Greyson shot her a riveting glare. "What is the bloody hound doing in your bedchamber? He hasn't tried this before, has he?"

Victoria shook her head, her heart fluttering in her chest. "No," she gasped. The murderous glint in Greyson's eyes sent her breathless to his side. "No, Greyson," she repeated, attempting a calmer tone, "he never touched me."

At once, Greyson lunged at the man and dragged him by the scruff of his collar to his feet. Lord Frankland-Foster exhaled a ghastly moan. His face was bleached of color. He gasped, inhaling desperately. Greyson shook him and tossed him onto the bed. He slumped like a rag doll, his head lolling between his knees. Greyson grasped at his shirt and jerked him upright.

"What do you think you are doing in here, you craven bastard," he grated. Teeth bared, he closed the scrap of distance between himself and Lord Neville. The man wheezed hoarsely, his mouth gaping.

"Please, Greyson," Victoria asserted as her delicate white hands clutched at his girded arm, "he is an old man; he is going to be sick."

"He is going to be more than sick," he ground out. He jogged the man viciously once again and then, with cold dispatch, let him collapse onto the bed. He eyed Victoria narrowly. "What is this all about?"

Victoria's mind whirled. If she told him about Lord Neville's advances, Greyson would no doubt kill him. He would be hanged for such a crime, no matter the provocation. "He . . . he wanted to read my poetry, Greyson, that was all. He probably came in here to see if I was awake."

Greyson's gaze hooded. "From the names he was calling you, I would have guessed he was here on another sort of mission entirely."

"He is such an old stick, you know that," she improvised desperately. "You remember the night you had dinner here. He considers himself an arbiter of morality." Her voice was pleading now. "Sir Neville is harmless, Greyson, I promise you."

"What is the matter!" Greyson and Victoria swung their gazes to the door. Vivien stood before them, clenching the opening of her night robe, her gray eyes bleary with sleep and terror. Victoria dashed to her side.

" 'Tis nothing, Vivien," she soothed anxiously. " 'Tis really nothing." She looked pleadingly to Greyson. "Tell her, 'tis nothing, Greyson."

"He is hurt," Greyson said tersely. "We had better get him into bed."

Vivien nodded and moved quickly to her husband's side. Greyson lifted the man over one broad shoulder and strode from the room with Vivien in the lead. Victoria followed, praying, pleading with the Lord to spare Sir Neville's life. No one dared to call a doctor.

Lord Neville Frankland-Foster awakened painfully, his head lolling on the pillow from side to side. Remembering little of what had happened, he questioned Vivien wretchedly about his injuries. Victoria managed to convince both he and Vivien that she had mistaken him for an intruder and simply defended herself. Through the day and night, Lord Frankland-Foster slept many hours. Neither he nor Vivien nor Victoria mentioned the incident again.

Chapter Twenty-two

" 'Twill never happen," said Abby Adams with certainty. "King George would never actually close the harbor." The other women agreed solemnly that such a tragedy was unimaginable.

"I have been in prayer since that awful day that General Gage announced the possibility of such a penalty," said Mrs. Warren softly.

"You forget, Mercy," stated Vivien not unkindly, "the Boston Port Bill is not a threat. 'Tis the law."

"I have no doubt that God will protect us," said Mrs. Higginson.

Mrs. Gannett agreed. "Why, if Boston Harbor were to be closed, we might all starve to death. Our ancestors did not come down here over a hundred years ago guided by Providence, only to have Providence desert us now," she asserted.

The women of the Wednesday Sewing Club were working diligently at their latest project, the creation of one of several quilts which they hoped to sell to make money for the town's homeless.

Victoria sipped at the coffee her hostess had offered and winced at its thick bitterness. Naturally, in the Adams household, tea was not offered. It was a good bet that after the event of the sixteenth of December, there would be no alteration in that custom for some time to come. Mrs. Adams smiled sadly at the girl.

"I am sorry, Victoria," she said softly. "You know this boycott is as hard on us as it is on you. Tea is *our* national drink as well." The other women joined in sympathetic and laughing agreement.

Vivien eyed them all sorrowfully. "I think you should all know," she said evenly, "that Neville has been advised to leave Boston as soon as possible."

Mrs. Gannett raised a brow. "The British have been advising *that* since the Massacre of '70, Vivien."

"The massacre that was not a massacre," said Abby Adams with a small laugh.

"Defend those lobster-backed blighters if you will, Abigail," said Mrs. Gannett, "but . . ." her voice trailed off as she glanced first at Vivien and then at Victoria. "Oh," she intoned, placing delicate fingertips over her lips, "I apologize to both of you ladies."

Vivien and Victoria exchanged a smile. The women of Boston had been determinedly bipartisan in the events of the last several years. They had decided that their effectiveness in this chaos would come in a demonstration of unity rather than in bitter confutations. The men were divided enough in these uncertain and perplexing times. The ladies were determined that history — and there was a great sense of history among these women — should record them as having been excellent homemakers, keepers of the flame and, if necessary, captains of the home front. They all shied from that last designation and all that it implied. They did not want to think of the possibility of war, though in truth, it was all people seemed to talk about these days. The Wednesday Sewing Club was the last vestige of civility among the divided factions. But it was becoming more and more difficult to remain untouched by the vast ideological chasm that separated the citizens of Boston. Even the most urbane and cultivated members of society — as these women certainly were — were affected.

Vivien, seated next to Mrs. Gannett, patted the woman's arm. " 'Tis all right, dear Deborah," she said gently. "We do not blame you for your feelings."

Deborah Gannett smiled and placed a hand over Vivien's. "So often I find myself feeling frustrated and even angry, Vivien. I know it must be just as difficult for you"—she looked quickly at Victoria—"and your household."

Mercy Warren laughed softly. "Sometimes I feel I must be in labor, but there is no baby at the end of all the pain."

"Something must come of it, though," said Abby Adams. "I cannot believe that this strife will amount to nothing."

"I think it will amount to a great deal," said Mrs. Gannett.

"I think you are right, Deborah," Vivien affirmed. "Neville has heard from the prime minister himself. He assures Neville that if we want to get out of the colonies at all, we had better leave immediately."

Victoria eyed her friend thoughtfully. "You did not mention that to me, Vivien," she said.

"I did not wish to worry you, Victoria," the older woman answered.

"For heaven's sake, Vivien, you sound just like a man." Mercy Warren puckered her lips as she manipulated a particularly complex stitch. Glancing up at Mrs. Adams, she commented, " 'Twould help enormously, Abby, if we had some pins."

"I know, Mercy," she sighed. "I have asked John if he cannot see to getting some for us. His circuit takes him to so many villages. One would think that somewhere in the colony of Massachusetts there would be a few pins."

"What we used to buy for seven and six are now costing twenty shillings," Mrs. Gannett complained, jabbing her needle with a decided annoyance.

"And they're not to be had for that here in Boston," affirmed Mrs. Warren.

The very pious Mrs. Higginson added her own observation. "I should go to battle myself for a bundle of pins."

Vivien set down her cup with a decided click. "You may have to do that all too soon," she said. Everyone glanced at her as she picked up her portion of the quilt to continue her sewing.

"Tell us, Vivien," asked Mrs. Warren, "is it your intention to leave Boston?" Victoria watched Vivien beneath lowered lashes. She was more than a little curious herself as to the Frankland-Fosters' intentions. Surely their plans would affect her own.

"I am not sure what Neville intends to do," Vivien answered. She looked up to realize with a combination of mild amusement and astonishment that everyone was watching her.

"You do seem to have an inside track as to the intentions of the British. Do you believe there will be a war?" Mrs. Gannett questioned.

Abigail Adams targeted them all with a riveting glance. "I

think we had best leave politics out of our discussion, ladies," she said sternly.

"This is not strictly speaking politics," stated Mrs. Warren.

" 'Tis only natural we should wish to know Vivien's opinion," added Mrs. Gannett.

"I admit to a certain curiosity myself," laughed Mrs. Adams, lowering her gaze. "Still, I think we should avoid — "

"The ladies are asking harmless questions," said Mrs. Higginson primly. She turned to Vivien, waiting for her answer.

Vivien sat back in her chair and smiled at each woman in her turn. She brushed at an errant wisp of her bright Titian hair. Her gray-green eyes sparkled in merriment. "I thought we had decided that we were above politics, ladies," she said, steepling her fingers before her.

"And we are," said Mercy Warren defensively. "But quite frankly, Vivien, you are an enigma." The other ladies nodded in good-natured agreement.

"We have never known exactly where you stood on any of this," stated Mrs. Gannett.

"Deborah is right, Vivien," said Abby Adams, abandoning for the moment her insistence on bipartisanship. "I remember you visiting several homes on John's behalf when he was elected to the House of Representatives." Vivien nodded, smiling.

"And yet, in this very room," stated Mrs. Higginson, "you as much as lionized King George. You said he was — what did you call him? Oh, yes," Mrs. Higginson went on. "You said he was a 'sympathetic figure.' Now, do not deny that, Vivien."

"I recall that day," Mrs. Warren joined in. "I was so embarrassed for you, Vivien. I would have said something, but the day before that you had baked all those pies for the Sons of Liberty rally in Dorchester."

"And *that* without your husband's knowledge or permission," stated Mrs. Higginson.

"If my husband had had any knowledge of such a thing, I can assure you all, he would not have given his permission." Vivien laughed.

"I hate to think what Lord Frankland-Foster might have said if he'd known," agreed Mrs. Higginson. There was a long pause as all the ladies waited expectantly for an explanation from their friend. Vivien watched them in tranquil silence.

"Vivien," Deborah Gannett finally said, "you are our very dear friend. You know how deeply we love you." She paused. "But the fact is you are an English noble woman living in America during very trying times. We are naturally curious as to where your political loyalties lie."

"Oh, pooh," Vivien scoffed, "I've no political loyalties." She leaned forward. "Let me tell you something about politics, my dears. It is a man's game. Men invented it. And I do not intend to play—at least not their way. Why do you imagine we are all here today, sewing this quilt? 'Tis because that silly war with the French nearly destroyed this town. Widows and their children walk the streets of Boston, unable to support themselves. Why? I shall tell you why. 'Tis because the men made a war. And why did the men make a war? They made a war because they wanted the Ohio Valley."

"And Canada and the southeastern seacoast," said Abby Adams flatly.

"Exactly," said Vivien. "And pray tell me what good the Ohio Valley does those pitiful specimens of humanity that walk the streets of Boston? What good does Canada do them, or the southeastern seacoast? If they have no home, no money and no opportunity to earn money, what good would owning the bloody world do them? And who can 'own' the world, in any event? Can the forests be 'owned'? Can the rivers be 'owned'? Can the mountains be 'owned'?"

"King George thinks *he* owns them," said Mrs. Higginson drily.

"Yes," said Vivien, "George Hanover *does* believe he owns them. But thousands of men in these colonies think *they* own them, too. And so they shall have their war." She sat back tiredly and lifted her cup. Taking a sip of the unpleasant brew, she scowled. "The men have decided to make a war over tea," she said softly. She glanced from woman to woman. "War," she said evenly. The word sent a shiver of foreboding through the room. Destiny loomed irrevocably over the gathering of women.

In an abrupt change of attitude, Vivien glanced at Sue Higginson. "By the way, dear Sue," she said, "if you are going to quote someone, you ought to quote them correctly." Mrs. Higginson regarded Vivien, a question in her eyes. Vivien smiled. "I did not say King George was a 'sympathetic character.' My exact words, I believe, were that George III is a fascinating psychological study. Remember that the House of Hanover has not been a model of dynastic effectiveness either in England or her colonies. For heaven's sake, George's father and grandfather were little more than laughingstocks. Have a pity, ladies. The poor man imagines he *has* to be masterful lest he be perceived as a milksop. George III is no tyrant, but if he says he will close the Port of Boston, believe me, he will do so. He is, after all, only a man."

"A very *foolish* man," stated Abby Adams.

Vivien nodded amiably. "You will get no argument from me on that point," she said. "But aren't they all? And that is precisely why I adhere to no particular political ideology. Until I am allowed a voice in the body that governs my life, I shall remain a silent observer of it."

"Why did you support Abby's husband, then?" asked Mercy Warren.

"I supported John because he is devoted to Abby," Vivien said with an impish smile. "John is one of the few politicians who might be enjoined to consider the female members of his constituency — if his devotion to you, Abby, is any indication of his feelings in general about women." Vivien returned her cup to the small table and picked up her sewing. "And that, ladies," she said, plying her needle diligently, "is where my political loyalties lie." There was a long silence as Vivien continued her work.

Abby Adams was the first to speak. "I know I speak for all of us, Vivien, when I tell you that for so many reasons, I pray that Sir Neville decides to stay here in America. We should hate to lose you."

" 'Tis so true," said Mercy Warren. Sue Higginson and Deborah Gannett agreed.

"Thank you all," said Vivien, lifting her gaze.

"Has Neville discussed any of this with you?" asked Abby.

Vivien shook her head. "I have no idea what my husband intends to do," she answered.

"Not everyone is fortunate enough to have a husband like yours, Abby," said Mrs. Warren. "John talks to you about absolutely everything." The women laughed.

" 'Tis too true," said Abby. "There are occasions when I should prefer he made his own decisions, though. As when he had the new privy installed at Braintree."

"I recall that," said Vivien. "He would not allow a shovelful of dirt removed from the property until his 'Nabby' had approved the site."

"I travelled all the way back to the country just so I could nod my approval at the workmen." Abby Adams laughed, and the women joined her, envying her, nevertheless, the devotion of her husband.

Victoria watched this company of sophisticated and worldly-wise women. She could not help but admire their courage and their boldness of spirit. Each one of them faced an uncertain — and possibly terrifying — future. And yet they were able to chide each other, bandy opinions and still remain friends, still laugh together. Vivien fit so perfectly with these clever and admirable women. She was as clever and admirable — and assured — as any of them. Her assurance was a side of Vivien Victoria had not seen often these days. She wondered at the woman's lack of resolution where it concerned her husband. Naturally, it was not something about which Victoria could question her. Surely, though, Vivien now knew of Neville's perfidy toward her. How could she not know of it? The incident in Victoria's bedroom had never been mentioned by any of them. Surely, Vivien was curious about it. Victoria sighed inwardly. If only Vivien could be spared the pain of a faithless husband.

"What will you do about all this, Victoria?" asked Mrs. Warren.

Victoria started as though the woman had read her mind. "About all what?" she asked hesitantly.

"About leaving the colonies, of course," said Mercy. At Victoria's blank stare, the woman went on tolerantly. "Will you be leaving the colonies?"

"I . . . I have not thought about it," Victoria answered. "I never thought it would come to this."

"Poor thing," said Mrs. Gannett.

Victoria glanced toward Vivien and noted that she was gazing keenly out the window.

"Whatever is so fascinating out there?" asked Mrs. Higginson.

Vivien turned back to her companions. " 'Twas just a group of young men passing by," she said vaguely.

Abby laughed softly. "I do not blame the two of you for

being distracted," she said. "You must make some very difficult decisions within the next few weeks." All the women joined her in her concern for the two English ladies.

Later, as Vivien and Victoria walked home from the Adams house, Vivien confided what she had seen through the window. " 'Twas a legation of young men, Victoria," she said, "a *legation,* I tell you. I know the difference between a 'passle of hearties' taking the afternoon air and a legation. Those boys had a mission."

"Whatever do you mean, Vivien?" asked Victoria, snuggling the older woman's hand more securely into the crook of her arm. It had rained through much of the late winter and early spring, and the narrow streets were pitted with deep puddles which the ladies were hard pressed to avoid.

"I mean," she said softly, "that these young men are through making public protests, they are through sending letters to the king and lobbying with parliament. They want action. If George closes that port—and as you know, I believe he will—there can be only one consequence."

Victoria eyed her worriedly. "Do you really believe that, Vivien?" she asked. The woman nodded with certainty. Maybe, reflected Victoria, they *should* leave the colonies. Maybe they should all leave. She could never convince Greyson of that, however. But maybe she should try.

As the two women stepped into the hallway of the Frankland-Foster mansion, Sir Neville charged toward them. His manner was uncharacteristically flustered, his face crimson, his waistcoat flapping open, his white wig askew. Before Vivian could even remove her shawl, he took her shoulders in his hands and swung her to face him.

"Do you have something to tell me, Neville?" she asked.

"We are leaving, Vivien," he said sternly. "I have booked us passage on Sir Dan's vessel. We sail tonight. Get what you can together within the hour." He turned, intending to leave, but Vivien stopped him.

"What is this all about?" she asked.

"Do not question me, woman," he rejoined, rounding on her. "I had a letter from our young Thomas today. He has been consigned to the military. If they are taking boys out of Harrow, for God's sake, there is no question—"

"Thomas," Vivien breathed. "But he is barely sixteen."

"Exactly," proclaimed her husband. "They have also accepted Derrick. Both boys expect to be sent here. I tell you, Vivien, there *is* going to be a war. I cannot believe it. I cannot believe the bloody colonists would—"

The tears had come slowly to Vivien's eyes. She swooned, and Victoria caught her in her arms. With the help of Sir Neville, she got her into the small parlor. "No," Vivien sobbed softly, as she was seated on one of the small sofas. "No, dear God, no," she said again and again.

"For heaven's sake, Vivien, control yourself," Neville scolded derisively. "I told you we are getting out of these damned colonies. We shall go back to Ipswich and—"

Vivien looked up at him through her tears. "Neville," she said softly, "do you really imagine I would go back to England when my sons are going to be here fighting a war?"

"Don't be absurd," he huffed, "of course you shall go back to England. I told you, we sail tonight. I have made us excellent accommodations on Sir Daniel Winthrop's very fine ship and we shall—"

"I am not going with you, Neville," Vivien said calmly. She dabbed at her tears as Neville regarded her in disbelief. He glanced at Victoria. That young woman offered no assistance.

His eyes narrowed. "This is your doing," he stated.

Victoria merely watched him. Vivien stood quickly. "This is none of Victoria's doing Neville," she said.

"Yes it is," he thundered. He grabbed at the girl, but Vivien quickly stepped in his way, thwarting his move. "Do not defend the little tramp," he grated and attempted to shove his wife aside.

"If you touch her," Vivien warned, "I shall kill you." Her eyes snapped gray fire. "Dammit, Neville, haven't you tortured her enough?"

His eyes widened. His face became a mask of righteous disbelief. "You dare say this to me?" he demanded.

"I dare," Vivien answered, her own face set in stern defiance. "Do you imagine I do not know what you have put this child through?" she clenched. "Do you imagine I do not know exactly what happened the night you entered her bedchamber? For God's sake, Neville, do you take me for an imbecile?"

"She has turned you against me," he roared, pointing at the silent Victoria. "She and her goddamned Whig husband, have twisted your thinking, Vivien, and I shall—"

"*You* shall shut your goddamned mouth, Neville," Vivien stated. "You shall—for once in your life—just shut your goddamned mouth!"

Both Victoria and Neville Frankland-Foster stared at the flame-haired woman before them. Neither of them could believe their ears or their eyes. Vivien's shoulders were drawn back, her chin lifted in abject rebellion. Her face was a mask of scorn.

"Vivien," Neville gasped. "How dare you speak to me that way. I am your husband after all."

"Yes, Neville," Vivien conceded, "you are my husband, and I respect that bond between us. *I* have always respected that bond. I have never broken one vow I made to you on the day we were wed over twenty years ago. You, on the other hand, have broken them all." Her tone was rigidly calm. She went on as much for Victoria's benefit—for she glanced at her—as for Neville's. "I have been hoping all these years that things would change between us, Neville. I have prayed every day that you would love me as much as I loved you. . . ."

"But I do love you, Vivien," Neville rejoined earnestly. "I know I have not been a perfect husband, but I do love you."

"That is your misfortune," Vivien responded quietly.

"How can you say that, Viv?" he cajoled. "We have been through so much together. . . ."

"In many ways, I agree with you," she said. "We have been through a great deal together. I have been a good wife. I have been supportive and caring. I have loved our children. I have made our homes as pleasant as they could possibly be. You on the other hand have been domineering, careless with my affections; you have taken my loyalty for granted; you have been a capricious father and—to put it mildly—an unfaithful husband—"

"Now, just a minute, Vivien," he interrupted. "This little slut attempted to seduce me. She is to blame. I never—"

"You never persuaded yourself into her bed," Vivien retorted. She glanced at Victoria. "I am sorry you must listen to this." She turned back to Neville and regarded him tranquilly. "You will refrain from calling this young woman names. Neither will you attempt to impugn her good name. I will not have it. You see, through all of this, Victoria has managed to remain my friend," she stated. She smiled, regarding the younger woman. "I do thank you for not tossing up your hands in despair of me," she said softly. "You must have wondered how I could have put up with him all these years." Victoria responded with a small smile of her own.

"Oh, this is perfect," Neville responded bitterly. "You are prepared to take her side—"

"If you wish, I shall call the little housemaid, Dory, into the room. I am not afraid to hear what she has to say, Neville, are you? And Dory is only the most obvious product of your philandering; over the years there have been so many others." Neville blanched. "Don't bother to deny it," Vivien said tiredly. "How many insolent housemaids I have put up with through the years, how many shop girls, how many pathetic little flower sellers and orange girls, I could not even begin to count them. The only reason I have endured your foolishness is because I truly believed that one day you would change. And I truly loved you, Neville. But you have destroyed my love. I do not love you anymore, and, believe me when I tell you, that will never change." Vivien regarded her husband wearily. "Do you know something?" she asked him softly. "You are a coward."

Neville puffed himself up to his full height and girth. He stood before his wife, his hands clasped behind his back. "I am no coward, Vivien," he said proudly, "and I will not allow you to call me one."

Vivien smiled sadly. "Whether you allow it or not, Neville," she answered, "a coward is what you are. Only a coward is afraid to commit himself to one woman, to one love. Only a coward would be afraid he was missing something by giving himself fully to one relationship. Only a coward would be so fearful for his manhood that he would attempt to conquer every vulnerable young woman he meets. Only a coward," she added pointedly, "would flee in the face of danger and leave his sons to fight a war that he has made." Another, fuller smile curved her lips. "I am quite a lovely person, I have recently decided. I deserve something better than a coward."

Neville snorted derisively. "Do you really think—at your age—you have much choice, Vivien?"

"At my age," she said with gentle certainty, "my choices are so much more clear. I may choose to live with you, Neville, or without you."

"Or without any man at all," he sneered with a thin smile.

"That may be a *result* of my choice, Neville. 'Tis not the choice itself. Whatever the result, I believe firmly that I have made the right choice." She moved to him and he stiffened. She regarded him placidly. "There is one result of my decision of which I am sure. Do you know what that is?" Neville shook his head. " 'Tis this," she said calmly. With the words, she reached up and snatched the pristine wig from her husband's head. His pate shown baldly through wisps of graying hair. His hands went immediately to his head as his horrified glance darted to Victoria. Both women hid their mirth. "I have always hated that wig," Vivien said reflectively. "As a result of my leaving you, I shall never have to look at it again." She swung away from him and seated herself primly on the little sofa. "You really ought to be on your way, Neville," she said. "You would not want to miss the boat."

Lord Frankland-Foster narrowed his gaze. He leaned down and swept up his wig from the floor where Vivien had let it fall. His nostrils flared. He said nothing. Turning abruptly, he left the room.

At his exit, Victoria eyed her friend keenly. She was not just sure whether or not to approach her, though she longed to. Vivien seemed hard-pressed to contain her emotion. Her elegant head bowed, and her hands covered her face. Victoria could not suppress the desire to comfort her. She moved slowly to her side and knelt down.

"Oh, Vivien," she said gently. "I know this was difficult, but I am so proud of you." She patted the trembling shoulders gently. To her amazement, when Vivien lifted her regard, her face was alight with mirth.

"Did you see his face?" She laughed. "Poor Neville. Poor, poor Neville."

Victoria's amazement was surpassed only by her own amusement, which she saw no need to repress any longer. She gratefully gave in to her own laughter. "I really thought you would be much more upset, Vivien," she said, once they had both managed to compose themselves.

Vivien nodded and swiped at her misted eyes. "I know, Victoria, isn't it terrible?" she said with another involuntary laugh. "You must think me totally depraved." Before Victoria could deny such a thought, Vivien continued. "I have done my crying," she said tiredly. "I have mourned our marriage over and over again, Victoria. Each night as I prayed that our marriage might be saved, I cried. I have cried for over twenty years. I am through with crying," she said, "at least for Neville." Her face became serious, and she touched Victoria's cheek delicately. "I do not know what the future holds for either of us, Victoria. But let us make a vow to each other that instead of crying, we shall take action. No matter what ever happens, let the others cry if they must. We choose not tears but life."

"And faith in each other," Victoria said warmly.

"And faith in each other," affirmed Vivien.

Chapter Twenty-three

The scream was real. It was her own. It raged through her being, impelled by another, and another. Like surging billows beating upon themselves against a rocky shore, the screams tore at the vortex of Victoria's consciousness. She had believed it to be a dream—a torrent of nightmarish horror. But the dream was real. The men, grasping her, restraining her, dragging her, were real. She stumbled, staggering, her feet barely touching the ground under their enforcement, down the main staircase of the Frankland-Foster house. By main force, they propelled her toward the front door. Now Vivien's screams joined her own.

"You cannot do this!" And, "You are hurting her!" And, "Oh, my God, my God, Victoria!" The red-coated soldiers seemed not to hear. Their intent was focused and grimly immutable. What that intent entailed neither Victoria nor Vivien knew.

Victoria found herself trawled from the house, across the porch and tossed onto a horse. Her hands were swiftly tied before her, her mouth gagged, her horse led at a pounding gallop into the night.

The office of General Roger Andros was a makeshift affair, not imposing but horrifying enough to a girl snatched from her bed in the middle of the night, wearing only her dressing gown, and having no concept of why she was there. For all her terror, Victoria faced the man squarely. Her gag was removed, though her hands remained tied, and the two people were left alone. Andros regarded her evenly. He did not stand. Victoria lifted her chin.

"I assume I have been arrested," she said. General Andros

nodded casually. "Am I to be advised of the charges against me?"

The man smiled. "I think we can arrange that," he said. Victoria watched him as he shuffled the pile of papers on his desk. The smile did not leave his weathered face. Roger Andros was not old, his physique spoke of youth and exercise, but his face had a hardness and a self-presumption that only men of their middle years acquired. He held out the parchment, but noting that her hands were tied, he drew the paper back, his lip curling. "I shall give you a conspectus," he said lazily. "You are being charged with consorting with known criminals, violently and feloniously assaulting His Majesty's property, and conspiring to defame and decimate the legal government of this colony." He looked up slowly from the paper. "Now I suppose you would like to respond," he said disinterestedly.

Victoria's gaze darkened. "The charges are false," she said. "I demand to know who filed them."

Roger Andros nearly laughed. "You . . . demand?" he asked.

"I am a British citizen," Victoria retorted.

"Everyone in this colony is a British citizen," Andros said mildly.

Victoria tilted an ironic gaze. "Is this how England treats its nobility?" she asked. Andros merely lifted a wide shoulder. "If we were in England right now, sir, I would be given every courtesy," she clenched.

" 'Tis unfortunate for you, in that case, that we are not in England," he answered.

In the face of this man's arrogance, Victoria's reserve snapped. "Dammit to bloody hell, you have no right to do this. I am no criminal. I'm a bloody baroness!"

"You," he chuckled, "do not talk like a . . . 'bloody baroness.' "

"Well I am," Victoria grated. "And I demand—"

Andros stood abruptly. The action both startled and frightened Victoria. "I think," he said, hooding his gaze, "that I am quite fed up with your demands . . . Baroness." His sniping tone sent a thrill of fear through Victoria's veins. The man continued. "I do not like spies," he said. "I do not like women who use their sex to get information from men."

Victoria's eyes widened. "What are you talking about?"

302

Her words came on an expulsion of breath. Roger Andros sat down. He leaned back comfortably in his chair, and again, he smiled. Victoria twisted against her bonds. The tousle of her pearlescent curls fell and blocked her vision. At last, breathing raggedly, she faced the man who so dispassionately watched her struggle. She tossed her proud head, sending her thick mane flying back over her slender shoulder. "Dammit," she ground out, "untie me."

Andros surveyed the trim figure beneath the gauzy film of her nightdress. His smile became reluctantly appreciative. "I must tell you, Baroness, I do understand how you managed it," he said silkily. Victoria stiffened. Her emerald gaze caught the firelight. Roger Andros knew a moment of hesitation. This feline creature of opal and ivory shimmering before him seemed more than merely mortal. A spy? he asked himself. A perfect spy, he decided grimly. Too bad. She might have been a goddess, but she was, after all, only a woman.

With a muttered command, he summoned his aide, who entered the little room. "Take her," Andros said. Victoria struggled against the young soldier's restraint. He merely lifted her over a broad shoulder and carried her across the compound. Without a word, he deposited her in a dark and narrow cell. The man had to bend nearly double as he made his way beneath the low threshold. Once he had left her inside, he exited, bolting the door from the outside. In the black emptiness of the room, Victoria felt an almost overwhelming loneliness. She might have been in the recesses of a hollow universe. She stood where she had been left for long timeless moments. There was no sound. Victoria attempted to believe she was dreaming. But of course she was not dreaming.

Endlessly, as the night wore on, she paced the airless room. Beneath her she realized was an earthen floor. She had raised her bound wrists to discover that above her — and not far above — was the ceiling. It was made of rough stones as were the walls. A slit in the opposite wall from the heavy planking that made the door served for meager ventilation and, she presumed, the cell's only light. In one corner, an oblong area had been laid with straw. The moment she had entered the tiny room, she had noted the ugly pungence of decaying human waste and realized as she explored that it emanated from that straw. She held herself as far from that circumstance as

303

was possible. She had long since given up the attempt to hold her breath. What little breath there was to be had in the tiny room, she finally accepted gratefully as the night slowly passed. She watched a certain lightening of the dark creep over the cell and reasoned that, at long last, it must be morning.

Breakfast was offered disinterestedly by someone who slipped a bowl of thin oatmeal into the small cut-out door at the bottom of the entry. Victoria started at the noise and scurried to the door. She banged against the rough, unyielding planking with her shoulder.

"Who is there," she demanded. There was no answer. "Who is it? I demand a lawyer!" Again no answer came. "Dammit," she grated, "answer me!" Silence resonated. Victoria glanced down at the disgusting concoction at her feet. In a thin gruel, gray clots of some substance or other had coagulated. She kicked viciously with a bare foot, and the little bowl flew across the room, smashing against the stone wall and spattering its uncertain contents to ooze where it landed to the floor. Victoria felt vomit, like an inverted bubble, rise in her throat. As she had throughout the night, she fought the nausea and the dizziness with which it was accompanied. She fought, as she had throughout the night, the angry tears that popped into her eyes. She must get out of this place, she avowed desperately. Twisting once again against her bonds, she felt, as she had throughout the night, the hot sting of the abrasive cord tearing against her flesh. She barely noted the burning pain. It was not until she saw the weals of bright blood coursing down her hands that she stopped.

With widened eyes — as tough she was watching some distant horror — Victoria surveyed the crimson rivulets that snaked her flesh. In that second, that breath of an instant, Victoria realized with heart-crushing terror, her appalling situation.

The pounding of the brass door-knocker resonated through the Frankland-Foster house. Vivien, alone there, felt a vibration of fear shudder through her. She ran to the front door and opened it cautiously. Relief washed over her as the figure of Jared Everett greeted her. He bowed grimly, and Vivien swept him into the house. As they passed through the nearly empty rooms to the kitchen, Vivien explained why she had contacted him.

". . . and they are keeping her in that awful prison on the common, Jared," she said at last as they seated themselves at the butcher-board table. "It has been three days, and they will not tell me a thing. They will not even allow me to see her." She looked into the tawny gold of his eyes, hopefully, wondering whether he felt any sympathy for the situation. Jared's mouth was set in a grim line.

"I heard of it only yesterday, Vivien," he said. "General Andros, who arrested her, is in charge of the investigation into that tea party incident, and I spoke with him directly. He says she has been arrested as a spy."

Vivien gaped at him. "A spy?" she breathed. "He must be mad."

Jared arched a brow, and his head of dark waves dipped in an apparent gesture of helplessness. "They have certain . . . documents. . . ." he said.

"What documents?" demanded Vivien. "Signed by whom?"

"That they will not tell me." His regard swung up, and he eyed her keenly. "Lord Frankland-Foster left under less than amiable circumstances, I am told," he ventured as he glanced around the empty, servantless kitchen.

"But Neville would not have —" Vivien stopped suddenly. She remembered his unreasoning anger as he had stormed from the house. She remembered that he laid the blame for Vivien's so-called betrayal on Victoria's slender shoulders. She recalled that he threatened terrible retribution. Both she and Victoria had decided that his threats were the last dying ejaculations of a beaten man. She remembered all this as at last she looked hopelessly into Jared's eyes. "Can we get her out?" she asked.

"We can try," the young officer said gravely. "We can damned well give it our best try." He rose abruptly and took Vivien's elbow, lifting her from her chair. "We are gong to see Andros," he grated. "If the son-of-a-bitch has not had her hanged without a trial, we can try."

Hustling Vivien along, he led them both from the house and with grim determination to the office, at the site of the Boston Common, of General Roger Andros.

* * *

The *Spectre* idled at the Long Wharf. Its prosaic, high-riding appearance belied the roiling fury taking place below decks.

"But, Captain," Edmund Harrt was reproving wearily, "you cannot just storm British headquarters."

Greyson turned the full power of his bronzed fury on the young officer. "The hell I can't," he roared. " 'Tis by my blundering she is there!"

"You did nothing, Cap—"

"Nothing! That is precisely the word, Harrt. I thought by leaving her alone, by expelling her from my life, I was protecting her. I believed she was safe in the arms of those Britishers. But I was wrong, I tell you! 'Twas that arrogant Brit bastard that turned her in. If I had kept her under my protection, she would be—"

"She might very well be in prison anyway," Edmund Harrt reasoned. Before he could take a breath, Tyrrel was upon him. Snatching his neatly groomed coat, the captain dragged him from his feet, and with bared teeth, he held the young man in a viselike grip.

"Don't say another word, Harrt," he growled menacingly. "Do not say one more word to me." He flung the young officer away. Edmund staggered over a chair and eyed the captain ruefully as he at last caught his balance, but he did not speak. Greyson expelled a harsh breath as he raked long fingers through his russet curls. "Oh, hell, Edmund," he groaned, "I have handled this situation as inadequately as it could have been handled." He turned and faced the warrant officer. "I apologize," he said softly. "I cannot say more than that." He lowered his regard as the younger man eyed him evenly. "Go ahead," Greyson intoned, "say what you have to say."

Edmund hesitated. "I suppose," responded the man quietly, "I run the risk of being manhandled again, but I shall tell you this, Captain: The British are not about to allow any risk to Victoria's captivity, for she is their only link to the tea party incident. With your and Adams' release, they lost what they considered to be their only connections to a possible indictment, and King George wants an indictment soon, *before* he is forced to close the port." He paused. Perceiving no reaction from Greyson, he went on. "Once he has that, there

306

will be no question of conviction. I believe Victoria is the lure," he added quietly.

Greyson's head swung up. "Andros wants me, then," he said.

"I believe he would be willing to strike a deal," Edmund acknowledged. "I must add, however, that in and of herself, your wife is quite a prize. The British have an excellent case against her."

"Would they be willing to drop the charges against her if I surrendered?" Greyson questioned.

Edmund nodded. "Remember one thing, Captain Tyrrel; if you decide to do such a thing, if you turn yourself in to Andros, you are surrendering not only yourself but fifty men. You will be expected to name names. Victoria's freedom will not come cheaply."

Greyson narrowed his gaze. "How is it you know so much about this situation, Harrt?"

Edmund cocked a shoulder and offered a sidewise smile. "You forget, Captain, you are not the only officer aboard who admires that lady." He splayed a defensive hand. "I know very well to whom she belongs, Captain," he said, his brown eyes twinkling mirthfully. " 'Twas me who performed the fateful marriage," he said. "But I cannot help my devotion to her. 'Tis the devotion of a loving brother, I assure you." He paused. Greyson saw in his countenance another sort of devotion—or . . . something—but he did not question it. Edmund had a right to love the very lovable Victoria—as long as his love remained brotherly, and unrequited. Greyson nodded a curt understanding of the young man's explanation and encouraged him to go on.

"As an objective bystander," Edmund said, "I am often included in political discussions. As one with absolutely no opinions, I am welcomed by both British and colonial complainers. Sometimes I do my listening at the Bull and Crown, sometimes at Sawtell's alehouse. Wherever I go, Captain—because I listen rather than speak—I learn a great deal. It was at Sawtell's that I listened very hard for news of Victoria. I have told you all that I have learned." He waited, watching Greyson's reaction to what he had said. A muscle worked tensely in the captain's jaw. At last he spoke.

"If it were only myself Andros wanted," he began reflectively, "I would surrender this minute. But they want Sam

Adams as badly as they want me." Edmund Harrt waited. Greyson shot him a glance. "Is that your understanding?" The younger man nodded. Greyson went on. "I may be expendable, but Adams is not," he said gravely. "We must get Victoria out of prison, and we must *not* do it at the expense of our cause."

Victoria was no longer avoiding the straw. She now gratefully accepted the one meal a day she was offered — the breakfast of thin, clotted gruel. She had lost count of the days, the silent lightenings and darkenings that were, along with the breakfasts, the only variations in her days. She no longer demanded lawyers. Her solitary imprisonment had taken its toll. Her hair had become matted, her flimsy gown tattered and grimed, her wrists dark and encrusted with blood. Worse than that, her mind had begun to create distorted pictures of her reality. The person who delivered her meal became her solace. She talked to that person — one day seducing, another day chiding, pleading, warning, sympathizing. She made up a life for that person. That person would come in, if only she could think of the right thing to say to him. He would carry her away, to his house in India. There would be green, there would be cool, and there would be comfort at his house in India. Her prison became India. It became the shaded teak forest. A golden tree — a very old tree — nodded in the warm breezes. Shadows lengthened; twilight encloaked her. The silence became the hush of evening. Darkness fell.

Chapter Twenty-four

A thin chinking sound above her startled Victoria from sleep. It swelled around her, cadent, reassuring. It might have been the patter of rain misting against her window in Kolhapur. She smiled in the darkness.

Outside, in hushed tones, Edmund Harrt offered to sell a young sentry a box of cheroots. The soldier eyed him suspiciously and tried to see him better in the dark. They discussed the price of the cheroots and where the scarce commodity had been obtained. The sentry wondered why he'd never seen the young British soldier before. Edmund laughed at the question; it was mentioned that there were almost as many English soldiers in Boston as there were civilians. Both men laughed quietly for a long time, and the question was not repeated. The soldier bought the cheroots. He offered one to Edmund Harrt, and they stood smoking their cigars together, exchanging stories, enjoying the balm of the spring night. Edmund Harrt offered the young sentry a drink from a flask. The soldier took a draught. Edmund offered him another. The soldier complimented Edmund on the fine whiskey. When the pint was gone, when the young soldier had enjoyed many draughts, he and Edmund sat, sliding down against the wall of the prison onto the soft spring grasses of the common. The soldier told Edmund, with wistful sweetness, of his home in Darlington and the North York Moors and of his mother. And the young soldier cried.

The chinking inside the dark prison grew louder. It grew more insistent. It grew to be annoying to Victoria. She wondered why Katje and Uncle David were allowing her to be disturbed. Where was Mrs. Jafar? Where was Joel? Where was . . . where was . . . someone? Why was no one coming to see what was wrong? She called to them in the delirium of her dream—the whirling, mindless treachery of her dream . . . of her reality . . . of her dream. Fragile crystals of light pricked at the darkness. Snowflakes danced in a prismatic galaxy. Moonbeams lifted her to the stars. The stars were blue in this magic world. In this magic world, the air was clean and plentiful, and Victoria breathed and smiled and lay her head back in serenity. She allowed the magic world to carry her to where it would for it was where she wanted to be . . . forever.

Bonny! The plump, painted woman leaned toward her, smelling of heady perfume and ale, her face distorted in the illumination of the yellow light. Victoria's scream tore from her breast. She gasped and fought the teasing vision. The vision vanished in a slow swirling dark.

" 'Tis a pity, Grey," said the sling-hipped Bonny Bowdoin. "And she so young and all." She glanced at the man who stood slumped near the narrow bed. His rugged face was unshaven, is eyes were red-ringed and the light pale skin around them tinged with blue. He looked toward the old man who sat and watched him.

"Can you do nothing, Pop?" Greyson pleaded hoarsely.

The comfortable-looking Dr. Poprik leaned more heavily on the curved stem of his umbrella. "If only I could, laddie," he said softly. He shook his head sadly and regarded the ice-white figure who lay on the bed. She was so still. Her stillness, though, was preferable to the sudden raging terrors that had haunted her for days now, he determined. "I've treated the infection," said Dr. Poprik, "bled the wounds . . ." his voice faded.

"Me and Mid have been cold-packin' her, Grey, to try to get down that damned fever," Bonny added helplessly. "Yet every time she wakes up, she goes into a fit."

Greyson leaned down, his big hands grasping the back of a chair. "Oh, God, *damn* it!" His voice was half moan, half sob—an animal sound. With the words, he lifted the chair and heaved it against a wall. It shattered into fragile sticks that clattered to the earthen floor. He turned and rammed his fist down onto a scarred wooden table. A pewter candlestick jumped; flames danced wildly casting flickering shadows. Ale sloshed from several pewter mugs as they were jolted into the air. Dr. Poprik lifted himself with a sigh and moved slowly to the table. Lifting one of the mugs, he took a long drink. He eyed Greyson worriedly.

"Have one, Grey," he said gently. "Have yourself two, son. Get yourself good and drunk, and sleep through the wait."

"I don't want to get drunk, Pop," said Greyson quietly. "I want to be here, ready for her to—" He looked at the old doctor. "She will be all right, won't she?" he asked.

Poprik noted, with a tightening of his old throat, the tears that coursed silently from Greyson's eyes. The doctor thought he was above—or beyond—caring about the pain of others. He thought he was beyond his own pain, certainly. He reached out and patted Greyson's wide shoulder. *We are such children,* he reflected sadly. *We need each other so much.* He wished that he could tell the boy that everything would be all right. In the end, he did tell him that. But, naturally he could not be sure. Whatever ailed the girl was surely beyond the old doctor's ken.

The three people regarded the pallid figure on the bed. Against the dark, gray ticking of the mattress, her hair and skin seemed almost transparent. Bonny had taken the time to wash Victoria's hair the best she could under the circumstances. Brushing it out, the jaded sybarite marvelled at its silken texture. "Oh, lord, Middy," she had ventured to the hardened creature who was aiding her in getting Victoria cleansed of her ordeal, "just feel that." The other woman had moved to the lucent mane and eyed it critically. "It ain't so bloody . . . remarkable," she sniffed. "*Feel* the flippin' stuff," Bonny had growled. Mildred did feel it and could not keep the awe from her tone. "I don't guess I ever saw nothin' like it," she breathed. As though they handled a rare gem, the two ladies took special care fussing over their delicate charge. Rather than dressing her in one of their stiff and flaunting gowns, they retrieved a shirt of Greyson's from a hook. They draped this most uncommon creature in the soft cambric with loving pride. They smoothed the opaline curls from her forehead and lay her on the best mattress in the house. And they sponged her and watched her—and even managed prayers of their own devising that she would recover.

They had shared Greyson's disgust, his awed horror, at the festered, gore at her wrists, the flea bites that covered her flesh, the dark and brooding wound on her shoulder, caused when she attempted to break down the prison door. Who would do such a thing to such perfection?

Their ministrations had not been entirely in vain. The ivory gloss of Victoria's skin, though ravaged was not dulled. The wound on her shoulder had already begun to heal, and Dr. Poprik had been optimistic — as optimistic as a hardened old doctor who had learned to live beyond pain could be. But the moment Victoria's lashes had fluttered up and Bonny Bowdoin had leaned down to encourage her awakening, the girl had begun the first of her waking nightmares. The fevered, emerald glisten of her eyes had appeared and widened, and screams raged up from some unholy terror that lurked inside the girl. Her arms thrashed wildly against the terrible, ugly inverted horror. And then she had collapsed into her fragile sleep, and Greyson had sent a message to Dr. Poprik that she had awakened.

That had been four days ago, and Greyson had not left the bedside. Bonny glanced at him now. She had known Greyson Tyrrel since he was boatswain on the *Blessing of the Harbor,* a small merchant ship out of Boston. Bonny Bowdoin smiled inwardly. How she had loved, how she had doted upon the young seaman. They had grown up together, really, in this thriving little seaport town. They had played together, sported together, laughed together. But Greyson's love of the sea had taken him far while Bonny had stayed right here. She and Greyson Tyrrel were of an age. He, however, had never lost his youthful vitality while she had lost much. Bonny regarded the angelic creature on the bed. Her radiance would never die. And, in Greyson's heart certainly, it would live forever. If Bonny had had any hope at all of luring the virile Greyson back into her sporting arms, she gave it up when she realized the great love that Greyson so obviously felt for the fallen Victoria. Greyson would never love her — not as he loved the luminous creature who lay now, so helpless, upon Bonny Bowdoin's bed. She sighed and glanced at the door as Mildred entered.

"I made up this beef broth for her," the woman said. "It's real thick, Pop, just like you said." The old doctor nodded.

"How's business, Mid?" Bonny inquired listlessly.

"Not good," the woman answered as she set down her tray. The two of them eyed Greyson worriedly. "Them Brit ships have been comin' in all day," Mildred intoned. "I think the harbor's really gonna close, Bonny," she whispered. Both women again looked to Greyson, but he did not take note of their words. His reddened eyes were for Victoria alone.

If only he could know what inner horror kept her imprisoned. Why did she not want to awaken? What fear of reality held her deep within her own ravings? Dr. Poprik had told them all that only such a fear could be keeping Victoria from rousing fully, giving herself to the world of consciousness. She was obviously experiencing recurrences of some desperate nightmarish reality from which she was hiding herself. Greyson moved now to the bed. He sat upon it, his weight rolling Victoria slightly toward him. He looked down on the opaline luminescence that lay so helplessly on the bed — Bonny's bed. His tears flowed unabated.

In Victoria's dark world, Greyson stood tall, broad-shouldered, heaven-eyed. His russet curls tossed lightly as he threw back his head in roguish laughter. Bonny stood by his side. She, too, was laughing, her bright blond head on Greyson's chest. They watched Victoria's struggles as she held out her arms and tried to reach them. She pleaded silently to Greyson to help her. Bonny tugged at him, pulling him farther and farther away. Other women joined them — faceless, silent figures. They moved away, drawing Greyson with them into a misting shadowed darkness. Suddenly, the face of Bonny appeared over her, shrieking triumphant laughter, and Victoria was alone. Hollow, empty, the world around her closed in — swallowed her. At once, Greyson was there, shattering in a tumult of blue stars the cavernous dark.

"Oh, love," he said softly as he smoothed the tiny opal curls from her forehead and cheeks. "I had not thought to need a woman. I had not wanted to depend upon anyone for my happiness. I believed I had the sea for that. But I tell you this." He leaned down so that his breath caressed her cheek. "I do need you, Victoria. I need your laughter and your trust. I need your gentle — and" — he smiled — "your not so gentle — reckonings of my character. I need to be reminded how alone we really are and how much we need to cherish

313

those we love. I have told you this before, and I repeat it now as a solemn vow. If everything else in my life were to vanish, I could go on if I had you by my side."

The persecuted and, therefore, rancorous Bonny Bowdoin swiped suddenly at an errant tear. Mildred, too, found herself possessed of a long-avoided tenderness of emotion. Old Poprik reached into his vest pocket for a handkerchief, but he did not offer it to the ladies. He used it himself.

A velvet twilight encloaked Victoria's consciousness. The world of magic, of possibility, of blue stars and plentious air and snowflakes, whirled slowly. It carried her upward into an inverted vortex. At the point of the vortex, Greyson's face appeared. Laughing sea-glass eyes offered tenderness. Roguish curls, falling in russet tousles, offered gentle playfulness. A firm, smiling mouth offered the breath of love.

Victoria's dark lashes fluttered, fanning the silk of her cheeks like ebon butterflies. She whispered a question. The four people in the room riveted their attention on the sudden animation. They girded themselves, fearing another turbulent awakening. But they watched, rather, a serene and gentle acceptance of reality.

Victoria raised delicate fingertips to Greyson's unshaven jaw. She smiled. "You look like a red-maned lion, love," she said softly. Greyson's astonishment translated itself into a joyously rambunctious embrace. Poprik rose with uncharacteristic abruptness.

"Easy, Grey," he commanded, tapping the overly zealous Greyson with the point of the umbrella. The doctor's own relief was blatant, but he reined his excitement and moved to the girl. "Let me have a look at her," he insisted, "before you squeeze the recently acquired consciousness out of her, lad." He brushed Greyson aside—the doctor's age and proven knowledge of healing allowed such boldness of spirit—and lowered himself onto the bed. "Hello, little one," he said with a barely concealed grin. "Nice to meet you. I am Dr. Poprik," he added, holding out his hand. Victoria regarded him uncertainly, but returned his greeting with a small smile. She liked the doctor's face. In his rumpled appearance, there was the promise of comfort, and a very private belief in his worth. He needed to announce to no man that he was someone of importance. He knew his own importance. The dull black of his waistcoat and doublet, the

314

crookedness of his tie, the absence of a wig told the world that he was comfortable with it—and with himself. And his name had a musical sound.

"Poprik." Victoria laughed once the word had been absorbed. "Poprik," she repeated. The old doctor laughed, too. The others in the room joined in the mirth.

"Poprik," he affirmed, and suddenly his name took on, even for him, a lyrical, childlike loveliness. His amusement deepened not only at the sound of his apparently wonderful name but at the girl's appreciation of it. His laughter softened. He regarded Victoria tenderly. "We didn't know if you would make it," he said gently. "I am awfully glad you did."

Victoria's gaze swung slowly to take in the other three people in the room. There was Greyson, of course, his relief obvious in the buoyance of his smile. There was the wispyhaired woman that Victoria recalled from the depths of some misty dream. And there was Bonny. Victoria's heart tilted. The grinning, full-bosomed woman moved cautiously to her.

"How you feelin', dear heart?" said the painted mouth. "We been so worried about you." The face swam and softened before Victoria's reluctant regard. Bonny knelt, lowering her countenance to Victoria's eye level. "I never been so worried in my life," she said warmly. She reached out and brushed Victoria's face with her smooth fingertips. "Lord, girl, you put a scare into all of us," she added, her smile tilting.

"You gotta have some of my broth," called the wispyhaired woman. "I made it special."

Victoria's regard was only for Bonny. She said the name softly at first. The woman lifted a penciled brow. " 'Tis me, dear heart," she replied. " 'Tis Bonny Bowdoin. You remember me?"

Victoria nodded. "I was afraid of you," she answered.

Bonny's smile became sad. "I know," she said gently. "I got a weakness for the young ones," she admitted. "And you were as young and as pretty a lad as I'd ever seen. Imagine my surprise when I tugged off your cap to discover you was a lass—"

"Not afraid of that," Victoria interrupted softly. "I was afraid of you . . . and Greyson."

The woman's face sobered. "You couldn't have been

315

afraid of that," Bonny gaped on a breath. "I won't have you bein' afraid of that." Greyson moved to the bed. Dr. Poprik allowed him space next to Victoria.

"As a matter of fact," Greyson said as he sat—cautiously, "I do love Bonny Bowdoin. Her tender care of you has earned my undying devotion, love."

Victoria regarded the woman. Her decorated face became a tapestry of soft colors. "Thank you, Bonny," she said.

Mildred peered into the scene, wanting very much to be a part of the tender reawakening. "Anybody hungry?" she asked.

Victoria's verdant gaze lifted to Greyson. "Oh, yes," she said happily. "I am very hungry—I am hungry for life."

Chapter Twenty-five

The transformation had not been difficult to achieve—not nearly as difficult as everyone thought it might be. By a little before noon the next day, Victoria had been metamorphosed from a fine and delicate English beauty into a frowzy bawd. She was as tawdry looking a wench as any who had ever graced Boston's dockside. Her hair had been colored with henna, causing the pearly strands to take on the hue of ripe strawberries. Mid and Bonny had scrupulously penciled her pale brows, forming saucy crescents over her eyes. Her cheeks and lips had been painted with bright rouge. Bonny had stitched all night to tailor one of her best gowns—a froth of lime-colored organza—so that it fit Victoria to perfection. With her matching parasol, kid slippers and bonnet, as well as the elbow-length gloves that were necessary to hide her bandaged wrists, Victoria was as meretricious a fallen sparrow as anyone had ever gasped to look upon.

If you wanted to hide something. Bonny proclaimed, you hid it right out in the open. Greyson could not disagree with the logic. It had been roundly publicized that Victoria Tyrrel had escaped from prison and the clutches of General Roger Andros. That man was extremely proprietary about his prisoners and had launched a town-wide search for the girl. He made it clear that he was looking for a woman who had, according to his information, no qualms about dressing as a boy to disguise herself. Andros had already questioned Greyson in the upstairs rooms of Bonny's establishment.

Greyson had made a great show for the general's benefit of appearing drunk and at hedonistic sport when Andros and his men had arrived, forcing their way into rooms and

317

surprising various couples in various stages of diversion. Greyson and Bonny, languishing on a rumpled bed, had seemed surprised at the general's questions.

"She out already?" Greyson had asked in uninterested tones.

"Yes," Andros had hissed.

"Well, if you find the chit," Greyson slurred, "you tell her to get her flippin' behind home with her husban'—" he hiccuped for effect— "where she b'longs . . . bloody defiant wench," he had finally groused as he fell into a snorting, grumbling sleep. Bonny had added her own bit of color to the scene. Lounging next to Greyson on the mattress, she had resignedly drawn the grimy coverlet over his muscular shoulders, and eyed him petulantly before looking up sweetly at Andros.

"I got some time now, Gen'ral," she said. "Long as you and your boys are here . . ." She allowed her voice to trail off as she twirled a bright blond tress over her generously exposed bosom. She noted the interest of several of the young soldiers and offered them a dimpled invitation. Andros had ordered his men out hurriedly, with curt and agitated commands as the pretty and plump Bonny had made to extricate herself from the tangle of covers.

As the legation left, their bootsteps fading on the stairs, Greyson had leapt from the bed. It was only Bonny's hastily reasoned dissuasion that kept him from storming the door and confronting Andros.

"It's *her* you need to be thinkin' about, Grey," she had cried. "For God's sake, wasn't that what all this was about? What are you goin' to accomplish, goin' after the bastard?"

In the end, Greyson had surrendered to reason, instead taking his retaliation out on the bric-a-brac. Grabbing up a slender statuette, he twisted the pewter as though it were only tin, and with a snarl of rage, he hurled it against the wall. Bonny eyed him speculatively as he smashed a chair and swept, with one clean motion of a muscular arm, the contents of the top of her bureau scattering about the room. At last, his fury spent for the moment at least, he stood breathing raggedly.

"That son-of-a-bitch," he rasped. Bonny Bowdoin was about to announce to Greyson that he really ought to stop punishing her innocent furniture, but she thought better of it, and only looked with philosophic despair at her twisted statue of the Venus de Milo.

The transformation of Victoria had taken place after that — after she had been retrieved from Dr. Poprik's nearby house. Bewigged and makeup smeared, Victoria had glanced, narrow eyed and disheveled, from behind Poprik's study door, and Andros and his men had been convinced that the old healer was something of a miracle himself. The young British soldiers eyed each other dubiously as they left the house. They agreed silently that as long as they were forced to be so far from home, perhaps this little seaside town was preferable to another, more given to demure recreation. Each young man made a mental note of the location of the Bull and Crown, and remembered well the succulence of its owner.

"What would you have done," Victoria asked Bonny as that woman worked over her, "had Andros accepted your invitation?"

Bonny lifted a plump shoulder negligently. "I'd of probably gone through with it," she conceded. "Then," she added with a mischievous tinkle of laughter, "I'd of kneed him where it counted, apologized for the 'accident' and told him there was no charge." Mildred laughed raucously as she applied rouge to Victoria's lips. Forming a definitive bow was delicate work, she reproached her friend in amusement.

"No more jokes, now," Bonny warned as she at last went back to her labor. The two women toiled diligently, extending all their professional skills to this important assignment. They decorated Victoria as though she was a Christmas cake. Standing back, they admired their work with unabashed pride.

Victoria was sent on a stroll that glorious morning — the first day of June — with every confidence that she was as ornate and desirable a daughter of joy as had ever graced a gentleman's arm.

Her new outfit and identity, Greyson noted dubiously, seemed to invade her very personality. She moved with a tantalizing fluidity, twirled her parasol invitingly and seemed to take excessive enjoyment in flipping her skirts insolently as she walked. Too bad, he reflected, she hadn't been able to make her first outing since her imprisonment dressed as Rod. Though Greyson was not entirely comfortable with the conversion, he had no problem enjoying Victoria's company as they strolled along the harbor in the noontime sun. And yet, Victoria noted, he seemed distracted. The sullen tolling of the bell in the Old North Church caught their attention. Greyson suddenly looked out to the harbor.

"What is it?" Victoria asked.

"Look," he said grimly, pointing out to sea. Within minutes, over a hundred ships flying Union Jacks anchored at the mouth of the harbor, literally sealing it off. The closing of the Port of Boston was to be no paper obstruction. Along the wharfs, hundreds of men abandoned their idled ships slowly, dejectedly, and marched from the sea into the streets. Red-coated soldiers guarded their way, muskets at the ready, as the docks became deserted. Victoria watched the terrible retreat. She glanced at Greyson.

"They are all wearing mourning bands," she murmured.

Greyson nodded. "A thankless protest," he grated, pointing to his own arm.

Victoria glanced sorrowfully down at the black band. "I am so sorry, Greyson," she said softly, touching the symbolic strip of muslin. A sudden thought assailed her. "Jack," she blurted.

Greyson could not help the smile that curved his lips. "Jack is safe," he said. "I have sent him to live with a family in Lexington. I wanted him away from Boston."

"You might have told me, Greyson," she reproved.

"And what would you have done, love?" he asked her.

"I would like to have had the chance to say good-bye to him," she said, lowering her gaze.

Greyson lifted her chin with a roughened forefinger. "You forget," he teased, "you went and got yourself arrested, love." The roguish amusement in his eyes did nothing to abate her sorrow. He drew her into his embrace. "I had no choice, Victoria, I promise you," he said gently. "I had to get him off the *Spectre* as quickly as possible. No one is allowed to live on their boats. Gage is so bent on avenging the imperial anger that he has even ordered that cows and sheep grazing on the islands in the harbor are not to be tended by their owners. Little boys swimming off private docks will be ordered out of the water.

"You must understand," he went on earnestly, "the town of Boston is, for all determinations, under siege. This is the worst thing the British have ever done to us, love. This town cannot endure such a blockade." He looked down into her eyes. "I hope you can begin to understand the reason we have decided to break our ties with our 'Mother Country'. She is a cruel mother, Victoria, and not worthy of our loyalty."

Victoria wanted very much to understand. At the moment, however, she found herself overcome with the need to rest. She and Greyson made their way back to the Bull and Crown.

The mood there was decidedly somber. Bonny Bowdoin would have traded all the business she was by default realizing, for the sight of one working sailor. She helped Victoria upstairs and into a dressing gown and bemoaned the heart-tearing sight of men in enforced conditions of idleness. Dr. Poprik came in to unbandage Victoria's wounded wrists and dress them with salve. He carefully inspected the raw and brooding welts. Though he had successfully fought the infection that had invaded her body, he noted worriedly the blood-tinged discharge that layered the area. With several oaths designed to describe in scornful detail the female ancestry of General Roger Andros, Poprik left the wounds unbound. He assured Victoria that they would heal faster that way and would be less likely to cause scars.

After examining her general health and finding her nothing more than exhausted, he enjoined her to rest. After a few hours, Victoria and Greyson enjoyed a dinner of potted beef and ale in an upstairs room and were kept abreast hourly through the late afternoon and early evening of the town's temper. By nightfall they had been joined by several of Greyson's compatriots. Victoria listened quietly as they talked long and seriously about the harbor's closing and about what was to be done next. Dr. Poprik was there along with several men whom Victoria had never met. One that she recognized was a gentleman she had seen on the night she and Greyson had arrived in town from Cambridge. He had been involved with the intimidation of Captains Hall and Bruce. He caught her attention because he seemed more determined, more angry, more sharply focused than the others. When he spoke, his orations were fiery and to the point, and then he listened keenly to what others had to say. He had been introduced to Victoria as Samuel Adams, and she realized that she was meeting the foremost agent of the colonial

321

rebellion in America.

He was a short and thick man. He wore no wig as the older men usually did; instead, his hair was long and peppered with gray and caught back in a queue. Like Dr. Poprik, his coat and breeches were a somber black, and he, too, wore a mourning band symbolizing his resistance to the events of that noontime. He studied Victoria, upon their introduction, with keen, marble-dark eyes.

"What is your business here . . . Mrs. Tyrrel?" he asked bluntly.

"Victoria is here as my wife," Greyson answered quickly, protectively as he drew Victoria to his chest. "You needn't worry about her."

Adams lifted his regard slowly. "I 'worry' about everyone, Grey," he said evenly.

Victoria twisted from Greyson's shielding embrace. "You needn't concern yourself about my discretion, Mr. Adams," she assured him.

"Your *discretion,* madam, is exactly what concerns me. You see, for all you are British, I do not doubt your loyalty to your husband. 'Tis only that women have a tendency to . . . talk. They rarely disseminate information wisely; rather they spread it like so much manure, imagining it to have little more value than that. I tell you this, madam. What we shall discuss here tonight has a great deal of value to a great many people, and if you plan on spreading it about, you shall be *de*valuing our very lives — giving them little more worth than manure." Samuel Adams spoke haughtily, and his lordly disdain of women sent Victoria's chin thrusting into the air. She regarded him coldly. Greyson watched for the anticipated confrontation with nothing less than a poorly disguised amusement.

"Oh, Mr. Adams," Victoria said softly, " 'tis so enlightening to hear your views on the insipidity of women. I am certain your cousin-in-law, Abigail, would be most interested in your thoughts." She felt a vaulting satisfaction as she watched Samuel Adams stiffen in discomfort. She went on. "Parenthetically, I should like to advise you — for your future reference — that we women do in fact realize the value of manure; we spread it on our gardens, and we make things grow. We make the world beautiful, Mr. Adams. We think beauty is a most valuable commodity. Don't you,

322

sir?" Before he could answer, Victoria's gaze shadowed. "As to my discretionary capabilities, I can only tell you this. I have no desire to see the British military advised of any information about anyone's activities including my own. You see, sir, I have, as you may have heard, recently been the victim of British martial 'justice' " She lifted her arms abruptly and flung back the full sleeves of her gown. Revealed, just beneath Mr. Adams' large-veined nose, were the terrible oozing wounds on Victoria's wrists. She smiled narrowly as his eyes widened. "You claim injustice and oppression and injury. Well so do I, Mr. Adams. After what I have been through, I might be justified in demanding *your* discretion." With that, Victoria spun away from him and settled herself defiantly into an upholstered chair in the corner of the room. She picked up a gown of Bonny's which she was resizing and began to sew on it.

Samuel Adams glanced sheepishly at his acquaintances. It was some moments before he dared look any of them full in the eye. "We have a great deal of business to attend," he muttered as he took his place at the large table. Many mouths were made that evening, many smiles hidden behind the back of the fiery rebel before business was at last conducted in earnest.

Victoria, having accepted with modest smiles the silent approbation of all the men, listened intently as she sewed. At last, losing all interest in her mindless pastime, she wandered to the table. Standing cradled casually in Greyson's arm, she heard described the consequences of the harbor's closing.

"Shipyards have suspended operations," Mr. Adams was saying. "Carpenters will be idle; sailors will walk the streets. Porters and stevedores will be thrown out of work; mechanics will leave Boston to find work in other towns. The great warehouses will close, mercantile houses will have no more business, and the clerks of the town will go without pay. Our economic life will be destroyed." He paused significantly before going on. When he did, his tone was suffused with an intensity of feeling. "A peaceful settlement of this controversy is no longer possible, gentlemen. 'Tis no longer a war of words between the British and the Americans, 'tis a war of deeds. They mean to punish us — 'to compel a full and absolute submission,' in the words of His Majesty, *Mr.* Hanover — but they have badly misjudged the colonial temper. In

323

the end 'twill be the Brits who endure punishment. Their punishment will be the loss of their American colonies."

"I agree," a Mr. Hancock asserted. "We must oppose these acts of oppression and misrule. Does anyone realize that there is, as we speak, one armed redcoat in Boston for every three civilians? That is, of course, unless the ratio has narrowed since this morning." The grumblings of the men showed their condemnation of such a circumstance. Mr. Hancock went on. "I would like to make a proposal," he said quietly. "I propose we contact the governors of the other colonies. I propose we convene a continental congress, gentlemen. 'Tis time we stopped fighting this scourge alone. We need the help of our friends — our fellow colonists. We need the help of important lobbyists against the British, such as Mr. Franklin and the young Mr. Paine of Philadelphia, the very young Mr. Hale of Connecticut and Mr. Henry of Virginia. We must *unite* in our efforts to free ourselves from tyranny."

"I assume," said Greyson, "that you would be willing to attend such a congress as our representative, John." The man nodded.

"I, too, would be more than willing to represent our numbers," said Mr. Adams.

"Then I would suggest," Greyson went on, "that once that congress has been convened, we organize a provincial congress so that we here in the Bay Colony may know what is being decided." He looked at each man pointedly. "I would suggest further that you inform the other colonies that a militia has been formed here in the Bay Colony and advise that they do the same."

John Hancock lowered his eyes. "They have, Grey," he said softly.

Victoria took this news quietly. She had, for some time, heard rumors of such a militia, but now the fact of a colonial force of trained fighting men was confirmed. She did not really know how she felt about such a thing. She looked around the table at the gathered men. Except for Mr. Adams, they were all under forty. Some were under thirty, and others were little more than boys. Mercy Warren's husband, Patrick, was there. He was a peach-faced young man with pale eyes. He and Mercy had, within the past year, become parents for the first time. Sue Higginson's husband, Willy, was there and so was Joshua Gannett, Deborah's husband. Victoria recalled the determined strength of the women. She saw now the determined strength of their men. She had begun to understand the elements of their contention with the British. She had endured British autocracy—felt something of what Greyson and the others must now feel toward their tormentors. But Victoria was also determined. She must, she decided, avoid being caught up in the emotionalism of a cause she did not fully comprehend—or approve. Causes could be dangerous to the undiscerning.

It was well into the morning hours before the men departed. Bonny had kept them well supplied with food and ale, and their bitter resolve had kept them well supplied with discussion. Greyson accompanied the gathering downstairs into the tavern's main room, avowing as he turned back to Victoria with a small seductive smile, that he would return within minutes. Victoria saw him off and vowed, with a seductive smile of her own, that she would be waiting for him. He twirled one of her hennaed curls on a roughened fingertip and commented on the fact that he might enjoy a night of sensual pleasure with a scarlet woman—just for old times sake, he added solemnly.

" 'Tis all right with me, 'Grey,' " she said softly, "as long as the 'scarlet woman' is me." They kissed tenderly and then he was gone.

Victoria turned from the door to undress for the night—her first alone with her husband since she had been imprisoned—but something caught her eye. She moved to a hook where she detected a flash of crimson. It seemed, she noted curiously, to be almost the same color as her hair. She reached beneath several garments, lifting them and drawing out the red one. It was a short cloak—a scarlet cloak. With a sudden chilling reverberation, the words her Uncle David had said so long ago in Kolhapur came back to her. "The man in the red cape," he had said, "may be the key to every frown of fortune where the American colonists are concerned." Was Greyson that fanatical dissenter? Had Greyson led those drunken ruffians up King Street that cold March night of 1770 and instigated the Boston Massacre? She remembered the flash of red she had seen the night of the tea party just before she fainted. Was it a red blanket as she had thought, or was it a red cape—this red cape? She knew she had seen Greyson wrapped in red. Had he incited the colonists to their present rage and provoked the final retaliation of the British? Victoria's mind whirled with supposes. Suppose the British had, as General Gage had said, merely been exercising their rights of patronage, all these years, over a colonial territory which was, after all, under their protection? Suppose certain power-hungry men, driven by greed and consuming vanity, had goaded the colonials to their wrath against the British? Suppose Greyson was one of those men? Suppose Greyson was the man in the red cape? A thrill of fear tingled beneath Victoria's flesh, for she remembered now some gossip she had heard regarding her escape from the British prison. Everyone knew that Greyson was her redeemer, but there was talk that in the area of the common the night of her liberation, someone had spotted a man in a red cape.

Chapter Twenty-six

By now the news of Victoria's miraculous and intrepid escape from the steely clutches of General Roger Andros had swept the town. Even those who believed that she might conceivably have been a colonial spy, breathed relief at her deliverance. Andros was well-known as a martinet. His own men applauded Victoria's liberation from his cruelty to her. The young sentry on whose watch she had made her getaway now suffered the same fate as Victoria had suffered — in the same stinking, airless cell. He, however, had the support of his comrades and was appropriated food secretly. Human contact eclipsed the loneliness of the boy's plight whenever it could be managed. The general's rancor, however, was a force to be deeply considered before one decided to attend the young soldier. Fortunately for him, much of his friends' diffidence was overridden by their hatred of Roger Andros. The lad was as well cared for as he could expect to be under the circumstances.

Victoria, too, found herself to be very well cared for — annoyingly well cared for. She had begged to be allowed to see Vivien, but Greyson informed her that it was impossible. Even if they could extract a vow of silence from Vivien, they could not risk a wayward reference or a dubious look. Vivien was, after all, seeing Colonel Jared Everett. Whether or not their relationship was intimate mattered little; Vivien had the British ear. Beyond that, Greyson feared that even if a visit could be arranged in absolute secrecy, and even though Vivien was the most trustworthy friend in the world, there was no guarantee that Andros was not watching her for just such a lapse. Vivien herself could be in grave danger. If Neville Frankland-Foster had even intimated at chinks in Vivien's loyalty to the Crown, she might find herself under arrest. Victoria could not argue with the logic, but she did not have to enjoy her enforced idleness.

"These are troubled times, lovey," Bonny had said resolutely when Victoria had complained to her. "Grey's doin' what he thinks best for all of us."

And so, Victoria spent her days in the upstairs rooms of the Bull and Crown, hiding from Andros, remaking dresses for herself, mending linens and missing Vivien. Her thoughts were occupied, too, by the nightly meetings. More and more, she began to see evidence of a growing firmness of resolution.

A continental congress had been called. It was to convene in September of that year in Philadelphia. Delegates were being chosen from all over the land to attend. Samuel Adams and John Hancock, the Bay Colony's representatives, were carefully instructed as to the specific demands of Boston. The Coercive Acts were to be repealed, strong economic measures were to be taken against the Mother Country, and a colonial army was to be created. This army was to incorporate the scattered militias of all the colonies and to organize them under one command. Eventually, the men determined, they must choose a commander in chief for their army. Each colony would no doubt have its own candidates for that appointment. Out of the war with the French, many good soldiers had evolved. Many names were suggested, so that Mr. Adams and Mr. Hancock would have much in the way of recommendation when the time came for the delegates to make such a choice.

One important consequence of these meetings was the formation of a band of local men who would be prepared — at a minute's notice — to fend off a localized British attack. It was jokingly suggested, after many tankards of ale, that they be called "minutemen." Greyson volunteered to ride the countryside and apprise the men of the colony that they were expected to be a part of this vigilant force.

"I shall ride with you, Grey," said the soft-spoken Paul Revere.

"I think not, Paul," said Samuel Adams. "There is other work for you. As Greyson suggested, we ought to form a provincial congress so that you here in Massachusetts may know exactly what is going on in Pennsylvania. We shall need an official courier to ride between the two colonies."

328

"You are the finest horseman in the country, Paul," John Hancock reminded the young engraver. "Will you do it?" The young man nodded. Greyson smiled at him.

"I might be able to compel another companion, Paul," Greyson said, cocking a glance toward Victoria. The sudden elevation of her spirit was obvious in the glitter of her green gaze. She saluted smartly and promised she would be as ready a companion as "minuteman" Tyrrel could hope for. All the men laughed.

Again, it was very late—nearly dawn—before Victoria and Greyson were alone. Her excitement at being liberated from her enforced idleness was boundless. As Greyson removed his doublet and shirt, and tiredly drew down their bed covers, Victoria talked endlessly about their adventure.

"This is why I came here, Greyson," she said finally, twirling and hugging herself. "To see the land where my parents were born, to know its people, to share its mysteries."

Greyson regarded her in aggrieved mockery. "And all this time, I believed you had come here because we were . . . how did you put it? Oh, yes, 'predestined to love.' Now I find the only reason you really made this journey was to ride horse with me to Concord." He offered an injured frown. "You have been toying with me, Victoria. How could you?"

Victoria placed her hands on her hips and smiled in wicked appreciation of his tall form. "You forget, sir," she said seductively, "that is exactly what can be expected of a lady of the evening. We love you and we leave you, sir," she added, lifting a negligent shoulder and flipping her hip saucily. "Call us callous, if you will, but—" Greyson swept her, in one swift movement, into the muscled curve of his arm. He looked down into her saucy gaze.

" 'Twould seem," he growled, "I had better make the most of you then, while I have you in my power."

Victoria fluttered her lashes piquantly. "Perhaps you should," she said impudently, "if you wish to get your money's worth." He pulled her roughly to his bared chest; her strawberry curls fell, cascading down her back as he arched her to him. She laughed a low enticing murmur. "Oh my, Captain, you are *strong,* aren't you." His eyes were like chips of blue steel as he lowered his lips, seizing hers in a rage of hunger. Victoria found herself captured by the force of his ardor. Apparently, their game was over.

She entwined her arms around the column of his neck and felt the heat of need grow between them. It swept them into a tide of whirling passion, even as he swept her from her feet and onto the bed. His hands abraded her flesh as he urgently tore at the fastenings of her dressing gown. His lips still upon hers, he groaned as he at last seized the quivering opaline mounds of her breasts. His big hands took possession of every part of her, roving her buttocks and belly, claiming her with the power of his need. Grasping a handful of her long, silken curls, he pulled her head back, arching her throat to his voracious appetite. He fed rapaciously upon the delicate flesh. His hot breath lingered over her shoulders as his mouth travelled to her breasts. He devoured each budded nipple with the moist torment of his lips, nipping with his teeth, tickling with his tongue at the thrusting ripened peaks.

Victoria arched to him as her own desire flamed. She moaned, writhing, compelling his mastery, stirring his savage hunger. Casting off the restraint of his breeches, he rose above her, lifting her to his thundering need. She was spread, stripped of all defenses, to his power. He drove, penetrating the essence of her woman's soul. She soared with his towering incandescence to the peak of her fevered need. Together they erupted into a flaming turbulence of completion, liberating the power of their love, transfusing the sweetness of their passion.

They held each other near. Tenderness encloaked their souls as they clung to that soaring moment of purest repletion, purest accord. Though Victoria found herself doubting and questioning, these moments alone with Greyson, in their rooms above the Bull and Crown, obscured the doubts — silenced the questions. In these quicksilver moments of torrential passion, she felt in complete communion with her husband — with the man she loved.

The sun rose in majestic harmony with the resplendent late summer sky. Victoria and Greyson had risen early. Bonny had prepared them a robust breakfast which they devoured in amused silence as the woman commented on their hearty appetites. Victoria, once more dressed as Rod — though Mr. Londgon's clothing had been replaced by those of a cooperative pot boy employed in Bonny's kitchen — mounted the

330

horse Greyson had procured for her. It was a sweet animal of uncertain lineage but nevertheless fair of face and form.

Victoria eyed Greyson curiously as he bound, in one powerful motion, onto his own steed. The animal pranced in excited readiness beneath his weight. Very soon — within moments — they would be on their way. Victoria wondered what the next few months would hold for them. She had noted as they left the room earlier, that the red cape had vanished. She wondered at its disappearance. Had it left, unnoticed by her, with one of the men? Or had Greyson packed it into his haversack in anticipation of its use on their expedition into the wilds of the Bay Colony? Victoria could be sure of nothing until she questioned Greyson directly, and, as was the usual case in their relationship, she abandoned all thought of rational conversation each time they were alone together. Naturally, she could not question him in front of others. She did not understand the significance of the cape, and its significance might be something that Greyson needed to keep to himself. Surely, though, he would share its meaning with her — if it had a meaning. And Victoria was sure that it did. Perhaps on their journey, as they rode the narrow byways of the countryside, she would have the opportunity to ask him about the red cape. She was to find, however, that they had few private moments as they travelled.

As they rode, farms and small homesteads abounded. They visited each and were enjoined, with avid anticipation of news from the town, to share food and drink with each family. Their grim intelligence surprised no one. In Roxbury, in Brookline, in Weston, in Sudbury, in Concord — no matter where they stopped — Victoria and Greyson were greeted with resolute acceptance of duty in the coming conflict. And no one doubted the advent of conflict. It was no longer merely a threat. The probability of war brought farmers and blacksmiths, cabinetmakers and tavern owners together in a pledge of unity. Up to now the colonists had been reacting to British authority, they agreed. It was time for the colonials to take the active role.

Squadrons of minutemen were formed in each village. Men were commissioned to enter Boston and collect muskets, gunpowder, shot and bayonets and carry the munitions in secret back to the outlying towns. Riders were assigned to scout designated areas and report to their squadron chiefs any unusual British activity. Each family had its assignment, and each—the Parkers, the Bowmans, the Barretts, all of them—accepted, with a terrible determination, the expected consequences of the stand they were now taking.

In Lexington, Victoria and Greyson stopped at the home of Tad and Eldora Wright. Greyson had adopted a self-satisfied grin that had not left him all morning. As they tied up their horses, he looked eagerly toward the house several times.

"What ails you, Greyson?" Victoria asked impatiently. "You have been positively *smug* since we started out today."

"You shall see, love," he said enigmatically. He moved to her and caught her waist in a warm embrace. "And when you do see, I shall expect a very special 'thank-you.'"

Victoria entwined her arms around his neck. "We shall have to camp out tonight, then," she said, tilting him a sun-kissed emerald gaze, "instead of accepting the hospitality of one of your countrymen."

"That we shall," he said lazily, "for I promise you; you *will* wish to thank me."

"In the meantime," Victoria offered with a mischievous smile, "we must make a pretty sight—two men in tricorns, embracing on the Lexington Road."

They were about to further astonish the population of the town when, from behind them, there erupted a joyful shriek. Victoria turned to find, to her own astonishment, that the figure of a young lad was bearing down on them at a pounding run. She realized with heart-thrashing joy that the running, shrieking lad was Jack. She bolted from Greyson's arms—as he had fully expected she would—and ran, her arms outstretched, to embrace her dear little friend.

"Oh, Jack!" she breathed when he was in her arms. "How long it has been." She held him away from her. "You have grown," she said in wonder. She tossed with her fingertips, the downy tangle of his brown, sun-burnished curls.

"I got to be nine, your ladyship, while we was apart," he stated proudly. "And guess what else I got to be?" Victoria listened attentively. "I got to be a real farmer. Never thought I could do it. But the captain, he said I could—and I did."

Victoria laughed. "I told you a long time ago, Jack, that you are a most resourceful lad." Victoria fought the tears behind her smile, but Jack noted the jewellike glimmers that

332

began to steal into her eyes. He touched her cheek with his little hand.

"Don't cry, your ladyship," he said gently. "If you cry, I might. And farmers and sailors ain't supposed to." The newly united friends laughed together as Greyson joined them.

"Who told you farmers and sailors don't cry, Jack?" he asked.

"I just figured," Jack answered.

Recalling Victoria's recent ordeal and his own reaction to it, Greyson responded, "Sometimes they do, lad, believe me; sometimes they do."

They were interrupted by the appearance of Thaddeus Wright. He smiled and held out his hand in greeting. "Hello, Grey," he said warmly. "What brings you so far north? From what I have gathered recently, you are not merely paying a friendly call."

Greyson returned the greeting. "We've come on a mission, Tad," he said. The young farmer nodded grimly—almost eagerly—and then glanced at Victoria. Greyson smiled. "As you may have guessed by now, my partner is no gentleman."

"We guessed it when we watched as you tied up your horses," the man said, smiling. "Jack noted the interchange between the two of you and let out a rather unmistakable indication that this was the much talked-about Mrs. Tyrrel." He offered his hand to Victoria.

"I'd of known her anyplace," Jack said proudly. Together, the four people walked the two hundred yards or so to the small frame house. They were greeted by Tad's wife, Eldora. That woman ushered them inside, and, Victoria noted, her welcome was friendly but guarded. Victoria also noted that Eldora Wright was, though not very far along, unmistakably pregnant. She introduced a little girl—about Jack's age—to the visitors, and a boy who was older.

"This is Elizabeth and Charles," she said, pride clear in her voice and manner. With appropriate politeness, the girl curtsied and the lad bowed. For all that their environment was, to say the least, rustic, they had most obviously been well-schooled in the more gentle procedures, Victoria thought warmly. The mother, too, seemed comfortable with all the proper amenities. She poured coffee for herself and Victoria and offered ale to the men. The children were asked if they preferred milk or cider. As they all sat down at the large wooden table, Victoria followed Greyson in removing her tricorn. Everyone stared with unabashed awe at Victoria's mane of oddly colored curls as it spun out wildly to frame her shoulders and face. The red dye had faded and her hair was a delicate shade of opalescent peach. Elizabeth and Charles were of course hastily enjoined, by their mother's admonishing regard, to drop their gazes. Jack, however, less formally trained, gaped openly.

"What've you done to yourself, your ladyship!" he blurted.

Victoria laughed. " 'Tis a disguise, Jack," she answered softly.

"You seem to have adopted all sorts of disguises," said Eldora quietly. Was it disapproval Victoria heard in the woman's voice, saw in her eyes? Victoria lowered her gaze.

"Yes," she murmured.

Greyson regarded the family seriously. "The necessity of my wife's disguise is at least part of what brings us here," he said.

"Would you children like to go out and gather some eggs for me?" asked Eldora quickly. The three young ones gleefully agreed when it was also noted that they might enjoy an afternoon swim in the pond. They left the table raucously, but immediately halted to offer their guests a decorous goodbye. Jack stopped before he left to give Victoria one last impetuous embrace, and then he, too, bubbled out of the house. "I do not mean to seem impolite," Eldora said stiffly, "but I would rather the children did not hear of the . . . unfortunate business that is going on in Boston."

"That unfortunate business, Ellie, is very unfortunately going to concern all of us very soon." Greyson's eyes were keenly upon the woman, and she lowered hers.

"In many ways," she murmured, "I am sorry you have come, Grey. We have been expecting you — or someone very like you — but I am . . . sorry." Her tone was vague and soft and filled with pain. Victoria could not help the ache that rose in her throat. All along their way, she and Greyson had seen much the same reaction as they were finding here at the Wright house. The men listened quietly, eagerly, for Greyson's news, but the women were less eager, more sad. Ellie Wright's reaction, however, seemed stronger. A profound suffering seemed to emanate from deep within this gentle woman. Victoria turned and looked directly at her hostess.

"Would you be so kind as to show me your farm?" Her words were offered evenly, but there was a decided gentleness in her tone. Eldora regarded her warily. At the warmth she at last realized in Victoria's request, she rose. The two women left the house.

The men watched them go regarding them with resignations " 'Tis hard on the ladies," Greyson said.

" 'Tis hard on that *particular* lady—quite particularly," Tad Wright intoned. He glanced over at Greyson. "My wife, I fear, has Tory leanings."

Greyson smiled sadly and took a long breath. "You are not alone, old friend, believe me."

The refulgent September afternoon spread out lazily before the two women as they walked the path along the split-rail fence that bordered the Wright property. Victoria eyed the woman next to her obliquely.

"Elizabeth Tudor and Charles Stuart," Victoria said reflectively, "were two of the Mother Country's shrewdest monarchs." Eldora glanced at her. Victoria smiled gently. "They were also popular and respected." Victoria tilted her gaze. "Do I mistake the significance of the names of your children?"

"You do not," said the woman. She looked out over the green and gold expanse of land. Willow grass undulated in the warm wind, animals grazed peacefully and small outbuildings leaned tranquilly in the sun. "When they were named," Eldora said after a pause, "there was . . . amity."

Victoria regarded her steadily. "From what I can determine, there was little . . . amity, ever."

"Well, there was at least no threat of real strife," Eldora shot back. She stopped and faced her guest. Folding her hands over the small distension of her abdomen, she spoke directly and flatly. "When Tad and I first settled this land eleven years ago, we were very young—and so full of hope. You see what we have made. 'Tis beautiful, is it not?" Victoria's gaze swept over the radiant landscape. Everywhere she looked, a rich profusion of fruitful life abounded. Everywhere, the bounties of nature swelled and sang of fertility, of regeneration, of promise.

"Yes," she answered softly. " 'Tis beautiful."

"Life *is* beautiful, Mrs. Tyrrel. 'Tis all we have—life." The last word was spoken on a breath. " 'Tis all I know of, anyway," she added. "I *believe* in God and an afterlife, but all I really *know* is right here." Again her eyes swept the land. "I do not want this war," she said. A small smile curved her lips. "My husband believes my feelings stem from some ingrained loyalty to Britain, but they don't. I love the Mother Country, 'tis true. I even have a certain . . . sympathy for poor King George." She chuckled softly. "He, too, is a victim in all of this. His stupidity is his nemesis, and he shall be punished for his pride. But then, so shall we all." Her gaze remained steady. "The reason I do not want this war is that in a war men kill each other for matters of principle. Principle, Mrs. Tyrrel, is the assumption of right. When we assume ourselves to be right, it follows that we must also assume others to be wrong." Her voice filled with wonder. "We assume all that, knowing little of ourselves and less than nothing of the people we must kill. How arrogant we are." Her gaze flitted timidly back to Victoria. "My own arrogance astounds me sometimes. Here I am saying all this to you, and I have no idea of your feelings on this subject. I am afraid I have forgotten my manners."

Victoria contemplated, with a frank admiration, the young woman before her. "Manners aside, Mrs. Wright, I do not believe I have ever heard my own feelings expressed so accurately." The woman lowered her gaze modestly. Victoria touched her slim shoulder. "Thank you," she said.

"I know we cannot stop the wars," Ellie Wright said softly. "We cannot stop the men; they will do what they will do. We can support them and love them; we can nurture them and have their babies. We can do all of that because we are no more than women—and no less."

Together the two young women walked the verdant land back to the house—back to their husbands.

Victoria had learned a great deal that afternoon. She could begin to sort out much of her ambivalence about this conflict. She hated Roger Andros for what he had done to her, but she did not hate the British. She loved Greyson, but she could not embrace his cause. She could begin, because of Ellie Wright, to understand her incertitude—and to forgive herself for it.

That night, the family ate a supper of roasted pheasants

and apple bread stuffing which they had all helped to prepare. Laughter and old stories abounded in the barely furnished, low-ceilinged kitchen room—one of only three—in the isolated farmhouse. Thaddeus and Eldora told of their beginnings, of their stops and starts as novice farmers on the virgin land. Greyson and Victoria had their own stories to tell—of plum groves and azure oceans. It was very late, after the children were securely abed, that the two young couples began to talk of serious matters.

Victoria was asked about her capture and incarceration by General Andros. She could not answer most of the questions that flew about her. The young couple, insulated by their distance from Boston, wanted naturally to know how a young British noblewoman could be forcibly taken from the mansion of a magistrate and thrown like any common criminal into jail. Both she and Greyson attempted to explain.

"We think I may have been slandered by Lord Neville," Victoria said. "He seems to have blamed me personally for his wife's decision to stay here in the colonies without him."

"From what Victoria has told me," Greyson added, "Lady Frankland-Foster's decision was based upon two things—the information that her sons were being consigned to the military and being sent here, and the fact of the old man's depravity of character. Apparently, he was quite the stalking cock, as I hear it."

Victoria eyed Greyson askance. "One stalking cock will," she murmured, "recognize another." She recalled only too well the echo of Lord Neville's assessment of Greyson's character when she had first arrived in Boston. She was surprised to hear Thaddeus laugh. She and Eldora glanced at him sternly.

Tad splayed his hands defensively. "Sorry ladies," he said, attempting to control his mirth. " 'Tis only that I have not heard old Grey described as such in many years." Victoria's brow shot up. " 'Tis true," Tad announced earnestly. "This boy was never a swagger." He eyed Greyson, who narrowed his gaze dangerously, but Tad continued undaunted. "While the rest of us were sowing our wild oats, old Grey was languishing on the decks of the *Blessing of the Harbor*. How he loved that old tub. I will not say that the lad is without ken on the subject of the fair sex, but his reputation far exceeds his actual achievements."

337

"You have had entirely too much ale," Ellie Wright scolded her husband. She glanced apologetically at Victoria. That young lady merely smiled and encouraged — much to Greyson's dismay — Tad to go on.

"There was a time," the young storyteller continued, "when Grey was forced by his friends to prove himself. We were no more than seventeen or so, and we set him up with the glorious Bonny Bowdoin, the most experienced of our rather inexperienced set — "

"We hear poor Bonny has taken to . . . business," said Eldora with barely veiled misgiving.

Victoria chuckled reassuringly. "Mistress Bowdoin is quite a successful . . . tavern owner," she said, patting the woman's hand.

"Is she?" Ellie breathed. "Oh, thank goodness. We'd heard . . . otherwise."

"Well, in those days," Tad interjected, "our young Bonny was as dear and generous a darling as ever there was, and we lads, concerned for Grey's lack of . . . well, shall we say exposure, decided they ought to get together. Naturally, we boasted on this monumental pairing, and Grey's reputation was born."

"His reputation as a rakehell, you mean," Victoria said, not concealing a certain amused triumph.

"Oh, he was a rakehell all right. He has never turned down a good fight — though he probably stopped more of them than he was ever given credit for — and he never turned down a pretty girl. But his attentions extended to picking wild flowers on the common and offering them with a blush at the lady's door. His courting techniques were, at the very best, awkward. And except for Bonny and perhaps a few others, our old Grey is just like the rest of us — skittish and scared. Sometimes," said Tad, slapping his knee delightedly, "the reputation a fellow acquires becomes more real than the real fellow. I think our friend Grey has begun to believe the hearsay himself." Eldora pushed at her husband's arm and admonished him that his raucousness would surely wake the children in the next room.

Victoria merely smiled. " 'Reputation, reputation, reputation,' " she intoned, quoting one of her favorite English poets. She glanced at Greyson, recalling tenderly his "courting" of her. She recalled his over-zealousness, his diffidence, his assumption of self-assurance—all, now obvious outward shows of uncertainty. *Oh, Greyson Tyrrel,* she thought warmly, *you were unsophisticated, too.* Her husband regarded her with a helpless concession in his narrowed gaze. He must depend a great deal in the next few hours upon her forbearance, he sighed inwardly. If she was lenient, she would refrain from scorning him too much. He could not know that gathering in her heart at that moment was all the love, all the gratitude, all the relief that any woman would feel upon discovering such a truth.

Things would never be the same for the Greyson Tyrrels, Victoria reflected, as the two couples made their good-byes. As always in her young life, she had learned a truth—and was reborn. Greyson's overconfidence that first night in the plum grove had been because he had found a certain boldness in that magical moment when he had discovered the mystical powers of love. Victoria had put her own initial eagerness that night to a masterful display on his part of seduction—perhaps he thought that, too. But Greyson had not seduced her. She, too, had fallen hopelessly in love the first time she had met him. She smiled inwardly. She would not destroy his illusion. Let him believe in his own manly power over her. She knew the truth—he knew it, too, she guessed, but his masculine pride might discourage such an admission. But one day—and very soon—all pretense would end between them. As Ellie Wright had pointed out, this life was all they really had together. They must live it as fully and as honestly as they could.

That night, beneath the canopy of a star-frosted autumnal sky, Victoria and Greyson came together with a new and a mutual tenderness. They caressed each other as if for the first time. They explored and collected for their memories those secret places of enchantment that only loving lovers cherished. They held each other as dear as any two lovers ever had. In that isolated grove, beneath a flowering tree, in the starlit warmth of that September night, Greyson and Victoria Tyrrel discovered each other.

Chapter Twenty-seven

If her house had been empty that summer and fall, Vivien Frankland-Foster's heart had been full. Her love for the handsome young Jared Everett had blossomed, even as the summer rains had brought the flowers in her garden to the gentle perfection of mature beauty. And now, as yet another winter faded and April brought the promise of another spring, the purity of his devotion kept promise in her heart. Vivien waited for him in elated anticipation. These evenings they spent together made her loneliness during the days more bearable.

It had been almost a year since she had heard from Victoria. There was no question that she had escaped the pernicious justice of Roger Andros. The militant colonials had used Victoria's arrest as an example of British dishonor even toward their own. It was roundly asserted that no British subject was safe on American soil. The speechmakers made speeches, damning the tyrant, warning the masses of British betrayal. If Victoria Tyrrel, a noblewoman, was not safe among these lobster-backed despots, then who could be safe? The British, too, used Victoria's arrest and subsequent escape as propaganda. General Andros had made it clear that no one — no matter their status — was above the law. The search for the Baroness Darby became the nucleus of the general's existence. Like a thing rotting inside of him and spreading to every organ, his hatred of Victoria dominated his every decision, his every action against the citizens of Boston. Vivien, herself, had been placed under guard — for her protection, Andros had snidely asserted. She endured, even as she waited for Jared, the knowledge that outside her home men stood ready to question and apprehend, if necessary, all visitors. She was followed everywhere by an armed escort.

Vivien had taken irreverent delight in flirting shamelessly with the lads who were assigned to guard her, dipping her elegantly bonneted head, smiling temptingly and fluttering her lashes each time she swept by them. Jared had informed her dubiously that the patrol of her was by now the chiefest goal of every soldier under Andros's command. "They argue among themselves for the *privilege* of guarding you," he had told her petulantly. It was only with a great deal of soothing that the young colonel was mollified—and assured. Vivien made her devotion for Jared Everett only too apparent. She was capable of great love and great loyalty, Jared often reflected tenderly. He could not dispel the thought—though it might have been considered a breach of British loyalty—that Lord Neville Frankland-Foster had been nothing less than a crackbrained nincompoop. Each time Jared regarded the empty house, much of the furniture sold off to support his beloved Vivien, he reminded himself that the earl was not a nincompoop after all, but a lunatic. Any man who would leave the elegant Vivien to dally with kitchen wenches and shopgirls, who would jeopardize a beautiful home and a marriage to such a wife, had to be the most unfortunate of imbeciles. The young colonel, however, wasted little time on sympathy. His time was taken up with simply loving his flawless Vivien.

She greeted him, as she always did, with love and with questions. "Have you heard anything of Derrick and Thomas?" she asked as she poured their brandy. Jared smiled, holding on to his news for just a little longer. His hesitation kindled her interest. "You have heard, Jared," she said excitedly as she moved to him. She paused, handing him his drink. "Tell me," she said softly.

Jared patted the seat beside him. As she sat, he cradled her in his arm. "Yes, dearest," he answered gently, "I have heard. I am praying you think as I do that the news is good." Vivien's attention was keen. Jared continued. "Both of your sons are being sent here to Boston. They have been assigned to General Gage's headquarters and . . . they will be directly under my command."

Vivien caught her breath in a sudden and audible inhalation. Her eyes closed. "Oh, Jared," she breathed at last, "if my boys must be here at all, if they must be consigned to soldierhood, then I thank God he has seen fit to place them in your care." She turned to him and looked directly into his golden eyes. "Thank you for that news," she said softly. "I know — and you needn't deny it — it comes of your influence. For that, too, I thank you."

The young colonel smiled modestly. Did this beauteous creature not know that he would do anything for her? Had she not yet learned that seeing to her happiness, her comfort, was his pleasure? He lowered his lips and took hers in a tender kiss. As always, Vivien responded warmly and completely to his tenderness.

"I will deny nothing," he said, his golden eyes laughing into the warm gray-green of hers, "that promises me such generous thanks. And I tell you this, sweet, in all the years that I pray we shall have together from this moment on, you may ask anything of me — and expect it to be fulfilled. I love you, Vivien," he added softly, "with all my heart."

"And I love you, Jared," she answered. They shared another lingering kiss. It was a long moment before the expected question came about Victoria. When the question did come, Jared sighed, for this news was not good, nor optimistic.

"I am afraid Andros is becoming more determined by the day," he said sadly. "Everyone, including Tom Gage, believes that Andros has lost his reason over the girl. He is convinced she is a spy of the worst order. He has closed the Bull and Crown because he had word that Victoria was seen there, posing as a prostitute. Fortunately, I have had word that Victoria and Greyson are not even in Boston. Unfortunately, their reason for being out of the town is one that I cannot approve. I am sorry to say it, sweet, but your friend and her husband are out there, even as we speak, rousing the gentle citizens of this land against the Mother Country."

"I think it is just possible, Jared," Vivien said, lowering her gaze, "that the gentle citizens of the colonial Americas were roused long before Victoria and Greyson came onto the scene." She glanced up and offered a modest smile. "That is only my opinion, of course."

Jared laughed and pressed her to his chest. "And your opinion is correct," he conceded. "I am beginning to believe my own British propaganda. But," he added, his tone becoming serious, "the fact remains that the Tyrrels are among those in the very center of this contention. They, along with several others, seem to be the core of the opposition to British rule. It is well they are not in Boston these days. For your sake, I hope they remain wherever it is they are for a very long time."

"Are there criminal charges against them?" she asked worriedly.

Jared shook his head. "Greyson is so far free from any actual charges. Only Sam Adams and John Hancock have been formally charged, and they are both subject to arrest. If they are captured, I am afraid General Gage will see to it that they are sent to England and tried for treason."

"But Greyson has not been charged," Vivien affirmed.

Again Jared assured her that that, at least, was true. "However," he added solemnly, "Victoria remains under formal arrest. Andros, I fear, will never free her from that onus. As far as he is concerned, Victoria Tyrrel will either be captured . . . or killed."

Vivien's heart tripped in her chest. "What do you mean, Jared?" she demanded, pulling away from him.

Jared sighed ruefully. " 'Tis as I have said, Vivien. I cannot soften that news. Would that I could tell you that Victoria might find some mercy in General Andros, but I cannot. He has made it known — he has given his men very specific orders — that if spotted, she is to be captured. If she attempts to run, she is to be shot on sight."

"But of course she will run," Vivien asserted. "What does Andros expect?"

"Exactly that," Jared offered grimly.

"Do you mean to tell me that he will not allow her the dignity of a trial?" Vivien gaped.

"Not if he can help it," answered Jared. "Listen to me," he said as Vivien rose abruptly, unable to contain her indignation, "I believe Victoria has been warned." He took her shoulders in his hands as he, too, stood up. "If I know Greyson Tyrrel," he added sternly, "he will not allow the first sighting by Andros's men. I cannot say for sure that this is true, sweet, but I know something of Andros and I know something of Tyrrel. They are both powerfully focused men. In any event," he said softening his tone, "I intend to do

343

what I can—for your sake—to see that Victoria is cleared of the charges. Next week," he continued, drawing her to him, "we shall go to Andros's office, and we shall demand to see the charges against her. We shall find out who her accuser is. If her accuser is Neville Frankland-Foster, perhaps you can convince Andros that there might have been ulterior motives involved in the accusation. Short of that, we shall go to Gage." Jared cocked a smile. "Gage is no more a defender of Victoria Tyrrel than Andros, but he is far more reasonable."

Vivien looked up at him quickly. "Why can we not go tonight?" she asked.

Jared threw back his head in appreciative laughter. "My redheaded darling is as impetuous as her bright hair would announce her to be," he said. He looked down at her in all seriousness then. "I wish we could, sweet," he said softly, "but the generals are, I am afraid, otherwise engaged tonight." Vivien's brows quirked in a question. Jared explained as much as he could to her. "Since as early as the middle of last month, Gage has suspected that the patriots—as they now call themselves—have been collecting and storing munitions in the smaller towns around Boston. On the twentieth, he went so far as to send Captain Brown of the 52nd Regiment and Ensign De Berniere of the 10th Regiment, and a private on a secret scouting trip to obtain information on the topographical features of the landscape and to learn the location of the military stores." Jared smiled. "I do not believe the mission of those soldiers was all that secret. These Bostonians, idle now because of the harbor closing, watch every move we make. They've set up Committees of Safety and Supplies as well as their Provincial Congress to organize every scrap of information on our activities. Your friend Victoria and her husband are very much a part of this organization," he said ruefully. " 'Tis one of the reasons they are traversing the byroads of the Bay Colony. And though I blame the colonists not at all for their actions, I do say that in the end, they are going to be very sorry for their aggressiveness." He sat down heavily, and Vivien joined him on the sofa, listening attentively.

"Is General Gage planning some reprisal?" she asked.

"I am afraid so," answered Jared. "He cannot allow this sort of organized aggression to go any farther. 'Tis tantamount to a declaration of war. And that, Vivien," he said softly, "would be an unprecedented tragedy—a bloodletting. These poor souls have no idea how vulnerable they are. Their hostility so far has been met with a great deal of forbearance. They do not seem to realize that if they go on with this, they will bring the wrath of all of Britain upon themselves." He shook his head sadly. "I do admire their valor, but I cannot condone their shortsightedness. They have no concept of what can happen to them."

"What are Gage's plans?" asked Vivien worriedly.

"He intends to send troops into the provinces—and a substantial number of troops, too. He has suspended the duties of all the grenadiers and light infantry in Boston in preparation of the action. Even now transports are being loaded to carry the troops by water across the Back Bay to the Cambridge shore. Naturally, because there is some sort of intelligence network among these colonials, he has also gathered a small legation of soldiers to travel south into Dorchester, but it is the eight hundred men being sent up to Concord that will seize the military stores and put an end to the aggressive actions of the colonial lads. By tomorrow, Vivien," Jared finished regretfully, "these valiant but imprudent Americans will see their dreams of . . . autonomy . . . or whatever the hell it is they hope to achieve drowned in a sea of British might. They haven't a chance."

"Oh, Jared," Vivien sighed, "we can only pray that Victoria and Greyson are safe from all this."

The young colonel nodded grimly. "We can hope, sweet, but all I can tell you is this, if they are within eighteen miles of Boston—if they are anywhere on the road between Cambridge and Concord—they are not safe. Gage sent out mounted officers yesterday to patrol the road in preparation of the march. Anyone seen will be questioned. If their loyalty to the Crown is suspect, they will be arrested on the spot. There will be no mercy for such people, I fear."

"But you and I both know—and so does Gage, if the question were pressed—that Victoria's loyalty to the Crown has never been in question," Vivien stated.

"Her husband's loyalty, however, is very much in question, even aside from Andros's irrational persecution of her," Jared reminded her. " 'Tis her loyalty to Greyson that will bring her down in the end."

Vivien stood in a rustle of velvet and lace. She paced the

wide unfurnished expanse of the small parlor. Stopping before the fireplace, she gazed down into the purling flames. "We must prove Andros wrong," she said softly. She looked up quickly. "I want to know who has accused her, Jared. If not for that, she might still be here with me, safe in this house."

"Unfortunately, sweet, I must be back at headquarters by ten o'clock; the embarkation of the troops is scheduled for ten-thirty, and I and three other men shall be the only officers left in Boston after that. I must see to it that my men are at the ready in the event that those 'high sons of liberty' take it into their reckless heads to attack us here." He smiled sadly. "One never knows what those impetuous gallants will try—"

"Then Andros will be gone from the town," Vivien said on a breath.

Jared nodded. "He will."

"What is to stop us from searching his office, then?" Vivien urged.

"Oh, sweet," Jared said, standing and moving to the fire. "You ask too much. How can I, a colonel in the British army—"

"You said I may ask anything of you, Jared," she reminded him, placing a delicate hand on his wide chest. "Has that vow been retracted so soon on the heels of its endowment?"

Jared watched her solemnly. His golden-brown eyes caught the firelight. In it, Vivien's determined countenance flickered with dazzling resolution. She would not be discouraged, this valorous creature. "Very well," he said at last.

Vivien and he walked hurriedly toward the common. On any other night, they might have been a handsome young British soldier and his lady taking a stroll in the pleasant spring air. But tonight, this portentous Tuesday, the eighteenth of April, 1775, they were two people caught in a reverberation of intrigue that would resound through the rest of their lives and the lives of everyone involved in their mission.

As they walked, they met Lord Percy, a loyalist who greeted his two fellow Britishers with a grim reminder that the secret of the night's march had not remained a secret.

"I was just crossing the common," he said softly, hurriedly, "and I heard a man say, 'The British troops have marched, but they will miss their aim.' What aim? I asked him. 'Why,' the man replied, 'the cannon at Concord.' " He tipped his tricorn grimly and rushed off.

Jared and Vivien glanced at each other. There was more to this night than either of them imagined.

"Look," said Vivien suddenly. Jared noted the direction of her riveted attention. Up in the belfry of the Old North Church, where no light had ever been seen before, two lanterns glowed. A lone rider galloped past them. And then all was silent. Above them, the two lights remained, glittering eerily against the dark, a reminder that some force, unknowable to them, was at work this fortune-starred night.

Chapter Twenty-eight

The thickening day roused Victoria. She and Greyson had by now made their several-months-long circuit of the provincial towns around Boston. They had been back in Lexington in time for dinner the previous night and had dined with Tad and the now very pregnant Eldora Wright and, of course, the children. This time they had accepted the offer of shelter and, for lack of a room in the house, had bedded down in the barn. The lowing of unmilked cows and the self-praising crow of an insistent and brightly feathered rooster roused Victoria with the coming of dawn. But it was the distant beating of a drum that caught her attention and brought her to her feet. Her glance darted quickly around the barn. Where was Greyson? Her heart pounded in cadence with the eerie, insistent beat of the drum. Brushing hay from her jacket and grabbing up her tricorn and haversack, she climbed down from her lofty bed and ran across the field to the house.

Inside, she found Eldora sitting grim and tired and holding tightly to the children. "What is it?" Victoria gasped, for she could tell that all was not right. "What has happened?"

"The Brits are here," Jack stated, gulping air. "They're not a half a mile away," he added. His trembling and his widened eyes reflected the fear of the others. "I don't think you're gonna be able to gull them this time, your ladyship. They got a million soldiers this time, not just one stupid Captain Stewart." Eldora looked quickly at Jack.

"Jack is referring to something that happened on the *Spectre* a long time ago," Victoria hastily explained. She went to the wooden sink and dipped water. Bringing it back to Eldora, she handed it to her, for she feared the woman

348

would faint. "You are so pale, Ellie," she insisted gently, "you must lie down." The young woman merely shook her head. She drank the water down, but immediately drew Elizabeth, Charles and Jack to her. She held them rigidly, her eyes staring, unseeing. Victoria nodded grimly at Jack and Charles, and the two boys lifted Ellie to her feet, while the little girl ran into Victoria's arms. "Take her to the bedroom," Victoria ordered. The two boys managed to steer Eldora to a bed and got her to lie down. Her face contorted immediately with pain. Victoria moved to her slowly, comprehension beginning to dawn. "Oh, my God, Ellie," she breathed. "How long has it been?"

"About four hours," the woman said wearily.

"Why didn't you wake me?" Victoria said, kneeling by the side of the bed and taking the woman's limp hand in hers.

"I didn't want it to happen yet," she said on a breath as another viselike constriction encircled her abdomen. "Oh, God," she moaned, "I did not want it to happen until . . . after—" Her tears came unabated. " 'Twill happen all too quickly now."

Victoria glanced at Jack. "Your resourcefulness—and mine, beloved Jack—will surely be tested this day." She reached out and took his arm in a reassuring squeeze, hoping to inspire confidence, though she felt none herself. "You boys must get buckets of water from the well, bring it here into the house and heat it over the cook stove." Victoria felt sure that water would be needed. She glanced at Eldora helplessly and then back at the boys. "Please, go," she snapped at them and then quickly glanced away, hoping they had not seen the uncertainty in her eyes. Charles and Jack left the room hastily to carry out their assigned chore. Victoria lifted an entreating gaze toward the heavens. She had seen animals born on the plantation in Kolhapur; she prayed that human births were similar. She looked down at the little girl, trembling in the fold of her arm. The child's bottom lip quivered, and her eyes filled with tears. "Elizabeth," Victoria said firmly, "you must live up to the valor of your name and help with this. Your mother is about to bring new life into the world, and you must be very much a part of that process. You must find lots of clean cloth—make certain it is clean—and bring it all to me." The little girl nodded and scampered out of the room. Victoria felt sure that cloths would be needed as well as water. The miracle of birth, she remembered with a lurch of her stomach, though a breathtaking spectacle of nature's splendor, was a messy business. Any inclination, however, to turn away from what was to happen was quickly brushed aside. Surely Eldora could not turn away from it, nor could the babe. Victoria patted her friend's shoulder and dismissed any personal aversion she might feel. "We shall see this baby into the world with as little stress to him and to you as possible," she said reassuringly. "Where are Tad and Greyson?" Eldora closed her eyes. The tears made little rivulets on her pale cheeks.

"What Jack said is true," she whispered. "They are assembling with the other men of the village on the Lexington Green." Victoria looked up. The beating of the drum had stopped abruptly. She glanced back at Eldora.

"They intend to take on the British army?" she asked in wonder.

Eldora nodded weakly. "I prayed he would not go, Victoria," she said softly, "but I knew he would. I would be with him now, but for this —" her voice became clenched with pain as she grasped at her writhing abdomen and drew up her knees — "this . . . life that so innocently demands . . . entrance into such a . . . world." Victoria lifted herself and took Eldora's hands in hers.

"Squeeze, Ellie," she said, "squeeze as hard as you must. I shall help you." Hands gripped together in love, in resolution in succor; the two women were bound at this hour of life. The children clattered into the room. Victoria bade them bring the water, for she sensed the babe was about to come. She drew up Ellie's gown and petticoats and arranged a clean sheet beneath her. "Hurry, children," she breathed as Eldora screamed a ragged cry of tearing anguish. Victoria smoothed a dampened cloth over the woman's forehead as the terrible pushing agony began. The children, their assignments completed, huddled together near the bedside, afraid and yet awed by the miracle that was about to take place. Victoria positioned herself at the end of the bed and waited as another scream raged through the quiet room. In the silence that followed, a tiny, radiant bud of human flesh appeared. It was the top of the babe's head. She motioned to the children. They gathered silently to watch this marvel of nature's wondrous power. The little bud of flesh popped from its imprisonment, and Victoria reached to catch it. Another tearing cry rent the silence as its mother at last released it fully. Victoria, with an exhalation of wonder, caught the liberated bundle as it slid into her trembling, but determined embrace. "Oh, children," she breathed, "did you ever see such a magnificent creation." The three youngsters looked down on the squalling, writhing, glorious little bit of humanity and gaped in silent and awe-struck fascination at what they had helped to bring into the world.

Victoria's heart pounded as she reached into her haversack and drew out her knife. She had seen enough of birth to know that a final cleaving must occur. With a firm hand that belied the quaking apprehension inside her, she cut the cord that had linked mother and child in a life sustaining bond. The final rending done, she brought the babe to be placed in the nest of its mother's welcoming arms. The little creature began to suckle gustily as together Victoria and Ellie wiped at it, cleaning it, preparing it for the world which it had so insistently entered. The children gathered, sitting on the bed near Ellie and Victoria and waiting their turn to swath the babe of its bloody birth. Victoria watched as the gentle Elizabeth took her turn. She looked up shyly at her mother and then at Victoria.

"She is beautiful," the child breathed.

Ellie began a low, quiet murmur of laughter, and she was joined by the others as she realized the child that had been born to her was a little girl. "I did not even think to look," she said as tears of joy swelled in her eyes. "Oh, Victoria, you must find Tad and tell him." She laughed. "You must tell him; he has a new woman in his life!"

Victoria glanced worriedly toward the window, her smile fading. She would deny Eldora nothing, and yet . . .

The drum had stopped. The air of the newly awakened April morn was absolutely still. No bird sang; no creature chirruped to welcome the dawn. The moon had not yet faded. It was barely five A.M. Victoria moved carefully, soundlessly, toward the Lexington Green. What she saw, as she stood behind a not yet blossomed tree, filled her heart with terror. About eighty colonials stood in a double row on the triangle formed by the Green. Their muskets were paused at their sides. Before them, not twenty paces away, a red-coated line of horsed soldiers was forming. Their number was uncountable, and it stretched for miles back along the Lexington Road, spread itself in an endless expanse before the tiny band of regulars. Faces grim, determined, the two lines faced each other.

A clear voice rang out from the courageous cordon of roughly dressed drably ununiformed patriots. "Stand your ground!" the voice called. "Don't fire unless fired upon! But if they mean to have a war, let it begin here!" Whereupon a crimson-coated, epaulet gilded major rode to the front of the ranks. His powerful steed wheeled and pranced in the gravel, raising clouds of dust.

"Lay down your arms, you damned rebels and disperse!" the soldier shouted.

The man who had called out initially seemed to slacken his stance. His proud shoulders lowered perceptibly. Victoria could see Greyson from where she stood, and she realized that he, too, seemed to sense the futility of their situation. He glanced around, grim-faced, at his compatriots. Several rag-coated men began slowly, dejectedly, to remove their tricorns and lay down their guns, but Greyson held his firmly.

Suddenly, unbelievably, a single shot rang out, and a volley from a British platoon answered. Another volley followed, and with bayonets levelled, the redcoats charged. Men scattered. Screams pierced the air as English bullets found their marks. Bloody cries of anguish merged with the harsh bark of the guns. One man, a man Victoria recognized as Jonas Parker, fired once then was claimed by a British bullet. Sinking to his knees, he attempted to reload. Bullets, wadding and flints fell with his hat as at last he was cut down by a bayonet thrust.

Victoria's hand flew to her mouth as her stomach writhed. The bile of horror rose to clench at her throat with a bitter grasp. Men flew past her, not noticing her, bent and wretching behind the tree. She looked up to find, to her terror, the main body of the British upon the Green. A cheer resounded in token of their victory and music — unbelievably in the midst of the screams and roar of the guns — began to play. As the troops started down the road for Concord, any illusion as to the secrecy of their mission had been dispelled.

Victoria felt herself lifted in Greyson's strong arms. She was swept along at a pounding run away from the Green and toward the house where so recently life had begun. Nearly to the house, Greyson stopped abruptly. He gazed down in disbelief at the ravaged body of Tad Wright. Victoria struggled, bounding from his arms, and knelt beside the fallen Tad. Greyson bent and felt for the man's pulse.

"He is not dead," he breathed. Lifting him over a wide shoulder, he carried the young patriot the rest of the way.

Greyson erupted into the quiet house, Victoria clutched to him and he still carrying the wounded Tad. "Where is your mother," he demanded as Charles appeared from the bedroom. Victoria's eyes darted over the boy's head as she saw, to her horror, Ellie Wright attempt to lift herself from her bed, the babe still at her breast.

She wrenched herself from Greyson's hold and dashed to Eldora's side. "Lay Tad on the table," she ordered over her shoulder. "You stay in bed, Ellie." Realizing what must have happened, Greyson laid Tad across the wide table and began shouting orders to the children. The hot water that had been used to swath the newly born child now served to wash their father's wounds. Tearing at the young man's clothes, Greyson discovered that the injuries Tad had received were superficial.

As the guns silenced, as the horrible gaiety of the British music faded, as Lexington quieted, Tad Wright roused and was taking small sips of water. The more serious of his wounds — a laceration caused by a musket ball — was bound up, and at long last, he was allowed to enter the room where his frightened, though reassured, wife lay with their new babe.

As the new parents were reunited, all four children surrounding them, Greyson urged Victoria, with a jerk of his head, into the other room. "I must get up to Concord," he said in a rasping whisper. "There are nearly a thousand Brits on their way, and the others must be warned they are ready to go to battle. We have roused their anger, but we have not dissuaded them one bit. The first American blood has been fatally shed, Victoria. The Concord men must be warned that we are at war."

Dreamily, as if she had not heard his words, Victoria touched the tousle of curls at his forehead. "Oh, Greyson," she breathed, "thank God you are alive." Her hand drifted to his shoulder but drew back in terrified dread as she touched something warm and sticky. Looking down at her fingertips, she realized that Greyson was bleeding. She glanced up quickly. His shoulder had been injured. "Let me see to it," she gasped.

"There isn't time," Greyson said, holding her hand firmly away from him. "I have to go. You must stay to tend Ellie and Tad."

"We will be fine," Tad interrupted. He leaned in the doorway of the bedroom. "And Victoria may be of some help to you, Grey. Go," he added, "and Godspeed."

With hasty good-byes, fervent embraces and a last look at the splendid newborn, Victoria followed Greyson to their horses. They led them as silently as they could through the early-morning fields and past the Lexington Green. Greyson had no idea if British troops had been left to occupy the tiny village, but if they had, they were not about.

They mounted once they were on the road to Concord, but realizing they could not just ride up past the slow moving British troops, they took to the woods. Victoria watched the oozing wound at Greyson's shoulder worriedly as they rode. Relentlessly, as the morning lightened to a stormy gray, they picked their way along overgrown paths. With a sudden and audible inhalation of alarm, Victoria pointed up ahead. Greyson had already spotted, through the thick growth of trees, the rear flank of a British regiment. His finger shot to his lips as he bade Victoria to silence. They drew their horses to a stop. He reached over, grabbing the reigns of her animal, and pulled her toward him.

"We must go deeper into the trees," he whispered. "If they spot us, they will kill us — nevermind bringing us in for questioning." He held her horse at tether and led them farther into the woods. Slowly, tediously, they passed the decorously-marching British troops. The music of fife and drum accompanied the deathly sonorous tramp of their boots.

At last, the couple was beyond sight of the flashes of crimson coats through the trees, and Greyson believed it was safe to travel the road. They made for the clearer way and spurred their horses to a gallop. As they approached the center of Concord, they observed that some of the minute-men had taken up a position on a ridge to the right over-looking the road and the town. Greyson waved an arm and the men waved back. Victoria and Greyson rode eastward toward the Concord River and the farm of Colonel James Barrett, in general command of the Militia at Concord.

All along the way, they saw vast numbers of men assembling at various sites. Gathered in fields, cemeteries, along brows of hills, men waited, muskets at the ready. Victoria rode in silent awe as she surveyed the numbers.

"There are so many," she whispered at last.

"The British have three times our number, Victoria," he said softly. They approached the North Bridge. Again, Greyson waved, and Victoria watched in disbelief as the hill-side leading up to the farm came alive. Drab-coated men rose up where before there had seemed to be only under-growth and a few trees. They crossed the bridge, and a group of fifers and drummers struck up the tune of "The White Cockade," and the men roared a welcome. As they reached the top of the road, they were greeted joyously.

"What news, Grey?" asked one of the men.

Greyson dismounted and helped Victoria down from her own horse. "Revere has been captured," he said gravely, "but Adams and Hancock have gotten away. The Brits have about a thousand light infantry and grenadiers headed this way."

"We have heard rumors about Lexington, Grey," said a young patriot who dipped out water and handed it to them. "Reuben Brown rode in just a few minutes ago. He said there were fatalities."

Greyson nodded, his face a mask of anger. "They fired on us," he said.

Victoria's gaze swung to him, and she viewed him over the rim of her cup. She did not know how Greyson could be so sure of that bit of information. In the wild confusion of the moment on the Lexington Green, could anyone have been absolutely sure who fired first? She remained silent, how-ever, until at last she was introduced. She nodded solemnly at the young man and offered her hand. His gaze slid over her as he returned her greeting. Several men watching nudged into the scene to make sure that they, too, might get an introduction.

"You will have to forgive us, Mrs. Tyrrel," one of the young gallants finally said. "We are more than a little overwhelmed to meet the notorious Baroness Darby."

Victoria's eyes widened in disbelief. "Baroness . . . Darby?" she gaped.

" 'Tis how you are known these days." The man glanced sheepishly at Greyson. "Sorry, Grey, but that's the word from Boston."

Greyson's brows plowed into a frown. "I don't understand," he said.

"General Andros has given her the title," explained one of the patriots. "He has sent men out to hunt her down. I am surprised you've not met up with them—and, I might add, thankful."

Greyson's gaze narrowed, but at that moment one of the assembled men noted the wound on his shoulder. A small dark stain had formed in the cloth of his coat. "Let us see to that wound, Grey," the man said hastily. Before anyone could react, however, a roar from the hill captured their attention.

"Will you let them burn the town down?" came an outraged cry from below. The assemblage saw smoke rising from fires in the town. The British had obviously set fire to several buildings. Just then, a company of grenadiers advanced to the bridge, and the force of four hundred patriots began to advance to a lower elevation. The men assembled on the brow of the hill scattered, muskets raised. Greyson and Victoria took up a position, and Greyson kept her protectively behind him.

"Do not move away from me," he ordered as he took aim. He did not fire. No one fired. In obedience to Colonel Barrett's order, the Americans would not fire first. The first full British volley followed several isolated shots, and then the balls whistled through the air, taking down two American men—one, shot directly through the head.

Suddenly, a man leaped into the air and fervently shouted, "Fire, fellow soldiers, for God's sake, fire!" The words ran down the ranks, and gunfire at last smashed into the English grenadiers. That one American volley unleashed the bloody virulence of the entire patriot force. The brown-coated American soldiers stood, firing their muskets, revealing themselves in all their astounding numbers, and began to advance on the bridge. The British, overwhelmed by the unexpected retaliation, scattered. And though a few more shots came from their ranks, the sudden violence of the American return sent them fleeing back to the town. In the end, two British soldiers lay dead on the ground at the foot of the North Bridge. Several wounded had hobbled away. Greyson grabbed Victoria's hand, and they ran first to the two fallen American soldiers.

Greyson leaned down and determined that the men were dead. He glanced up at the gathering of patriots. "They are Acton men," he said. Victoria recognized the two, a Mr. Davis and a Mr. Hosmer. Both had provided the Tyrrels with hospitality as they travelled.

"We cannot leave them here, Greyson," she said softly. Greyson nodded grimly. Victoria then looked down the hill to the foot of the bridge. "Two of the British soldiers are dead as well," she added. "Can we not see them properly buried? They are so far from home."

"We cannot be sure what the Brits will do next," he conceded, "but we cannot just allow these men to lie here. We must see that all four of them receive proper burial. Some of you," he said standing and gazing over the assemblage, "stay here and see to the burial of these men. I shall attempt to discover the British intent. 'Tis my guess they will reassemble in town and make their way back to Lexington and then go on to Boston. Those lads have not slept all night, and they shall be needing attention for their wounded." He targeted several men. "You are to ride north, to Billerica, Chelmsford, Reading, Woburn, and you are to apprise those companies of minutemen that they are to rendezvous at Meriam's Corner. Some others of you," he said, pointing out another group, "will ride south to Framingham and Sudbury. We need all the reinforcements we can get, gentlemen, to take up the pursuit of those Brits. They've wanted a war with us for a long time. Today they will get their wish." He led the soldiers he had indicated to follow him down the hill. As they reached the foot of the bridge, he glanced down at Victoria, who had stopped abruptly. Her eyes were wide with disbelief. "What is it, love?" Greyson demanded.

"Look," she cried. One of the English soldiers thought dead was moving, attempting to rise. "That man is alive!" Her voice carried over the assemblage, and before anyone could make their way to aid the fallen soldier, a shriek arose from the depths of the crowd of patriots. A young man, barely more than a boy, broke from the group, and hatchet in hand, he bounded past the others and swung the weapon at the Englishman—burying the sharp blade of the weapon into the man's scalp, instantly killing the red-coated soldier. With a gasp, Victoria and the others stared in horrified disbelief at the unimaginable mutilation. The boy, glassy-eyed and smiling proudly, raised his blood-stained weapon in triumph.

Victoria looked directly at the boy. His face was familiar, but even more familiar were the several silver rings he wore on his fingers.

Chapter Twenty-nine

As Greyson had suspected, the British were indeed planning a march back to Boston. Slowly, arduously, their crippled numbers began the trek south along the Lexington Highway. In the vicinity of Meriam's Corner, the number of the American Militia were increased to as many as eleven hundred as more men from neighboring towns appeared. British flankers were joining the main column on the road, and the American soldiers were advancing through the cover of the trees. It was a volley fired by the retreating grenadiers that began a deadly attack by the Americans. From that moment on, and for the next few hours, a bloody battlefield only a few hundred feet wide but sixteen miles long was created.

Greyson and Victoria travelled the wooded route back to Boston, not twenty feet from the red-coated column, as they took cover from tree to tree. As shots rang out, the British soldiers fell, their blood staining the dusty road.

"For the love of God," Greyson hissed, as he reloaded his musket, "why don't the bloody fools take to the woods? They offer themselves like tenpins for the picking." He sat with his back to the bole of a tree and wiped at his forehead. Victoria realized in alarm that the stain of blood was spreading rapidly within the fibers of his coat. As he started to rise, she held him back.

"Greyson," she whispered into his ear, "let me look at your wound."

He smiled roguishly as he arched her a glance. "If we are to stop for a few moments, I can think of better ways to occupy our time," he said softly, the sea-glass blue of his eyes twinkling in the shadowed woodlight.

"You are hurt," Victoria intoned sharply. They both looked quickly to the road, but the line of crimson kept moving. "You are hurt," she said, whispering again, "and I want to look at your shoulder." Greyson allowed her to partially remove his shirt and coat and examine the wound. As she was doing so, a musket shot rang through the trees. A shrill scream sounded. About ten yards down the road, an American soldier suddenly lurched from behind a tree and fell to the ground. Victoria and Greyson huddled together as they crawled through the underbrush to the injured man. Rolling him onto his back, they recognized the now all too familiar open-eyed amazement of the face of death. Victoria stifled a cry and turned away as Greyson drew her to his chest. Then setting her aside, he reloaded his weapon. Taking careful aim, his face a mask of forbidding resolution, he fired. A British soldier shrieked and fell in the road. Greyson flattened Victoria beneath him as a roar of retributive fire shattered the surrounding foliage. More shots rang out. They pulled themselves with the dead man far down into the blanket of crusty leaves and undergrowth.

The red-coated line moved on slowly, stopping only to shoot or to break up into flanking movements. But nothing the British did had any real effect upon the devastation rained on them by the American soldiers. By late afternoon, their retreat was characterized by a scattering of the closely maintained column, the fatigue, thirst and hunger of those who stayed, and sudden outbreaks of unprovoked violence on innocent onlookers.

Victoria and Greyson came upon a legation of British soldiers storming a roadside tavern, dragging out the benign patrons and mercilessly bludgeoning and stabbing them to death. Greyson got off many shots, and more than half the soldiers were killed. By the time that bloody encounter was over and the surviving grenadiers had fled, more than twenty men — British and American — lay dead before the tavern in a common pool of blood. Several incidents of horrible mutilation were reported throughout the day before, as the sun went down, the Battle Road was at last abandoned by both British and Americans.

Exhausted and overheated, frantic with thirst, Victoria and Greyson at last dragged themselves into Boston. The

360

town, by comparison to the Lexington Highway, was serenely quiet — almost eerily so. Few British soldiers were on the streets, and the couple made their stealthy way along Milk Street to the Bull and Crown.

No warm light greeted them as they stepped up to the door. In the salt breezes off the harbor, the wooden sign swung, squeaking indifferently. They moved quietly, testing doors and windows, but the building had been sealed. They rapped fervently on boarded apertures and called hoarsely, hoping to rouse someone inside, but no one answered their pleas.

Victoria glanced at Greyson fearfully. In the last few hours, he had been losing strength, and though he had attempted to cast off her concern for him and make light of his wound, she had regarded his increasing pallor with alarm. The blood stain now encompassed his right shoulder, and his arm hung heavily at his side. She had insisted, as they entered the town, on carrying his musket. Victoria glanced up the street from the alley where they stood, to where Dr. Poprik's house was. That house, too, remained dark and broodingly silent against the thickening night.

Behind her, she heard a thunk. She looked back. Greyson had slid down the clapboard siding of the Bull and Crown and was sitting with his back to the building and his head slumped.

"Oh, Greyson," she gasped, moving to him. She lifted his chin with her hands.

He smiled weakly. "I am fine, love," he said, but Victoria could see he was not. The terrible day had taken its toll. She must get help for him.

"I shall be right back," she assured him in a hoarse whisper. She stood, and glancing around in all directions, making sure the way was clear, she made her way up the street to Dr. Poprik's front door. Banging as loudly as she dared, she tried to rouse the old healer, but her attempts were in vain. She leaned heavily against the door, pleading silently for someone to answer her, but only the uncanny quiet of the night responded. She looked hastily back at Greyson. He sat so still in the encircling shadows of the moon. She must not indulge in fits of melancholy. She ran to him and knelt beside him. "We have to get you help," she whispered desperately. He attempted to lift his gaze to hers; but his sea-

361

glass eyes closed, and his head fell back against the siding of the building.

Victoria's frightened heart thrashed wildly against her chest; her mind whirled. There were other houses where Greyson might be safe. She regarded the lighted windows up and down the street. They stared back with sinister dispassion, giving no evidence of the loyalties inside the houses. Any door on which she knocked might offer sustenance — or death. There was only one house of which she could be sure. That house was Vivien's. And yet, how could Victoria know such a thing? She and Greyson had had no contact with Vivien for over a year. Since Victoria's arrest and imprisonment, they had not dared get in touch with her. Victoria looked back at Greyson. She brushed at the tousle of russet curls that clung to his perspiring forehead. She could not know whether Vivien's friendship had endured their separation, but it was Greyson's only chance.

Hesitantly, she slapped lightly at his beard-stubbled jaw. "Greyson, love," she intoned fervently, "you must wake up." He grasped her wrist abruptly.

"I am not brutalizing you, Victoria," he ground out. "I am loving you . . . I love you . . ." His words deteriorated into incoherent mumbles as his head shook from side to side. "Let me . . . love . . . you," he intoned over and over, holding on to her wrist.

"Oh, I will, Greyson," she breathed as she attempted to extricate her delicate wrist from his grasp. "Oh, please . . ." In a sudden, desperate inspiration, she leaned to him, her lips taking his. He succumbed, grabbing her waist, pulling her into the hot steel of his embrace.

"Oh, love," he groaned, his lips still on hers. He drew her across him and held her to his chest. She felt the cadent power of his heart. The golden stubble of his beard abraded her flesh as his lips, hot against her, ravaged her arched throat.

"Oh, Victoria, Victoria," he groaned. He shuddered against her, forcing her closer as though he would draw her inside him. His big body, his overpowering possession, encircled her. Within the confinement of his arms, his thighs, his chest, Victoria breathed his sea-scented passion. She was surrounded, encloaked in his ardor. As though awakened to reason by the force of the singular perfection of

362

their union, he looked down into her eyes. "I love you," he breathed. "Oh, I love you."

"And I love you, Greyson." She drew him close, for she, too, needed that quick infusion of life that his passion always created. They were that for each other and would be—always. No matter where the fates, the dark forces carried them, they knew, in the sudden soft warmth of their lambent desire, they would always come back to this. They held each other against those dark forces for long moments before, at last, Greyson slumped in Victoria's enfolding embrace. She rolled them over, gazing down into the opalescence of his fever-bright eyes.

"Oh, my God, Greyson," she whispered, tears welling suddenly in her own eyes, "I've got to get help for you." She untangled herself from his clutching embrace. He groaned softly as she stood, pulling herself away.

"Don't go, love," he murmured, reaching for her.

"I must go, Greyson," she said. She noted that in his sudden passion, Greyson had torn her bodice. She attempted to cover her near nakedness. "I have to find some help, Greyson. You are losing blood," she said hurriedly.

"Please . . . don't," he gasped.

"I won't," she promised, knowing that in truth, she could never leave him there. But what could she do? "We must get you out of here," she moaned. Furtively, she knelt in the dust of the moon-shadowed alley and tried to lift him. His body was an unyielding weight. She cradled his head in her lap. She glanced around, then leaned down toward him. "You must help me, Greyson," she whispered. "You must. I cannot move you."

He nodded, seeming to comprehend. As she again made an attempt to lift him, he struggled, pulling himself up. Victoria retrieved his musket, as they stumbled to their feet, and shrugged it over her shoulder. Greyson's impossible weight weakened her knees, but with his help, she led them around to the back of the Bull and Crown. There they stopped. Breathing raggedly, she decided on their next move. They must not be seen, and so she decided upon a roundabout route to Vivien's house. They must travel up Milk Street, to Cornhill, over King Street to Traumount and then on up to Hanover. It was not the quickest way, but they had tempted fate too capriciously already this day, and

Victoria decided it was the only way for them to travel.

With determined resolve, she heaved herself up beneath Greyson's shoulder, and they began their painful journey. Half dragging him, she led them along dark streets that boded betrayal. They kept to alleyways whenever they could. She inched them along the pebbled byways, never resting, only stopping when Greyson's moans threatened to expose them. By the time they reached Hanover Street, Victoria was, for all her slightness of frame, fairly carrying Greyson's ponderous weight. Outside the huge wrought iron gate, they stopped. Victoria let Greyson and herself slide to the ground among the lush vegetation that bordered the street.

From the shadows, she noted the approach of a redcoated sentry. She held her breath, but the man merely crossed the path in front of the gate and then turned to retrieve his steps. Vivien must have been placed under some sort of guard—if this was, in fact, still Vivien's house. Greyson slumped against her. She straightened herself and then gently eased him into a prone position. She glanced from the shelter of the foliage. The sentry was approaching once again. He was armed. *But,* she suddenly realized, *so was she!* She glanced down at the musket she had so carelessly heaved onto her shoulder. She drew it hurriedly down her arm and regarded the weapon keenly.

She had no idea, of course, how to use it. She hefted it once, wondering at its weight, realizing that she only had to threaten with it, not actually use it. Before her thoughts could go any farther, several men approached.

"More wounded have come in," stated one of them. The sentry saluted and unlatched the gate. Pushing it wide, he stood at attention as men were brought in on stretchers. From her dark bower, Victoria watched the procession of crimson-uniformed soldiers file past, bearing the shattered bodies of their comrades. "The poor blighters," said the first man, "never had a chance against those swarming fiends. They might as well have been invisible." The sentry nodded dully.

"I've seen enough of it tonight to last me the rest of my life," he said as he swung the gate closed.

"Your bloody life may last a lot longer since you pulled this cushiony duty. While you're holdin' high tea with the lofty Lady Frankland-Foster, the rest of us blokes've got to go out there again, I fear, to face those flippin' crawlers." The man turned away, saluting indifferently. "There'll be more straggling in before the night's over," he said resignedly, and strode off into the night.

This was still Vivien's house, Victoria reflected, and Vivien *was* under guard. In any event, the house appeared to be a hospital, she reasoned excitedly. Nevermind that it was a British hospital, there would be doctors there. Somehow she must get Greyson inside and under medical supervision. She looked down on him, lying next to her. She touched his forehead and was deeply alarmed at how hot it was. His breathing was shallow. She must get him inside. She glanced out and saw that the sentry was at the opposite end of the gate. Before he had returned, she had devised a plan.

Grabbing a twig from the ground, she snapped it deliberately. She watched as the young soldier halted and peered into the darkness. She grappled in the brush, not caring how much noise she made, and found another twig. Again, she snapped it loudly. The man approached slowly. Suddenly Victoria lunged from the cover of the undergrowth. Her gun was levelled steadily. "Drop your weapon," she commanded. The man did—immediately. The vision that materialized before him could be nothing more than a dream, after all. His eyes flitted over the trim, half-naked figure of a young woman. Spun-sugar curls drifted out in a moon-struck aura around the perfect oval of a glorious face. An emerald gaze, framed by thick dark lashes, glittered jewellike. The young soldier stood open-mouthed, noting the tatters of her colonial garb. Beneath it, flashes of ivory flesh shimmered. This could be no other than the notorious Baroness Darby, the man gaped. This, then, was the woman who had engaged the sadistic Andros and who had emerged triumphant. Tales of her had come down from both Lexington and Concord this day. Soldiers, wounded, nearly incoherent with fatigue, had spoken of catching glimpses of her at the Lexington Green, at Barrett's farm, at Meriam's Corner, on the Battle Road. And now, here was this magnificent creature standing before him. He could not disguise his euphoria at meeting her, in the flesh.

"Baroness Darby?" he asked, just to be sure.

Victoria nodded curtly. "Take off your clothes," she directed.

"My clothes?" the young man breathed. Again, Victoria offered him a nod. Oh, Lord, he thought in bemused astonishment, what was this miraculous witch going to do to him? He already envisioned the tales he would tell his comrades when he arrived back at the barracks. Breathing raggedly, barely taking breath into his lungs, he obeyed.

"Your small clothes, as well," Victoria ordered sternly.

"My-m . . ." he rasped.

"Everything." The gun was lifted almost imperceptibly, and the young man hastily complied. Completely naked now, he stood before the radiant apparition—wondering, hoping. "Now start running," she said quietly.

"Running?" the man asked, bewildered, disappointed.

"You heard me," Victoria snapped. "Start running and don't stop—ever!" She steadied the gun.

The soldier blanched. The insurrectionist noblewoman had not earned her reputation idly. Perhaps, and probably, in fact, she was as dangerous as Andros said she was. The British soldier spun from the blackened barrel of the much-used gun, and without a backward glance, he did as he had been ordered. He ran as fast as his lean legs would carry him, and he did not intend to stop—ever!

With a sigh of profound relief, Victoria lowered the heavy weapon. Thankful to have been delivered from her role as combatant, she immediately began to gather the soldier's garments. She hurriedly stepped into them. She might have attempted to hold the young man hostage, to have him, with her gun in his back, lead her and Greyson inside, but she had no idea of what she would find in the house. She had no idea how many arms they had and no idea how she might have managed to propel all three of them into the house. The deciding factor in her hastily made plan was that she would never have been able to use that weapon even if she had known how to use it. She must make her way into the mansion—unnoticed, if possible—and seek out Vivien. Vivien would know how to get Greyson inside.

With trembling fingers she fastened the buckles of the breeches and slipped into the blouse, white vest and scarlet

366

coat of the British uniform. *Oh, Greyson,* she thought wistfully, *if only you had such fine raiment in which to fight your war.* She glanced down at his darkly-clad figure as she tucked her curls beneath the black tricorn and pulled on the white gloves. It was this very lack of raiment which had won Greyson and his men their victory today. She buckled on the gunbelt and scabbard. She eyed the French pistol at her hip. This looked to be a more manageable weapon, if she needed it, she thought. She fastened the gold buttons of the vest and coat and leaned down awkwardly, touching Greyson one last time before she went to the gate.

Shuffling in the huge leather boots, she made her way to the gate's latch. It was locked. The soldier had opened it, she remembered, and hurriedly reached into the pockets of his vest and coat. Searching out the key, she was about to open the ornate barrier when a voice from behind her told her that she was not alone. Her heart constricted in terror as she turned and nonchalantly saluted. The man was the same one who had approached before, and as before, several other men, carrying stretchers, trailed after him.

The soldier eyed Victoria sharply and did not bother with a salute. "Who are you?" he demanded.

"Percy," she muttered, recalling that Vivien's acquaintance Lord Percy was also a high-ranking officer in the British armed forces.

"Percy what?" the man demanded.

"*Earl* Percy," Victoria responded quickly.

"What happened to Reed?"

"Got off duty," she answered. The man eyed her suspiciously. This was not the time that watches changed. "He got sick," Victoria added.

The older man nodded in understanding. The boy had admitted to a certain queasiness at seeing the wounded file past. These youngsters had no bones, he thought disgustedly. He peered into the darkness at this one. Younger than most, he reflected. And his uniform didn't fit properly. Well, he reasoned, what did the powers that be expect when they lifted them out of the cradle? There probably wasn't a uniform in all of Great Britain small enough to fit such a tadpole. "Open the gate, lad," he said almost gently. Victoria did so hurriedly and stood at attention as she had seen the other man do, as the wounded were conveyed through. Once they were inside, the man patted Victoria's slender shoulder. "Try not to think about it, boy," he said. Then he returned Victoria's salute and again strode away.

Victoria breathed relief. She once again attacked the latch, and glancing back once at Greyson to make sure he was safe, she slipped inside. The entire front courtyard was serving as a triage area. She stepped around the bodies of groaning, writhing men as she made her way to the front entrance. The great front door hung open with the passage of men in and out. Awkwardly, in her big boots, she shuffled her way into the brightly lit dining room. It was there she found Vivien, her sleeves rolled up, a bloody apron tied at her waist, assisting the doctor. She glanced up at Victoria's entrance and blew at a flame-colored tress that had fallen over her eyes.

"What is it, lad?" she demanded.

"I . . . uh . . . wanted to . . . uh . . ."

"Speak up, boy," Vivien snapped. "We're busy as all bloody hell in here, now what is it—quick!"

"I'd . . . uh . . . like to see your ladyship—for a minute." Victoria kept the brim of her tricorn down so that it shadowed her face. The doctor standing over the long dining room table glanced up from beneath graying brows.

"You'll have to get out of here, son," he said sharply.

"There's someone at the gate—says he knows you," Victoria persisted. Vivien looked up at the doctor and that man nodded curtly.

"Why doesn't he just come inside?" Vivien questioned the young—the very young—soldier as she hurriedly moved to him, drying her hands with a begrimed towel. "What is the problem?" Victoria could barely keep up with the swift-moving Vivien.

"He . . . he doesn't think he'd be welcome," Victoria muttered. Vivien arched a titian brow and eyed the lad keenly. With a surreptitious lift of her tricorn brim, Victoria looked up and directly into Vivien's eyes.

"Victo—" Vivien exhaled suddenly. Her hand flew to her lips. "Victory to the Sovereign Rule," she intoned, glancing with a serene smile from side to side at the various men being treated, and grabbed Victoria's arm, hustling them both out the door.

"I'm sorry, Vivien—" Victoria began when they were safely outside.

"Oh, my darling," the older woman breathed, clasping Victoria to her. "Where have you been? What are you doing here? Look at you." She laughed, holding the girl away from her. Then, pulling her back into her arms, she held her for a long moment. "I have missed you more than I can tell you. Oh," she said finally, glancing over her shoulders and then looking at Victoria, "you should not be here at all. Andros has—"

"Vivien," Victoria interrupted her, "you have to help us."

"Us?" Vivien asked.

"Greyson and me." She grasped her friend's arm and pulled her to the gate and outside it to where Greyson lay, totally unconscious now, in the underbrush. "He has been wounded," Victoria said, looking up desperately into Vivien's eyes. Vivien knelt down immediately to inspect the wound at Greyson's shoulder.

" 'Tis hard to tell anything in the dark," she said worriedly. "We must get him inside, Victoria."

The younger woman nodded."But how can we?"

"Take off your clothes," Vivien ordered. She began to undress Greyson rapidly. As soon as Victoria was out of her British uniform, she and Vivien began to try to fit Greyson into it. "I shall get you something to wear," Vivien said as she heaved Greyson up so that Victoria could struggle him into the blouse, vest and coat. "His uniform is far too small," Vivien lamented. "But it will have to do for now." Making sure that Victoria was safely hidden, Greyson's clothes hanging about her, she called for a stretcher. "I shall be right back," she told Victoria and supervised the loading and conveyance of the "unfortunate soldier who had walked down from Concord and collapsed on the doorstep."

Within minutes, she was back, handing Victoria the clothes she had brought out for her and, at the same time, dragging the girl through the courtyard to the back of the house.

"Halt!" a stentorian voice shouted. The two women stopped abruptly.

"Be calm," Vivien whispered. She turned, holding Victoria behind her. Victoria tucked her curls deeper into her tri-

369

corn and hunched into Greyson's big coat.

"What are you about, Lady Frankland-Foster?" asked the soldier as he moved toward them.

"About?" asked Vivien innocently.

"Who is the lad?" the man demanded.

"This? Oh, this . . . boy is . . . um . . . Rod . . . He bring me my . . . rags." She nudged Victoria's arms that held both her and Greyson's clothes. Victoria held out the heap of clothing for the man to see. "He brings me rags to . . . make . . . my . . . blankets," Vivien improvised weakly. Would the man believe her? "His mother saves rags for me," she added to strengthen the lie. Then, to emphasize her plight even further, she lowered her pale lashes, and they fanned out in golden luminescence against her delicate cheekbones. She dabbed at the supposed tears that formed as she made her distressful admission. The soldier knew only too well the poverty to which the beauteous Lady Frankland-Foster had been consigned since her husband's leaving. Everyone knew she'd had to sell off most of her furniture simply to eat. And now, to have to collect rags to make blankets for herself. . . . This was no circumstance for a lady of quality to find herself in, and he hated being witness to it. He cleared his throat in embarrassment. Nodding tersely he strode away.

Vivien and Victoria turned then and began a more decorous retreat. Vivien led Victoria to the end of the house. With one last backward glance, the two women vanished quickly around the corner. The dark quiet back garden was empty of blossoms. Dry leaves covered the winter-chilled ground, and each stealthy footfall was greeted with their soft scattering.

"No one knows of this root cellar," said Vivien softly as she kneeled and felt among the debris of the untended garden. At last, revealed beneath a wide-growing, ragged thorn bush was a small declivity in the earth. "Neville had it built in case of an Indian attack," Vivien whispered, laughing as she groped. Her fingers finally curved around a small metal handle encrusted with dried earth. She pulled, and a hole, barely large enough to accommodate a small man, gaped in the darkness of the ground. "I doubt if Neville could have fit into this opening," she said reflectively. She glanced quickly up at Victoria. "But you shall," she added. Victoria looked down into the aperture, her eyes wide and fearful in the shadowed moonlight. " 'Tis large enough inside," said Vivien, consolingly. She laughed softly. "Neville Frankland-Foster was a man, you will remember who would not think of surrendering his luxury even under threat of siege. This underground room is well-stocked with brandy, candles, waxed cheeses, dried meats and fruits . . . " her voice trailed off as she recognized Victoria's apprehension. She stood and placed her arm around the girl's slender shoulder. "Try not to be afraid, darling. You and Greyson have come so far. You must not submit to fear now." Victoria looked piteously vulnerable as she faced her next trial. "Greyson is safe inside," Vivien said softly, "and this is the only safe place for you."

Suddenly, loud voices could be heard from around the corner of the house. "The lad said she stole his clothes!" railed the unmistakable injunction of Roger Andros. Apparently, the young man whom Victoria had ordered to strip *had* stopped running, and he had stopped at the headquarters of General Roger Andros. "Dammit to bloody hell, I want her. Search this house, you blighters, and find that unholy Jezebel!"

"But, General, we would have seen the Baroness if she had come in" came another voice.

"We'll *all* see the bitch before the night is out, or I'll know the reason why!" Andros shrieked. "Now begin the search. I know she is here!" The men scattered, the loud cadence of their boots echoing in the cold night. They were coming around the house. Vivien shoved at Victoria, and without further thought, the girl scrambled down into the hole. Vivien replaced its earthen lid and hastily brushed dried leaves over the small declivity. She stood and brushed at her gown and hair and ran to the front of the house to meet the oncoming scrutiny of the soldiers. She stopped abruptly as a man confronted her. The moon erupted from its cloud cover, and there before her was the mottled face of Roger Andros.

"Where is she?" he demanded.

"Where is who?" Vivien responded with a hard swallow.

"The Baroness Darby," Andros ground out.

Vivien stood silent, regaining her composure, knowing that Victoria's life depended upon her self-possession. "I am afraid you have me at a disadvantage, General," she said and managed a sweet smile. In the blaze of moonlight, the man's face contorted by his acrimony came down, and he glowered at the woman.

"I want her, Lady Frankland-Foster, and if you have her, you'd better tell me now. 'Twill go easier on you when we find her."

"Again, General," murmured Vivien, "you have me at a disadvantage." She lowered her eyes, attempting to disencumber herself from the terrible, stabbing glare. Andros grabbed her arm and Vivien looked up sharply.

"Tell me where she is," he grated, shaking her roughly.

"I do not know where she is," Vivien retorted, "and if I did, you can bloody well bet, I'd not tell you." Her eyes blazed. Andros's anger erupted in a moonstruck frenzy.

"You had better tell me," he ejaculated, "or I shall kill you!"

"Kill?" Vivien sneered. Her eyes shot to the men who were suddenly gathered at the general's back. "Kill me then, you bloody whoreson, but if you do, be prepared to die yourself — for committing the crime of murder!" She felt an overwhelming satisfaction and relief as the man's glance swung to his witnesses. The soldiers stood watching as the moon faded behind a cloud. Only their dark shadows remained to avert his rage. He glanced back quickly to Vivien. His eyes narrowed, taking in the arrogant angle of her chin. He took a long breath.

"All right," he clenched, "You have the law on your side, but so have I. I shall search this house until I find that woman. And when I do, you have my word, you will be arrested for harboring a criminal." Vivien offered him a measuring look but said nothing. Andros paused and smiled thinly. "You *would* protect her, would you not, Lady Frankland-Foster?" He watched as Vivien lowered her eyes. Roger Andros raised himself contemptuously. "Oh, yes, Lady Frankland-Foster, you would protect the wench *and* her rebel husband. You, who bear no loyalty to the Crown or to the sanctity of your own marriage, would harbor that virago and protect her from my wrath." His hand still grasped her arm and his hold tightened until Vivien cried out. With almost ghoulish reluctance, Andros released his hold. His smile deepened. "You have made a powerful enemy this night, madam," he said quietly. "You shall not have one moment's peace until Victoria Tyrrel is found." He turned abruptly, and gesturing to his men, he led them away. Vivien glanced fearfully toward the back garden. She knew Victoria was well-hidden, and Greyson could be moved to the cellar as soon as she could divert attention from him. Her mind flew. She must find someone she could trust to help her in this. There was that old rebel doctor that everyone was talking of. What was his name? It was an odd name, a musical name, if she recalled. She must ask Victoria. They must work together to keep them all safe from the remorseless wrath of Roger Andros. Whatever else had happened tonight, the general was right about one thing. Vivien had made a powerful enemy.

Deep inside the dark ground, Victoria breathed a long sigh. She had no idea how her surroundings looked or felt. In the deepest darkness she had ever known, she waited for Vivien's return.

Chapter Thirty

"She is in Boston," Roger Andros grated, "and by God, I shall have her."

Jared Everett eyed him speculatively. There was no question that the general had information on Victoria, he was so positive of her whereabouts, but where the information had come from remained the question. "How do you know this, General?" he ventured.

Andros's face contorted, reddening dangerously. "I have my sources, Everett, and my sources have seen the bloody she-demon." He leaned across the desk menacingly. "Now I ask you a simple question; does Lady Frankland-Foster know her whereabouts?"

"She does not, sir," answered Jared, standing at attention, unflinching, before the twisted countenance. If Jared had hated the man before, he now found himself wishing profoundly that he could tear him apart and exorcise his brand of fanaticism from the earth. It was the fifth time in less than a week that Andros had called him into his office. And it was the fifth time in less than a week that Jared had denied any knowledge on Vivien's part of the whereabouts of Victoria Tyrrel.

"How do you know she does not, sir," spat the general.

"Lady Frankland-Foster does not—to my knowledge— sir," he answered as sedately as he could, "know the whereabouts of the Baroness Darby."

From a corner of the room, General Gage's voice attempted to soothe the agitated officer. "He's told you the same thing before, Roger," Thomas Gage said quietly. "He tells you the same thing every day—sometimes twice—"

"Keep out of this, Tom," Andros snapped.

Thomas Gage sighed audibly and stood. "I think we'll be

getting on, Roger," he said resignedly. He saluted Jared. "You are dismissed, Colonel Everett."

Jared was halted mid-salute at the sudden slamming of Andros's fist onto his desk. "He is dismissed when I say he is dismissed, by God!" he shrieked.

General Gage faced his fellow officer. "You may consign your men to search after search of Lady Frankland-Foster's house," he said evenly, "you may waste your time and theirs on this demented compulsion, Roger, but I will not have you wasting the time of *my* officers. I do not say your cause is a waste, mind you, I too would give a great deal to find that lady, but if Colonel Everett says — "

"The Baroness Darby was *seen,* Tom," Andros persisted doggedly, "and this man, not one week ago, came in demanding to know who accuses her." His narrowed gaze swung to Jared. "Why did you want to know that, Colonel? Of what concern is it to you, who accuses her?"

Jared shifted uncomfortably, hoping his discomfort was not apparent. Vivien and he had searched the general's office that fateful Tuesday night and found nothing. Vivien had insisted they go back several days later, when the confusion of the nineteenth had died down, and question Andros himself. Her nearly frantic insistence had bewildered Jared, but he had finally agreed. It had been the biggest mistake of his life. Andros had plagued them both mercilessly ever since. He looked to General Gage, but that man, too, seemed to want to know his reasons. Jared sighed inwardly.

"Lady Frankland-Foster feels that her husband may have accused the Baroness Darby falsely from the first. Neither Vivien nor I have ever known her to be anything but absolutely loyal to the Crown," he said finally, hoping the explanation would appease the two generals. Neither seemed in the least appeased.

"You must admit, Jared," said General Gage, "the woman is not above reproach. She began her career by marrying one of the most notorious rebels in Boston. She went on to be spotted at the Bull and Crown — the most notorious of rebel haunts. She was also seen, not incidentally, in the vicinities of not only the Boston Tea Party but two of the most fateful battles the world will ever know — "

"And now — not one week after those battles were fought, not one week after those arrogant rotters had the audacity to fire upon the soldiers of the king—the Baroness Darby is back in Boston, seen at the house of your lady, Everett. It has been reported to me," Andros seethed, "that she attacked one of my men and, at gunpoint, stole his clothes. I want that bitch, Everett, and by God I will have her!" He pointed a finger at Jared, and that man tried very hard not to flinch. "Your *Lady* Vivien Frankland-Foster had *better* not know the whereabouts of the Baroness Darby, Everett, because if she does, she and her *friend* will *hang from the same rope*," he finished, clenching out the last words.

Jared looked to Thomas Gage, who nodded, dismissing him. He saluted both men smartly and turned, exiting the office with a profound sigh of deliverance. Vivien's house would be searched again before the day was out.

This whole damned situation was getting beyond him, he decided as he made his way across the Boston Common. He stepped carefully across rain puddles. Jared Everett wanted nothing more after his duty in these rock-bound American colonies than to return to his home in Coventry. He longed to take Vivien there, to share with her the gentle pleasures of the English countryside. He would welcome her sons and call them his. They would all be at peace in those benevolent environs. He looked up to the thickening sky. Clouds, begrimed and foreboding, hung swollen with impending rain. He would welcome Vivien's warm fire tonight, and the warmth of her company. Though, of late, he reflected, her company had been something less than attentive. She had become more and more distracted over the past two or three days. Jared had put it to the arrival of her sons.

The boys had arrived on the twentieth—and handsome, vigorous lads they were. Vivien's devotion to them was heartrending—sweet, yet marked by elements of profound suffering. She obviously felt that somehow, by ending her marriage to their father, she had injured them. In truth, thought Jared, she had done them a favor. Lord Frankland-Foster had never been a conscientious parent, from what the boys had told him. Their mother had been the light and strength by which they had been guided all the years of their young lives. And now he, Jared Everett, would be their father. He would offer them the manly vigilance and love of which they had been deprived. He allowed a smile to curve his firm lips. He would offer them all that. He would offer all that to their mother as well — if only she would allow it.

As he made his way to the house on Hanover Street, resolve weighed upon him. He must get Vivien to speak of what was troubling her. There were so many things that might be diverting her usually serene bearing. The separation from her husband of over twenty years must have been traumatic to this gentle and loyal creature. It was a decision that had not come easily, Jared was sure. Her recent poverty, after she had lived a life of at least material security, must have put enormous chinks in her sense of well-being. Jared had tried — and believed he had succeeded — in smoothing those obstacles to her happiness. But he knew that Victoria's arrest and involvement with the infamous Greyson Tyrrel had left Vivien deeply anguished. And these days — every day — Roger Andros entered and searched her house. This shameful practice was now legal in the American colonies under British law, and Jared had no doubt that Vivien had been appalled by it. He did not blame her. She had nothing to hide after all — or did she? This was what Jared must discover.

He had never fully accepted her assertion that she knew nothing of Victoria's whereabouts. Perhaps the girl was up at the Beacon Hill with Bonny Bowdoin and that crowd. Undoubtedly Tyrrel had fled there to be in the company of his Bull and Crown cohorts after the terrible cleaving events of the nineteenth. But Tyrrel would never have allowed Victoria to contact Vivien. He would not have allowed either of the women's lives to be placed in danger by such contact. Perhaps Victoria had overridden Tyrrel's vigilance and gotten in touch with Vivien secretly. That was very possibly the reason for Vivien's increasing uneasiness during the past week. Each time Andros left her house, she seemed less and less anxious to speak with Jared — less and less anxious to share with him the reasons for her apprehensiveness. Today, he determined, he would discover her reasons. He would allow no turning away, no evasion, no affronted denials on Vivien's part to keep him from discovering the truth. He would question the obstinate Vivien until she told him exactly what she knew of Victoria's whereabouts.

Jared's smile deepened. Once they had had their battle over this matter, once he'd gotten the truth out of Vivien, he would enjoy assuring her that he would not betray her secret.

And assure her he would.

He stepped through the gate and onto the porch, relieved that the temporary British hospital had been moved to the granary on Park Street. That, at least, was one thing less Vivien needed to worry about. The front door hung open. Jared frowned and closed it behind him as he entered. Why was Vivien being so careless with her scarce supply of wood on this damp and cold afternoon? He strode down the hallway and into the small parlor. At the entry, he stopped abruptly, his heart turning cold at what he found.

Vivien was seated on the small sofa. Trembling, pale, her eyes brimmed with tears, she slowly swung her gaze to him. He dashed to her side.

"What is it, sweet," he questioned, kneeling and taking her icy hand in his. "Tell me."

"He was here again," she breathed.

"Andros?" Jared exhorted.

Vivien shook her head slowly. "No," she answered softly. "The other one."

"Who," Jared demanded.

"That little man . . . that ugly little . . . man." Vivien's eyes dimmed with misting terror.

Jared's face became grim. "Bouchard," he said coldly. Vivien nodded. "Did he want money again?"

Again Vivien nodded. "This time, he brought his friend Clough the mute. Bouchard told me that Clough had killed before — silently, he said — without compunction. He . . . he rubbed his hands together as he said it, Jared." Vivien shuddered. "He and Clough just . . . stood there, where you are, right over me and . . . and . . . smiled. . . ."

Jared stood, his jaw clenching. "Those two smarmy bastards need a lesson in discretion. 'Tis one thing that they are spies for the British and live among the citizens of Boston as one of them. 'Tis another thing entirely that they now threaten women in the name of British intelligence. They have undoubtedly been sent by Andros to intimidate you. In their own self-abasement, they will do anything for money it appears."

At once the front door exploded open, kicked by the big boots of General Andros's men. "Stand and be searched!" came the now all too familiar command. Vivien rose and stood with Jared as, once again, her house was ransacked.

All three stories resounded with the heavy tread of armed soldiers. Again, nothing was found. Again, Andros stormed, red-faced and glazing, wildfire in his blood-shot eyes, into the small parlor to face Vivien.

"I want the Darby bitch!" His crazed tone resounded through the empty house. "And I want her, goddammit, *now!*"

"Lady Frankland-Foster does not have her, General," Jared said, saluting stiffly.

The general's glare swung to the impudent young colonel. "We'll just see about that, Everett," he seethed. "We'll just see what is revealed when I burn this house to the ground."

Vivien shot Jared a horrified glance. As General Andros and his men charged from the house, her voice was clenched with dread as she said, "We have got to get her out of here."

Jared gazed at her, bewildered. "What did you say?" he asked.

"Jared," Vivien said softly as she sat them both down, "we have a great deal to discuss." She paused, and then continued slowly, "I do know where Victoria is."

"I thought so," Jared assured her. "Well, sweet," he said gently, "why don't you tell me about it. Start from the beginning."

Jared's complexion paled as Vivien told her story. "Are you telling me she is . . . here?" he demanded, rising from the sofa and looking down at her. Vivien nodded helplessly.

"What was I to do, Jared?" she insisted. "I could not toss her to Andros."

"But you have endangered yourself and her, Vivien. How could you have been so reckless." His golden eyes flickered angrily, impaling her with their accusation. Vivien lowered her own gaze.

"Rather than reproaching me," she murmured, "you might think of some way to help." Vivien's irritation was obvious, and Jared knew he must attempt to gird his impatience. He knew that she'd felt she had no choice in the protection of Victoria and Greyson—he would have done the same thing himself, he supposed. But he wondered that she had not trusted him enough to confide her secret. Jared realized he had far to go in inspiring trust in this woman he adored. She had been wounded deeply and required a man of patience to help her heal those wounds. They went as deep as her generous heart.

"I want to help, my darling," Jared said, raking his fingers through his dark hair. "My anger lies in the fact that you have kept this from me. Do you realize what might have happened if Andros had discovered that root cellar?" Vivien nodded. Jared took her shoulders and lifted her to face him. "When will you realize there is nothing you cannot share with me? I could have helped in this."

"How?" Vivien asked. "You are a British officer and Victoria is—"

"—a human being and your friend," he finished for her. Jared shook her gently. "That fact makes her very important to me, Vivien. Don't you know that? Couldn't you have trusted me? I might have been able to help." He splayed a hand when she would have protested. "Dammit, Vivien, I am not saying I could have stopped Andros, but I might have been able to throw him off the scent. As it is," he continued, turning from her, "we have few options open to us. Andros might do anything at this point to find the 'Baroness Darby.' In his desperation, he just might decide to put a match to this house." Jared paced for several moments. Vivien watched him in silence. Though she had been forced to face his anger, she felt great relief now that she'd told him the truth. Why had she doubted that in the end Jared would be her ally? He was, after all, her best friend. Together they would find a solution to this problem. Though it seemed insurmountable, it was now at least shared and therefore lightened. Vivien wondered, though, what Jared would say when she brought him down into the cellar and he discovered not only Victoria but Greyson and Dr. Poprik there. She was about to tell him that further truth when a sharp knock on the front door interrupted them. They both turned abruptly, fearing another invasion by Andros and his men, when a figure appeared in the arched entrance to the parlor.

"Hello," said the gentle friendly voice. "I am looking for Victoria Quayle."

"Who are you?" demanded Vivien.

"My name," the visitor said quietly, "is Edmund Harrt."

380

Chapter Thirty-one

The rain-swept road to Salem wound darkly along the coastline. The three travelers, huddled against the dashing mist, were tossed together as the rickety cart jerked and skittered in the mud. Along one side of the narrow byway, rocky banks descended to the roiling waters of the Salem Harbor. The moon—released from its skudding cloud cover—cut a silver path through the foaming surf as it broke along the shore. The cart groaned to a stop. One of the riders jumped down and made to the front of the conveyance to see to the horses. Rubbing down their muzzles, the cloaked driver grabbed the reigns and walked the animals for a way into the darkness—into the town of Salem.

The village rose darkly from the ocean mist. Small houses, weather-boarded and shuttered against the storm, lined the narrow bystreets. Lofting more darkly, more austerely, more ponderously than the rest was the rusted oaken siding of the house the driver identified for the other two passengers as the "Gables." The driver said it was the home of the local historian and storyteller, Mrs. Samuel Ingersoll. The passengers watched as the many-gabled house disappeared into the misting drizzle while they continued up Turner Street.

After several turns of the twisting, shadowed streets, the cart at last pulled into a constricted drive. A small causeway brought them to a stable area. The cart stopped. The two passengers were helped down by the driver, and they all repaired to a nearby house. The door opened and they were ushered inside.

The woman who greeted them was tall, and her long

coiled hair was streaked with gray. Her warm brown eyes flitted over her guests, but her regard was really only for the young man who introduced them.

"Edmund," the woman said. The word was a tender breath. She moved softly toward him and took him in her arms. "Oh, my darling boy," she whispered as she brushed his cheek with a kiss. Her smile drifted to the two women who her son had accompanied inside.

"We thank you, Mrs. Harrt, for your very generous hospitality," said Victoria softly. Vivien murmured her own profoundly felt appreciation as well.

"You are most welcome," responded their hostess, but her gaze remained disconcertingly riveted on Victoria.

"Mrs. Tyrrel and Lady Frankland-Foster," said Edmund Harrt quickly, "are fugitives from Boston. Neither is a criminal, Mother," he assured the woman, "and both are . . . friends of mine." The woman nodded, her smile deepening. A look of . . . something—relief?—swept over her weathered face. She moved to the two women and directed them each to small upstairs rooms.

"You must be very tired," she said gently. "I shall bring up some refreshment in a few moments." Both women thanked Mrs. Harrt and retired gratefully to their chambers. Edmund came in shortly to bring water and to build a fire in each little hearth.

The journey up from Boston had been long and arduous. Victoria stripped off her damp clothing at last and hung it near the low purling fire. She wrapped herself in a dry night robe and fluffed out her hair. Its silken sheen snapped and popped as she brushed it dry before the fire. A tentative knock roused her. She moved to the door and found Mrs. Harrt standing there with a heavy tray.

"Oh, let me take that," she said and brought the laden tray into her room.

Mrs. Harrt began to unload the contents. "I shall bring some of this into Lady Frankland-Foster as well," said the older woman. "You must both be starved."

Victoria nodded and smiled. "Let me invite Lady Frankland-Foster in here," she said. At her hostess's consent, she padded down the narrow hallway and knocked on Vivien's door. When the three women were together in the little bedchamber, sipping hot cider, Victoria and Vivien began an abbreviated tale of how they had come to be in Salem. Mrs. Harrt listened attentively and with deep interest to their story.

"We got in touch with Edmund," Victoria said softly, "when we realized that there was nothing else for us to do. We would never have involved your son, but we were desperate, Mrs. Harrt."

"And what of your husband, my dear?" the woman asked her. "How is he faring?"

Victoria lowered her lashes, and tears welled in her emerald gaze. "He is well, Mrs. Harrt," she murmured.

"He is *very* well, Mrs. Harrt," stated Vivien. "He is under the care of the best doctor in Boston. His wounds are healing, and his spirits are elevated—especially since your son intervened and offered to escort Victoria and I out of Boston." She placed an arm around Victoria's shoulders. "Captain Tyrrel's spirits are much better than those of his wife, I might say."

"You did not wish to leave your husband," said Mrs. Harrt with a sad smile. Victoria shook her head, her pale curls undulating in the firelight.

"We practically had to drag her out of town," Vivien said, drawing Victoria closer. "But as I said, Mrs. Harrt, we had no choice. Even as we speak, Victoria's and Greyson's hiding place and my home are undoubtedly being burned to the ground." She turned to look directly at Victoria. "Dr. Popik will care for Greyson better than we might have, darling."

"There are no formal charges against Captain Tyrrel?" asked Mrs. Harrt.

"There are none now," said Vivien, "but there would have been if Victoria and I had stayed in Boston. Greyson could have been accused of harboring a spy—two spies, actually. Just before we left, I, too, was about to be charged."

"Can you tell me anything about the incidents of the nineteenth?" asked Mrs. Harrt leaning forward. "We have heard so many rumors about what happened down there. We heard there was actual *combat* between the Americans and the British. We have heard that . . . blood was shed." Victoria and Vivien confirmed at least that rumor. But Mrs.

383

Harrt went on. "So many rumors . . . " she said, shaking her head sadly. "We have heard of a young American boy — a musician, I think someone said — boldly mutilating a British corpse. We have heard of a man in a red cape who has instigated every hostility between the British and the Americans. We have heard of a mad British general who hunts down a young English noblewoman — and that woman being something of a turncoat — who dresses in men's clothing and steals uniforms from the British soldiers. We are told she is called the 'Baroness' and that she is a wild creature bent on destroying the very people by whom she has been nurtured. Can you tell me about any of that?" she asked. Victoria and Vivien eyed each other.

Victoria leaned toward the woman. Her words were as much for Vivien, though, as for their hostess, for she, too, was curious. "The boy you spoke of, Mrs. Harrt, was a young man of my acquaintance. He was, in fact, a musician — a very talented lad of Cambridge. He did . . . kill a British soldier. That man was apparently fatally wounded, and the boy, caught up in the excitement of the moment, and no doubt fearing for the lives of many Americans, took his hatchet to the man. 'Twas a stunningly sad moment — to see a gentle boy so enraptured by the killing spirit of the day. 'Tis one of the penalties of war, I fear. But he did not . . . mutilate the corpse as so many have gossiped. He simply did what his elders had been doing all day. I think he believed, as did they, that his duty was clear.

"As to the man in the red cape; no one is sure who he is — or, in fact, if he exists. I, myself, have come to the conclusion that he will remain one of those fantasy figures that rise like smoke to spread and tower over any legendary time. English folklore is rife with such figures — Robins Goodfellow and Hood are two that come immediately to mind." Victoria smiled softly. "They represent the best and the worst of us in times of stress. If there is such a man, Mrs. Harrt, he is no more *responsible* for this war than you or I." She paused, glancing at Vivien. "The matter of this 'Baroness' is something else — though no less embellished by the spirit of the times." Feeling a sense of obligation to her hostess, Victoria took a long breath. She must speak the absolute truth so that Mrs. Harrt would know exactly whom she had welcomed into her home. "The 'mad general' you mentioned is General Roger Andros, and the woman he seeks is . . . me. He believes he has cause. As I mentioned, Mrs. Harrt," said Victoria sorrowfully, "I was inadvertently involved in some militant and apparently well-planned exchanges between the British and the Americans. And though you might have your own opinions as to where my loyalties must lie, I can assure you that I see virtue and imperfection in both sides. I understand the deep frustration of the Americans, but I also comprehend and empathize with the expectations of the Sovereign Rule. I am only deeply sorry that the conflict between the two had to come to a force of arms."

Mrs. Harrt nodded sadly in understanding. "I feel much the way you do about all this, Mrs. Tyrrel," she said. "Unfortunately, 'tis anyone's guess how long we may remain neutral."

"It may come to nothing," Vivien said, hope clear in her tone. "Negotiation may well redeem us all from this ugly business. I hope so," she added, "for the sake of my sons. They have both been sent here from England to join the British armed forces."

Their hostess stood and moved to Vivien. Placing a gentle hand on her shoulder, she said, "You are a mother, too, Lady Frankland-Foster. Then you know heartbreak."

Vivien looked into the woman's eyes. "I do," she said softly.

Mrs. Harrt shifted her gaze. "I shall leave the two of you now," she said, forcing brightness. "I would suggest you get right to bed. Tomorrow, Edmund will show you the town." She regarded Victoria, and again that unspoken and dusky reflection of vague relief shown in her eyes. She turned and left the room abruptly.

Vivien and Victoria regarded each other quizzically, but put the woman's odd demeanor to their own fatigue. They snuggled beneath warm covers that rain-swept night in their cozy rooms in that cozy Salem house, and both women slept heavily, safely at last.

Jared Everett regarded the stolen papers darkly. He raised

385

the nearly guttered candle just high enough to read once again the date of the first accusation against Victoria. May 1st, it read as it had read before, 1774. Jared lowered the candle slowly and stared into the darkness. His golden eyes caught the flicker of the dying candlelight. Then all was black. He stuffed the papers into his vest pocket, and setting the candlestick aside, he stole from the office of General Roger Andros. Out on the street, Jared attempted to sort out the question of who had accused Victoria as a spy. As he strode along, down toward the river, he realized, as he had realized upon first reading the accusation, that the signer — a Mr. Spector — could not possibly have been Lord Neville Frankland-Foster. By May 1st of 1774, Lord Neville had been well on his way to England. He had left in April of that year, if Jared remembered it correctly. Yes, he reflected, it was just a year ago that Vivien's husband had sailed. It was just one year ago that he and Vivien had begun the friendship that would finally and forever bind them in love.

Jared stood leaning on the harbor rail. He gazed out over the silvered waters of the bay. He wondered what his beloved Vivien was doing right at this moment. In many ways, he was sorry to have sent her away, but there was no choice for any of them. Andros had become increasingly virulent in his tactics. His threat to burn Vivien's house to the ground had not, by the time she'd left Boston, seemed an idle caveat. They had all feared Roger Andros was just irrational enough at that point to do such a thing.

He recalled with some regret his anger when he had discovered not only Victoria but Greyson Tyrrel and that old rebel witch doctor, Poprik, in Vivien's root cellar. Jared had stormed and ranted and scolded Vivien about the recklessness on her part of doing such a thing. In the end, he conceded that it was, in fact, the only thing she could have done. He conceded as he regarded the sweet gratitude in Victoria's eyes for her friend's support, as he regarded the fallen Greyson, lying so still on a hastily arranged pallet that what Vivien had done had been right. Jared had even come to feel a certain warmth in his heart for the old medicine man and had managed to congratulate Vivien and Victoria on their courage in sending for him. Poprik and he had shared a mug or two during the several days during which they had awaited Greyson's recovery. And Greyson had recovered — his rage against Andros increasing in direct proportion to the increase in his strength. By the time it was decided that Greyson could be moved to the residence of Bonny Bowdoin up near the Beacon Hill so that his recovery might be completed, he was threatening violence. It had taken a great deal of reasoning on the part of all of them to assuage his wrath. In the end, it was decided that they must accept the offer of Edmund Harrt — the only man of their acquaintance who had remained untainted in this contention — to secrete Victoria out of Boston. Edmund had a home in Salem, and Victoria trusted him completely. It was decided that Vivien should go with them, for Andros had threatened to charge her with harboring a spy. And there was always the possibility that the man just might make good his threat to set fire to her house. In any event the root cellar had been no longer safe. Andros had very nearly stumbled upon it one day as he stalked the back gardens. They had all agreed in the end that Victoria and Vivien would be far safer waiting out the general's obsession in Salem. But that did not stop Jared from attempting to discover who had started this whole ugly business. If it had not been Neville Frankland-Foster, who was it? Who was the faceless Mr. Spector who had dogged Victoria's steps practically since the day she arrived in Boston?

The scrape of tinder against flint caught Jared's attention. He swung abruptly to see, flaring in the darkness, the rugged face of Greyson Tyrrel.

"They are in Salem," he intoned. "I've just had word that they arrived there last night."

"Thank God," Jared breathed. He turned back to his contemplation of the water. Greyson joined him at the rail. Jared glanced at the man. "You boys have an amazing network, Captain Tyrrel," he said softly.

Greyson arched him a small smile, his cheroot clamped firmly in his teeth. "We have to," he said, "to keep up with your lads, Colonel Everett." Both men stared out at the moon-washed bay for long moments. Jared pondered the question of whether or not he should share the information he had just procured with this rakehell. His decision made abruptly, he turned to Greyson.

He snatched the crumpled papers from his pocket. "I found these," he said, holding them out.

"What are they?" Greyson asked as he accepted the bundle.

"They are private files. Andros has kept them very well hidden up to now. I have a feeling he carried them with him. They are accusations filed against Victoria since May of '74. They are accounts of sightings, vilifications of her character and, finally, charges of conspiracy against the Crown."

Greyson looked down in disbelief, attempting to read the writing in the dark. "Who filed the accusations?" He glanced up at Jared. "Was it Frankland-Foster?"

Jared shook his head. "That's the mystery, Tyrrel," he said grimly. "They were filed — every one of them — by a Mr. Spector." Greyson frowned. Jared eyed him evenly. "Spector," he said. "The name does conjure one image for me; what about you?"

"What image?" Greyson asked, honestly bewildered.

"I am thinking of a certain ship," he said flatly. "I am thinking of the *Spectre of the Bay*."

Greyson regarded him levelly. "And what is that supposed to mean, Everett," he inquired.

"I don't know what it means," he said, turning back to the water. "I am only commenting on the coincidence of the—"

Greyson grabbed the colonel's lapels and swung him sharply to face him. His teeth bared, his face a mask of bronzed anger, he jerked Jared to him. "I am asking you what you mean by that," he shot out.

Jared calmly surveyed his assailant. His eyes drifted down to the scarlet cloth of his coat, crushed in Greyson's big fists, and then back up into the diamond-hard glare. "Don't you think the name just might have some significance, Captain?" he asked calmly.

Greyson slammed him away. "Only an imbecile would imagine I had anything to do with those accusations," he ground out. "I will not even respond to such lunacy." He swung his gaze out over the harbor and leaned upon the rail, his jaw working tensely. After a pause, in which Jared tranquilly brushed himself off, Greyson turned back to him. "Do you think someone on the *Spectre* may have filed those charges?" he asked.

"Do you?" Jared responded. He moved back to the harbor rail to stand near—but not too near—the headstrong rebel. "Listen to me, Tyrrel," he said narrowly, "I have only one interest in all this. I want to see justice done. I want to see Vivien and Victoria exonerated of charges that are obviously false. If that is your interest, then by the bloody devil, help me. And—" he added quietly, "do not lay hands on me again."

Greyson's gaze glinted blue fire. "What will you do, Everett?" he grated. "Will you punish me? Will you take my ship away from me? Will you take my bloody livelihood? Will you destroy my homeland, force me to raise my bloody guns against you in order that I may keep my dignity—in order that I may live in peace with my wife?" The two men stood apart, regarding each other in grim silence. At last, Greyson turned away. He snatched off his tricorn and raked his long fingers through the russet tousle of his curls. Taking a long breath, he pushed the hat back onto his head and at last glanced back at Jared. "All right," he said evenly, "I shall cooperate with you." His eyes danced roguishly. "And," he added, "I shall try to refrain from rumpling that dandy red coat of yours."

Jared made a vain attempt to hold on to his stern bearing, but he failed miserably. The smile came finally, appreciatively, to his lips. "Don't worry too much, Tyrrel," he said genially, "I have several more like it at home."

That night the two men—avowed enemies united, at least temporarily, by their love for two remarkable women—made plans. They would question everyone concerned with the case. They would seek out every particle of information relating to the question of Victoria. They would find her accuser, discover his . . . or her reasons, and then they would see Victoria's name cleared of any stain. They shook hands. The elegant, fine-coated English colonel and the rugged and arrogantly ununiformed American rebel had found a common ground.

Chapter Thirty-two

Edmund had kept his mother's word. He had squired the
two women about Salem until they laughingly begged to be
taken home. Refreshed and at the same time pleasantly
weary, they had arrived back at the Harrt home in time for
tea. Naturally there was no tea, but there was cider and coffee and a generous array of cakes and breads from which the
hungry trio could choose. Mrs. Harrt, it was soon discovered, was an excellent and a prolific cook. She offered pre-
served fruits for the breads as well as a number of different
sauces. Vivien and she happily exchanged recipes while Edmund and Victoria talked quietly by the fire.

"Mother owns a small cent shop in back of the house,"
Edmund said softly, pridefully. "She has run it for many
years now. The ladies of Salem, those who prefer to allow
others to do their baking and canning, are her most grateful
customers." They laughed together, and once again, as she
had been throughout the last several days, Victoria was
struck by Edmund's attentiveness. He had looked at her
constantly, practically ignoring Vivien. He was polite to
both women, but to Victoria he was positively courtly. Her
discomfort had increased as his vigilance became more avid.
His gallantry knew no bounds. He bowed her into and out
of shops and restaurants, he held her arm as they crossed
streets and paid her extravagant compliments. And, as he
had just now done, he conducted her into quiet corners and
private conversation whenever he could.

Victoria had expressed her concern to Vivien on several
occasions. She could not allow Edmund to go on imagining
there might be hope for some sort of romantic relationship

between them, and Victoria was sure that was what he hoped for. She must, she determined, make it clear to him that there could be nothing more than a friendship for the two of them. Victoria hated hurting him. Over the last years, since she had first met him on the *Spectre,* Edmund had been nothing but generous in his behavior toward her. She must be equally generous in her discouragement of him. She must be, above all else, kind.

And so it was, that night at supper, when he invited her to stroll out with him on the morrow alone, that she agreed. Her glance toward Vivien told the woman that it would be best if she had this private moment with Edmund to deter him gently from his obvious campaign to win her heart.

She and Vivien discussed it that night, and it was agreed at no matter the consequences, Edmund must be told before his ardor proceeded any farther that Victoria was deeply in love with her husband and intended to remain faithful to him. Vivien offered much needed support and said she would enjoy, in any event, browsing Mrs. Harrt's little cent shop the next day.

Edmund's mother was all too pleased to show Vivien around the sunny, shelf-lined room. She displayed with pride each little statuette, each trinket that had been brought to her from one exotic port or another. Sailors, she said, always thought of her in their travels, finding pretty things for her to sell. The shop reminded Vivien, in many ways, of Misty Molly's in Cambridge. Though, from what Victoria had described, Molly's business was not nearly so organized as this one, it was surely just as diverse in its offerings. Vivien described Boston and the surrounding towns to Mrs. Harrt and Mrs. Harrt listened with pleasure, offering observations and information about Salem. The two women chatted amiably, and by afternoon their acquaintance was on a first name basis. When it was decided that Edmund and Victoria were not going to return for dinner, Lenore Harrt suggested that Vivien might enjoy a stroll.

"Did Edmund take the two of you to Mrs. Ingersoll's?" he asked.

"No," Vivien answered curiously, "where is that?"

"You must have passed the house on your way here," Mrs. Harrt said as she wrapped herself in a heavy shawl. " 'Tis the most arresting house in Salem," she added.

391

"Ah, yes," Vivien said as they strolled down to the street. "I believe you are referring to that many-gabled structure on Turner Street."

Lenore nodded. "Mrs. Ingersoll also runs a cent shop," she said. "I think you would enjoy seeing it."

"I surely would," Vivien said genially.

The two women strolled arm in arm until they reached the "Gables." Mrs. Harrt rapped lightly on the cent shop door and was greeted by the owner. The two women were ushered inside.

Susannah Ingersoll was an attractive woman with deep, intelligent eyes and a shy manner. Her delicate, expressive hands lingered lovingly over each little artifact. She explained that each treasure, as in Mrs. Harrt's shop, represented a different port of call. There were trivets from Holland, mugs from Germany and baskets and brooms from the West Indies. There were plates, elaborately and delicately hand-painted, from Canton, China. Mrs. Ingersoll told Vivien that these were often used, in great numbers, as ballast on sea-going vessels.

"What is for some people merely ballast, others consider treasure." Susannah laughed. Lenore joined her in a special understanding of the cent shop philosophy. "That is really the advantage of living in a seaport village," Mrs. Ingersoll said softly. " 'Tis of course also the advantage of being married to a sea captain," she added, laughing. She insisted when the two women would have bought their afternoon meal, that they join her instead in the house. "I have not yet had my dinner," she urged them, "and I hate to eat alone." The three women took their meal in the pleasant, wide-panelled kitchen. The low ceiling and huge hearth fire kept the sunny room warm and cheerful. They sat at the wooden table near the window overlooking Turner Street and observed the passersby. It was not long before Mrs. Harrt had enjoined their hostess to tell them one of her famous stories.

"Susannah is something of a historian," said Lenore Harrt. She turned back to their hostess. "Tell Vivien about the Cranches. They have the most fascinating history. Mrs. Cranch writes *romance* novels!" She laughed.

"I do enjoy reading up on the local families," affirmed Mrs. Ingersoll. "Lately, I have developed an interest in . . witchcraft. As you know," she said, offering Vivien a blique smile, "we in Salem are rather expert at sniffing out he witches among us."

Vivien noticed that Lenore Harrt had turned pale. She tood quickly. "I have left my shop far too long, Susannah," he said. "You don't mind, do you, Vivien?"

"Of course not," Vivien said politely. "Perhaps, we might neet another time, Mrs. Ingersoll." The lady nodded and er glance toward Lenore was knowing. She bade the two adies good-bye.

As Lenore and Vivien strolled hurriedly up Derby Street way from the harbor, Vivien could not help but note her ompanion's uneasiness. Once they had reached the Harrt ome, she questioned her as discretely as she could. Lenore Iarrt poured coffee for them and successfully evaded each uestion.

"I really do not know why Susannah dotes so on that parcular bit of Salem history. Actually it only lasted a few nonths. And it was nothing more than a product of fear. 'he fanatical Puritans began to believe that the loss of relion here in the colonies meant that Satan was among us." he managed a light laugh. " 'Twas nothing more than emoonal hysteria. Puritans, as you know, get *terribly* emoonal over Satan." Vivien offered a smile, but she wondered t Lenore's discomfort. "I would hope," Lenore Harrt said nally, with heightened feeling, "that the town of Salem ight be remembered for the diversity of its architecture, ne gentility and individuality of its people, and for the fact at it was at least temporarily the capital of the Bay Colny—not for those silly witchcraft trials."

Vivien knew little of the history of the Salem witch hystea, but she realized that for Lenore Harrt at least, it seemed be something of an embarrassment. Vivien did not press e issue. The two women spent a pleasant afternoon, and it as not until suppertime approached that Vivien began to ecome uneasy about Victoria and Edmund's long absence.

The little man sniffed miserably. He swiped at his oozing ose with a tattered sleeve. His companion stood near, silent always, his arms folded across his chest.

"We are not going to harm you, Bouchard," said Jared, ting back his impatience.

"Yes you are," said the skinny, twisted informer. "A
me'n Clough's been a *friend* to the Brits all this time; it ain'
fair," he whined.

Greyson threw up his big hands in exasperation. "For th
love of God, Everett, why don't we just break the little snak
in half?" Clough stiffened—he seemed about to run.

Jared eyed him, a warning in his regard. The big mut
slackened his stance. "Listen to me both of you," he said
attempting to reason with the dim-witted spies, "we are in
terested in nothing more than finding the Baroness Darby'
accuser. Nothing will happen to you, if you tell us the truth.

"What about him?" asked Bouchard, pointing towar
Greyson.

Jared's gaze swung to his companion. "Captain Tyrrel wi
not harm you, I guarantee it." He regarded Greyson na
rowly. Greyson nodded surreptitiously, reluctantly. H
folded his arms across his chest, imitating Clough's postur
Clough immediately let his heavy arms fall to his side:
Jared continued. "Now," he said in as gentle a tone as h
could manage, "we know that Andros hired you and yo
friend Clough to intimidate Lady Frankland-Foster, and—
Bouchard and Clough exchanged a glance. Jared eyed the
keenly. "Andros *did* hire you, did he not?" The two me
remained steadfastly expressionless. Greyson approache
slowly. There was menace in his bearing. Jared splayed
hand. "For God's sake, Tyrrel—relax." He glanced back a
Bouchard. "We won't hurt you, Bouchard," he assured th
little man. "Our question is, were you hired to frighten Vi
ien Frankland-Foster?" The little man nodded uncertainl
his eyes never leaving Greyson. "Were you hired by Gener
Roger Andros?" Jared persisted. When the frightened pro
ligate hesitated, Jared reached into his pocket and retrieve
a coin. He held it up before Bouchard. "You understan
this coercion, don't you, little miscreant." The man's mol
like eyes glittered darkly. Jared glanced at Greyson. "Yo
could threaten physical violence all day, Tyrrel," he intone
"and get nothing out of these two." He turned his attentic
back to the little man whose gaze was fixated greedily upc
the money. "You don't mind beatings, do you, Bouchar
And you, Clough," he said looking up at the mute, "you ca
take any abuse, can't you? You particularly enjoy bullyi
women, I have heard, but you can take a man's punis

ent — if there is coin in it for you." His voice became seductive. "Now I am going to give the two of you this coin. But I will give it on only one condition." His eyes impaled Bouchard, and the man's small head hunkered ferretlike between his shoulder blades. "I am going to give you this money if you will say who hired you to frighten Lady Frankland-Foster."

" 'Twas a feller . . ." Bouchard began, his voice a whimper. "He wanted me'n Clough t' scare 'er t'death," he said. Jared and Greyson both noted with disgust the small smile that crossed the mute's countenance. Bouchard snivelled on. "The feller gave us good money for it. Each time we went over t' th' mansion, he give us a shillin'."

"Well, this is no shilling, Bouchard," countered Jared enticingly. "This is a whole crown. 'Tis worth five times that little shilling." Bouchard nodded avidly. In an ecstasy of avarice, he grabbed with grimy serpentine fingers at it. Jared pulled it away.

"First, the name of the man who hired you," he said tranquilly. Unbelievably, the pathetic little creature who huddled before him began to cry. Great tears slopped down his sunken cheeks. He began to hit himself, pounding frenziedly on his own head.

"I . . . don't . . . remember," he moaned over and over. "Gi' me my coin, gi' me my coin, gi' me my coin . . ." he blubbered as he continued to flagellate himself. Jared's eyes widened in horrified disbelief. Bouchard continued the self-scourging. Greyson turned away in abhorrence. Blood appeared beneath Bouchard's eye and at the corner of his mouth. Clough smiled fully now as he looked down dispassionately on the self-destruction of his little cohort. The big man slowly stepped forward. He indicated to Jared that he wanted the coin. Jared regarded him warily.

"Do you remember the name of the man who hired you, Clough?" he inquired. Clough nodded complacently. He held out his big, roughened hand. Jared glanced at Greyson and finally placed the money in Clough's palm. "Who was it?" asked Jared. Both he and Greyson waited silently, expectantly, wondering how the mute intended to tell them the name, but somehow confident that he would. At last, the creature, still smiling triumphantly, lifted his hand. With one finger, he pointed to his heart.

Chapter Thirty-three

The room was barren, shadowed with the wavering light o
only one candle. Victoria pressed back against Edmund'
wide chest as they entered. His presence seemed an unyiel
ing barrier behind her. She glanced back at him tremulousl
She offered a hesitant smile and ran her tongue over her dr
lips.

"I do not mean to seem childish, Edmund," she venture
forcing a lightness in her tone, "but for some reason . . . th
place frightens me."

Edmund looked down on her. His smile was almost seren
"Does it, Victoria?" he asked.

Victoria nodded ruefully, her smile sad. "I hope you wi
forgive me. I am not usually such a frail creature," she chuck
led in embarrassment, "but I really would like to go."

"Oh, I am afraid not," Edmund breathed. His voice, ve
near her ear, was seductive, calm — certain.

Victoria's gaze swung to him. "I beg your pardon?" sh
asked. Her heart quickened as she noted the triumph in h
brown eyes. She turned to him slowly and swallowed th
quick clench of apprehension that tightened her throat. '
. . . really do think we should go, Edmund," she murmure
The lightness in her voice had deserted her. She lowered h
gaze. The silken fans of her lashes swept out over the delica
roundness of her cheekbones. "I am ashamed to say it," sh
conceded, "but I am feeling unwell."

"I do not doubt that," Edmund purred. She looked up
find that his regard was steadily upon her. No concern,
solicitude, no affectionate anxiety for her welfare trouble
his expression. In the narrow smile that curved his lips, Vict

ia found, to her bewilderment, the hint of . . . what? Was it malevolence she discovered there? Her heart pitched in her breast. She must be mistaken. Edmund Harrt was her friend. She trusted him implicitly. And yet . . . She blinked, hoping to clear her uncertain vision. No! An expression of purest hatred could not be twisting his aspect. The glitter in his fixed glare came from the light of the one flickering candle — not from some terrible malice within. Victoria backed slowly, cautiously away from him.

"Please, Edmund," she said on a breath, her emerald gaze pleading, "I really would like to leave."

Edmund's smile coiled. He advanced on her as she backed farther into the room. "I know you would like to leave, Victoria," he said dispassionately, "but that, of course, is out of the question."

Victoria stopped abruptly. "I don't understand," she said.

"You will," Edmund answered. "Remember this morn when I suggested we come here? I told you I had built this house." Victoria nodded uncomprehendingly. Edmund went on quietly. "Remember I told you that one day I planned to live here? Well, Victoria, I lied to you. I do not plan to live here. I built this house for only one reason. I built this house for you."

"For me?" she asked in a small voice. What could Edmund mean by this admission? Did he plan to steal her away from Geryson, to hide her here?

" 'Twas built for you, Victoria," he went on. "This house was built for you not to live in . . . but to die in." Victoria's eyes widened. Her heart thundered in her breast. Edmund threw back his head in laughter. The sound resonated darkly in the empty room. *But the room was not empty!*

To Victoria's disbelieving horror, she saw for the first time undulating shadows begin to take shape on the room's periphery. Her terrified gaze swiveled wildly as the black figures advanced from all directions, descending relentlessly upon her. Beads of cold perspiration sheened her flesh. In a heart-clutching panic, she lunged toward Edmund. He held out his arms as a lover might.

The motion of the room slowed. She saw Edmund before her, smiling, his face a writhing mask of preying pleasure. Victoria tried to stop, but it was too late. Her mouth opened in a silent scream as she crashed into his hard chest. Her blood turned to ice, and then all was black.

Victoria fell back, arched over Edmund's forearm. The silken fleece of her hair spun out, pearlescent in the candle's lambent flicker. He swept her up into his arms and looked down on the perfect oval of her face.

"At last," he breathed triumphantly.

The din of voices, like the cadent thrumming of a hellish chant, was the first thing Victoria heard as she awakened. Her eyes flew open. She looked up to find herself somewhere in the depths of a dark pit. The pit began to move around her and she realized that its walls were made up of the bodies of men, gathered together, standing over her. The sudden comprehension overwhelmed and horrified her that she was on the floor tied down, stretched immobile on her back. The wall of men widened to reveal a lighted circle. Her prison, she realized as her eyes took in the oddly designed floor surrounding her, was some sort of symbolic representation. Twining, undulating shapes and colors revealed themselves as she lifted her head slightly and strained to grasp the significance of her surroundings. She allowed her head to fall back at last. Her eyes drifted around the circle of faces above her. They stared down at her, their gazes fixed, their features stony.

"Who are you?" she whispered.

Edmund's face appeared over her. "I will introduce each of these men, Victoria," he said, his tone almost casual. "Heed their names and faces well," he added, "for they will be the last you ever encounter." The circle backed from the light. "This," began Edmund Harrt softly, "is John Osgood." A man, crag-faced and glaring, stepped over her. Victoria shuddered at the ferocity of intent she felt emanating from him. The man stepped back. "This," said Edmund Harrt, leading another man to stand above her, "is Charles Wendell." Again Victoria felt her heart recoil as she viewed that man's rancorous countenance. "This," repeated Edmund, drawing the man back and urging another to take his place, "is William Sawyer . . . " his voice droned on. Face after face appeared above her in a ritual of hate, in a litany of evil. Finally, Edmund himself stepped forward. "And I, Victoria, am Edmund Harrt." He stood above her for a long moment. At last, as though he savored the moment, he continued. "Eighty three years ago, Victoria, your ancestor, Purity Quayle, was

398

accused of witchcraft. She was never tried or convicted, but our great grandfathers knew what she was. Our great grandfathers, Victoria, realized the evil that lurked within that maidenly exterior. Those men—those Godly men—took the exorcism of that demonic creature into their own hands. But she escaped them, Victoria. Purity Quayle escaped . . . but you did not."

"And now, I am to pay for her imagined sins against your ancestors," Victoria said softly. She was beyond fear now. Survival was her only spur. She must try to understand—she must try to reason with these men—she must try to escape them.

Edmund was smiling. "The sins against our ancestors are not imagined, Victoria," he said, his tone one of reason and tolerance. "You must understand that Purity Quayle has, for four generations, haunted our families. For four generations we have vowed to nullify the evil that she bred. Unfortunately, for me—and for you—my own revenge has an entirely veritable origin. You see, while it took four generations for the others to know the true evil that lurked within your ancestor, my own great grandfather fell victim to that evil on the very night he tried to eliminate it from the world. Beneath the floor on which we stand, Victoria, beneath the very circle in which you are imprisoned, is the site where my great grandfather was killed . . . by Purity Quayle." He paused, and his regard congealed to a flintlike hardness. "I built this house as a memorial to that terrible sin perpetrated by your ancestor against my ancestor."

"Tell me this, Edmund," Victoria said, her tone matching his, "how do you know I am Purity's descendant?"

Edmund shrugged. " 'Twas not hard to know it, Victoria," he answered negligently. "You confided in me so thoroughly the lack of evidence concerning your past, that I could only conclude your parents meant to keep it hidden. They had good reason. My father and his father before him were bent on revenge. You would have been the target of that revenge. Then there is the matter of your appearance. Legend has it that Purity was a most extraordinarily beautiful woman; she had pearl-colored hair and emerald eyes, just as you do. When you boarded the *Spectre* and I realized your name was Quayle," he added craftily, "I suspected you were the woman for whom generations of my family had searched. As I came to know you, I had no doubt you were that daughter of evil whose blood my family craved." His face became contorted with hatred as he lowered himself on one knee between Victoria's bound ankles. "Oh, yes, Victoria, there was no doubt that you were the issue of that evil seed. I wanted to see you dead, Victoria, and so many times over these past years, I hoped it would happen. The day we were boarded by the English ship, I prodded Captain Tyrrel to throw you below decks among the colonists sailing back from India. I knew they would hate you. I hoped they would take out their frustrations against the British on you. I hoped they would kill you. But they did not. Then, when you posed as Rod, I gave you the most hopeless tasks—the ugliest work aboard the ship—and still you survived. And, really, Victoria, you survived on your own. Tyrrel was an idiot. He thought he could lighten your burden by cocking his male feathers and acting the protector, just as I suspected he would. But you knew the way to the men's hearts was to go quietly about your work, uncomplaining, diligent." His voice had taken on a mocking cadence. "I saw that happening, Victoria, and realized I had to do something. You were about to win back the sympathy of the men, and that would never have done. I sent you to your cabin; remember that? I put a bug into the ear of poor duped Mr. Curry, and he discovered you there. What good fortune you had your jewels in your hand at the time you were discovered. You were to be flogged, but Captain Tyrrel saved you by marrying you. 'Twas the only thing that saved you at that point, Victoria. I had manipulated you to the point where you were hated by both the seamen *and* the passengers. They would all have gladly taken you to task for your deception. 'Twould have been a glorious end, Victoria. But, as I said, you were saved. Your evil star saw you through the crisis.

"And then in Boston, Victoria, I lodged accusations against you. The accusations were not hard to prove." He made a sound that was an ugly distortion of a laugh. "Oh Victoria, you nearly hanged *yourself* in Boston. It was only for me to *report* your reckless behavior. It was unnecessary for me to *do* anything. But, once again you survived." He paused for a long moment. "And your marriage survived, Victoria. I did my best to come between you and Greyson Tyrrel. I intercepted messages between you, but somehow

400

you kept finding each other. Together, the two of you are an unbeatable force," he finished contemplatively. Victoria remembered that terrible long period when Greyson and she were apart — when he seemed to have tossed her from his life. She recalled how desperate she felt, how lonely for his love. Her eyes closed, remembering that time. Edmund's voice droned on. "Perhaps everything worked out for the best, though. I have always wanted you to die right here, with all these good men as witnesses. They deserve to see you die, Victoria." He paused again. "You are such a poor fool," he said at last, "such an evil little fool." He reached down and lifted a tress of her opaline hair onto his forefinger. "I shall bet you really thought you had escaped your destiny," he said thoughtfully. "And you know, you might have. Had you allowed me to save you, I might have done it. There was hope for you even as late as this afternoon, but then you vowed your love for the unworthy Tyrrel. How foolish you are, Victoria. How foolish and . . . evil. Don't you know 'tis evil to reject love that is offered you?" He regarded her steadily, almost sadly. Then, abruptly, he threw down the curl and stood. "And now our moment has come, gentlemen," he proclaimed. "Our way is clear. Prepare her!"

Victoria struggled wildly against her bonds as several men descended upon her. Drawing their knives, they began the crazed ritual of cutting off her clothing, while others spread straw around the parameter of the circle. Victoria writhed madly; screams raged from her throat. Frenzied activity swirled all around her. A live chicken was plucked from a sack. It squawked insanely as a man twisted its neck, violently killing the animal. As the bird's body jerked crazily, the man swung it directly over Victoria. Its blood spurted out, covering her naked body. She gagged, screaming and choking, twisting frantically against the warm spattering flow.

"You slimy ghouls, let me go!" Victoria shrieked.

Edmund Harrt lit a torch, and its sudden flare caught the glitter of Victoria's emerald glare as he held it high above her. She looked at each man as, again, they formed a living wall around the circle. She saw the fever of hatred in their eyes.

"The evil must be exorcised!" one of the men cried.

"Kill the she-demon!" another shrieked. In an orgy of vindictive triumph Edmund held the torch aloft, and with a final victorious cry, he threw it into the straw. Flames shot up and circled the bound Victoria.

The door of the house exploded. Greyson and Jared blasted into the room. Twenty men descended upon them. Fists flew. Blood spattered. Flesh was ground into pulp, muscle rended from bone. Greyson lowered one shoulder and rammed his muscular body into a wall of men. They fell back into the flames that now swept the room. Seeing Jared being held by two men and pummelled by a third, he grabbed the assailant and threw him off. Jared flung away the other two and immediately lunged at a man who was about to plunge a knife into Greyson's back. Jared whipped the man across the room as Greyson heaved himself into a pair who were ready to attack. Swinging his fists wildly, he battered them both to the burning floor. At last, through the inferno of roaring flames, he spotted Victoria.

The sight of her stretched, bound and blood-smeared enraged him. He lashed out in a delirium of wrath, sending four men crashing into the thundering furnace. Their panicked howls echoed above the sonorous roll of the blaze.

"Keep them off me," he shouted to Jared. "I'm going to get her!" Jared immediately pitched off his own attacker and ran to Greyson's back. There, he systematically repelled with savage, slashing thrusts each would-be combatant. Greyson, arms over his face, thrashed through the conflagration that threatened to engulf Victoria. Suddenly, Edmund Harrt lunged into his view. Greyson grabbed at him, but the man slashed the air between them with a glinting blade. His face alight with a horrible bare-toothed smile, his eyes reflecting the flames that surrounded the two of them, he swung the point of the blade down to Victoria's bared breast and held Greyson at bay.

"I will not be robbed of my revenge," he hissed.

"Back off, Harrt," Greyson clenched.

"Never!" he shrieked.

At that second, Jared reared into the engulfing circle of the blazing straw. He rammed into Harrt, propelling him from his feet and onto the floor.

"Get her, Grey," Jared shouted, as he and Edmund battled, the knife between them reflecting the carnivorous sheet of flame. Greyson reached Victoria and sliced her bonds. Wrapping her in the brown cloth of his big jacket, he threw her over one muscular shoulder. "Let's get the hell out of here, Everett!" he bellowed, grabbing the red wool of Jared's collar and dragging him toward the door. They rammed through the flames once again, leaving Edmund Harrt to struggle dazedly against the encircling pyre. The three people erupted in a crazed dash from the house. Immediately it exploded in a spume of red flames.

Rolling on the chilled ground, over the husks of grass and winter-killed vegetation, they lay in the dark, gasping raggedly for breath. They did not even notice the sting of their own fire-scorched flesh as they watched the evil caldron of hate-filled destiny burn to the ground.

"Did any of them get away?" Jared asked finally.

"I don't know," Greyson answered, "but I don't think so." Victoria's crystalline gaze reflected the glow of the flames. Greyson and Jared both regarded her.

"I am fine," she breathed at their unspoken inquiry. Her eyes darkened to jade as the fire waned. "A long time ago, I believed my life was guided by an evil star. Now I know that if we allow ourselves to be manipulated by what we *believe* to be our 'destiny,' we have no one but ourselves to blame for the outcome." Greyson wrapped her more tightly in the protection of his embrace. Jared, too, added his arm to her protection. The three of them had learned a great deal this night. The British soldier and the American rebel had discovered a common ground. They realized that as men, they were not so very far apart. As human beings, fighting for a common good, they were closer than they had anticipated. Victoria, too, understood this. When left to their own necessities, good people, people innocent of bad intent, would find a way to save themselves, and each other, from forces seemingly beyond their control. They knew that true peace was to be found within the discovery of individual values and not in the dogma of an implied or imagined destiny. No matter what happened to them after this night—no matter where the necessities of their chosen paths carried them—they would not forget the lesson they had learned in the flames of Edmund Harrt's personal hell. They huddled together on the ground, in their newly flowered empathy, watching the inferno die— listening as the roar of the flames merged at last with the gentle thunder of the sea beyond.

A hush settled over the seaside village. The only sound was the lap of moon-washed waves on the silvered shore.

Chapter Thirty-four

"Purity Quayle was no witch," said Susannah Ingersoll softly. "She was a beautiful, intelligent creature of the air and the water and the sun. She was everywhere — and always." She smiled and patted Victoria's hand.

Everyone had gathered in Mrs. Ingersoll's pleasant parlor. The springtime sun streamed through the big windows that overlooked Salem Harbor. Low beamed, white ceilings caught and reflected the sea-washed light.

"She was not evil, then," said Victoria.

"Oh, far from it," Susannah answered with a light laugh. "She was as good and as gentle a woman as ever lived in Salem."

"I blame myself for this," said Lenore Harrt sadly. She splayed a hand when the others would have protested. "No," she went on, "do not interrupt me. I feel much guilt over this, and 'tis well that I do. I could have prevented it. I saw in Victoria the legend that has haunted our family for four generations. I suppose I knew from the moment I met her why my son had brought her to Salem. I simply chose to accept his simple explanation of her presence here. I prayed so hard that the hatred that had raged through the Harrt family had ended with my son. His father died with his hatred of Purity Quayle on his lips."

Everyone looked at her, pity and understanding in their eyes. Her son was dead. He had fallen victim to the same maddening, soul-destroying hysteria that had overwhelmed the little village in 1692. Lenore lowered her gaze.

"Why did they all hate her so?" asked Victoria quietly. "I know that so many citizens of Salem were subjected to un-

404

imaginable horror because of the idle prattlings of little girls, but what was the particular sin of Purity Quayle?"

Vivien and Jared, sitting together on a small sofa, watched Susannah Ingersoll with interest. Greyson took Victoria into a protective embrace. Susannah stood and moved slowly to the window. She looked out over the lapping waters of the harbor.

"Edmund Harrt — the first Edmund Harrt — was deeply in love with Purity Quayle," she said gently. She turned and gazed sorrowfully at her rapt listeners. Her gaze became fixed on Mrs. Harrt. "I am sorry to say it, Lenore, but your husband's grandfather was obsessed by Purity. She — being a gentle soul — allowed him to visit her on occasion. When at last his attentions became more than she could handle, more than she wanted to handle, I imagine, she rejected him flatly. She turned him from her life. It was at this time that the witchcraft frenzy hit Salem. Being a Puritan of deep religious conviction and married to another, Edmund suddenly found a rationalization for his obsession. I would guess that he could not understand his own lustful behavior. Instead of putting it to a flaw in his character or the normal, if excessive, impulses of a healthy man, he became convinced that Purity had bewitched him. He would not charge her formally, because that would have exposed his own sin. Instead he and several other men went to Purity's house one night and burned it. In the confusion, Edmund was killed and thought by some to be a martyr to the onslaught of satanic influences. From that night to the day the last of them died, the sons of those men have believed in Edmund's martyrdom. They believed, I am sorry to say it, in the evil of Purity Quayle. I think," she added, moving softly to Victoria, "from what you have told me, that young Edmund and his compatriots believed you to *be* Purity."

Victoria lowered her lashes. "And perhaps I am," she murmured. "No one knows where I came from. Everything about me is a mystery."

Vivien reached over and took Victoria's hand in hers. "Have you no idea of Victoria's parentage, Susannah?" she asked.

Susannah only smiled. "I wish I could help, but I fear that much will have to remain a mystery," she said.

Victoria glanced up at the shy and gentle woman. "You

said Purity was . . . 'always,' Susannah."

Their hostess nodded. "I said she was a creature of the air and the water and the sun. I said she was everywhere and always. I meant all that. Purity Quayle was a mystery, too."

"But you do know a great deal about her," said Greyson.

"Oh, yes," affirmed Susannah. "I know everything about her — and nothing at all." The guests eyed her curiously. She crossed the room to a small secretary. Opening it, she drew from a pigeonhole a sheaf of parchments. "This is what I know about Purity Quayle," she said. "One day — one fine and gloriously sunny day — I was strolling along the shore. I often find treasures there, little shells and sea glass, and that day was no exception. My foot struck something as I walked. I leaned down and found a box. 'Twas an ordinary box, not made of metal or any other hard substance, just a plain wooden box. How long it had been there, I cannot tell you. I opened it. Inside, I discovered these papers. As I retrieved them, a wave surged up onto the shore and directly over the sand where I stood. I watched in wonder as its powerful ebb pulled the little box out to sea. I stood there for a long, long time, not even aware that the wave had wetted my shoes and the hem of my gown. I knew, before I even read what was in the papers, that I had found a truly great treasure. I knew I had discovered someone's life." She held the papers now as she must have held them that day, clutched to her breast. Her eyes closed and her face was filled with some deep inner knowledge of a vital force. "These tell the story of Purity Quayle." Susannah looked tenderly down on the treasured bundle. She moved to Victoria and stood over her. "I cannot tell you where you come from," she said gently. " 'Tis really within each of us to know that, after all. We — every one of us, if asked — has our own truth to tell about ourselves. Our mothers cannot tell our truths for us." She lifted her chin and looked with assurance at Lenore. "They do not know our truths . . . and . . . they are not responsible for them." The two women smiled together. Lenore's regard held a profound gratitude. Susannah looked back at Victoria. "Only we know who we are. It is up to each of us to build our own truth about ourselves. The *influence* of fate, however, cannot be totally eliminated from our lives. We must deal with that influence — overcome it or embrace it every day of our lives. With that in mind, I offer you this, Victoria." She held out a yellowed sheet and Victoria accepted it hesitantly. "Purity Quayle was a poet. All of these poems tell her story . . . but this one"—she indicated the one that Victoria held—"tells her story best of all. Read it. Read it aloud for all of us, and let us each decide who was Purity Quayle."

Victoria looked down at the paper. She read the lines silently at first, then raised her eyes. Slowly, without looking back at the paper she began to recite the words.

I live to write my life; my quill essays
A verse; the poem bears thoughts a perfect birth.
I'll wait to die until I've lived my ways.

How I've longed to breathe the peace and warm my
    days.
With gentle verse I'd sing to friends with mirth.
I live to write my life; my quill essays

To reason dreams; I glean from words at play.
I can be me or whom I choose to be.
I'll wait to die until I've lived my ways.

Though fires burn my flesh, my eyes now jades
And my heart carved rock cannot quell my rage—
I live to write my life, my quill essays

To refresh my soul's seas with sun's spun rays
And soft refrains of moon gold's tender earth.
I'll wait to die until I've lived my ways.

I'll rhyme until life's time burns out its stays.
I live to write my life; my quill essays.
I'll wait to die until I've lived my ways

"I believe," said Susannah softly, after a pause, "that Purity Quayle was guilty in the eyes of those men so long ago of an unpardonable sin—*the* unpardonable sin for a woman. She was guilty of desiring fulfillment as a human being." She turned and walked slowly toward the windows and looked out over the harbor. "She paid a terrible price for her sin." She regarded Victoria. "She was forced to kill a man in defense of her freedom, as you now know. She must have lived with that

407

terrible deed for a very long time. She was a gentle soul—no burning firebrand—and she must have hated what she did. I showed you that particular poem, Victoria, because I believe it tells her story as completely as anything she wrote. In that little villanelle, I find, as well, a longing, a sweet and gentle longing, to resolve and . . . perhaps . . . to absolve herself of her so-called transgression. At the *Final* Assizes, I believe she will be absolved.

"Purity Quayle loved someone, I think, though I do not know if she ever married, but she would not allow that love to override her freedom of spirit. That, too, I suppose engendered a certain guilt. There is not a woman among us who has not felt the weight of her own reproof upon discordance with the man she loves." Susannah smiled as each woman nodded in understanding—and agreement. "I do not know," she went on, "whether Purity continued to write poetry, but from her words, and from the spirit of her poem, I believe she continued—and perhaps continues—to follow her free-spirited ways. Those men, like their ancestors before them—with their sabbat circle and ritualistic blood of freshly-killed game, and their fires—were not trying to exorcise true evil, Victoria," said Susannah, moving to her quickly, "they were trying to exorcise their own perception of evil. They were trying to rid the world of the spirit of women's independence from them. They will never do that, for there will always be men like Greyson Tyrrel and Jared Everett, and there will always be women like Vivien and you—and Purity—to stop them." She took Victoria's hands in hers. "And you must stop them. Let them kill all the imagined witches they can, in their own insecurities, ferret out. Never, never allow them to quell your rage to live as you must." She smiled. "Whether Purity is alive or dead, her spirit lives in you, Victoria." Susannah raised her eyes and regarded Vivien and Lenore. "I hope it lives in all of us. I believe after today it will."

Victoria nodded—as did the other women. As with Purity, Victoria's rite of passage had begun with the sea. There could be no turning back; the chasm between where she had been and where she was now was too wide. She had known what it was to oppose the power of men's opinions. She had faced and dispensed with her Uncle David's belief that the American colonials were savages. She had done the same with Steven Kensington's belief that she ought to be content to be

408

made his mistress. Victoria had felt the weight of her own reproof in disagreeing with Greyson's belief that the Americans must sever their ties with the Sovereign Rule. This particular conviction had not been so easily maintained in the face of Greyson's certainty and his commitment to that ideology, but she had done it. She glanced around the room. In their own ways, each of the women, and women like them everywhere, had faced the question of their right to independent thought. Was Purity's dream worth the struggle? Would she and these other women find it worth the struggle to continue to "write" their own lives? Born women, were they preordained to subjugate their thinking to that of their men? Could they fight their destiny? Would they continue to risk the disapprobation—and even violent reactions—of certain men? Oh, yes, Victoria thought smiling, holding Purity's poem to her breast. They must continue in their struggle. She looked up into Greyson's loving gaze. There would be no question of his respect for her newly awakened cause. That was good, she reflected. She would have hated—though it might have been the case—to have continued the struggle without him.

Chapter Thirty-five

The people of Boston had begun to gather at dawn. Slowly, silently, they assembled to watch the evacuation of the nine-thousand-man British garrison. A flotilla, escorted by six-teen warships, was to sail the British soldiers out of Boston Harbor that afternoon. The winter of 1775-76 had been long and debilitating for both the citizens and the soldiers. Icy winds and freezing rains had torn through the town, leaving in their frigid path a shortage of fuel, a staggering scarcity of food, and a ravaged population. By now, there were only about six thousand people left in the town of Boston. General George Washington, a Virginian and the newly appointed commander in chief of the colonial forces, was to find, when at last he marched into the liberated town, a tragic shambles. Trees had been cut down everywhere, fences had been ripped up, and barns and warehouses had been razed to the ground to supply the townspeople with fuel. Churches and meeting houses had been used for stables, private homes had been turned into hospitals, and monuments and public buildings had been defaced. Slowly and painfully, however, the town was beginning to pull itself together after the ordeal of siege, occupation and plunder.

The battle that had turned the contention between the Mother County and her colonies into an all-out war had taken place on June 17, 1775. British and American forces had clashed at Charlestown, just across from the Boston pe-ninsula, when a force of twenty-five hundred redcoats, sup-ported by ships of the royal navy, sought to dislodge colonial troops from their entrenched positions atop Breed's Hill. The battle had demonstrated clearly that the clashes at Lexington and Concord two months earlier had not been accidents.

And now, through the strategies of General Washington and his troops, the long-occupied town of Boston was at last to be set free. On this frosty morning of March 17, 1776, the people gathered to watch — and wonder what would happen next.

General Roger Andros was among those men who had been ordered by an agreement between Lieutenant General Sir William Howe and General Washington to leave Boston. He had done so without ever making good his threat to burn Vivien's house to the ground. Such an act would have been illegal, and whatever Andros was, he was a stickler for the law — though he often bent it for his own purposes. That fact, along with General Gage's respect for Jared and the incredible — though undoubtedly true — story he told concerning Edmund Harrt, had succeeded in clearing Victoria's name. It was also decided that in order that she might be freed of all persecution, Andros must be shipped out of Boston along with the rest of the troops. Even now, the ship that carried Andros idled at Nantasket Roads, waiting to catch the winds that would sail him north to Halifax. Jared could not even venture a guess as to where Andros would be stationed after that. The war had just begun. At least — to the relief of all who had suffered under his tyranny — Andros, it was certain, would never again reside in Boston.

Jared and Vivien stood on the long front porch of the "biggest, grandest house on Hanover Street." Vivien's divorce from Neville Frankland-Foster had become final that morning. She held Jared very close as she smiled at her approving sons. Derrick and Thomas, given leave by their commanding officer for this day of liberation, had joined them. The three men, along with their regiment, were to remain in Boston as advisors to local law-enforcement officers for the duration of the war. Their function was benign and absolutely — under the law — nonofficial. They had been advised by the Boston constabulary to "relinquish and forgo" the "display of arms or uniforms." They watched as some two thousand American soldiers began to form a train. Marching from Roxbury, through Dorchester, the rag-coated Americans made their way silently through the town. The early-morning sun broke through the clouds.

The big front door of the house opened, and Victoria and Greyson stepped through it into the bright morning chill.

Greyson carried their week-old baby boy cradled in one strong arm, and with the other, he supported his pale, determined wife. He glanced sheepishly at Vivien as she shot him a withering glare.

"I told you not to let her get up, Greyson," she reproved.

Victoria laughed and drew her woolen cloak more snugly around her chin. "You did not really think I would miss this, did you Vivien?" she said brightly. She turned and tucked the babe more securely into the warmth of his father's embrace. Greyson gazed down on them both. These two wondrous beings belonged to him. His Victoria — his beautiful and gallant creature of the air and the water and the sun — had given him a son. She had given him his immortality.

Victoria's attention was caught by a familiar voice down on the street. She broke into a warm smile and waved frantically.

"Your ladyship!" Jack exulted as he made a dash for the porch. The vigorous, nearly adolescent lad, bound up the steps. Victoria swept him into a loving embrace, from which he quickly broke free. Apparently, Jack had not yet developed a liking for shows of affection. One day, he would, thought Victoria with a wide smile — and from the looks of him, that day would not be long in coming. After being introduced to the others, Jack offered Greyson a smart salute, then eyed him curiously. "What're you holdin', Captain?" he asked.

" 'Tis a babe, lad," said Greyson, holding out the thickly wrapped bundle for Jack's inspection. The boy looked down on the sleeping bit of copper-haired humanity, and then raised his eyes to Greyson.

"Well," said Jack finally, "now I guess I got me two brothers." Everyone agreed, congratulating the lad on his rapidly expanding family. "But that don't mean you and the captain are my parents, your ladyship," he said sternly.

Victoria lifted a quizzical brow. "It doesn't, Jack?" she asked, curious as to where his observation was leading.

"Nope," he said with certainty. "Tad and Ellie are my parents now. They adopted me full out." His smile was broad. " got me a name, your ladyship, and a family."

Victoria smiled warmly. She regarded the lad whom she loved so well and on whom she had depended so constantly during her voyage to this time and place in her life. He would soon be a man, and she prayed silently that their friendship would continue and flourish during this time of his voyage into adulthood. "Do you know something, Jack," she said softly. "You have always referred to me as 'your ladyship.' Now that we are both practically grown up, won't you start calling me Victoria?"

Jack's brow wrinkled in consternation. "I don't think I can do that, your ladyship," he said gravely.

"Why not, Jack?" Victoria asked in surprise.

"Well . . ." the boy answered, his lips pursed solemnly, "if I did that, why, I'd get the two of you mixed up."

Before Victoria could question him on his odd remark, Tad and Ellie Wright approached the porch.

"There you are, Jack," Ellie chided gently as she smiled up at those gathered before the house. "Hello, Victoria," she said softly. In her arms, she carried her year-old daughter. Apple-cheeked and bright-eyed, the babe laughed delightedly in greeting.

Victoria moved slowly down the steps. "Oh, Ellie," she breathed as she embraced the woman and child. Eyes welling with soft tears, she drew away so that she could better see the little girl.

"Meet *Victoria*, Victoria," said Ellie. " 'Tis not a monarch's name," she added smiling, "but a regal one, nevertheless, and one of which I believe she will be most proud."

"Thank you, Ellie," said Victoria softly. They regarded the pretty child. "We shall both try to live up to our 'regal' name."

The two women laughed together as Victoria brought Ellie and Tad and the children up onto the porch. Introductions made, Vivien decided that they had all better come into the house and warm themselves. A large breakfast would not be out of order, she assured them — if she could depend on at least one of them for assistance in its preparation.

"I am not much of a cook," she lamented. "But Jared is," she added with a mischievous wink. They all bundled inside. When Victoria insisted on enjoying the air for a few moments longer, Vivien determinedly took the babe from Greyson. "If the two of you insist on catching pneumonia," she reproved gaily, "at least let me save the little Tyrrel from the sins of his parents." With the promise secured that Greyson and Victoria would let the diners know when General Washington himself marched into the town, Vivien went inside.

The sunlight had diffused the bitterness of the morning

chill, and Greyson and Victoria stepped out of the porch's shade and along the walk to the street. They strolled arm in arm, beneath a sky filled with soaring gulls and late winter sunshine. Greyson now wore the official uniform of the colonial armed forces. His waistcoat was made of fine black wool, piped with beige. His vest, blouse and hose were a shimmering white. Victoria eyed him obliquely and hid a smile. His black, finely molded tricorn sat jauntily atop his tousle of russet curls. He would never change — this rogue of hers. They had been married three years now. They had a son. Greyson was a proficient sea captain, a valued soldier and a respected member of this colonial community. There was talk that he would be invited to attend the Continental Congress in Philadelphia. Abigail Adams's husband John had been appointed to a special committee that had been formed to draft what they were referring to as a "Declaration of Independence." Mr. Adams had requested that Greyson join him as his aide. He had even raised Greyson's name as a candidate for the General Assembly which was now being reformed and revitalized. Greyson was distinguished by all this, Victoria reflected as they walked, and yet, in her heart he would forever remain that carefree vagabond who had stolen plums from her orchard in Kolhapur all those years ago — and, so unstintingly, taught her the meaning of love. No matter where his fortunes took him — whether or not she believed in or embraced his causes — she would be by his side. And one day, she thought mischievously, she would bring him back to that plum grove in Kolhapur. She would saucily insist that there beneath the blossoms they fulfill a certain promise made there on a certain night so long ago. She smiled inwardly. So many joys awaited her in the life she was to share with Greyson Tyrrel.

She could not wait to introduce this rebellious rogue of hers to the haughty and acerbic David Newton. What verbal duels those two would enjoy. Katje d'Aumerle would love Greyson because Victoria loved him. Their days would be warm and sweet in Kolhapur once this war was over and Victoria could plan a visit. She might even convince David and Katje to make a journey to these shores. Those gentle English rebels who, searching for their own autonomy, had settled the green hills of India in the early part of the century might just enjoy meeting a very different sort of rebel. And surely

Katje would thrill at seeing the happiness found at last by her dear friend Vivien. Oh, yes, there was much, even in the face of this war, to hope for and to fondly anticipate.

Victoria and Greyson made their way to the common. General Gage's unit had been deployed and were now beginning their march down to the harbor. As they passed, Victoria caught her breath. There, among the retreating soldiers, she saw a familiar face. Leading his own small battalion, looking polished and elegant as always, was Steven Kensington. His eyes straight ahead, his neatly combed hair shimmering golden in the sun, he looked every bit as handsome as he had during all the years of her youth. He had not changed one bit. Or had he? Was there a certain hardness about the mouth, a vague hint of disappointment in the eyes. *Oh, Steven,* Victoria mused, *what if you had defied your father? What if our childhood expectations had been fulfilled?* She looked quickly up at her husband and drew him a little closer. Greyson smiled down at her.

"Would you like to go back, love?" he asked softly. Victoria nodded. They turned to make their way back to the house. Over her shoulder, in the periphery of her vision, she saw Steven. She supposed, with a small knowing resignation, that that was where Steven would always remain. She would never completely forget him. Some little part of her would always wonder what would have happened . . . if . . .

They heard the faint trill of a fife and the cadent beating of far-off drums. They knew that they must hurry if they were to apprise Vivien and the rest that General Washington was about to enter Boston. Seeing them all gathered on the porch, however, Victoria and Greyson realized that they, too, must have heard the approach.

As the now finely uniformed troops began their march into the town, Victoria noted the swelling of prideful tears in Greyson's eyes. She touched his shoulder, and he drew her into his arms.

"I wonder where the man in the red cape is today," she said softly.

Greyson looked down on her and arched a brow. "What do you know about the man in the red cape?" he asked with a smile.

Victoria matched his smile. "I suppose you could say, he is an old friend of mine," she answered.

415

Greyson laughed. "The man in the red cape, love, is a friend of mine, as well."

"Were you that man?" Victoria asked seriously.

"In a way I was," he said. His sea-glass blue gaze drifted over the passing soldiers. "In a way, we all were—all those who have loved freedom, who have made a conscious decision to take action against tyranny—every man in Boston has worn that cloak. Sam Adams wore it, and John Hancock wore it, and—yes—I wore it once myself." He laughed, looking down into her eyes. "Great myths will arise from the ashes of this conflict, love," he said at last. "Great myths always do. We will be thought better than we were—and worse. But in the end, we are only men and women doing what we need to do. We are no more than that."

Victoria nodded and returned his tender gaze. "We are no more than that," she agreed, "and no less."